ABOUT ROBERT MOORE WILLIAMS...

During his career, prolific author Robert Moore Williams published more than 150 novels and short stories under his given name as well as a variety of pseudonyms including John S. Browning, H. H. Harmon, Robert Moore, Russell Storm, and E.K. Jarvis.

Williams was born in 1907 in Farmington, Missouri and earned a journalism degree from the University of Missouri, Columbia. He had a full-time writing career from 1937 through 1972 and cut his teeth on such publications as *Amazing Stories*, *Fantastic Adventures*, *Astounding Science Fiction*, *Thrilling Wonder Stories,* and *Startling Stories,* just to name a few.

He also became a stalwart contributor to Ace Books in the '50s and '60s, with many fine novels, including "Conquest of the Space Sea," "The Second Atlantis," "The Day They H-Bombed Los Angeles," "The Blue Atom," and many others. One of his more unusual books was a fictional autobiography: "Love is Forever—We Are for Tonight'" where Williams presents a description of his childhood and then goes on to discuss his experimentation with hallucinogenic gasses, Dianetics, and 1950s-era communes. After a long, distinguished career, Williams passed away in May of 1977 in Dateland, Arizona. This collection contains some of his finest tales from the 1950s.

TABLE OF CONTENTS

MASTERS OF SCIENCE FICTION

Volume 10

ROBERT MOORE WILLIAMS:
"TIME TOLLS FOR TORO"
and other tales

ARMCHAIR FICTION
PO Box 4369, Medford, Oregon 97504

For more information about Armchair Books and products, visit our website at…

www.armchairfiction.com

Or email us at…

armchairfiction@yahoo.com

Time Tolls for Toro

*He awoke as an amnesia victim, beset by unknown enemies. Could his
hurt mind recover soon enough to preserve his life?*

CHAPTER ONE

HIS MEMORY was bad but he didn't know it. He knew
only that there was vague dissatisfaction in him and that he was
hungry. The roar of homeward-bound evening rush-hour traffic
pounded in his ears, rousing the vague wish to live in a land
where they didn't have so much noise. He said to himself: "I
am walking along this street—" and let the thought die without
wondering how he came to be here.

On the corner an elderly newsboy with a face like a sinful
gnome yelled: "Killer Hunted." His ears heard the sounds but
somehow they did not register on his mind. Nothing really
registered. He was like a man walking in a dream without
knowing he was dreaming.

There was a restaurant on the corner, reminding him again of
the gnawing in his stomach. He went in. The place was familiar
somehow. He knew he had been here before though not often
enough to be remembered even by a waitress. Nobody ever
remembered him, he thought wistfully...

"Blue plate special?" the waitress said without really looking
at him or waiting for him to give his order. He nodded. Driven
by hunger, he ate with relish. The cigarette afterward tasted
good. He found the cigarette in a package in his pocket. He
found the diamond-studded cigarette lighter there too, lit the
cigarette with the lighter without ever really noticing what he
was using. The waitress noticed. Her eyes widened. "Gosh,"
she whispered. She looked with new respect at this man sitting
at the counter. "Some more coffee, sir?" He didn't hear her.
She filled his cup anyhow, hoping he would notice. He didn't.

There was a thought in the back of his mind. Like a fretful, restless ghost, it kept telling him that something was wrong— somewhere. He was watching the thought. It faded away, became formless and vague, leaving restless dissatisfaction behind it. Abruptly he rose to his feet. He managed to remember to pay the check and to leave a tip for the waitress before he left the restaurant.

"Killer Hunted!"

He gave the gnome with the sinful face a dime, took the paper thrust at him but forgot the nickel change, started down the street, stopped abruptly as the dateline caught his eye. October 16, 1950. The chilling wind moving from the northwest said it was October. The leaves in the gutter at the edge of the sidewalk said it was October. The newspaper said it. It ought to be right. Only the ghost lurking in the back of his mind whispered a protest. He turned back to the newsstand.

"I'm sorry but I believe you have given me the wrong paper." He was polite about it. The newsboy had made a mistake that was all.

"Huh? What mistake?" The sinful-faced gnome, thinking the customer had come back to demand the nickel, was indignant. "No mistakes corrected after you've left the stand."

"But this paper has the wrong date."

"Huh?" The gnome thrust his face near the paper, lifted indignant eyes. "October 16, it says."

"But—"

"But what, Mister?"

"WHAT DATE DID you think it was?" the girl said, gently. He turned quickly, startled and surprised. The girl had come up so quietly he had not heard her. She stood there now staring at him from compassionate, friendly, violet eyes. They were the most beautiful eyes he had ever seen. The color was blue shading indescribably into violet, the color of far-off skies. The girl herself was as beautiful as her eyes. Wearing a street dress and carrying a small purse, she looked as if she had just stepped out of the most modernistic bar, where she had sipped a cocktail, or out of the oldest museum on earth where she had served as a model for the world's best painter.

"Eh?" He was startled. He had never met a girl like this, though he had always wanted to.

"What date did you think it was?" she asked again.

"Well—" The date had been in his mind, in the card index there, on one of the cards, all pulled out and ready to use. But when he tried to speak, the card slipped furtively back into the file, became one of millions of similar cards, lost and gone. Finding it again would be an incredibly difficult task. "Something is wrong with my card sorter," he thought. "It isn't working right. Time was when it found instantly the card I wanted." He frowned. "Do I know you?"

"Of course you know me," the girl answered.

He smiled at her. "I would like to know you. But I don't. Goodbye now." Turning, he moved quickly down the street.

He did not want to go away like this but fear was rising in him. He did not know what he feared or why, only that the fear was there, a rising apprehension that something was wrong. In his mind, the card sorter was working frantically, searching for something that was missing. Meanwhile it was trying to conceal from him the fact that anything was missing.

A taxicab moved in a U-turn to cross the street, pulled up at the curb beside him. The driver leaned out. "Taxi, mister?" The driver had the wizened, lined face of a dwarf and the alert eyes of a watchful bird.

"No, thanks."

The cab tooled along the curb beside him. "Drive you to the lab, mister," the driver said.

"What lab?"

The cabby shrugged. "Any lab?"

"What makes you think I might be going to a laboratory?"

"To your hotel, then."

"No thanks." He walked on. The cab remained at the curb, the driver sitting in it. Lighting a cigarette, he glanced back.

The girl was coming along the sidewalk. Was she following him?

Why would she be following him? Why would anybody follow him? He wasn't important enough to follow. He wasn't— *Who was he?* The fingers lifting the cigarette began to shake. The card sorter, growing sullen, quit entirely. He did not know who he was. Or what he was.

Or how he had gotten here on this street.

Or what city this was.

Or his name.

Or his occupation.

In his brain, the sullen sorter refused to pull a single card out of his memory.

The mental shock was terrific, like running full speed into a stone wall. He realized that he had been operating automatically, like a robot or a well-oiled machine, responding to stimuli like hunger and curiosity. Because he had been hungry, he had gone into the restaurant. Because he had been curious, he had bought a newspaper. No doubt in this transaction his mind had followed a well-rutted reaction pattern—see paper, want paper, buy paper.

But the date on the newspaper was wrong. Did this mean something? If so—what? What did anything mean? What did he mean? Who was he? What was his name?

"WARREN!" The sound burst on his ears. Hand outstretched a man was coming out of a doorway toward him. It was this man who had called him Warren. Warren who? Warren what? Did he know this man? The name-caller was tall and skinny with something of the look of a hawk upon his narrow features. Beaming good will and friendliness, he advanced. "Long time no see, Warren. Where have you been keeping yourself?"

"Oh, hello." At the word Warren, the card sorter stirred, once, as if it was about to begin selecting cards again, then, tired by the effort, relapsed again into indifference.

"This calls for a drink," Hawk-face said. "It really does. You old goat. You sure are the medicine for sore eyes. Only last night the missus was asking about you. She said, 'Have you seen Warren lately? Why don't you bring him home for supper some night?'" Hawk-face had his hand and was shaking it. Hawk-face hooked an arm through his arm. "Come on, let's get that drink."

"Thank you. Very generous of you, I'm sure. But—some other time."

"No time like the present."

Hawk-face applied pressure on the arm. "You old rascal, you." He beamed fondly.

"Look, I'm in a big hurry. I simply don't have time—"

"Take time," Hawk-face said.

Hawk-face had him and both knew it. Hawk-face urged him along the street, making a great show of friendliness, but never once relaxing the pressure on his arm.

"Just a minute," the girl said, behind them. Hawk-face jerked around. The girl with the violet eyes had caught up with them.

"What the hell do you want?" Hawk-face said.

Hawk-face made a noise like the growl of a trapped wildcat. "You'll play hell getting him."

"Will I?" she smiled, casually, as if this matter was of no great difficulty. "Either let him go or—"

"Or what?"

"Or I'm going to start screaming," the girl said. "You've never really heard a girl scream until you have heard me."

Hawk-face looked like a trapped animal. "Damned witch. Who the hell are you? Where do you figure in this?"

"I'm going to count to five. Either you let him go or listen to me scream. One."

"But—"

"Two."

Sweat was on Hawk-face's features. "Look, we'll cut you in."

"Three."

9

"Woman, you don't know who the hell you're monkeying with!

"Four."

Hawk-face looked as if he was about to choke.

"Five," the girl said. A look of determination appeared on her face. Her breast swelled as she took a deep breath preparatory to screaming. She opened her mouth.

Snarling, Hawk-face let go of the arm of the man he had called Warren.

"Thank you," the girl said. Smiling, she took hold of the arm Hawk-face had released. "Come, dear," she said. "Come, Warren."

He didn't resist. He trusted this girl somehow, without knowing why or how. Hawk-face walked rapidly away. The girl saw the taxi, still at the curb. She waved toward it. The driver got it into gear, opened the door for them.

HE ENTERED the cab first. Perhaps it wasn't the gentlemanly thing to do but he had the impression that it was definitely expected of him. The girl stepped in behind him. She crossed her legs, opened her purse, took out a package of cigarettes, offered him one. He took it, found the lighter in his pocket, lit both cigarettes. Then he settled back on the cushions. If there was calmness in him, it was all on the surface. He thought: "Something is going to happen. Well, let it."

The girl watched him. She seemed awed. "You are really rather remarkable," she said.

"Am I? Why?"

"You don't know who you are or what you are and yet you sit there as if the only thing on your mind is what a nice day it is. There must be a maelstrom going full blast inside your mind but the only sign of it is just a trace of moisture on your upper lip."

"My card sorter is out of order," he said. His hand went up to the trace of telltale sweat; he wiped it away. "Maelstrom is a weak word for what is happening inside my mind."

"You will get over it," the girl said. "The worst will pass in a few days. Of course there will always remain startling moments when you think you are remembering events that haven't happened yet. But you will learn how to control these moments."

He nodded as if what she said made sense. In fact, it didn't. He fingered the cigarette lighter. It was a beautifully made little instrument, apparently of solid gold set with diamonds. It must have cost a fortune. Could he afford to own such cigarette lighters? It was another question he could not answer. There were so many… One of the diamonds caught his eye. Something was wrong there, some slight imperfection. What was wrong? The top surface was a little too curved, for one thing, for another, a tiny hole was visible in the back of the jewel.

At the sight of the hole in the back of the jewel, cold water splashed on his spine, a dripping spongeful of it. This was not an ordinary cigarette lighter, it was something else. But what? Reluctantly the card sorter stirred, went furiously into action, brought a dozen cards up before his mind for inspection at the same time. His mouth fell open. He remembered, now, what this lighter was and how it could be used. A gaping chasm opened into his mind and he remembered. Also he remembered where he had gotten it.

Sweat appeared again on his upper lip. He could feel it there but he made no attempt to remove it. His mind was completely engrossed in the information the card sorter was bringing him. Stunning, bewildering, blinding information. He could hardly believe that what he was remembering was true.

But it had to be true. The lighter proved it was true.

Then the card sorter, like a defective relay functioning for a moment and then erratically refusing to function, went off the job again. It left one card plainly visible before the eye of his mind.

The card that told him what the lighter was and how it could be used.

CHAPTER TWO

THE GIRL had not told the cab driver where to go but he slipped the cab into gear and swung expertly into the traffic as if he knew, exactly where he was going.

"Who was that man who had you by the arm?" the girl said.

"I don't know." He knew only one thing—what the lighter was and how to use it. He kept it out of sight in his sweaty hand.

"But what was he trying to do to you?"

He shook his head. Hawk-face was as much of an enigma as he was himself. Hawk-face had seemed to know him but he did not know the man, had never seen him before in his life. What had Hawk-face wanted? To buy him a drink? It didn't seem likely. Hawk-face had been after something. But what?

The driver was watching them in the rear-vision mirror, he was leaning back in the seat and trying to listen to what they said. Was this fact important?

The girl was frowning. She seemed to be concentrating, trying hard to remember something. "This must be the beginning of the pattern that takes you out of history," she said. "It can't be anything else."

"W-what?" he said.

"I can't explain it because I don't know what is to happen," she said, frowning. "Nobody really knows. It's one of the great mysteries of all time."

"What are you talking about?" He heard bewilderment in his voice, knew that the bewilderment was an accurate echo of the feelings in him.

"I'm talking about you," she answered. "You are one of the big men of history, as big as Einstein and Newton."

He stared at her. "Are you out of your mind?"

"No." The answer was simple, short, and direct. "I came

before you and I have finished the transition process. My mind is working again. No, I know what I am talking about when I say you are one of the great men of all time. I also know what I am talking about when I say that you are one of the great mysteries, one of the great enigmas of the ages. But I don't know the part that Hawk-face plays in what is to happen. However, I strongly suspect that you had better be very wary of that man—*Eek!*" She gave a sound like a frightened mouse as the cab slewed on two wheels into a side street. Tires screamed on asphalt as the cab was jerked to a halt. The driver spun and started over the back seat toward them. He had a gun in his hand.

Warren remembered that this cab driver had tried to pick him up. He suspected instantly that the cab driver and Hawk-face had been working together. Certainly the intention of the cab driver was similar to the intention of Hawk-face.

"Get your hands up!" the driver ordered.

The girl said, *"Eek!"* again and dived at the driver.

Warren, lifting his hands, brought the lighter into focus and pressed the right spot. From the jewel with the tiny hole in it sprang a cone of radiation that looked a little like light. It struck the driver in the face. How the light produced its result was not obvious but the result itself was very plain.

The driver said, "Uck!" His face froze in the grimace that had been contorting it at that moment. He dropped the gun, which he had been swinging around to point at the girl. It went out of sight in the front seat. The driver went out of sight behind it, sliding down like a gargoyle coming loose from the base that supports it. Lunging at him, the girl fell forward over the seat.

Before Warren could turn it off, she fell into the spray of light.

She collapsed over the top of the seat.

HORRIFIED, Warren stared at her. He had not intended to harm her. Without knowing quite how he knew it, he knew the results of the light were not permanent. Used at this intensity, the light stunned but did not kill. Used at a higher intensity, it produced much more devastating results, but at this low power, the driver and the girl would both recover in the matter of half an hour, the exact length of time needed for recovery depending both on how the beam had struck them and their physical and mental condition at the moment of impact.

She would be all right. All he had to do was to get her to a place where she could lie down for half an hour. He could keep her in the cab, dump the driver, and drive the cab around until she recovered. He started to get out of the cab, intending to go around and slip under the wheel.

Tires screeched again as another vehicle made a quick turn into this side street. In the dusk the features of the man crouched over the wheel were dimly visible.

Hawk-face.

The man had followed the cab. There was a second man with him. The car was driving straight toward him. Warren knew that he had no time to get the cab started, no time for anything except one thing. Ducking around the cab, he jumped a fence into the backyard of a small private residence. Rubber yelled on the asphalt as the car was jerked to a halt beside the cab. Warren ran to the alley, slid into it, ran along it.

Behind him voices shouted, feet pounded.

"Where in the hell did he go?" he heard Hawk-face yell.

"I saw him jump that fence," a second voice answered.

"Find him. The boss wants him bad."

Warren ran like a rabbit from hounds. He hated to leave the girl behind him, but if he stayed to try to help her, both might be captured. If he could get away, he could help her later. Helping her was important to him somehow, but at the moment other things were more important. The first was escape. The second was finding out who he was.

Bigger than Einstein and Newton, the girl had said. He could not believe she knew what she was talking about. Nobody was bigger than those two men. Behind him the shouts and the pounding footsteps died down. He crossed to the next street. A green bus was pulling in to a stop. He climbed in it. Five minutes later, he got out and changed to a taxi. He breathed a little easier now. Hawk-face had been left behind.

Changing to a second taxi, he asked the driver a question. "Do you know a good cheap hotel where they will put me up without baggage?"

"I know a dozen."

"Take me to the nearest one."

Reaching the hotel, he paid for his room in advance. The desk clerk paid him no attention, evidently check-ins without baggage were no novelty in his life. The room to which he was taken was small and uncomfortable but it was a room. It was also protection, of a sort, against the menace outside in the growing night.

"Who am I?"

He began an examination of his clothes. In the right pocket was some loose change and eight dollars in bills, held in a large paper clip. There was no billfold with its identifying data. His coat pockets yielded what was left of the package of cigarettes and the lighter. And nothing else. No scraps of paper, no keys. He picked up the lighter.

THE CASE was gold plated but a scratch revealed the existence of some other metal under the gold, duro-steel he suspected. With the exception of the one that served as a lens for the devastating beam, the diamonds looked to be real. He judged each to be about half a caret in size. There was no maker's name on the lighter, somehow or other he had not expected to find one. People who made lighters like this one did not advertise them with their names.

He did not like this lighter.

Through it, he could glimpse dimly and vaguely the civilization around it. Life in a land where people carried deadly weapons disguised as cigarette lighters was a tricky, unfair business.

Because he had grim suspicions as to what would happen, he did not try to pry into the operating parts of the lighter. A ray weapon that could be held in the hand... Genius had made this lighter, but it was a sick genius, turning its high art to weapons of destruction, tearing down rather than building up.

The lighter told him nothing about himself. He began to examine his clothes. There was a maker's name in the suit but the garment had been factory made. Cleaner's marks were visible on the pockets. If he had time, they would tell him who he was, if he could locate the cleaner. He stripped down to his skin.

The skin was smooth and light brown in color, muscle tone seemed to be excellent and the muscles seemed to be well developed. He guessed offhand that he was about thirty years old. He seemed to be in good health, his hair was black, the mirror in the room told him that his face was well-formed and pleasant. There were no tattoo marks, he had known there wouldn't be any.

He still didn't know who he was, what he was, where he lived or where he worked. He did not know his occupation or profession. He lit a cigarette, cautiously using the lighter for this purpose. When used to light cigarettes it worked just like any other lighter.

There was a radio in the room, a quarter in the slot type. He found a quarter in the change he had taken from his pocket, slipped the coin into the slot, began to dress.

"Police report a new development in the case of Mike Toro, notorious killer who escaped two days ago from death row at the state penitentiary. While they are unwilling to state the exact nature of the new development, recapture of the killer is expected soon."

Listening, in the back of his mind fear opened a fanged mouth, and grinned at him. Was he Mike Toro? He pushed the thought resolutely out of his mind. The card sorter in his mind was still sulking in the corner, refusing to work. Was he Toro? The card sorter refused to answer the question for him, or any other question. "Give me the password," the sorter complained. "Give it to me before I work."

Password? Was there such a thing? If there was, he didn't know the answer. The girl had said there must be a maelstrom raging in his mind. The maelstrom was there all right. It consisted of questions, pounding ceaselessly. Are you Toro? If you are not Toro, who are you? What happened to you? What are you doing here? How did you lose your memory?

A sound caught his ear. He turned quickly. The door was opening. Hawk-face was coming in. He had a gun in his hand. There was another man with him.

"Take it easy, Sumner," Hawk-face said. "We're not going to hurt you. It's just that the boss says we are to get you."

HE HEARD the word Sumner. In his mind, the card sorter yelled: "That's it—that's the password. That's your name. Warren Sumner." Like a well-oiled machine beginning to function, the card sorter swung into high-speed action, bringing in regular order the cards of his life for his inspection.

Warren Sumner, age 31, a mathematician. In graduate school the professors had called him potentially the greatest mathematician alive. He had never attended college. A sweeping entrance examination had revealed that he had the mental capacity to skip the four-year college course and jump straight into the graduate school. Everything that had ever happened in his life came back to him, his childhood and his youth, the games he had played, the girls he had kissed. Memories of his work came back, the long patient mathematical exploration of the universe that he had attempted. Back early in the Twentieth Century the scientists had begun to suspect that if the enigmas of the universe were ever unlocked, they would yield themselves to a mathematical key. He remembered some of the articles he had published in scientific journals, mostly math, they had been. He remembered his search for the mathematical key that would unlock the complex inter-relationship between mind and matter, that would include in its analysis the way the mind formed concepts, the way the mind abstracted essential qualities from the world outside of it, the way the mind formed symbols. The mind was a part of the universe, it had to understand itself before it could understand the whole. He had gone through the work of the mathematicians and philosophers of past centuries, seeking understanding. He had found something. What?

The card sorter told him what he had found. Just a hint it had been, a clue. He had developed the equations and they had been published, attracting only jeering comment. Then he had begun to develop the equipment the equations described. He had rented space over a garage as a laboratory, had worked for years. Even the tools he had needed had not existed, he had had to invent them, then fabricate them before he could build the machine.

What was the machine?

"Are you sure you want to know?" the card sorter questioned.

He was sure. The sorter brought out the card. He looked at it, in his mind's eye. The sorter hastily put it back into file. He had built the machine. Two months past he had finished it. What had happened after that?

"Those cards are all locked up," the sorter explained. "I can't get to them, can't tell you what happened."

"Try and get to them."

"No use trying. They're locked. The lighter was all I could tell you about."

Two months were missing from his life. He had no memory whatsoever of the previous two months. It was this missing memory that had made him think the date on the newspaper had been wrong. Instead of the date being October 16, he had thought it should have been August 16.

His memory was sound again, except for this period. He looked at Hawk-face there in the room, the gun covering him. In his whole life as he recalled it was no memory of Hawk-face. "Take it easy, Sumner," Hawk-face repeated. "Just get your clothes on and come along with us. And no tricks, nothing like that trick you used to knock out the cabbie. This gun's got a mighty soft touch on the trigger."

"Did I ever see you before tonight?" Sumner questioned.

"Nope."

"What do you want with me? I don't know you."

"The boss wants to talk to you."

"Who is the boss?"

Hawk-face shook his head. This was a question he did not choose to answer.

"What does this boss want with me?"

"He'll tell you that."

"How did you find me?"

This was a question Hawk-face could answer. "We figured you'd try to hide out in a cheap dump somewhere. So we called on the hotels asking about people who had checked in without baggage during the last half-hour. We got you first crack out of the box."

"I see," Sumner said. He had had no experience in hiding and he had chosen a poor hiding place. He pulled on his clothes, pulled a cigarette out of the package, reached over to the dresser and picked up the lighter.

"Are you going under your own power or are you going to try to kick up a fuss?" Hawk-face said.

"How would you like to be dead?" Sumner said.

"Huh?" Hawk-face's eyes narrowed. As if his collar had suddenly become too tight, he reached up and thrust a finger between the cloth and the skin. "I don't get it."

"What did you do with the girl?"

"Huh? Oh. She came to and took air. We didn't do anything with her. Look, Sumner, the boss is waiting."

These men were tools, intermediaries. If he blasted them, others would take their place. He made up his mind. "Okay, I'll go," he said. He used the lighter to light the cigarette, then dropped it into his pocket.

He went out of the dingy hotel room between them. Probably there were not two more badly deceived men in the

19

whole continent of North America than Hawk-face and his partner. They thought they had him trapped. In point of fact, he could have destroyed both of them, and walked free.

But if he did this, he might never discover the identity of this mysterious boss behind them. Nor what the girl had meant when she had said that this must be the beginning of the pattern that was to take him out of history.

Out of history? What had she meant by that?

CHAPTER THREE

DOWN ON the street, they put him in the back seat of a Chevrolet sedan. He got the impression that this car had been chosen because there were literally millions of other cars like it on the street. Hawk-face sat beside him on the back seat. Under the streetlights, the gun Hawk-face was holding was evident. Sumner lit another cigarette and grinned at the gun.

"Pretty soon you're going to have to get down on the floorboards," Hawk-face said.

"Sure," Sumner answered. "You don't want me to see where I'm going, eh?"

"It safest that way. What you don't know you can't tell." A little later, he said, "Time to lay down now. And don't try to raise up a stink."

"No stink," Sumner said. Doors opened somewhere, the car slowed, stopped. Doors closed. "Here's where we get out," Hawk-face said. Sumner found himself in a basement garage, empty now, except for the car that had brought him here. They went up a flight of stairs.

"Watch him, Steve, while I go see if the boss is ready to talk to him," Hawk-face said. He disappeared up a flight of stairs, then returned, opened a door and motioned for Sumner to pass through it.

Sumner found himself in a room that might have been located anywhere. There was a green studio couch, a couple of chairs and a desk, all used, all worn. Two windows were closed off by lightproof cloth. The ceiling light shed a dull glow that was more concealing than revealing.

Behind the desk sat a man. Thick black unruly hair rose from a forehead and face that were too white. A trace of a scar showed along one cheek. Sumner noted these things as being unimportant. It was the man's eyes that held his attention. They were shiny black with a hot glint in them that told all the world to go to hell.

A man with eyes like these was automatically a big shot. The eyes were a plain warning to everybody to get out of this man's path and the devil take anybody who ignored the warning.

"This is him," Hawk-face spoke.

Almost imperceptibly, the man at the desk nodded. Hawk-face moved soundlessly away. The door closed softly.

"Won't you sit down, Mr. Sumner?" The tone was courteous, almost pleasant. It would have been pleasant except for the note of compulsion in it. Because of this tone, this man would naturally lead other men. Others would follow him, because of the eyes and the tone. But they would not love him, for the same reasons.

Sumner sat down.

"Cigar, cigarette?" The scientist took the cigarette that was offered, took the lighter from his pocket. Keeping it cupped in his hands, he lit the cigarette. When he had finished using the lighter, it was still in his hand but below the level of the desk. The black eyes searched Sumner's face. "You are Warren Sumner?" Privately he seemed to feel reason to doubt the identity of the scientist.

"Yes."

"I—ah—well I was sort of expecting—"

"A bigger man?"

"Sort of." He stared curiously at Sumner as if he found in the scientist an object of intense interest. "Well. You're Sumner." He shook his head. "I guess you are, all right. I saw a statue of you once—"

"I beg your pardon," Sumner gasped. The remark had been

made so casually and carelessly that he thought he had misunderstood. "A statue of me?"

"Yeah. There's a statue of you. Several of them, I expect. Didn't you know?"

SUMNER felt his mouth sag open. He snapped it shut. This man was insane. There was no other conclusion. A statue of him? Not a hundred people even knew that he existed.

"To hell with that." The man behind the desk shrugged away a dozen statues with one twist of his shoulders. "Do you know who I am?"

"No."

"Do you want to know?"

"I—I guess so." Confusion was putting his self-control under vigorous attack.

"I'm Mike Toro."

"Huh? I mean—" At the moment his mind was simply too busy with other tasks to recall this name.

"You mean you've never heard of me, never heard of Mike Toro?" The man behind the desk seemed to find this hard indeed to believe.

"Oh," Sumner said. His memory gave him back the name that he had heard on the radio broadcast. Again confusion assaulted his mind. He pushed it away, forced himself to think of Mike Toro and what Mike Toro could possibly mean to him. He had never seen the man until this moment, had not known that he existed until he heard the radio broadcast. But Toro seemed to know about him. Toro had certainly sent men seeking him.

"They—they're looking for you." Sumner couldn't think of anything else to say.

"I know. They've got a special cell wired for gas all ready for me." Toro's laugh was brittle and without point.

"What did you do?"

"To earn a trip to the death cell? Nothing, really. I killed a fool. The trouble was, several people saw me do it." He shook his head, dismissing from consideration the unnamed fool who had died by his hand. "Do you know why I sent for you?"

"I do not."

"I want you to hide me."

"Hide you?" Of all the answers Sumner had been anticipating, this was the one he had least expected. "I should think you would have connections adequate for that purpose."

"I got connections all right but they won't hold up long. I killed another fool on the getaway and this one was a cop. Sooner or later another cop will get me under the sights of his gun. No, I got to get away."

"I should think you would have planned a hiding place when you planned an escape."

"I did."

"Well—"

"You were it."

"I?"

"You still are."

"Eh?" Was this man mad? "I don't understand you."

"Sure, sure," Toro answered impatiently. "I'd put on that act too, in your shoes."

"What act? What are you talking about?"

"Quit kidding." Toro was becoming more and more impatient. "I know about you and you won't do yourself a nickel's worth of good by trying to act innocent. I want you to hide me in time."

"What?" Sumner gasped the single word.

"I said to quit kidding. Didn't you develop the time equations?"

SUMNER was more surprised than ever, mostly at the fact that this man knew about the equations. They had been a mathematical development of the concept of time as the fourth dimension of space inadequately perceived and distorted in the human eyes and the human mind. In effect, they said that time was a fourth dimension of space, but that the human perceptive mechanism perceived this fourth dimension inadequately as time. The theory was not new, the equations were. "What has this got to do with hiding you?"

"Didn't you say that the equations meant that a time machine could be built?"

"I said no such thing. True, there was a story in the newspaper about me, but the writer misquoted me."

Toro seemed not to hear. "Didn't you build a time machine?"

"I?" Sumner gasped.

"Please," Toro said. "Where have you been the last two months?"

Sumner was silent.

"You've been in time," Toro said. "When the boys said they couldn't find you, I knew where you were. I had them on the watch for you all around your lab. We were waiting for you to come back—*out of time.*"

Sumner was still silent. Up to two months ago his memory was clear and complete. He had been constructing a time machine, he had been working on it for years, working secretly. Although Sumner had not been willing to admit it, Toro had been telling the exact truth—up to a point. That point was two months in the past. It covered the period of which Sumner had no memory.

Had he actually used the time machine, had he actually been in time during these two months? He had no memory of using the machine, merely of getting it ready for use. He had no memory of being in time. So far as he was concerned, the two months were formless, foggy, without definition and without clearness, a period from which the card sorter could produce no memory cards. Had he actually been in time? He started to laugh, then stopped abruptly as his eyes caught a flicker from one of the diamonds on the lighter in his hand.

In the year 1950 this lighter could not exist. Science could not construct such a device.

Yet he had it.

Where had he gotten it?

Where, if not in time?

Sweat appeared on Sumner's face. Fear turned a double somersault in his mind, laughing like an idiot. His frozen gaze came up to Toro's face.

The killer was watching him and was nodding. Eager lights were burning in the black eyes. "It's like this, Sumner. A man in my shoes doesn't have much choice. If I as much as show my nose outside this room, the chances are I'll be picked up. I'll be lucky if they even take me in, if the first cop who sees me doesn't put a bullet in me first, before he bothers to take me in. Even if I get taken in alive, all I'll get will be a fast trip to the death chamber... If I stay here, sooner or later one of my own boys will turn me in, for a shot at the reward money. I can't get out of the country. The airports are watched, the ships are watched, the border is watched. Every cop in the country has a picture of me pasted right up behind his eyes. Every bulletin board in every police station and in every post office and in every sheriff's office has a poster of me. I'm just about as hot as any human being can get and stay alive. I kinda like living. Which is where you come in."

"But—"

"There are no 'buts.' I don't have any place to hide. Try and understand that. Try to understand also that if you don't help me, I'm a dead man. So far as money is concerned, I've got some of it stashed away. Anything you say will be all right. A hundred grand—" The voice became persuasive but the eyes did not leave Sumner's face. The scientist sweated. He was glad he had the lighter, glad because it was his only way out, or the only one that he could see.

Aiding a fugitive from justice was a serious criminal offense.

"Suppose I refuse to help you?" Sumner said.

"Huh?" For a moment Toro was startled, then he laughed, a sound without mirth in it. "You don't have much control over the situation."

"Don't I?"

"No." The black eyes were hot. "Sumner, get it straight—I'll kill you if you don't help me."

Toro meant every word he said. His meaning was clear in the tone of his voice and in the glitter of his black eyes. There were many questions about this man, which Sumner would like to have answered—how he lad gotten his knowledge of the time equations was one of them—but there was no chance of asking them now. Toro would kill him if he did not obey. Probably if he did obey, if he sent Toro into time—presuming he was able to do that—Toro would kill him anyway, to protect himself.

Either way the answer was the same. Sumner shrugged. "I guess you've got me." The lighter in his hand, he rose to his feet. As he moved, his finger sought the tiny firing stud. He brought up the lighter.

Toro saw it. His eyes glittered with hot flame. He could not have recoiled faster if he had seen a rattlesnake. He came to his feet in a single lunging motion, his left fist driving straight at Sumner's chin.

Smack! The fist connected.

Sumner saw the fist coming, tried to dodge. Too late and too slow. He knew when the fist landed on the point of his jaw, knew he was going over backward. Falling, his head rammed hard against the door facing. Lights flashed in front of his eyes like exploding fireworks on the night of the Fourth of July. Then the lights were engulfed by darkness.

Sumner felt himself fall, crashing, into that darkness.

CHAPTER FOUR

AMMONIA stung his nostrils, biting, eating its way into the lining of his nose. He sneezed violently and tried to shove the ammonia away. "He's coming to," a voice said.

"Get that damned stuff away from me," Sumner muttered. The ammonia was irritating, there was also nausea in his stomach. What had happened to him? His card sorter was out of order again, his memory flickering like a badly-run movie.

The ammonia was taken away. "I'll handle it from now on," Toro's voice came. "You go outside and watch in the car. If anything suspicious shows, honk twice." Footsteps faded away. Sumner sat up. Agony clamped a hard vise around his stomach. He held his head in his hands and waited while the agony settled itself a little. His head felt like it was going to split wide open.

"Feel kinda bad?" Toro said.

Sumner nodded.

"Sorry I had to hit you but you shouldn't have tried to use Kovenair beam on me," the killer said placatingly.

"Kovenair beam?" Sumner muttered.

"A fellow by the name of Kovenair invented it," Toro explained. "It got its name from him."

"You mean the lighter?"

"Yeah."

Sumner thought of that. He had never heard of anybody by the name of Kovenair but his ignorance proved nothing. He twisted his head, was somewhat relieved to find that it did not fall off and that his neck was not broken, as he had halfway expected. Little by little the shooting pains inside his skull began to subside. He lifted his head, looked around. He was in his own laboratory.

"You move fast," he said.

"Yeah. I thought we might as well bring you over here before you woke up."

It wasn't an elaborate place. The lab occupied the second floor over a run-down garage, a spot he had chosen because the rent was low and because the people living in the neighborhood were elaborately unconcerned with the activities of a scientist. They had regarded him as just another queer duck in a world that already had too large a supply of that commodity. Yes, this was his lab. There was the three-wire input lines bringing 220 volt current into the room from the big transformer outside the window, there were the workbenches with the equipment piled in disarray, just as he had left them, there was—

He looked once, blinked, then looked again. In one corner

was an array of equipment grouped together into a machine of some kind. Heavy power leads ran from a motor generator to a series of radio tubes that had been designed to produce vhf (very high frequency) oscillations. He stared at the array. In his mind, the card sorter reluctantly brought him information about this machine, its purpose, its function.

Toro was watching him. "There it is," the killer said.

"I see," Sumner said. "If you knew it was here, why didn't you just go ahead and use it, why did you have to kidnap me?"

"If they had pushed me hard enough I would have done just that," Toro answered. "But I would rather have you around working it for me. I'm a little bit scared of the thing."

"How did you know it was here, how did you know about me?" Sumner questioned. This question had been rising in his mind all the time, demanding an answer, but he had been pushing it aside in favor of other questions.

"I had the boys start looking for you and when they couldn't find you, I had them start looking for it," Toro said.

"But how did you even know I existed?"

"How?" Toro seemed astonished. "I finally remembered about you."

"But how could you remember about me when we had never met, when, so far as I know, you had never heard of me?"

"I remembered reading about you. I told you I had seen a statue of you."

"Where am I famous?"

"Why, in the future," Toro answered, surprised. "Don't you yet know about yourself? You're one of the most famous men who ever lived—*you're the man who invented time travel!*"

"I—WHAT?" Sumner choked. His gaze lifted, went back to the machine. Astonishment reeling through his mind. He knew he had been working on the problem of time travel, he knew he had been trying to design a time machine, but he did not know that he had succeeded. There the machine stood. Like the lighter, it was evidence that could not be brushed away.

He had built it. But the functioning of the machine, if he had used it, belonged to that blank period in his life. He had no memory of using it. When he tried to remember if he had used it and what had happened to him, the card sorter in his mind patiently told him that those cards were in the forbidden section.

"How do you know I invented time travel? How do you know I am famous because of that?"

"Because I came from the future," Toro explained. "Hell, man, they used your invention to shoot me back here into time. I had enemies in my own world. They got rid of me by kicking me back into time." Hot anger directed at those enemies showed on the swarthy face and in the dark eyes. "After I landed here, I kept quiet until I had learned the language and the customs. Both change, you know. Then I began to branch out. I was doing fine until I got into trouble. Only when they had me on the way to the gas chamber did I remember that I had come back to the exact time when the inventor of time travel was alive. That was when I had the boys start looking for you. If I could find you, I could not only save my neck here but I could get you to send me back to my own time where I can get even with the dirty doublecrossing rats who trapped me and sent me here."

Bang! went Toro's fist on the table. "I'm killing two birds with one rock, Sumner. I'm escaping to a place where the cops here will never find me—and I'm returning to get even with the rats who sent me here. They've forgotten all about me by now. Won't they be surprised when I give 'em a dose of the Kovenair beam!" He gloated at the thought. "I've got it all planned out already, just exactly what I'll do and how I'll do it. They'll get the Kovenair beam all right—at full power."

Listening, Warren Sumner felt sickness rise again in his stomach. He had developed the time equations and had designed and built the first practical time machine. His purpose, aside from the actual pure thrill of discovery, had been manifold. First, he had thought of using time travel for exploration, and he had actually collected gear, rifles, axes, knives, all the tools an explorer might need, for trips into the remote past, into those periods of earth about which history tells little or nothing. They were all here in the lab now, in the big wooden box in the far end of the room.

The idea of using time travel to explore the past had tremendous appeal to him. Historians had wrangled for generations about the real cause of the fall of Rome. If time travel was possible, trained historians could be sent back to the time of Rome to make an on-the-spot investigation of the cause of the fall of that mighty civilization. Cro-Magnon man had vanished, leaving behind him a mystery that puzzled anthropologists. With time travel, scientists could go back to the days of the Cro-Magnons, follow this ancient race to its final resting-place. There was, for instance, the mystery of the great Pyramid. Who had built this great stone monument, and why. What methods had been employed? How had the gigantic blocks of stone been transported from the quarries to the building site? Science had no real explanation. There were other mysteries hidden in the depths of time, challenging the mind. There was the puzzle of the Sumerians, the inhabitants of the ancient land of Sumer. Where had they come from? There was the puzzling question of the origin of the planet Venus? Had Venus actually been a comet that had wandered into the solar system. Or had it been torn from the planet Jupiter? Time travel would solve the problem. Time travel would solve a thousand problems. Or so he had thought. So he had planned, so he had dreamed.

HIS SICKNESS came from the fact, clear now before his eyes, that his invention had been perverted to other uses. Somebody had used it as a weapon, a way to get rid of an enemy. Taro was planning to use it as a way to escape from the law. Thus men had made a mockery of his dream, had trampled it in the dust, had spat upon it, had used it for selfish purposes. He wondered about the unknown Kovenair who had devised the beam that now was used as a weapon hidden in a cigarette lighter. What had been Kovenair's dream when he had discovered the beam? It hadn't been destruction, Sumner thought. No real scientist ever willingly built a weapon, except for his own defense. But vicious men perverted the discoveries of science to selfish purposes.

"But why did you come to me?" Sumner protested. "Why didn't you just build your own time machine?"

"Because I don't know how," Toro answered.

"But you came from the future, you've been in a time machine."

"Sure, but they aren't exactly common things even in the future. You've seen a jet plane fly, haven't you?"

"Sure."

"Could you build one?"

"No."

"Well, I've seen a time machine work, but I couldn't begin to build one."

"How far into the future do you want to go?"

"To 2930," Toro answered promptly.

Sumner was silent, thinking. There was a way out of this situation, but it was a way he did not want to take if he could avoid it. "What do you know about the laws of time travel?" he asked.

"Nothing. I didn't even know there were any laws."

"What if there is a law, which says you can't go back to your own time?"

The black eyes fixed themselves on Sumner. "I wouldn't do any kidding, if I were in your shoes." He reached into his pocket, brought out the lighter. "There's a lot of ways to use this thing. Do you know all of them?"

"I guess not."

"Well, here's one you may have missed." He focused the lighter on the scientist's hand. At low power, the beam shot out. Sumner choked back the scream that leaped to his lips. The sensation in his hand was one of unbearable agony. He jerked away. Laughing, Toro turned off the beam. "That's just a sample." He slid the lighter back into his pocket. "Get busy, Sumner."

Sumner slid from the table, moved unsteadily toward the equipment in the back end of the room, Toro following like a watchful shadow. The equipment was exceedingly complex but the main function was clear. There was a seat, a place for an operator to sit. Directly in front of the seat was a control panel, containing among other things a two-way switch and a finely graduated dial. The two-way switch was marked F and B, F for Forward, B for Back. The radiation from the machine was focused on the operator in the control seat. The dial registered the number of years for which the machine was set. There was a final switch, which set the whole machine in operation.

The operator made the setting in advance, then shoved home the final switch. The setting of the instruments determined where he went in time. When he reached the designated year, the machine turned off automatically. After that, the operator was strictly on his own. The machine did not go with him. It remained here, in this time.

The effect of the operation of the machine was simply the drawing of a quick veil between the operator and reality. When the machine turned itself off, the veil disappeared. And the operator found himself in a new time.

Outside, in the night, a horn honked—twice.

TORO SPUN, ran toward the light switch. "I got to see what that is. Don't try anything funny in the dark." He reached the switch, snapped it off. From his pocket, he jerked a flashlight. The beam caught Sumner. "Be still, you." Sumner was still.

The horn did not honk again.

Crash!

A window in the back end of the lab exploded in a shower of breaking glass. Something thudded against the ceiling, fell to the floor. Simultaneously a window on the other side of the lab burst in a shower of glass. Again something struck the ceiling, fell to the floor.

Two soft *phuts* sounded. They weren't loud noises, they didn't sound dangerous. Sumner wondered what they were. Apparently Toro knew.

"Gas grenades," the killer shouted.

An instant later, Sumner caught the first whiff of the raw gas and began to choke. He heard Toro curse again, heard other gas grenades land in the room and explode softly. He dropped on the floor, rolled himself into a ball, covered his nose and his eyes and tried not to breathe.

This was tear gas, he vaguely recognized. From outside came a babble of voices, growing in intensity.

"Surrender in there or we'll blast you out."

The police, Sumner thought, with vast thanksgiving. Even though his eyes were closed, he caught glimpses of bright lights playing on the ceiling, knew that squad cars with searchlights were outside.

"The place is surrounded," Taro gasped. "We're taken."

From the grenades, the gas poured into the laboratory in a blinding, choking, torturing flood.

CHAPTER FIVE

THE TRIP to the police station blew some of the gas away but it left both men still sneezing violently and still trying to see from eyes that were made worse by rubbing. Both were handcuffed with their hands in front of them. In the station, they were lined up in front of the desk. Behind it a burly sergeant gloated at them.

Flashbulbs were already popping, the news bureau man on duty at the station had already called in a flash on this story and the regular reporters were on their way as fast as cars could bring them.

The contents of Toro's pockets were emptied out on the desk in front of the sergeant. Sumner was given similar treatment. No thought or effort was given to removing the handcuffs from either man. Already the headlines were screaming:

KILLER CAUGHT!

Taro's eyes were red, he coughed constantly, but he still maintained something of his composure. "All right, boys, all right," he kept saying. "You'll all get your picture in the paper. No need to push, no need to shove." He joked with the men who had captured him, they didn't joke back, but that made no difference to him. "How'd you find out where I was?" he asked.

"A dame tipped us off," a pompous captain answered. The captain was giving instructions to the desk sergeant and was obviously waiting for the arrival of the newsmen before booking the prisoner.

"What dame?" Toro questioned.

The captain did not answer. In truth, he did not know the identity of the unknown woman who had called the station, but he was not prepared to admit his ignorance. He turned to Sumner.

"What's your name?"

"Warren Sumner," the scientist answered, and waited for the name to be recognized. Somehow he expected this captain to know his name.

"Probably a phony but book him that way anyhow," the captain said to the sergeant.

"Book me? What for?"

"Harboring a fugitive."

"But I wasn't harboring him; he had kidnapped me," Sumner protested, and saw that the captain wasn't listening. Nor was anyone else. The whole big station was crowded with men but no one was paying him any attention. They were all watching Toro. "I want to talk to my lawyer," Sumner said.

"Huh?" The captain gave him a look of disgust. "Aw, hell, shut up. You can talk to your lawyer tomorrow."

"But he kidnapped me."

"Why?"

"So he could force me to send him through time," Sumner answered. It was the truth, if he had ever spoken it.

A strained expression appeared on the captain's face. For the first time, Sumner had his thoughtful attention. "When did you get loose?" he said.

"Loose—"

"From the nuthouse."

Sumner was suddenly silent. He knew instantly that he should have kept his mouth shut. He saw what he was facing. The pompous captain was not kidding him when he said the scientist would probably face charges for harboring a fugitive. In view of Toro's reputation, and the wide publicity that had been given his escape, there was no chance that Sumner could plead innocent of the identity of the man. And if he claimed he was kidnapped, how could he prove it? If he told the truth— He saw the trap that waited for him in that direction, too. In the year 1950 no jury would be willing to believe in the reality of time travel.

THE NEWSMEN and the photographers arrived. Flashbulbs began popping again. Reporters yelled questions. Sumner was elbowed to the side. "Scowl, Toro," a photographer yelled. Toro scowled accommodatingly. "Grin, Toro." It was a lop-sided grin with no mirth in it, but he tried it. He seemed to be willing to do anything for the reporters. The pompous captain was in seventh heaven.

"Want one of me lighting a cigarette?" Toro asked.

"Sure," the photographer yelled.

Toro leaned forward, picked up the crumbled package from among his belongings on the desktop. His hands were cuffed together but he managed to extract a cigarette and stick it between his lips. Grinning, he reached for the lighter.

And Sumner at last understood why Toro had co-operated so willingly with the reporters and the photographers. Every action he had taken had been directed toward this moment.

"Watch him!" Sumner screamed.

Even if they had known what to watch, his voice was too late. Toro already had the lighter in his hands. He used it at full power.

The head of the pompous captain vanished in a blur of red mist. His headless body fell like the chunk of dead meat that it was. Toro turned the lighter in another direction. A photographer with his camera ready to shoot did not get the picture of the killer lighting a cigarette. In a half crouch, he stumbled and went down. Behind the desk, the sergeant reached for his gun. He did not complete the motion.

The jammed police station was suddenly a bedlam of sound. Sumner threw himself flat on the floor. Around him men were falling like trees growing down. Toro had turned on the death-dealing Kovenair beam at full power. At full flow, it was as deadly a weapon as has ever come from the brain of inventive man. At close range it literally dissolved tissue, made flesh creep and crawl. At longer range, ten feet or more, men were knocked unconscious, blistered, and badly burned. Whether or not the falling men were dead Sumner did not know. Toro certainly did not care. He used the lighter like a spray.

One cop got his gun free. It barked once. Toro turned the lighter toward the cop. The gun did not bark again.

The room was suddenly empty of men on their feet. At the rear a detective was trying to crawl. Toro saw him, lined up the lighter. The spray of light lanced out. The detective screamed and went limp to the floor.

Toro grunted with satisfaction. Bending down, he searched the pockets of the dead captain until he found a set of keys. He grunted again, applied the keys to the cuffs on his wrist. A key fitted. The cuffs came free. He threw them across the room, looked around again. His eyes came to focus on Sumner. He bent over.

"Okay, get up. You're not hurt."

Sumner rose to his feet. Toro unlocked the cuffs from his wrists. "Come on," he said. Sumner followed him. Outside,

Toro moved toward the nearest police car parked at the curb, opened the door, slid behind the wheel.

"Where are we going?" Sumner questioned.

"Back to your lab," Toro answered. "I got away this time but I was lucky. Next time I won't be so lucky. Next time they'll shoot first and take pictures afterward."

"But they will trace you by this car."

"Sure. They'll trace me to your lab. But by the time they get there, I'll be gone."

WITH THE siren going full tilt, he drove the car through the streets. Traffic got out of his way just as it would have gotten out of the way of any other police car. Brazenly he drove the car up to the front door of the lab. "They probably left a guard staked out here," he said. "That's the way they work. Ah, here he comes now, like Rover looking for a burglar. Well, he's found one."

The policeman came on the run toward the squad car. He thought it was occupied by his own kind. As he came up Toro lifted the lighter.

The cop died without a sound.

They went unmolested up the stairs and turned on the lights. The odor of gas still lingered in the laboratory. "Get busy," Toro said.

Sumner nodded. His mind was already made up. He turned current into the time machine, checked its function as it warmed up. "What was that year again?" he asked.

"2930," Toro answered. "And no tricks."

"There will be no tricks," Sumner said. "You asked to go back to your own time. I'm sending you there."

Toro stepped into the machine, slid into the seat. Somewhere far off in the night a siren began to howl. Toro cocked his head to one side, listening. The siren went into silence. "Maybe coming here, maybe not," the killer said. "Well, they'll never get me. Is this the way I turn on the juice?"

"It is," Sumner said.

Toro shoved home the switch.

The transformer hummed heavily as it sucked power from the lines. The framework of the machine began to glow and flicker like a neon light trying to turn on.

Toro went out of time like a ghost going out of existence. He became insubstantial. Then he was gone. Gone like a man going into nothingness, gone across a dimension interspace, gone back to his own time. The machine cut off automatically, automatically it reappeared. The seat was empty. Toro was gone.

Long after the current had been cut off Sumner stared at the space Toro had occupied. The girl came out of the darkness of the laboratory and stood beside him. He looked around at her. "Hello," he said. He was not surprised. It seemed natural for her to be there.

She was the girl with the violet eyes.

"Did you tip off the police?" Sumner said.

She nodded. "I was trying to find you again. I thought, when you regained your memory, you would be sure to return here. So I watched and waited. You came with him."

He was silent. She was silent. When she spoke, her voice was odd. "I heard you say he was going back to his own time?" He nodded.

"But—" she hesitated, her voice faltered into silence, then came again. "The law—"

"I know," he said. "I developed the time equations from the original law, which says: *Two bodies cannot occupy the same space at the same time.*" This had been his starting point on the time equations. The law was valid. But from it another law could be deduced.

The girl's face whitened. "The same body—" Again she faltered.

"I know," Sumner said. *"The same body cannot occupy the same time twice.* This means you cannot appear twice in the same time. If you have lived from January through June of the year 1950, you cannot go back in time and live this period over again. That section of time is forever barred to you. You can go around it, to reach a year you have not previously occupied, but you cannot go back to a time in which you have already lived. If you did, you would meet yourself. Hence the law."

"But Toro—" She could go no farther.

"I know," he repeated. "He insisted on going back to his own time again... In doing this, he violated the law." His voice sank into silence while he thought of what happened to men who violated nature's laws. Man-made laws could sometimes be violated with impunity. Nature's laws—never. Nature always exacted her penalty.

"What do you think happened to him?" she whispered.

"When the machine released him, in his own time, he was in violation of the law. He could not occupy that time again. I think—mind you I don't know for sure—but I think he was forced entirely out of time, completely out of our space-time continuum. What happens when two bodies try to occupy the same space? One gets pushed aside into some other space. What happened to Toro when he tried to occupy the same time twice? He got shoved aside, into some other time." He tried to think of what had happened to this violent killer, then tried not to think of it. It had been a ghastly end, he suspected. Toro's twisted, distorted, wretched body had been shoved into subspace, in effect, it had been hurled out of existence altogether.

SUMNER SHUDDERED. The picture would haunt his dreams for many nights to come. But he knew Toro had gotten exactly what was coming to him.

"Yes," the girl said. "He had earned what he got."

"Who are you?" Sumner spoke.

"I'm a sort of guard," she answered.

"Guard?"

"Yes. There's a missing period in your life."

"Two months," he said.

"You spent that time in the future. Developing the time equations and building a time machine, you came forward to the future. We recognized you for who and what you were and tried to make you welcome. But you would not stay in our time. You didn't like it there. You insisted on coming back here. We sent you back. I came ahead of you, to help you."

"You volunteered for this task?" he said.

"Yes. It wasn't a task, it was an honor. To a few of us in my time, you were a sort of a god, to the scientists, to the real thinkers. We sent you back as near to your own time as we could. In this case, two months was as near as we dared to try for. Otherwise, we might have miscalculated, and send you back into a time you had already occupied. If that had happened, you would have vanished like Toro." She shivered, forcing her mind away from this thought.

"Thus to you there were two months missing from your life."

"I can't remember the future," he said. "I can't..."

"Who can?" she answered. "There is some kind of a psychic block that keeps you from remembering, or at least from remembering clearly. Later, after a week or two, we can remember better. I came back ahead of you. When you returned, I was waiting. But you did not remember me, you couldn't, from the very nature of the mental block in your mind. When I met you, I could see you were in some kind of trouble. I tried to help you but you did not understand what I was doing."

"I see," he said. He still could not remember. His mind was busy with other things.

"Also, I was curious," she said. "About you. Much is known about you, but much has been lost. The time equations that you developed were not really used until over two hundred years after your original lifetime. Then they were rescued from the long-forgotten technical publication that printed them and their value was at last understood and recognized. But you, Warren Sumner the man, remained a mystery. You vanished from history. Why?"

He nodded. He was pretty sure now, that he could tell her

why. It was a complex problem and it was tied up with his dislike for the time in which he lived. He moved toward the heavy chest at the back of the room. How close was the squad car that Toro had heard? Or had it gone on another call? Whether it was coming here or not, certainly a tremendous search was beginning, for Toro and for him.

"What are you going to do?" the girl questioned.

"I think I've known all along what I was going to do," he replied. He opened the chest, began to take objects from it. A rifle with cartridges. An axe, a hatchet, a case of hunting knives. There were other tools, needles, thread, bolts of stout cloth, such things as an explorer in a primitive world might need. Or a man going into the dawn of history. The girl watched him.

"You're going back into time?" she whispered.

"Yes," he answered.

"So that is the solution to the mystery about you? You went into the past. You left your time machine here, but nobody understood what it was."

"That's right, I guess."

"But why did you go back into the past?"

"Why?" He fumbled with the word, tried to find other words that would explain his motives. "Down on the street there is a squad car and dead policeman. Sooner or later, they will be discovered. The trail that starts there will lead inevitably to me. I shall be captured. I shall be recognized as the man who was with Toro when he disappeared."

"Can't you explain?"

He shook his head. "No. Any explanation I could give would get me either the penitentiary or the insane asylum. Before they took me to the penitentiary, the police would literally beat me to death, or hound me to death, trying to find out what had happened to Toro. If I tell them what really happened, they won't believe it. If I don't tell them—" He shook his head. "No. Anyhow I've always wanted to live in some other time, when the world was cleaner and fresher and better. That's where I'm going."

Outside, on the street, tires screeched. The sound was not repeated. A car had stopped there, suddenly. From the distance came the roar of a racing motor. He began quickly to move the contents of the chest to the time machine.

The girl came with him. "I—I— Do you mind if I go too?" she said.

"Do I mind?" He hardly knew what to say.

"I feel the same way you do, that the past world is cleaner and better. I would like to see it, to live in it, with you."

He grinned. "There is nothing I would like better."

Moving the switch over to the B position, he set the time dial, then turned power into the equipment. The girl stood very close to him. There was no hesitation in her manner, no faltering. Where he went, she was going. He liked that.

The glow came up around them like a protecting and concealing flame.

WHEN THE nervous police came up the stairs, they found an empty laboratory. But they didn't find Mike Toro or Sumner.

The newspapers carried headlines: Killer Eludes Police. Riot in Police Station. Hunt Still in Progress. Obscure Scientist Missing.

Neither the police nor the reporters were ever able to make sense out of the equipment in the laboratory. As for Sumner, in the year 1950, he was a minor figure, unimportant. True, he had developed the time equations—but nobody understood them. In the future, he was known as the inventor of time travel, his name was honored, he was a scientific colossus walking across the pages of history.

The mystery of his disappearance was never solved. Here and there a few discerning souls, reading aright the signs he left behind him, may have guessed what happened to him. But they, like he, are in a minority, and are unimportant.

THE END

Find Me in Eternity

In every physical way they seemed to be identical. But one question remained a mystery: which one of them was a superman?

CHAPTER ONE

WHEN Harold Miller returned from his fishing trip, he was a day late in getting home and he was expecting to catch a little hell from his wife for being late but he wasn't expecting to run slam-bang into the problem that was waiting for him. Pulling into the driveway beside the house he occupied in the suburbs, he stopped the car in front of the garage and got out, expecting his wife to come out the back door and say "Hello" and maybe give him a big hug, she being an affectionate girl who could usually hardly wait. But she didn't show.

One of the neighbor's kids had been playing in the drive, getting out of the way of the car. When Miller got out, he said, "Hi" to the kid. The youngster didn't answer. Instead the kid, who was about eight, took a long steady look at him, then went yikety-yikety straight for the back door of his own house, yelling for mama at the top of his voice.

The kid's actions surprised Miller. Just the sight of him didn't usually scare kids into conniption fits, especially not ones who knew him. But this kid had acted scared. He saw the kid and his mother in the kitchen of the house next door, the kid pointing at him and the mother staring hard at him through the glass. He waved at her, to show her he hadn't run over or otherwise damaged her offspring, then went up the back steps of his own house, expecting to find his wife in the kitchen and maybe cooking up something good for him to eat. But the door was locked and his wife wasn't in the kitchen.

"Probably shopping," he thought. Unlocking the back door, he went into the house. The place smelled musty, the way a house does when all the windows are closed. Thrust under the front door was a yellow envelope, a telegram, which he opened. It was his own telegram, which he had sent the day before telling his wife he would be a day late in returning home.

Obviously, she had not received it. Since the time stamp showed it had been delivered the day before, she hadn't been home since yesterday.

It was a situation that will cause a man to wonder. Miller and his wife got along fine; he didn't think she was stepping out on him or had left him. But the telegram under the door took the wind out of him. He searched the house for a message from her, found nothing. The place was in order, there was no sign of a struggle, she hadn't been robbed or attacked, at least not here. Then where was she?

Miller was a biochemist—the calm type. He was employed as a research assistant by the Gerontology Foundation, a large, privately-financed foundation doing research in the field of gerontology, the scientific study of the phenomena of old age. It was quite a field. In actual fact the Foundation was not so much interested in the phenomena of old age as it was in discovering a method to keep men from growing old. Its aim was simple—immortality. Since it never expected to reach that goal and wasn't too sure the goal was worth reaching, its more practical goal was to discover ways and means by which men could live to the age of a hundred—and retain their physical and mental powers. Or two hundred.

WITH THIS goal in mind, the Foundation had no difficulty in finding all the money it needed to operate. All it had to do when it wanted money was to reach out and tap the nearest millionaire who was getting along in years and ask him if he wanted to make a small contribution to the Fountain of Youth, and stipulate that if the research was successful the donors would get first crack at the results. How to keep from growing old, how to keep from dying, how to dodge the old man with the scythe, this was the problem they were trying to solve. The rather pompous but usually pleasant director, Dr. George Claxton, always managed to find money when it was needed.

The research program was getting results, too. Not practical results as yet, not the way to take a sixty year old man and turn him into a kid of thirty, but hints, clues, tips, which led them to believe that the problem would eventually be solved. Another ten years of research might do it. A lucky break might do it. Lucky breaks had solved many a problem in research. Why not this one?

Harold Miller was thinking of going next door and asking his neighbor if she knew where his wife was when he saw the squad car pull up in front of the neighbor's house. Two cops got out of it and started up the walk. Mrs. Atkinson, his neighbor, her eight-year old son with her, went running down to meet them.

"What's going on?" Miller thought. A conference immediately began in front of Mrs. Atkinson's house. She pointed toward his house, and was apparently talking a blue streak. The cops nodded. They moved toward Miller's house, one going toward the front door, the other moving around to the back, apparently to cut off his line of retreat in case he chose to try to flee in that direction.

The sight of the law moving in on him gave Miller a shock. His wife gone, the cops coming for him. At least he assumed they were coming for him. As a knock sounded, he went promptly to the front door. Mrs. Atkinson, the kid, and the cop were there.

The kid yelled: "That's him."

Mrs. Atkinson said: "There he—" Then she shut up, staring at Miller as if she was seeing a ghost.

Harold Miller said: "Okay, here I am." He was irritated.

The cop said: "What are you doing in this house?" He wasn't very polite about it either.

"What's it to you, what I'm doing in this house? I own it, me and the mortgage company, that is." Since he was a homeowner and a taxpayer and he was in his own home, he didn't propose to take much guff from cops, especially from cops who asked silly questions. "Why can't I be in this house?"

The cop was taken aback. He looked Miller up and down and turned to Mrs. Atkinson. "Do you know this man?"

"Why—" She said the same word three times, her voice getting fainter each time she opened her mouth. When she finished, she was down to a whisper.

"Just what is going on?" the cop demanded. "You call us to come out here. You say there is an intruder in this house. The intruder comes to the door and says he owns the house. I ask you if you know him and all you say is—'Why—' Is this man a trespasser or isn't he?"

MRS. ATKINSON swallowed hard. She kept looking at Miller and then looking away and then looking back at him as if she was expecting him to disappear between looks. "He—he looks like Mr. Miller. He—he talks like Mr. Miller. But he just can't be." She was wringing her hands and looked as if she wasn't a bit happy with Harold Miller, with herself, or with the police.

"Why can't I be Harold Miller?"

"Because you're in the hospital," Mrs. Atkinson answered. "You were hurt in an automobile accident yesterday afternoon. The hospital called your wife. She came over and told me what had happened and said she was going to the hospital right away. Later, she called me from the hospital and said you were there, that you were unconscious but that you didn't seem to be too badly hurt, and that she was going to stay there, with you last night. She asked me to keep an eye on things. When I saw you come—well, I called the police."

"Uh," Miller said.

"How can you be in the hospital and here too?" Mrs. Atkinson said.

"It does seem to be a problem," Miller answered. He was beginning to feel a little dazed. Obviously a mistake had been made. He didn't quite see how it could have been made, since presumably his wife would recognize that the man in the hospital was not the Harold Miller she had married, but apparently it had been made. "What hospital am I supposed to be in?" he asked.

"Presbyterian Memorial," Mrs. Atkinson answered.

"And my wife is there, too?"

"I—I guess so. That's where she went."

"Then that's where I'm going too."

Convincing the police that a mistake had been made was not difficult. His driver's license did the trick. He got back into his car and burned the wind to the hospital.

"Harold Miller?" The receptionist at the hospital consulted her file. "Room 713. Visiting hours three to five." Miller went up in the elevator. But he didn't reach room 713. Or not right away.

Just to the right of the elevator as he got off was a conference room where members of the patient's family could get together with the doctors. A conference was in progress when Miller walked past. His wife was there. So were two of his best friends, Ed Groff and George Clairborne. Both were biochemists working with him for the Foundation. Apparently, thinking he had been hurt, they had come to the hospital to see him. They were talking to his wife.

Miller made a sharp right turn and swung into the room. "Hi," he said.

All talk ceased instantly. The room got very quiet... Clairborne took one look at him and moved two steps away. Groff blinked at him from behind thick spectacles. His wife sat in her chair. Her eyes were focused on his face but from the way she looked, he was willing to bet she wasn't seeing him clearly.

"Who—who the hell are you?" Clairborne said.

"Harold Miller," he said. Ruth, his wife, sat in the chair and continued to stare at him. Clairborne moved still farther away. Groff, in the manner of a man who is seeing a ghost but is determined not to run, moved closer to him. "What is my name?" Groff said.

"Edward Huggins Groff," Miller told him. "You are 37 years old. You are a biochemist doing research in gerontology. Married, two kids, ages five and three. Boy and a girl. Names are Robert and Alice." He laughed. The situation was perfectly clear to him and he could see the funny side of it.

Clairborne, Groff, and his wife needed more time to see the funny side. His wife moved her lips. "If you are Harold Miller, who is in room 713?" she said.

"I don't know," he answered. "Did you identify him as me?"

"I did."

"But how could you do that? Was his face bandaged?"

"His face was not bandaged. And you go in there and look at him and tell me how I could do anything else." The expression on his wife's face was strained. Even her footsteps sounded strained as she followed him down the hall to room 713.

Harold Miller went into the room. There was a bed, with a patient sitting up in it. He looked up as his visitor entered. Harold Miller looked at him. Miller got a nasty shock.

The patient was the spit and image of him. They were as alike as two peas in a pod, as alike as twin suckling pigs. Hair color, eye color, shape of face, shape of the nose were similar, hands, skin color, everything was alike. Perhaps they were not identical but they were so much alike that only the closest examination would reveal any difference between them.

"Hell on wheels," Harold Miller said. He saw now how his wife had been fooled. This man looked enough like him to fool his brother. But even if appearances had fooled his wife, the names should have been different. "Who—who are you?"

"Harold Miller," the patient answered. "Who are you?"

CHAPTER TWO

HAROLD MILLER felt shock shake him. The patient not only looked like him, the patient also had the same name. No wonder his wife had been fooled.

On the bed, the patient looked shocked, too. He stared at Harold Miller as if he could not believe his own vision, then passed a hand in front of his eyes, and looked again. "Crimantely," he gasped. "Who are you—one of my great-great-great-grandsons?"

"Great-great-great-grandsons? Yikes," Harold Miller said. He understood now how the eight-year old kid had felt when he had gone yipping for his mama. Automatically he stepped away, backing into Groff, Clairborne, and his wife, crowding into the door.

"What did I tell you?" his wife said. She was pale and was breathing heavily.

"He asked me if I was one of his great-great-great-grandsons!" Harold Miller said. Not even their resemblance and the fact that they had the same name had shocked him as much as this question. The words had popped out of the patient's mouth in shocked surprise. Men speaking like this usually speak the truth. But how could this patient be speaking the truth?

The room was silent. The patient stared at them. His mouth was open. The expression on his face said he wished he had kept it shut. He closed it with a snap.

Harold Miller started to back up, to get out of this place. It was damned unsettling to run unexpectedly into a man who not only looked enough like you to be your twin brother but also had your name. Miller wanted to get away, to take time to think about this.

Ed Groff quietly closed the door. Groff was the kind who always went toward ghosts, discovering later that he should have run instead. Groff moved toward the bed. "Did you say great-great-great-grandsons?" he asked. The tone of his voice was calm and reasonable. The tone said he was asking a courteous question and he expected a courteous answer.

The patient seemed confused. He looked at Groff, looked again at Harold Miller, opened his mouth to speak, closed it again as if he had changed his mind. "Go away," he said. "This beats the hell out of me. Go clear away."

"But you did say great-great-great-grandsons," Ed Groff persisted. "I heard you."

Ed Groff was a digger. He never left a buried bone alone but always tried to dig it up.

If he had not been present, probably the whole situation would have been dropped. Harold Miller, feeling greatly confused, would have left the hospital. The patient, probably equally confused, would have left later.

"How can you have great-great-great-grandsons?" Ed Groff continued. "You don't look to be a day over thirty years old."

"Looks are sometimes deceiving," the patient answered. He still didn't have his mind on Ed Groff or on what he was saying but was concentrating his attention on Harold Miller.

"I know that looks are sometimes deceiving," Ed Groff said, patiently. "How old are you?"

"Oh, hell, I've forgotten," the patient answered. "Something over nine-hundred years—" This time he realized instantly what he had said. A shocked expression appeared on his face. "Forget I ever said that. I'm nuts, I'm out of my mind. I got a lick on the head in that accident and my mind is still fuzzy."

"You don't talk as if your mind was fuzzy," Ed Groff said. "You talk as if you have been surprised into speaking the truth."

"Well—"

"How can you be over nine hundred years old?" Ed Groff continued.

"WHY IN the hell are you asking all these questions?" The patient was irritated and he was becoming more and more confused. "What are you, a reporter?" He waited for the answer to his question as if he was afraid of reporters.

"No," Groff answered. "I'm a biochemist. We are all biochemists, except Mrs. Miller."

"And what is a biochemist?"

"A biochemist is a chemist who studies the chemistry of living organisms, the cell and its products, the organ and its products. It is a study of living processes, the changes that take place in living bodies, it is a study of life itself."

"I see," the patient said. He seemed to consider problems of his own. His eyes went to Harold Miller and he nodded, as if he approved of what he saw, then his gaze came back to Ed Groff. "What difference does my age make to a biochemist?" He didn't sound friendly.

"Well—" Groff began. To answer this question properly would require a long explanation, which he was reluctant to give. The answer would also require a statement of the aims and purposes of gerontology, and of the Foundation, which he was even more reluctant to give. The research of the Foundation was not exactly hush-hush but it was not front-page stuff either, for obvious reasons. Men who worked for the Foundation were constantly cautioned to keep their mouth shut, not because the Foundation was a secret organization but because the research it was doing was more potent than an H-bomb. Unwise publicity, which hinted that the Foundation had solved the problem of old age, might result in calamity. If the notion got abroad that they could make old people young again, the old people would come, first a few individuals asking for new life, then a trickle, then a stream, then a sudden flood pounding ceaselessly against the doors of the Foundation. If the Foundation could not make them young again, or could not give them a few additional years of life, the results would be heartbreak, despair, and bitterness too deep to measure.

All of which was in Ed Groff's mind when he hesitated.

"I see," the patient said. "You want me to trust you, but you don't want to trust me."

"But—" Groff said.

"Go on, get out of here," the patient spoke.

"I'll answer your questions for you," Harold Miller said. "Your age might make a lot of difference to a biochemist. If you are actually as old as you said you were, you might be the most important man alive." Groff clucked warningly at him, he ignored the sound. "We're working on gerontology," he said. He began to tell the part biochemistry played in gerontology, the aim and the purpose of the Foundation's program. The patient listened with acute interest. Harold Miller spoke eagerly, there was eagerness in him, it showed in his face and in the gestures of his hand, expressive symbols revealing the pressure in him.

Perhaps he was being naive, he did not know. No man could live nine hundred years. Science itself was not that old. The problem of old age could not have been solved before the science of chemistry itself had been invented, except in one way. Was this man a living representative of the one way the problem could have been solved? Had he actually lived before Newton had been born, before Roger Bacon had existed, before the scientific method itself had been discovered, before the tools for licking the problem had been invented or even thought of except in fairy stories?

Was it possible that this man had inadvertently revealed the truth about himself?

"We're working on the problem of old age," he finished. "If you are actually nine hundred years old, it may be that you can help us."

Only a pathetic disbelief in common sense made Harold Miller hope. Common sense said this man was deluded or was lying. But Harold Miller hoped anyhow.

"Were you telling the truth?" He waited for an answer.

ON THE bed the patient was quiet. From outside, from the street down below, came the distant muted hoot of an automobile horn. Over in the park on the other side of the street, Harold Miller was vaguely aware of movement, a ball game between teenagers. To the right of the ball diamond was a golf course, with men driving from the first tee.

Although they did not know it, the drivers of the cars on the street, the kids playing ball, the men playing golf, were also waiting for this man to answer.

A trace of a grin appeared on the patient's face. "I'm kind of proud of you, son," he said. "To hear this story from the lips of a man who must be one of my own grandsons was worth waiting nine hundred years for."

The hospital room became very quiet. In the hallway outside the room, rubber tires whispered as a hospital carriage went past. There was a distant muted rattle of tin pans. Ed Groff seemed to have stopped breathing. Ruth Miller stood with her back to the wall, her face white, her eyes going from her husband to the man on the bed.

"Then you were telling the truth?" Harold Miller whispered.

The patient nodded.

The story, as they eventually got it from him and pieced it all together, started back in the tenth century. He had been born in Dartmoor Forest, in Devonshire, near the peak of Yes Tor, in old England. He didn't have the name of Miller then, he got this name in 1086, when the compilers of the Doomsday Book came to an English stream, found a mill there and asked the name of the miller. Harold was his name, he had no other and needed none. So he became Harold the Miller, later shortened to Harold Miller, and he got his name in the Doomsday Book as the owner of eight cattle, eighteen swine, five hides of land, and one water mill.

For the next five hundred years he had lived in England, Ireland, Scotland, and Wales. He had come to America in 1638, in the ship, Rose. The Pilgrims had just gotten themselves well settled down then. At different times, he had been a blacksmith, a coppersmith, a sailor, master of a whaling ship, and many times a farmer or a planter, as farmers were called then. He had taken pains never to become too rich and never to meddle in politics or religion.

"If you get too rich, people envy you," he explained. "If you go in heavily for politics or religion, they notice you too much."

His existence had always been tied up with the problem of not being noticed, of not attracting attention to him. He had spent much of his life on the fringes of the settlements, moving into the backwoods of Virginia, over the Appalachians into Kentucky when that land was known as the *Dark and Bloody Ground.* He had been a '49er.

"Found a little gold, but not much," he said. "I didn't look for much."

"But where do I come into this story?" young Harold Miller questioned. "You said I must be one of your great-great-great-grandsons? Is that right?"

"It must be," the patient answered. "We look so much alike that we must have a common ancestry somewhere. It is my guess that so far as physical appearance goes, you have thrown back to me. I don't think there is much doubt that you are a grandson of mine, though I'm not certain how many greats are involved. I think you throw back to the brood I fathered shortly after I landed in this country. I was using the name of Miller then—"

Each generation he changed his name and his occupation. He also moved to a new state or a new country and started all over again, moving far away from the home he had had before. Sometimes he had married, and had raised a family. But this had produced problems. His wife grew old and he didn't. His children grew up. They did not inherit his ageless quality and the time came, or would come, if he let it, when his children looked older than he was. When he saw this time, coming, there was only one thing he could do—disappear.

"I always left my family as well fixed financially as I could and drifted out of the picture. In a few years, they decided I was dead and forgot about me."

"Wasn't that kind of hard on your wife and family?" Ruth Miller asked.

"Maybe, maybe not. When the kids were grown, they didn't need me. And my wives, well when they grew old, we sort of drifted apart." His voice sounded sad, as if he hadn't liked this part of life.

"But if you had used the name of Harold Miller once, how did you happen to use it again?" Ed Groff questioned. Clairborne stood silent and stiff, taking no part in the questions.

"Thinking back, the only solution I can see is that I just forgot I had used the name in this country," the patient answered. "When you have had so many names, it's kind of hard to remember all of them. I didn't realize what I had done until you came through the door of this room." He looked at Harold Miller.

"The minute you came in, I knew I had made a mistake. I had used the same name twice and I had also run straight into one of my own grandsons."

There was a coherence about the story, a relevance of detail that gave it an unquestioned air of authenticity. Ed Groff was nodding. Even he had ceased trying to pick holes in the story. As for Harold Miller, he had long since accepted as simple fact the story of this man.

He had met his great-great-great-grandfather, a man who was over nine hundred years old.

Standing against the wall, Clairborne cleared his throat and spoke for the first time.

"How have you kept from growing old?"

CHAPTER THREE

"I DON'T know the answer to that," the patient said. "I've puzzled about it some and had to give it up. I'm no chemist. All I know is that my heart beat is much slower than the average, about forty to the minute instead of the average seventy. There's something inside of me that keeps me from growing old, but I don't know what it is."

"What about diseases?" Ed Groff questioned.

The patient snorted. "I've had 'em all, cholera, small pox, and the black plague. Typhus and diphtheria and pneumonia and flu. But whatever it is in me that keeps me from growing old also keeps me from becoming very sick. Typhus lasted two days, small pox one. Cholera was the worst, it tied me up for almost a week. I guess I'm immune to most diseases now, I've had 'em all."

"Then you don't do anything to keep from growing old." Harold Miller spoke.

"Not a thing," the answer came. "I had a long babyhood and a delayed childhood. I didn't really mature, wasn't really a man until I was almost forty years old. Whatever it is that keeps me from growing old, I was born with it."

"Then you are actually a biological mutation," Harold Miller said. This was the one way in which the problem could have been solved before the days of science, and then it could not have been solved by men but by nature. Nature, as a result of an accidental combination of genes, could produce an individual that aged slower than the average. This was the solution Miller had had in his mind when he first realized that the patient might be telling the truth. It probably could not happen oftener than once in a billion births, but it could happen this way.

Could man discover what nature had done, could the human mind penetrate the secrets of natural processes? All of scientific endeavor was based on the belief that nature's secrets could be discovered.

Harold Miller started to speak, changed his mind. The question was so important he did not know whether or not he wanted to ask it. "Will—?" For a moment he hesitated, then blurted out the words. "Will you help us, will you let us examine you, will you let us try to find out why you don't grow old?"

"I do grow old," the patient corrected. "For every thirty years that an average man ages, I age about one year, as near as I can figure it."

"But—"

"I've gone this far, I might as well go the whole way," the patient answered. "Yes, I'll help you, if I can. But I will have to impose one restriction."

"Anything you say," Harold Miller said. He was too excited to think clearly. Here they had in their hands the one man on earth who might be able to solve their research problems for them. A careful, competent examination of this patient might reveal one of nature's most closely held secrets. "What is the restriction?"

"That you keep secret the truth about me. That you tell no one—and I mean *no one*—what I am."

"Of course," they answered in unison.

"Then I'll help you," the patient said.

THEY TOOK him out of the hospital that afternoon, over the protest of a young doctor who was worried about the slow heart beat and wanted to do something about it. He waved aside the young medico's fears. Harold and Ruth Miller took him home with them. Since he and Harold resembled each other so closely, and since the names were the same, they decided to introduce him to their friends and to the personnel at the Foundation as a cousin. He would not let them tell the people at the Foundation who he was and what he was. "A man in my shoes learns to keep his secret," he explained. "No publicity. Nobody in on this secret but the ones who already know it." His tone suggested that in his opinion perhaps too many people already knew his secret.

He was installed in the guestroom at the Miller's home. Ruth Miller found his presence raised a rather perturbing problem. "I ought to make you chew Sen-Sens," she said to her husband.

"Why?" he asked.

"So I can tell you two apart in the dark," she answered.

"Oh, he wouldn't do anything like that."

"How do you know he wouldn't? He's a man, isn't he?" Her manner said that a man might be capable of almost any action.

For the first time, Harold Miller realized that from her viewpoint the situation might not be quite so ideal. "We'll have a password," he decided. "Something like Jack Frost. You say, 'Jack', and if I don't say 'Frost', don't let me into the bedroom."

"What if he learns the password?"

"We'll change it if he does."

"Change it when? After?"

"You're making a mountain out of a molehill. This man is important. Be reasonable."

"It's important for me to know who is sleeping with me too," Ruth answered.

Her fears proved to be groundless. Old Harold, among many other things, was a gentleman. Moving in with them, he seemed to feel he had found a happy home. Young Harold realized that this man was incredibly lonely.

In the biochemistry lab at the Foundation, they began their tests. Queer birds were always wandering in and through the Foundation building. Old Harold was accepted by the rest of the staff as just another of this species. He cooperated completely and willingly. He was not only lonely but for the first time in his life, he had found people he could talk to, people who understood him, people who didn't laugh at him. Groff wanted to take notes on what he said, he could offer evidence on many of the disputed points in history, he had been there. Clairborne scoffed at the idea.

"We're making history. To hell with what has already happened." Clairborne, a little man with a pinched face, but a competent biochemist, seemed to be laboring under a suppression. "Just think, if we can lick this, we can make millions out of it. Billions!" His eyes narrowed at the thought and he shut up quickly.

"If we are going into this with the idea of making money, you will have to count me out," Old Harold said.

"Why?" Clairborne challenged. "Money is important." His manner said that in his opinion money was about the most important thing that existed.

"Sure, enough of it to get along on is important," Old Harold answered. "But I've seen too many men ruin their lives by getting greedy to be hoggish about money, or to want more than just enough."

"That's the way I feel about it," Young Harold spoke. "We're not working for money here, we're working for the whole human race. If we can perfect the process of slowing the onset of age, it must be made available to all people, regardless of race, color, or creed."

"You're a couple of sentimental idealists," Clairborne answered.

"I would rather be remembered with gratitude by one man than to have a million dollars," Old Harold said. "I'm not helping you in order to get rich. I could have gotten rich a hundred times over, if I had wanted to."

He was emphatic on the point. Clairborne said nothing more.

THE WORK began, and continued. The four of them formed a tight group. They were part of a much larger team working at the Foundation, much of which was financed by a man by the name of Morganstahl. Morganstahl paid them a visit. He came into the bio-chem lab unannounced but accompanied by Dr. Claxton, research director. Young Harold looked up from the microscope in which he was studying a blood sample to see the two men standing in the doorway. Old Harold was sitting down. They had just taken another blood sample from him for analysis, they did this so often that he had begun to complain they ought to put a zipper on his arm so they could open the vein easier. Clairborne and Groff were working with the centrifuge.

"We've got visitors," Old Harold said, from his chair. His voice was quiet but it contained a warning note as if he had seen and had not liked these visitors.

Morganstahl stood just inside the doorway. He was about sixty-five years old, his face was beginning to show gray blotches marking the real onset of old age, he wore dark glasses and he walked with a cane. He was worth more millions of dollars than he could count—oil was the source of it, rumors from his past indicated that he had not cared how he got his money, just so he got it. During the last few years he had acquired a reputation for philanthropy. MORGANSTAHL GIVES ANOTHER MILLION TO CHARITY, the newspaper headlines often reported. If critics sometimes whispered that his gifts were actually conscience money, to the general public he had come to be regarded as a big-hearted philanthropist.

He donated immense sums to the Foundation and he paid them regular visits. Since they were spending his money, he always claimed he had a right to make certain it was spent wisely. His eyes focused on old Harold.

"Danby," he said. His face whitened.

For a split second Old Harold hesitated. "Danby?" He rolled the word around his tongue. "Never heard of anybody by that name."

Morganstahl continued to stare at him. "I never forget a face."

"You must be mistaken, sir," the director said. "This is Harold Miller, cousin of our Harold Miller. You will note the strong family resemblance they have to each other."

"I note it," Morganstahl said. "I also note the strong resemblance this man has to George Danby." A hoarse note had crept into his voice and on his forehead a vein was throbbing visibly.

Old Harold was nonchalance itself. "When did you know this Danby?" he questioned.

"Forty years ago. We were young men together," Morganstahl answered. He poked out with the cane, jabbed Old Harold in the knee with it. "You look like him. I think you are Danby." Again he poked with the cane as if he was trying to satisfy himself that a real man was sitting in the chair.

Old Harold moved his knee. A trace of color appeared on his face. "Poke that cane somewhere else," he said. An edged note crept into his voice.

PERHAPS Morganstahl did not like the edged tone in Old Harold's voice. Perhaps he did not like to let anybody tell him what to do or what not to do. Perhaps he had no concern whatsoever for the feelings of anyone except himself. At any rate, he kept poking. The pokes were not painful but they were annoying. Old Harold moved his legs again.

"Are you Danby?" Poke, went the cane.

"How much did you steal from him?" Old Harold spoke.

The pokes stopped. Watching, Harold Miller thought that Morganstahl was going to have a stroke of apoplexy. His hands began to shake and his face started to turn red. Claxton, the director, didn't look much better than the millionaire, with his mouth hanging open and his eyes bulging out. The bio-chem lab got very quiet. The centrifuge hummed softly. There was no other sound.

"I beg your pardon?" Morganstahl spoke.

"It's probably the first time in your life that you ever begged anybody's pardon for having poor manners," Old Harold spoke.

"I did not come here to be insulted," Morganstahl said. His voice sounded like a buzz saw hitting a knot in a log.

"I didn't come here to be poked by a cane either," Old Harold said.

"Gentlemen—" the director begged.

"If you're calling him a gentleman, then include me out of that classification," Old Harold said, looking at Morganstahl.

"I beg your pardon—"

"Twice in one morning. This really sets a record," Old Harold spoke.

Dramatically, Morganstahl pointed his cane at Old Harold. "Fire this man." All his life he had solved problems like this by firing somebody. If a clerk didn't serve him fast enough—fire the scum. If a bookkeeper made a mistake—fire him. Old Harold had spoken disrespectfully to him. Fire him!

"Yes, sir," the director said. He was almost out of his mind. If he wasn't treated right, Morganstahl might withdraw his support of the Foundation.

"Kind of hard to fire me," Old Harold spoke.

"Why?" Morganstahl demanded.

"I've never been hired. I'm donating my time and myself. What are you donating—money?" From Old Harold's tone and manner, Morganstahl and all his millions didn't matter a spit in the street to him.

Morganstahl looked like he was about to choke. "Who do you think you're talking to?"

"Hell, I know who I'm talking to—the biggest unhung thief alive," Old Harold answered. Bitterness crept into his voice. "I know you—I mean, I've seen your picture in the papers often enough to recognize you if I met you in hell."

"This is slander. This is actionable. I will instruct my attorneys—"

"To sue me for defamation of character?" Old Harold inquired. "Go ahead. Before they can show I have defamed your character, your lawyers will first have to prove you have a character to be defamed. From what I have heard about you, even the shysters you employ will have their hands full trying to prove your character is worth a tinker's damn."

The agitated director managed to get Morganstahl out of the lab. He went vowing vengeance.

An awed silence remained behind him. "You shouldn't have treated him like that," Young Harold protested mildly. Actually, deep in his heart, he had heartily applauded every word Old Harold had said. "But, we need his money."

"Sure, I know. Because I insulted him he will threaten to cut his donation to the Foundation. But he won't cut it off. Do you know why?"

"No."

62

"Because he isn't giving his money away, he is spending it in the hope that you people will find some way to make him young again. He's trying to buy life with his money."

"You seem to know a lot about him," Clairborne spoke.

"Some few things, none of them good."

"How do you know so much about him?"

Old Harold grunted tonelessly. "He wasn't wrong when he thought he recognized me. I was actually George Danby once. How do I know about him? Because, forty years ago, I was in the oil business with him. He sold me out, he ruined me. That's how I know about him." For a moment anger showed on his face, then it faded. "Well, what does it matter now? He got the money, which was what he wanted. And a lot of good it did him. I don't begrudge him a cent of it." He broke off as the door opened.

Claxton, the director, appeared. His face was red and he was puffing as if he was out of breath. "Fellows, I try to be a good guy. I try to keep everybody happy. We need money to run the Foundation, we've got to have it, lots of it. While I admit that I despise Morganstahl as much as you do—he's pompous, overbearing, and tyrannical—still the fact remains that we need him. Under the circumstances there is little excuse for deliberate bad manners." His eyes came to rest on Old Harold. "I'm sorry, but I'm going to have to ask you to leave. No arguments, please." Lifting his hand and shaking his head, he gently closed the door behind him.

CHAPTER FOUR

"HE'S A GOOD GUY," Old Harold said. "He hates to give me the boot but he's got to do it. Well, I had it coming, I spoke out of turn."

"But we need you, we can't let you go, we've got to have you," Clairborne, Groff, and Young Harold spoke almost in the same breath.

Old Harold grinned. "I didn't say I was quitting, did I? All I have to do is stay away from the lab. And in order to protect you, son, I had better move to a hotel. This way you can see me daily and nobody can kick about it. You can ask all the questions you want and you can tap me for blood, take X-rays of me, examine me in any way you wish. It takes more than Morganstahl to lick us Harold Millers." He grinned at them.

That afternoon he moved out of the guestroom at the home of Harold Miller and into a small hotel. The next day the biochemistry lab continued operations as usual. In the middle of the afternoon the director entered again. If he had been worried before, he looked frantic now. "Mr. Morganstahl is in my office," he said.

"Tell him to go soak his head," Ed Groff said. "What's bothering him now? We followed orders, we got rid of the man he didn't like."

"I'm afraid it is much more serious than that," the director said. "Mr. Morganstahl is convinced that your cousin is actually somebody that he calls George Danby, whom he knew years ago." He looked at Miller questioningly.

"Well?" Miller answered. Because of Old Harold's firm request, they had not taken the director into their confidence. Nor could they do it now, without breaking faith with Old Harold.

The director wet his lips. "I'm afraid you don't see the problem. He thinks your cousin is this George Danby. Danby ought to be an old man. But he isn't. So Morganstahl has reached the logical conclusion that we have treated Danby and that we have discovered a method of making a man young again."

In the silence that followed, Groff spoke slowly. "Tell him he's crazy."

"Did you ever try to tell a man worth forty million dollars something he doesn't want to believe?" the director asked. "He *wants* to believe your cousin is George Danby. If this is true, then it is also true that we have discovered a way to make a man young again. Morganstahl wants to believe this more than he wants anything else on earth."

"Tell him very politely that he is mistaken," Harold Miller said. "Tell him that if we succeed, he will be the very first one to know about it."

"I have told him that," the director answered. "He isn't satisfied. He is firmly convinced that your cousin is this George Danby. He is so certain of himself that he has begun to shake me, to raise questions in my mind." Claxton's eyes came down to Harold Miller. "Morganstahl claims we are holding out on him. I happen to know that this is nonsense. I am not holding out on him. But are *you* holding out on me?"

"Eh?" At the lab bench, Miller uttered a single grunt, then was silent. Neither Groff nor Clairborne spoke.

"Just who is this man that you introduced to me as your cousin?" the director continued.

"Well—"

MILLER'S face must have given him away. The director said: "So you *are* holding out on me."

"I didn't say that."

"Maybe your lips didn't, but your face did. What's going on here, Miller? I have a right to know."

"I can't tell you," Harold Miller answered.

"I have a right to know," the director spoke. He didn't shout, bluster, or wave his arms. He didn't threaten and he didn't coax. He just stated the facts, calmly and gently. Harold Miller squirmed. This was harder to take than any amount of bluster. "I would tell you if I could. Something is going on, in fact, I would say we are closer to our goal than we have ever been."

"What?"

Miller nodded.

"What have you got?"

"The secret is not mine to tell. But this I promise you, if we succeed, the first person we tell will be you."

"By God." There was a glow in the director's eyes. "Do you mean you have actually come close to licking this problem?"

"Not yet, but I think we will. We've just begun, just started."

"And this man, your cousin, has a part in it?"

"Yes."

"But you can't tell me what it is?"

"No."

From his face, it was obvious that the director was taking this decision hard. "All right," he said slowly. "I will respect your right to secrecy, but—" A gleam appeared in his eyes. The door slammed behind him and he was gone.

"Now we're in a spot," Clairborne said sullenly. "He'll fire the whole bunch of us."

"I don't think so."

Ten minutes later, the door opened again and the director entered. He was breathing hard and he was taking his coat off as he came into the room. He reached for a white lab jacket hanging from a hook on the wall. "I don't know what you boys have or what you're doing but I'm declaring myself in on it."

"What?"

He nodded his head vigorously. "Somebody else can handle the front office from now on. Or it can go unhandled. I'm coming back to doing research, I'm moving in with you. I will take any oath of secrecy that you require of me. I will keep your secret no matter what it is or what it may require of me, but I've been in this work for years, and nobody is going to keep me from being in at the kill."

He spoke like a man who knew exactly what he was saying and meant every word he said. The three stared at him in incredulous disbelief.

"What about Morganstahl?" Harold Miller questioned.

"To hell with Morganstahl. I just kicked him out the front door."

Round-eyed the three biochemists looked at him. "Do you mean that literally?" Miller questioned. "Did you actually kick him in the behind?"

"I almost broke my foot on his tail end. Don't look at me like three old maids peeking into a pool hall. Secretly, for years I've been wanting to kick Morganstahl in the hind end. I finally did it. Brief me, boys, tell me what you've got. I'm working right here in the lab with you from now on."

They spent the rest of the afternoon telling him what he wanted to know. The wondering director listened, alternately nodding, then shaking his head. "It's inconceivable. Yet it could have happened like you say. As a matter of fact, if our work is to have any real meaning, it must have happened to somebody. Chance alone would produce a mutation, a man who aged very slowly. But for us to find such a man to use for research is almost too good to be true."

He was a changed man. "We'll want this man Harold Miller, or George Danby, whichever is his proper name, back in here tomorrow morning to continue with these tests you boys have started."

"But what about Morganstahl?"

"To hell with him. He can stick his money—I mean he can take his money and—I mean to the devil with him." The director grinned. "Get Harold Miller back in here the first thing in the morning. He is more important than all the Morganstahls on earth."

Young Harold called Old Harold on the phone, to give him the good news. "Fine," Old Harold said. "Pick me up first thing in the morning. I'll be waiting in the lobby for you."

THE NEXT morning he called at the hotel. Old Harold was not waiting in the lobby. Ringing the room, he got no answer. Vaguely alarmed but not quite knowing why, he got the desk clerk and they went up to the room. The bed had not been slept in.

Old Harold was not there.

The clerk knew nothing about him and no message had been left. Young Harold drove quickly to the Foundation lab, hoping that Old Harold would be there. Perhaps he had risen early and had walked to the lab.

He wasn't there.

"Maybe he—uh—found himself a girlfriend," Clairborne suggested.

They waited all morning for him, all of them growing more and more worried. The day passed. They didn't hear from him. They kept calling his hotel without response. The next morning he still had not returned. The hotel had not seen him and knew nothing about him.

Young Harold went to the police, to the Department of Missing Persons. He got scant comfort there. An unimpressed sergeant took down a description of the missing man, noted that he was not wanted for any crime, and said that the police would do their best. Young Harold wondered how many times in the past some department of missing persons had looked, indifferently, for Harold Miller. And had not found him. It struck him that Old Harold must be an expert at dropping out of sight, at hiding and at staying hidden.

"So far as you know, he left of his own free will?" the sergeant questioned.

"Yes."

"Is he a relative of yours?"

"A cousin."

"Any money involved?"

"No."

The sergeant shrugged. "We'll put it on file."

Had Old Harold left of his own free will? Leaving the police station, Young Harold wondered about this. The old man had seemed eager and willing to help them. He knew how important their research was. Under the circumstances, it did not seem reasonable that he would have quit cold, walking out without even telling them he was leaving.

"But from his own story, he was in the habit of leaving without telling even his closest friends," Clairborne said, back at the lab. "And another thing, there's a lot about him he hasn't told. He may be one jump ahead of the law. Actually we don't know anything about him except what he has told us. For all we know he may be a murderer in hiding."

"I don't believe it," Young Harold said hotly. "He wasn't a killer, he was an honest man, if I ever saw one."

"How many really honest men have you ever seen?" Clairborne questioned acidly.

"I don't believe he's hiding and I don't believe he is in trouble with the law," Young Harold said. "I think he's in trouble of some kind, and it's up to us to help him."

"First, we've got to find him," Clairborne said. "I've got a hunch that finding him will take some doing."

In this respect at least, Clairborne turned out to be a good prophet. A week passed. Old Harold not only did not come back but they heard nothing from him. Young Harold found himself growing more jumpy each passing day as he waited for the ring of a phone that did not ring, as he looked for a telegram or a letter that did not come. The director was going quietly crazy. Each day, Young Harold went back to the hotel, hoping against hope that each time he would find a message. There was no message. The luggage had been left behind. He searched it carefully, finding nothing. Old Harold's car, badly damaged in the auto accident in which he had been hurt, had been repaired. The garage that had done the work called to find out where it was to be delivered. Old Harold hadn't taken his car, then. He hadn't taken his clothes. What had happened to him?

Had Morganstahl had him kidnapped? The second the idea occurred to Young Harold, he had a hunch he was on the trail of something. So far as he knew, Morganstahl was the only man on earth who might have a motive for kidnapping the man. Morganstahl, thinking Old Harold was George Danby, might have had him kidnapped, in order to learn from him the secret of the process by which he had been made young.

Ordinarily, millionaires do not take chances on violating the law, but Morganstahl considered he was a law unto himself.

There was no doubt that he desperately wanted life and that he would be willing to pay for it.

COMING out of the hotel in the late afternoon, Young Harold did not notice the two men fall into step beside him.

"Mr. Miller?" one of them spoke. He was short and powerful, with heavy shoulders and long arms. He had his blue coat off and carried it over his arm. His shirt was white, it was dingy and open at the collar, revealing short chest hairs trying to climb upward. The man's face was round and heavy.

"Yeah," Young Harold said, without really noticing the man who had spoken. Vaguely he was aware another man was on his left side, keeping in step with him.

The one on the left was slender and waspish. He walked daintily, as if he was about to step on an egg and wanted to be careful to put each foot in exactly the right spot. He had his coat on. Looking straight ahead, he was darting side-glances at Miller out of the corner of his eyes.

"You want something?" Harold Miller said.

"Yeah," the man on his right answered. "We want you to take a little ride." He made jabbing motions with the coat held over his right arm. Where the coat formed a fold, the round hard muzzle of a gun was visible.

"Just take it easy," Blue Coat said. "Just don't get excited. A man wants to talk to you…"

At the sight of the gun, a wave of cold passed over Miller. "Who—who are you? What do you want?"

"Just take it easy, I said. A man wants to talk to you. Just do as you're told and you won't get hurt. Act funny and you'll get a bullet in the guts."

They put him in the back seat of an inconspicuous sedan. The man who walked daintily drove the car. He drove as daintily as he walked, taking great care to observe all traffic rules. Blue Coat sat in the back seat beside Miller. Keeping the coat over his arm and the muzzle of the gun out of sight, he chewed on an unlit cigar.

"But what do you want with me? I can't pay a ransom. I haven't any money. I haven't anything."

"A man wants to talk to you," Blue Coat repeated monotonously.

To Miller, this kidnapping made no sense whatsoever. He had no enemies and he certainly had no money. His wife might be able to scrape up a couple of thousand dollars, as ransom, but that would be the absolute limit. What did they want with him? Who were they? Who was this man who wanted to talk to him?

Dusk came softly and quietly. The car seemed to be moving aimlessly, the men seemed to be waiting for something. Miller eyed the streets, keeping close watch on their movements. They were making a mistake in letting him see too much. Dusk faded into darkness. The streetlights came on. "Okay?" the driver called.

Blue Coat grunted an assent. The car pulled swiftly into a side street and was tooled slowly along. "I'm going to put a blinder on you," Blue Coat's voice came.

"A what?"

"A blindfold."

"But—"

"I can knock you on the head, if you say the word," Blue Coat's voice became blunt. "Make up your mind which way you want it, with or without a knock on the head."

"Okay," Miller said. He was helpless and he knew it. The car was a two-door sedan. To get out of it at all, it was necessary to push the seat forward. If he tried to get out, Blue Coat would certainly club him with the gun. If he tried to slug the man, he might get a bullet for his trouble. He submitted to the blindfold. After that, they seemed to drive for hours. He lost all sense of direction.

All he could tell for sure about their destination was that they had left the city. When the car finally stopped, he could hear frogs croaking in a pond somewhere near. Holding to his arm, they guided him through a door, and into a place that was damp and musty. Voices echoed hollowly here. Then they passed through another door and the blindfold was removed.

He was in a small room. A single bulb set behind a metal grill in the ceiling shed a wan glow downward. The walls and floor were concrete. A cot was in the corner of the room.

"Set down and take it easy," Blue Coat said. "The man who wants to see you will be here in a few minutes."

They went out. As the door closed behind them, he saw that it was made of metal. He heard a clank from the other side as a heavy bar was dropped into place.

He was a prisoner, in a small room that looked as if it had been designed for storage.

CHAPTER FIVE

THE METAL bar rasped and the door opened. Miller looked up.

The man who entered was well but not flashily dressed. Miller knew hundreds like him, rather dull looking but clean and neat. Professors, research men, chemists, physicists, lawyers who didn't get many cases to try, doctors who didn't get many patients. This man had black hair and prominent ears. Miller could tell this much about him. But no more.

A thin rubber Halloween mask had been slipped over his face, giving him the features of a grinning gnome.

Gnome Face said: "Don't be startled by the mask. I don't wish to be identified by more possible witnesses than are necessary."

"I don't blame you," Miller said. "Kidnapping is a serious offense, especially if the FBI gets in on it."

"The FBI won't get in on this one," Gnome Face answered. "Nor will any other law-enforcement agency. On the contrary, I think you will agree that you came here of your own free will." He made it as a minor point that wasn't really important.

"What makes you think I will agree that I came here of my own free will?"

"A hundred thousand dollars," Gnome Face answered.

"A hundred thou—" Miller would probably never earn this much money in his whole life. "Just for saying I came here of my own free will?"

"For that and for co-operating."

"Um. Whose throat do I help you cut?"

"Nobody's throat," Gnome Face said hastily. "Nobody will be hurt, especially not you." He was most emphatic on this point.

"What do you want me to do?" Miller said.

"I want you to reveal the process by which you regained your youth," Gnome Face said calmly.

"What?" Miller said, not so calmly.

"The process used to make you young again," Gnome Face repeated.

"But—" This made high order nonsense to Miller. He didn't get it. Then he got it. Or thought he did. "Who do you think I am?"

"I know who you are—George Danby, alias Harold Miller," Gnome Face answered.

"Uh," Harold Miller said. He started to laugh. What had happened was quite clear, too clear maybe. "You've got the wrong man."

"What's that you say?" the rubber mask writhed with alarm.

"There are two Harold Millers. We look so much alike it even fools my wife. You jackasses made a mistake, you got the wrong man. You can tell Morganstahl that he ought to be a little more careful about selecting thugs who can kidnap the right man."

"What?" Gnome Face said, as if he wasn't hearing correctly.

Miller repeated what he had said. Gnome Face got it this time. For a moment he seemed shaken, then he regained his composure. "Who did you say?" A cold note crept into his voice.

"Whoever is back of you," Miller said. He had the impression that he was now the jackass, he was the one who had made a mistake.

OBVIOUSLY Morganstahl had to be back of these men. Probably the millionaire was completely removed legally and physically from the kidnapping but he was the only person rich enough to sluff off a hundred thousand dollars in return for the cooperation of a prisoner. Also, he was the one person with this much money who knew for sure that Old Harold and George Danby were one and the same man. Groff, Clairborne, and Claxton knew it, but they were automatically eliminated from suspicion by the amount of money Gnome Face was offering. Morganstahl had to be back of this kidnapping.

Gnome Face studied him. The eyes were hidden by the mask and Miller could not tell their color or the expression in them. "You had better be George Danby," Gnome Face spoke at last. "I would hate to think we have made a mistake."

"But even if I was Danby, so what?"

"So what? So you could tell me what I want to know."

"Do you think you could understand it?"

"If you mean the technical details might be beyond my comprehension, forget it. I am a competent biochemist and I can understand any explanation you can give."

"I see," Miller said. So this was the way it was. He did not doubt that the man was telling the truth. "You seem to have an excellent grasp of the situation."

"The whole matter has been carefully explained to me."

"And what are you getting out of it?"

"A hundred thousand dollars in gold deposited in a bank in Tangier in my name. This amount is already there, whether I fail or succeed. My passport is in order. If I succeed, four hundred thousand additional dollars in gold will be deposited for me."

"But gold is illegal."

"In this country, yes, but not in Tangier."

Tangier, Miller knew, was an international settlement on the northern coast of Africa, a sort of no-man's land, a place of refuge for international swindlers, political refugees so hot no country would take them, and for other law violators of the western world.

"You seem to have planned well," he said.

"I had help."

"Would you mind telling me where I am?"

"Not at all. You are in a deserted factory outside the city. We have fitted it up as a biochemical lab."

"You have moved fast."

"Money in large amounts will buy almost anything, including speed."

"And life?"

"And life. Also life's opposite—death." The voice grew harder, colder. "Are you willing to cooperate?"

"But what if I am not George Danby, as you think?"

"Then we will have to get Danby."

"But what about me in that case?"

Gnome Face shrugged. "What to do with you will not be my decision." The twist of his shoulders said he suspected what the decision would be. "You can spend the night making up your mind. I'll see you in the morning and you can give me your decision."

The door closed behind him, the bar rattling as it was dropped into its slot. Miller wiped sweat from his face and fumbled in his pockets for a package of cigarettes. Gnome Face was working for Morganstahl. This much was obvious. It was also obvious that Morganstahl had had nothing to do with the disappearance of Old Harold.

Which left unanswered the question of what had actually happened to him.

MILLER could not see where the answer to this question made much difference to him. He was in a bad enough spot himself without worrying about the troubles of somebody else. "I guess I had better be George Danby," he decided.

As long as Gnome Face thought he had Danby, he would not start looking for the real man. In the meantime, Miller thought he could stall Gnome Face for days, maybe for weeks. Surely, in this length of time, he would find a chance to escape.

"I'll go along with you," Miller said, when Gnome Face returned in the morning.

"Good." They started promptly. First, questions. Gnome Face brought a chair into the cell, he provided cigarettes, poised himself with a notebook and a pen. The door was closed, the bar was dropped in place from the outside. Blue Suit or somebody else was on guard out there.

"First, how long does the treatment take to begin to be effective?"

"It produces results immediately, that is, within two weeks."

"How long does the complete treatment take?"

"That depends on how far you want to go. As near as we can calculate it, for each week of treatment about one year of age is taken off. If the treatment lasts thirty weeks, the patient ends up thirty years younger."

"That seems pretty fast," Gnome Face said doubtfully.

"It is fast, to the patient. You understand, there are profound physiological changes taking place. The arteries are regaining their pliability, circulation is improving. The hair is beginning to grow again, the bones are losing their brittleness. The liver, the kidneys, the lungs, and the heart begin to renew their proper functions. In fact, every cell in the body undergoes a deep-seated change. The patient must be hospitalized. Nurses and doctors must be in constant attendance. The patient's diet must be regulated, increased input of vitamins must be arranged. His heart action must be watched, sometimes the heart just stops under this treatment. A doctor must be on hand to meet such emergencies."

"I quite well understand. Doctors will be provided."

"These are just the physiological changes. The psychological changes are even more pronounced and more important. A seventy-year old man who finds himself going back to become a mere thirty years old is due for a tremendous mental upheaval. A complete treatment team is necessary and must be in attendance at all times, doctor, nurse, psychologist, and psychiatrist."

"This sounds really expensive," Gnome Face said.

"It *is* expensive. Hundreds of dollars a day. Of course, it's worth the price. I don't imagine there is a seventy-year old man alive today who would not pay the cost, if he had the money. Of course, large-scale developments will reduce this cost to a more reasonable figure." Miller rattled off the talk easily and readily. So far, he was on safe ground. The process of age reduction would work this way, once it was perfected. All these factors were involved. It was not a simple process, not a matter of taking a pill one night and waking up a young man in the morning, at least not the first time, although, once the proper age was reached, it might be possible to hold a man at the same age by the pill-at-night treatment.

GNOME FACE spent the whole day taking a case history. Sandwiches and coffee were brought in at noon, handed through the door, then the questioning went on.

"Tomorrow we will begin on the technical aspects of the treatment," Gnome Face said, when the day was over. He went out. The door was closed behind him.

The next day he began with technical details. After he had asked a dozen searching questions, Miller knew that Gnome Face was actually what he had pretended to be—a competent biochemist. Miller went much more carefully here, he didn't want to make a mistake. Much of the chemistry of the body has already been worked out. He gave standard formulas, told where they were to be modified, and why. Gnome Face wrote them carefully in his notebook, then frowned.

"To check these formulae properly would take months," he said.

Miller was quiet. He had known that checking would not only require much time but that elaborate and expensive equipment would be needed, this was the reason why he had given the formulae in this manner.

"I wouldn't want to make a mistake," Gnome Face continued. "After all, this treatment must be used on a human being."

"Go down to Skid Row and catch a bum and run the tests on him," Miller said.

"That's an idea, that's what I'll do," Gnome Face said, brightening.

"You don't mean it," Miller said, appalled.

Gnome Face shrugged. "Why not? Somebody has to be a guinea pig, in case you're lying."

"But I didn't mean it, I was just kidding."

"I wasn't."

"But you can't make a guinea pig out of a human being without his consent."

Behind the mask the eyes glinted at him. "Why not? We didn't have your consent when we brought you here, did we?"

On the third day Gnome Face laid down his pen. The words shot out:

"You're not George Danby!"

CHAPTER SIX

"WHY NOT?" Miller demanded.

"Because Danby doesn't know any biochemistry and you know too damned much," Gnome Face answered. "No, you're not Danby. You were telling the truth when the boys first brought you in."

Miller felt his mouth fall open. He saw the trap he had walked into, the trap of knowing too much about an extremely difficult subject. The questions had come so naturally and had been asked so casually that he had answered them without realizing the real George Danby didn't know enough about the subject to answer such questions.

"Well, I told you I wasn't Danby and you wouldn't believe me. So you just got what you asked for. Now what are you going to do?"

Gnome Face rose to his feet. "I'm going to find Danby."

"I mean what are you going to do with me now?"

He got a shrug of the shoulders for an answer. "I don't know. Does it matter?" The eyes were expressionless holes, the mask an emotionless stretch of leering rubber. Gnome Face yelled for the door to be opened. The bar was removed, Blue Suit looked in. Gnome Face went out. The bar rattled as it was dropped again into place.

An hour later, the door opened again and Gnome Face entered. The door closed behind him, the bar rattling into place.

"Well?" Miller said.

"Whether you are Harold Miller or George Danby makes no real difference," Gnome Face said. "George Danby received the treatment. Harold Miller was one of the men who administered it. Probably Harold Miller knows more about the treatment process than George Danby. So, I am ready to start taking notes."

He was polite enough. He sat down and poised the pen over the notebook.

"What would you say if I told you there was no such treatment in existence yet?" Miller asked.

"Other people think it is in existence and I am taking my orders from them," the answer came. "I advise complete accuracy this time. Because I have found a guinea pig."

"Who?"

"You."

"Eh?"

"The necessary tests on the treatment process will be made on you," Gnome Face answered.

Miller's left arm jumped as his fist started automatically for the masked chin. He caught the motion and disguised it as a part of rising to his feet. "But there isn't any rejuvenation process yet. We were working on it but we hadn't solved it. The solution is years away yet. We've just begun." The words came from his lips in hard gusts of sound.

For all the impression he made on Gnome Face, he might as well have keep quiet.

"There isn't?"

"No." Sweat was on his face. Sweat was making his palms sticky. It seemed to him that sweat had replaced the blood in his veins.

The rubber mask stretched as Gnome Face opened his mouth to yell a single word: "Mack!"

In response the door opened quickly. Blue Suit, a gun in his hand, looked in. "What's wrong?" he said.

"Nothing, yet," Gnome Face answered. "I just want you in here." The expressionless eyes sought Harold Miller. "I don't know much about the methods of Torquemada, haven't had a chance to learn. However, I shall do the best I can, with my limited knowledge."

"Torquemada?" Miller faltered. He didn't like the sound of the word. Torquemada had been famous in history for the use of torture. "Do you mean—?"

Gnome Face nodded. "I mean exactly that." He glanced at the impassive figure in the blue suit standing just inside the door. "Mack, when a guy won't talk, what would you recommend?"

BLUE SUIT rubbed a dirty hand on an unshaven chin. "Sometimes matches on the soles of their feet helps them to talk," he said.

"Do you really mean it?" Miller faltered. He was dazed, the idea of torture appalled him. Yet he knew beyond a shadow of a doubt that they would use torture on him in an effort to extract from him a secret that he did not possess, that nobody on earth possessed.

"I told you before I mean it," Gnome Face answered. "Just make up your mind which way you want it."

In the back of Miller's mind a vague thought formed, let go, formed again. Blue Coat, when he entered, had not closed the door. It stood six inches ajar. Miller laughed, a little shrilly. He carefully kept from looking at the door.

"You've got me," he said.

He hurled himself against the door, knocked it open with his flying body, caught it and shoved it shut again. Desperately he set his back against it.

"You had me," he grunted. The bar was standing beside the door. He grabbed it. Vaguely from the room behind him came the sound of an explosion, a gun shot. The metal rang from the impact of the bullet, then jumped as Blue Coat drove his weight against it. Miller shoved with all his strength, holding the door closed. He got one end of the bar into its socket. The door thudded again as Blue Coat rammed himself against it. Miller's feet slipped. He caught himself, shoved again. The other end of the bar slid into place.

Like a mighty wave, exultation shot through him. He was out of the storage room and Gnome Face and Blue Suit were in it. Now to find his way out of this place, fast.

He was in a basement, this much was obvious from the thick concrete pillars stretching off into the distance. Dim ceiling bulbs cast a wan glow over the scene. Beside the iron door behind which he had been held prisoner was a cot with blankets, chairs, magazines, a worn deck of cards. Paper cartons that had once held food were scattered on the floor.

The iron door vibrated from the force of the blows being rained against it. To Miller, the sound was satisfying. He wondered how Blue Coat and Gnome Face felt at finding themselves caught in their own deadfall. From the way they were pounding on the door, they didn't seem to like it. In this case, they would just have to lump it. A light burning far across the basement revealed a flight of steps leading upward. He moved swiftly in this direction.

Footsteps sounded up above. Miller heard them, flattened himself against the wall. Somebody was coming down the steps, in a hurry. At the bottom of the steps, he let out a single yell:

"Mack!"

The man was yelling for Blue Coat. His identity was obvious. He was the second of the duo who had kidnapped Miller, the one who had looked as if he was walking on eggs.

Egg Walker didn't see Harold Miller crouched against the wall. He headed across the basement for the room with the iron door. If he reached this door; he would certainly release the two men held prisoner there. Miller went after him, low along the concrete, like a football tackler coming from behind to bring down a runner who has just broken into a clear field.

Egg Walker heard him coming, glanced over his shoulder, saw the body hurtling at him, tried to dodge. Miller hit a pair of twisting knees. They went down. Egg Walker had never played football, he didn't know how to fall. He went down with his head leading the way, his chin hitting the concrete. Miller heard a sharp pop of teeth snapping together. In his arms, Egg Walker squirmed. It was purposeless squirming, it was without intention. Egg Walker was just squirming a little because he was unconscious, knocked out cold by the driving tackle that had been thrown at him.

From under the man's shoulder, Miller took a flat automatic. The mechanism snicked as he pulled it back. A shell popped out, another was fed into the barrel from the magazine. Miller hadn't known for sure whether or not there was a shell in the gun ready to be fired. Now he knew. He moved toward the steps, gun in hand, stopped again.

SOUNDS OF conflict were coming from up the stairs. Men were grunting up there, he caught the sound of moving feet. Then a man came down the stairs. Unlike Egg Walker, he came down a single step at a time—bump, bumpety-bump, bump,

bump. End over end, falling, sprawling, the man came down the stairs. He fetched up with his body on the floor, his head on the last step. A little trickle of blood ran from the corner of his mouth. He was bald-headed and unmasked. Miller had never seen him before. The blood trickled from his mouth and formed a little pool on the steps.

Miller did not hear the second man come down the steps. He moved quietly, soundlessly down them. Miller caught just a flicker of a moving shadow. He stepped quickly behind a concrete post, the gun covering the steps.

The man was standing in the stairway surveying the basement. He was keeping out of sight. Just a part of his head was visible. Miller waited.

The man moved into full sight. Miller almost dropped the gun he was holding.

"Old Harold!" he yelled.

It was Old Harold who had thrown the man down the steps, then had come so cautiously after him.

At the sound of the voice, Old Harold turned and dived to the protection of the stairway. "It's me," Young Harold yelled. He moved to the stairway. The old man was coming down again. They stood facing each other.

Old Harold had a gun in his hand. There was a bruise on the side of his face, he had lost his hat, his hair was frowsy and his coat was torn. He glanced once at his great-grandson; then looked quickly across the basement, seeking something or someone. His gaze came to rest on the body of Egg Walker. He grunted approvingly. "Your work?" he said.

"Yes."

"Good. There were two men upstairs. They're accounted for. How many more are there?"

"Two more. And they're accounted for."

"What happened to you, boy?"

"I was kidnapped, brought here. They were after you but they made a mistake and got me. They wanted the rejuvenation process." Swiftly he explained what had happened.

"Morganstahl," Old Harold grunted.

"I figure he is back of it but I don't know for sure. What happened to you?"

For days this question had plagued him. What had happened to Old Harold?

"I was kidnapped, too."

"What?"

Disgust sounded in the old man's voice. "I ought to have seen it coming, but I didn't. He just walked into my room with a gun in his paw and walked me out again."

"Who did it?"

"Clairborne," Old Harold said. His face was grim and hard.

"CLAIRBORNE," Young Harold gasped. The statement bewildered him. He had known Clairborne for years and had thought him trustworthy.

"Nobody is trustworthy when they've got their nose into my secret," Old Harold said. "It was so big it addled Clairborne's wits. He knew if he could solve the problem of rejuvenation, he would automatically become one of the biggest men on earth. He kidnapped me so he alone could solve the problem. He was going to organize a corporation and sell life. He held me prisoner in a farmhouse and was getting ready to start experimenting on me, just continuing the research of the Foundation." Disgust sounded in Old Harold's voice.

"What—what happened to him?"

"One night when he came to work on me, he ran into a little trouble. Somehow or other, his neck got broken in the fracas. I don't quite know how it happened..." His voice trailed off.

"You mean, you killed him?"

"Oh, no. It was an accident. Nobody with any sense ever admits anything except an accident. His body hasn't been found yet. Maybe it won't ever be found..." His tone changed. "When I got loose from him, I discovered you were missing. To my mind, this meant that Morganstahl had got you. I started hunting for you."

"How'd you find me?"

"It wasn't too hard. I just had Groff and Claxton make up a list of the best biochemists in the country. Then we cross-checked until we found one who had been hired, at a whopping big salary, by a lawyer who was retained by Morganstahl. Then we located this biochemist and I started trailing him. His name was Hendrickson. He led me here."

"Gnome Face," Young Harold said. "I don't know him but I know about him. He's over there with Blue Suit now."

"We'll leave them there, for the time being," Old Harold said. "Later, we'll call the cops and tell them where these two lads can be found. First, we'll get out of here. Then we'll call your wife. Then we'll call Groff and Claxton. I don't know who has been the most worried about you. We'll let 'em know you're all right..."

"Then what?" Young Harold said.

"Then Groff and Claxton are going to pull out of the Foundation and we're all going into hiding to work on the secret of rejuvenation." There was a glow in his eyes and a note of triumph in his voice. "Within five years we'll have that secret licked. Then we will make it available at cost to all the people of this earth..."

He was planning the future. Listening, Young Harold thought it was a good plan. In many ways it ran parallel to his own dreams.

"We have to go into hiding," Old Harold continued. "That's the only safe way for us, until we know the whole secret and are ready to announce it. If anybody is going to have life, everybody must have a chance at it."

"But what about Morganstahl? Are we going to have him arrested?"

"We're not going to touch him. He'll be paid off, but good, for what he tried to do here. We will just let him alone, let him grow older, day by day, until he dies of old age and his own meanness, while we hunt for the secret of immortality."

Again his voice went into silence. "How does all this sound to you?" he asked.

"It sounds fine to me," Young Harold answered.

"Come on, then. It's time to be moving, time to be getting started."

Side by side they went up the steps together, son and great-great-great-grandfather. Somewhere ahead of them, perhaps near, perhaps far, was a new world in the making, a world without old age. Perhaps in some far-removed future, was a world without death itself, a world, which they would help to create. Somewhere in the mind of each was a feeling of vast triumph.

THE END

The World of Reluctant Virgins

*A weird blue light filled the caverns of the moon. Was it the real reason
no woman from Earth could ever hope to bear children?*

HE WAS the first man to set foot on the moon. His name
was John Holden. He had just arrived by rocket ship. His
money had built it. So much of his money had gone into it that
he was a pauper back on Earth.

He didn't care. He wasn't back on Earth. He was on the
moon.

He was forty-nine years old, he had a little pot belly, arteries
that were threatening to go stiff, almost no hair, and eyes so
weak he had to wear thick lenses to see at all.

He didn't care about these things. He was on the moon.

Behind him, three other men came down the steps. A
woman came last, an order of precedence that had been
determined by drawing lots. Back on Earth, they had drawn lots
to see who was to make up the crew. Over a hundred men and
several women had worked very hard building this ship. Each
had volunteered to ride it to its destination.

Holden felt someone slap him on the shoulder. "Well, we're
here, Johnny." That was Noddy Warzicki speaking the first
word.

"What was it Columbus said?" Sam Gosset asked. Gosset
sounded as if he was trying to remember what Columbus had
said, to say it all over again, but he wasn't able to remember.

"I was fourth," Fred Samson said. "The fourth man on the
moon. My grandchildren will talk about that." Samson's niche
in history was now secure. He sounded pleased.

"And I was fifth, damn it," Jane Tovara didn't sound at all
happy. "Fifth. I could have been at least second if I had cut a
higher card. But I'm the first woman. Remember *that.*"

"How do you spell your name?" Warzicki said. "We want to

get it right, for the history books. Hey, Johnny, where are you going?"

They had landed on the level floor of a valley. To the right, the sun was sinking behind high mountains. It threw long dark shadows across the volcanic ash, which made up the moon's surface.

On the left, the slanting rays struck full against a cliff, illuminating it clearly.

Holden had already seen it. He had already rubbed the glassite helmet with a heavy glove to clear away the distortion. He had discovered that the distortion was not in the glassite but was up there on the cliff. When Warzicki called, he had started walking toward it.

He kept on walking. The voices of the others went into quick silence as they saw what he had seen. Automatically they followed him.

Ten feet away from that cliff, Holden stopped. The letters carved in the face of the cliff were head high.

WE PASSED THIS WAY

Below them were other letters:

Follow the Arrow

The arrow was there too, pointing an enigmatical finger toward the right. There was a third line, four figures, which made a date:

1887

The four men and the one woman stared at them.

"No," Warzicki's voice came explosively over the inter-com sets. "This can't be true. Goddard didn't publish his paper on the technical aspects of rocket propulsion until 1919."

"And Oberth didn't publish his treatise until 1923," Fred Samson added, his voice full of astonished pain.

"And it wasn't until the end of the war that rocket experiments got under way in earnest in America," Gosset gasped. Gosset sounded hurt too, as if these words on the cliff were trying to take something away from him.

John Holden said nothing. He stood looking up.

"This is a monstrous practical joke," Noddy Warzicki continued. "Somebody got a ship up here last year and carved these letters just to confuse us."

"Us?" Holden said. "Just to confuse *us?"*

"Well, to confuse anybody who landed here," Warzicki amended.

"I'm still the first woman," Jane Tovara said. "But you guys are not the first men. Not any more. And you were so puffed up about it. That's a laugh." Because that was what it was, she began to laugh.

"We ought to have dropped you out of the air lock," Noddy Warzicki said. "I'll do it too, on the way back, if you don't shut up."

The tone of his voice made her stop laughing.

THEY STARED uneasily at the cliff. "It's got to be a joke," Warzicki said. "In 1887 the only people who knew anything about rockets were the Chinese and they used them to scare away devils."

"Maybe somebody knew then," Holden said.

"You're nuts," Warzicki answered, appalled. "Those letters are as clear as if they were cut yesterday. There are the stone chips on the ground. No weathering. You can see for yourself—" His voice went into troubled silence.

"Where there is no weather, there will be no weathering," Holden said, gently. "It would make no difference whether the letters were cut yesterday or a century ago, they would still look the same in both cases."

"All right, I'm nuts," Warzicki muttered.

Holden moved forward and touched the letters. Through the thick gloves, he could feel them. Yes, they were there. Two senses said they were.

"Perhaps we had better get back to the ship. This is all so new to us. We need time to think." Turning, he walked away. A stoop showed in his back now. And even under this light gravity, one-sixth that of Earth, his legs seemed to have lost their spring.

The others followed him.

Long shadows were reaching jagged edges from the opposite mountains. But they had not reached the ship, yet. Out of those shadows something came walking. It looked at them, at the ship.

They stared at it.

It moved toward the ship, sat down on the bottom step to await their coming.

"It's a man in a space suit," Holden said. "He is waiting for us." He moved quicker now, but if there was eagerness in him, it was hidden under deep layers of fear.

If a ghost appeared, John Holden would walk straight toward it. He was that kind of man. He walked toward this ghost now. The others followed him as if they were glad, this once, to have somebody out in front of them.

The ghost did not have a radio aerial projecting about his helmet. Presumably he had no radio. His space suit was strange, it fitted him as if it had been built for somebody else and he had borrowed it. As they approached, he rose to his feet, made signs to them. Through the window in the helmet, something looked out at them, they could not tell exactly what. The plastic window was obscured.

"He wants to go into the ship," Gosset said, interpreting the signs.

"We can't let him in that ship," Warzicki said. "We don't know anything about him."

For the first time, Holden showed signs of strain. "God damn it, he could have gone into the ship if he had wanted to. This is not the time nor the place to hesitate." He moved past the gesturing figure, stood in the air lock. Here he made a sign of his own, an extended sweeping open hand that invites the guest to precede the host into the ship.

THE STRANGE figure bowed like a cavalier. He moved past Holden into the lock, waited there, looking at the strange controls. The others followed. They closed the outer door, opened the inner one. Inside the ship, they hastily took off their helmets. Oxygen was all right but the lungs needed more than that. Talk over the radio was better than no talk, but the ears and the mind needed more. The friendly always-present fringe sounds, the noises from the distance, the honk of an automobile, somebody laughing in the next room, the rattle of an elevated train, the fall of a leaf, without these sounds the mind and the ears felt lonely, a little lost. These sounds were missing on the surface of the moon.

The strange figure had already unlocked his helmet and had swung it back. His voice rang out.

"Howdy, howdy, howdy! I'm sure glad to see you! Who are you and where'd you come from? What's it like on earth these days? When are you going back?"

It was the voice of a man hungry for news, for talk with his own kind. Holden pointed in the direction of the cliff. "There are some words and a date there—"

The man laughed. "I saw you looking at them. You wondered how they got there, I bet. Well, if you had landed in any of a dozen other places, you would have seen some more just like them. We scattered them in most of the likely places. It just happens that you hit the one nearest the old landing." He talked easily and freely, saying much or nothing. It was hard to tell which.

"There was a date—" Holden said.

"God, I'm glad to see you," the man said. "My name is Brad Stinson. What's yours?" He extended a hand. "The others will be glad to see you, too. It just happens I was at the top of the slit and saw you land."

As if he did not see the hand and had not heard the words, Holden spoke again. "Is that date right?"

"Oh, I see what you mean," Brad Stinson answered. "Didn't understand you at first. Sure, the date is right."

The ship became very quiet. The five humans stared at this one human who had come walking in to see them. His skin was tanned a deep brown, it was without wrinkles, his eyes were clear. A net thrown across the United States would catch a million like him. A net thrown a million times on the moon ought not to catch any like him. Or so they had thought.

For the first time, Holden seemed to see the outstretched hand. He took it, gave his name. "This is Mr. Warzicki, this is Mr. Samson—" He went through the introductions. Then he moved over to a chair and sat down. His legs had grown tired and his heart was acting fluttery. He would sit there and rest and let the others ask the questions.

They asked dozens of them. Stinson answered readily enough. The ship that had landed here in 1887 had been powered by a "green stuff that Thad invented." It had been built in a valley in the Great Smoky Mountains, in western North Carolina. It had carried a crew of three young men and their wives. And one other man: Thaddeus Juvenal. Respect sounded in Stinson's voice when he mentioned that name. Thaddeus Juvenal had imagined, designed, and built that ship. He had called her the *Egg Tooth*. Each baby bird has a small tooth on the top of its beak, which is used for only one purpose—to break, the shell of the egg. After this is accomplished, the tooth disappears. After hearing that name, John Holden wished he had thought of it for his own ship.

THERE WERE other questions. Holden hardly listened. He was busy subtracting the difference between 1887 and 1955. The answer he reached was 68. Because even genius requires time in which to operate, Thaddeus Juvenal must have been at least forty years old at blast-off time. That would make him 108 now. "No," Holden thought with real regret. "We won't meet Juvenal. He's dead. We won't meet any of the original crew. They're gone too. We'll soon be gone ourselves…" He choked off such thinking. It got him nowhere.

"I assume you are the son of one of the original crew," he said.

"Grandson," Stinson answered.

"Ah. Did Juvenal leave any descendants? No, I guess not." He broke off hastily, remembering that there had been three couples but that the leader had been an odd man.

Stinson laughed. "Sure he did. You can meet his grandson tomorrow, if you want to."

"But I thought—"

Stinson nodded as if he understood this objection. He could also shrug it aside. "But when you've got a real genius, it isn't right for his line to die out just because he was too busy all his life to find a wife. They lent him a woman."

"I see," Holden said, embarrassed and despising himself for it. The solution seemed reasonable and natural somehow, and in the absence of personal friction and personal possessiveness, it could have been worked out. "How many of you are there now?"

"Still seven," Stinson answered. "Three granddaughters and four grandsons of the original crew. I know, it seems likely there would have been more, but it hasn't worked out that way."

"But how have you managed to survive? No air, no water, no vegetation—"

"None on the outside. But on the inside—" He hesitated and seemed to pick his words with care. "Somebody was here before *us* too."

"What?"

"We call him the Moon Man but we don't know much about him. He made the suit I'm wearing. He built cities underground. Thad knows more about it than I do but there's air down in those cities and water and plants. The original bunch found them soon after they landed."

"Where is this Moon Man?" Holden asked, excited. "I want to see just what he looks like."

"Can't," Stinson said. "He's gone."

"Gone where?"

"Gone dead. He didn't last until men got here. If you want to know more, I'll talk to the others and if they're willing, I'll show you around tomorrow."

They wanted to see more. "By the way, can this ship return to earth?" Stinson asked, moving toward the air lock.

"Certainly."

"Well, see you tomorrow." Snapping his helmet into place, he stepped into the lock. It was dark outside now, except for star—and moon-shine. He moved into that darkness and out of sight.

"That was the damnedest story I ever heard," Noddy Warzicki said.

"We'll get the rest of it tomorrow," Holden spoke. There was wonder in his voice. It was a pale echo of the real wonder existing deep inside of him.

"You can go hear the rest of it if you want to," Warzicki said. "I'm not leaving this ship."

"Eh? What could harm—"

"I don't know. I just don't like the feel of things. Damnit, shut up, I told you I don't know." Warzicki went moodily toward the galley where he began to rattle pots and pans. They could hear him cursing dehydrated foods in there. Holden looked thoughtfully after him, shrugged. Tomorrow would answer all questions. Or raise new ones; he didn't know which.

THE SUN was a white-hot ball in the sky when they glimpsed Stinson returning. Another figure was with him. The two walked easily across the plain of volcanic ash, came up to the ship, and were admitted. They removed their helmets.

"I want you to meet Thaddeus Juvenal, the Third," Stinson said.

Juvenal was tall and thin, his face was open and frank, his eyes were almost without expression. He glanced curiously around the ship, a sweeping look that seemed to probe every detail. When he spoke, his voice had the courteous tones of the

Old South hidden somewhere in it. "Glad to meet you folks, mighty glad to meet you. Brad tells me you have come to pay us a visit. Others are coming behind you, I reckon?"

"That's right," Holden said.

Juvenal seemed to think darkly for a moment of that prospect. "A big migration to the moon, I suppose?"

"That is coming," Holden said. He glowed a little at the thought.

"Well, we can't have it," Juvenal said.

"Why the hell can't you?" Warzicki spoke, his voice hot. "You can't turn back the clock. Nor can anybody else."

For a moment Juvenal studied the defiant Warzicki, then he shrugged and smiled. Holden got the impression that the man had reached a decision, though on what point he could not guess. Still smiling, Juvenal shook hands all around. "Brad tells me you want to see where we live," he finished. "Come along and we'll show you."

They put on their suits and helmets, including Warzicki, who went through the air lock with them, but went no farther. "I'll wait here," he said. "If anything happens, you can reach me over the walkie-talkie."

They moved off. By signs, Juvenal asked if Warzicki did not wish to go with them. By signs, Holden said no. Juvenal and Stinson conversed rapidly by hand gestures.

They reached a huge crack in the moon's surface, one of many similar cracks that astronomers have seen but have not understood. It was at least a mile deep. Steps cut into the stone led down into it.

Jane Tovara took one look and squealed in dismay. "I'm not going down there. I get the willies just looking at it."

"Who cares what happens to the fourth woman on the moon?" Warzicki said, over the radio.

"Fourth woman?" she yelled.

"That's what you are," Warzicki said, from afar. "No, by golly. Three landed here. They had three daughters and the daughters— You're the tenth woman, kid." His laugh came from the distance.

Jane Tovara went down the steep steps without further protest. Her voice was an almost inarticulate mutter over the radio. "That dirty dog, I'll cut his throat yet. The tenth woman. I'd rather not be here at all than be tenth."

The steps passed over a ledge and went down again. Juvenal stopped, pointed toward the bottom. They could just barely make out what looked like a toy space ship down there. Juvenal made signs, which they did not understand.

"Probably the wreck of the *Egg Tooth*," Holden commented. "She must have landed in this slot." He thought of that first landing and of the horror the crew must have felt when they realized they were trapped.

HALFWAY down to the bottom of the crevice, Stinson stopped. A metal door covered with hieroglyphics was in the wall. He opened it, made gestures for them to pass through. Inside was an air lock, which served the same purpose as the one they had on the ship though the design was entirely different. Stinson closed the outer door. A line of blue radiance circled the walls of this place, providing illumination. He opened a valve, then opened an inner door, then took off his helmet.

They were in a tunnel that led off into some far distance. The streak of blue light went down each wall.

"What would you all like to see?" Juvenal spoke, removing his helmet.

"Everything, I guess," Holden said. When his helmet was off, the radio was disconnected. He could no longer hear Warzicki. It did not matter, he guessed. There was too much to be seen here to worry about that lone rebel back at the ship. "Everything—"

"That's kind of a big order," Juvenal drawled. "But we'll try. You've got tomorrow, maybe a lot of tomorrows, to see this place. Personally, I've seen it so long I've got kinda sick of the sight of it."

"It's all new to us," Holden said. "New and bewildering."

Hours later it was not so new but it was even more bewildering. They had seen subterranean caverns that generations of Moon Men must have excavated, vast spaces where edible fungi grew, a machine that had once supplied air to this system. And supplied it still.

"They built their air machine to last forever," Juvenal said. "They didn't last as long as their machine." His voice was dry and tangy, a whisper lost in the vast reaches of these caverns.

"But what happened to the Moon Men?" Holden asked.

"They died," Juvenal said. "If you will come this way, you will find the quarters where they lived." He turned toward a vaulted arch that marked the entrance to another tunnel illumined with blue radiance.

"I've seen enough," Jane Tovara said. "Please, let's go back now." Her voice had a pleading note in it.

"Don't you like this place, Miss Tovara?" Juvenal said.

"I don't like it even a little bit."

"Do you know why?"

"I don't have any idea except it's gloomy and it's dead and it scares me somehow. What difference does it make? Please, let's go back."

Juvenal nodded as if he understood exactly what she meant. "Nor did Mary or Grace or Helen like it either," he said. "They sensed what was wrong with it, just as I suspect you sense what is wrong."

His words were little jarring notes in the quietness.

"Who were they?" Holden asked.

"The wives of the men of the original crew," Juvenal answered. "Certainly, we will go back to your ship. Incidentally, are you certain it is in condition for an immediate return to earth?"

"Of course it is," Holden answered. He looked at Stinson. "You asked me the same question."

"Did I?" Stinson answered.

"Say, where are the others who are supposed to be here,"

Gosset spoke. "We haven't seen them."

"They're busy," Stinson answered. "Lots of work to be done here."

"Come, please," Juvenal said. He moved purposefully across the cavern and opened the inner door of an air lock. "Put on your helmets. We are going up."

OVER THE radio when the helmets had been replaced their voices were a babble of sound.

"John, Noddy doesn't answer. I called him and he doesn't answer." This was Jane Tovara speaking.

"John, there's something wrong here."

"They may be trying to trap us."

"John, we've got to get out of this place." Now, Jane Tovara sounded frantic. "I still can't hear Noddy."

"We're too deep here to reach Noddy with walkie-talkies," Holden said. "As to the rest, they have made no move against us."

"But we may walk right into a trap any minute. How would we know a trap before we were in it?"

"Be on the alert," Holden said, trying to be calm.

The outer door opened. Outside was the knife gulch in the moon with the steps leading in both directions.

"They may try to shove us off these steps," Samson whispered. "Look, no guard rail. You could fall a mile."

"Stay close to the wall," Holden answered. "Keep your eyes open. There are four of us and only two of them."

In the lead, Juvenal was already moving upward. They followed him.

"It seems forty miles up these steps," Jane whispered.

The top was visible above them. It was closer, closer. They were there. They were safe.

Across the plain of volcanic ash, the ship was plainly visible. Figures moved around it. Now Warzicki's voice came over the radio.

"Try to hit me over the head, will you? I'll show you!"

They could see him in the lock. He was wielding a heavy wrench as if it was a club, fighting off five figures who were trying to pull him down.

"There are their pals," Gosset whispered.

Holden turned toward Juvenal and Stinson. They had drawn apart and were staring at the ship. "Come on," Holden said. "Noddy needs help."

In this light gravity, running was no effort. Stinson and Juvenal, after an exchange of hand signals, followed them, but at a distance.

They were seen before they reached the ship. The attackers drew off and stared at them. Noddy Warzicki stood in the air lock. Like a victorious but tired gladiator, he leaned on his wrench. The sound of his heavy breathing came over the radio.

"It's about time you got here," he greeted them. His nod took in the attackers in one contemptuous gesture. "They came up here and tried to talk. Hell, we couldn't talk when all they could do was make signs, which I couldn't understand. Then they wanted to enter the ship. Not past me, they weren't. They hung around, making signs to show they were friendly. Then one tried to hit me over the head when he thought I wasn't looking. John, they want this ship." He sounded outraged and terribly angry. "Get in here, all of you, and we'll turn a jet blast on them. That'll singe them."

They reached the lock, entered. Holden looked back. Juvenal was coming across the plain of volcanic ash. His hands were held high above his head. At the gesture, Holden hesitated. "Wait. He wants to talk to us."

"To hell with him!" Noddy answered. "Let him talk to himself."

Still Holden hesitated in the lock door. The suited figure came up to the steps. With his hands high above his head in the ancient gesture of submission, he stood looking up. The others stayed far back, watching, waiting—for what? The gesture touched Holden, he did not know how. They were pleading in silence for something. What?

"Get into the ship, Johnny," Warzicki growled. "I'll start warming up that blast—"

"You will do no such thing."

"But—"

"Damnit, he's a man and he's here on the moon. And we've got to talk to him. We'll take him into the air lock. You, Noddy, go inside and get the pistol out of my drawer. You come back into the lock and watch him while I talk."

"All right," Warzicki grumbled. "But if he doesn't talk right, I promise you I'll blow a hole in him you can stick your fist through."

HOLDEN motioned to Juvenal to come forward. They entered the lock, closed the outer door. The inner door opened and the others went through. They went fast, as if they were in a hurry. Juvenal started to follow. Holden caught his shoulder. Juvenal stopped, turned mute eyes toward him. Holden shook his head. The man did not protest.

Then Warzicki was back in the lock alone, a .45 caliber automatic in his hand. He closed the inner door, removed his helmet. Juvenal and Holden did the same. Warzicki snicked back the slide on the gun, let it slip forward. Juvenal stared at the weapon. "What is that?"

"An automatic pistol," Warzicki answered. "We want to hear your story. It better be good. Why did your pals try to steal this ship? And don't tell me you didn't plan to get everybody out of it and then grab it."

Juvenal did not answer. His eyes went to Holden almost in pleading. "You said other ships would be along," he said.

Holden held himself steady. "Yes. It is the rocket ship era on Earth."

"Why are you asking about other ships?" Warzicki demanded. "Are you going to try to steal one?"

"No. This one will be enough—I hope."

"You *hope?*" Holden echoed.

"Yes. We weren't really trying to steal your ship, we were

just trying to get control of it and to make certain it returns to Earth immediately."

"What's the rush?" Noddy Warzicki said. Some of the anger was going out of his voice. Uncertainty was replacing it.

"*This* is the rush," Juvenal said. "This moon, this place everybody is trying to reach, is a floating death trap."

His words left complete silence behind them.

"Eh?" Warzicki said . "You look pretty healthy to me."

"I am. It's a different kind of death trap—a racial death trap."

"What?" Holden said.

"You saw the civilization of the Moon Men," Juvenal answered. "You asked what had happened to him. Well, apparently late in his history, he discovered a method that he thought would make him immortal."

If there had been no sound before, there was even less sound now.

"Sounds like a fairy story," Warzicki grunted.

JUVENAL spoke tonelessly. "Hardly that. As to the method the Moon Man tried to use to make himself immortal, I don't understand it. It ties up, somehow, with the blue light that illuminates those caverns, and it ties up also with something that happens inside matter itself. They did something to matter to make it explode inside itself—"

"Radioactivity," Holden whispered. In that single word, he suddenly understood everything. And nothing.

"I never heard that word before," Juvenal answered. "But this I know, both from what I have found in the caverns themselves and from what I have managed to decipher of the Moon Man's writing he left behind. He almost made himself immortal. But not quite. He discovered how to live a long time, but not how to live forever. There is indisputable evidence in those caverns that the last of the Moon Men lived for hundreds of years."

"Why did the race die out?" Warzicki breathed.

"For this reason. The method that made them live a long time also made them sterile. Babies stopped being born, there was no next generation. Somebody once said that death was nature's greatest invention. If you thwart nature, you seem to pay a price for it. In this case, the race pays the price for you. The race of the Moon Men paid that price, by perishing."

The silence was heavy.

"About two months in this place is all a human can stand. After that, he is sterile forever. Miss Tovara sensed what was wrong in the caverns, all women sense it. Something deep inside them tells them to get away from this place."

"But—" Warzicki breathed.

"There is a disease here. Or something. I call it the sterility disease. The whole moon is alive with it. Even the surface has it but it is ten times worse inside. I can't understand it, but that is the way it is." His hands came up in a helpless gesture.

"Can you take this ship back at once? About us, it does not matter. We do not want to go back. There would be nothing on earth for us now. But if other people are coming here, they must know what they are getting into. Sure, they can land but they must understand that about two months is all they can stay without becoming sterile."

HE BROKE off as a sudden metal click sounded. Warzicki had released the safety catch on the automatic.

"You are a damned liar and your own words prove it. I don't know what you want but you are a liar," Warzicki said. His face was contorted, his eyes had suddenly became bloodshot. "You are the grandson, the third generation, of the original Thaddeus Juvenal who first landed here. If two months here makes a man sterile, how could you exist?"

The question thundered back from the walls of the lock. Juvenal's face twisted into an expression that had once been a smile but now was something a little less than that. "Maybe Brad had to do some fast thinking when you showed up here. Maybe he had to tell you something he knew you would believe, not something he was afraid you wouldn't. Am I Thaddeus Juvenal, the Third, or am I Thaddeus Juvenal himself, alive here sixty-eight years after landing?"

He swallowed as he spoke and a choked note crept into his voice. "What if the Moon Man's method of making himself almost immortal had also worked on me?" he said.

"My God," Warzicki said. Slowly he lowered the pistol.

John Holden nodded. He did not know when he had guessed the truth but the revelation had not come as a complete surprise. Inside, he was glowing.

"If you will open the outer door, I will go back to my caverns," Juvenal said. "As to warning those who are coming, you can make what arrangements you please." He swung shut his helmet.

They opened the door for him.

His comrades waited outside.

"Wait," Holden called, forgetting he could not be heard. "Wait." He ran after them. If he could not be the first man on the moon there was still something here for him, something so big it almost took his breath away. There was something here too, for other people back on earth, when proper plans could not be made. He could imagine the migration that would be coming here, of those past the age of child bearing.

If the Moon Men had made the satellite bloom once, inside its rocky shell, other men would make it bloom again.

"Wait," a voice called in his earphones. "Wait—"

He looked back. It was Warzicki who had called. Noddy was coming out of the lock, running across the plain.

The two fell into step behind the little group following Thaddeus Juvenal. The volcanic ash lifted in little puffs around their feet. They walked lightly, as do old men who have suddenly discovered they have new springs in their legs.

THE END

The Soul Makers

Embattled, doomed, they waited for the end, the handful of survivors of a blasted Earth—and wondered why the metal servants of Man's last days trooped silently out into the wilderness—carrying sculptor's tools!

THE DOOR of the headquarters hut squeaked on unoiled hinges as technician Ralph Harrison entered. He looked at Lieutenant Colonel Martin seated at the desk, seeing the fret and the worry, the strain of a war already four years old—and ending God alone knew when—on the face of the man, seeing also the deeper, unexpressed fear that looked out from the CO's eyes.

It was not a new sight, this fear. Harrison had seen it before, in the eyes of every intelligent soldier helping man the radar warning net being operated out of Station Blizzard, Alaska. Each time he looked in a mirror, he saw it in his own eyes, lurking in the background like some monster crouching in the back of his mind, waiting the slightest relaxation of human vigilance to leap out, all grinning fangs and sweeping talons, to rend and destroy.

Behind Harrison, the door slammed as Joe Connors, his companion, entered. Both had come here in response to the CO's order. They saluted together. Martin answered the salute mechanically, his mind on some other problem, hope and fret mingling on his face, hope as if here at last were two men who might solve one of his problems for him, fret because he knew they couldn't solve it. No man could. Martin looked at them. They waited for him to tell them what he wanted.

From a desk piled high with official papers, morning reports, special orders, a calendar peeped out at them, revealing the date: 12 August, 1987. On the wall behind the desk complicated instruments reported the recording of air pressure, humidity, wind direction, velocity—and radiation count. Harrison could not see the dial of the radiation counter but he knew what it read—the count was going up, and had been going up since the first atom bomb had been dropped, by the Euro-Asian Union, led by Premier Chukovich, in a drive for world dominion.

When would the count stop going up?

No man knew. Hence the uneasy fear in their eyes. There was a point beyond which all living matter would be so saturated with hard radiation that disastrous changes in cell structure and germ plasm were inevitable. What was that point? Again no man knew. Would it be reached before the shooting stopped? The knowledge belonged to no man.

Martin consulted a memo on his desk. "You men are from the non-human-personal control division?" he said.

"Psycho technician, sir," Harrison answered.

"Mechanic," Connors said. Neither he nor Martin noticed that he had left out the "sir." But Harrison noticed. It was in such little things as this that men first revealed the extent of the pressure on them.

"I sent for you men because you are familiar with the non-human personnel at this station. Orders have come through from Topeka to take extreme security measures—"

He broke off as the door on his left opened.

The robot, a member of the non-human personnel group at Station Blizzard, had entered without knocking. For an instant, as the myriad of photoelectric cells in his eyes took in the three men in the room and the brain behind the eyes adjusted to the situation, the robot hesitated. Ralph Harrison, who knew as well as any man alive the intricacy of the brain substance to which the robot sense organs reported the world outside, never ceased to wonder at the sight of a robot meeting a new situation—even so simple a situation as this—

and deciding what to do. The stack of papers the robot carried indicated he was assigned to station headquarters as messenger. Obviously he—all robots were called "he"—was accustomed to enter this room at all times. Usually he found the commanding officer alone. This time, he found the CO with two men. What to do?

From the robot's viewpoint, the situation was complicated by the fact that these were two special men—robot technicians. Unquestionably he remembered them from trips to the repair and conditioning shops, where the robot body was kept in working order—by robot technicians, supervised by mechanics like Joe Connors—and the robot brain was kept obedient to human masters, by psycho technicians like Ralph Harrison. Finding these two men talking to the CO might mean trouble for robots.

Or so Harrison felt the robot reasoned. Theoretically, the conditioning of the robot brain substance prevented any such thought sequences. But Harrison had never been sure of the effectiveness of that conditioning. So he watched. For a split second, the robot hesitated, then moved on silent, sponge rubber shod feet, into the room and laid the papers on the CO's desk. "Special orders, sir." The voice was as impersonal as the speaker from which it issued.

"Thank you," the CO said, abstractedly. Aluminum body gleaming, the robot turned and left the room, not quite closing the door behind him. Martin stared at the door. "I didn't order him back to his post," he said. "He went—without orders." His voice taut, with ragged edges, he stared at the door, then turned back to the two men. His fingers sought among the papers on his desk. "Where's that damned morning report?" He found the missing document. "This morning another robot was reported AWOL from this station. That makes twenty-one who have disappeared, over the past two years, from this command. There's your problem. Find those robots." As the CO finished, he was pounding on his desk.

Ralph Harrison's eyes, straying to the door, saw it was open a crack. He moved quickly to it, jerked it open. The robot was a dozen steps away, walking purposefully toward the communications hut.

"Were you listening at this door?" Harrison asked.

The robot stopped, turned. "Sir—?" he began.

The tone was blank. Harrison knew by experience how impossible it was to get a robot to answer a question he didn't want to answer. "As you were," he said. Irritation sounded in his voice. He turned back into the headquarters hut, to face the questioning eyes of the CO and to listen to the story the CO had to tell. It was a story that scared Ralph Harrison in a way that he had never been scared before.

"WHAT I have to tell you comes down from headquarters classified Top Secret," the CO said. "As robot technicians, I know you are familiar with the details of the development of the non-human personnel serving in our forces and with the enemy—"

Ralph Harrison nodded. It was an old story, but no matter how often he heard it or how much he thought about it—and it disturbed his dreams at night—there was still something of a miracle in the development of the robot brain, miraculous in the sense that in their hour of testing and of trial some benevolent force outside their comprehension had sent the allied nations, faced with the challenge of the Euro-Asian Union, a mighty helper in time of trouble.

The brain substance had been discovered by a man named Jorgenson, a jack-of-all-trades scientist. Jorgenson had started out to be a biochemist, then had switched over and become a physicist, then had decided that psychology was really his field, with the result that he had a smattering of many sciences but was master of none. Yet it was this man, utterly undistinguished, and actually earning his living by working in a bookie's office, where he computed track odds, who invented, in a flash of intuition, the magic electrochemical substance that was capable of storing impressions and of sorting out these impressions and giving them back as electrical impulses, which were in turn capable of actuating relays that stopped and started motors. In other words—a brain.

Jorgenson made his discovery just one day before an atom bomb converted Washington from a thriving, beautiful city to a hole in the ground.

Eventually, when new government functions had been established in other cities and military headquarters had been set up in Topeka, Jorgenson accomplished his second miracle—not only by getting through to high brass with his robot brain substance but by forcing high brass to sit still long enough to listen to him.

When high brass realized what this robot brain was potentially capable of doing, they immediately clamped Top Secret classification on it and gave Jorgenson a blank check to build robot-manned rockets with atomic warheads. It was, they felt, the secret weapon that would end the war. The brain could be conditioned to steer the rocket on a certain set of coordinates that would deliver a few pounds of the inner essence of hell to an enemy city. That city would cease to exist. Another robot-manned rocket would be fired, another city would cease to exist.

They shot off the first rocket and sat down and waited for the enemy city to blow up.

No boom-boom.

No boom-boom anywhere on earth.

So far as the intelligence service could learn, the rocket had simply vanished. Considerably worried, but obstinate, high brass had ordered the second rocket launched. This time they took the precaution of stringing high altitude jet fliers along the path of the projectile, to track it by radar.

The radar reports showed that the rocket had gone up strictly on course but when it reached the top of its arc, where the robot brain was scheduled to take over and guide it to its destination, it had kept right on going-up. What had happened after that, no one knew. Beyond the stratosphere, the radar beams had lost it. It might have taken up an orbit around the earth, it might have gone on to the moon or to some planet, depending on how skillfully its fuel supplies were utilized.

There had been no other explanation for the action of the rocket except that the robot brain had realized the nature of its mission and had deliberately taken the rocket away from the earth, to stop the warhead from exploding.

Life, even in a robot brain, once called into being, clung grimly, with tooth and claw, to existence, not relishing disintegration a few feet from an exploding atom bomb.

The failure of the robot-manned rocket was a disappointment to everyone concerned except possibly the robot.

The next step was the construction of robot tanks, artillery, and specialized foot soldiers. The high brass had visions of a gigantic D-Day in which robot armies landed on the enemy shores. But this time, with the pilot models built, they took the precaution of testing their robots tanks and artillery under simulated battle conditions.

It didn't work. The robot brains could not be made to fire the weapons and at the first HE burst near them of a shell fired by a human soldier, they tried to run away.

There would be no robot warriors.

Pending the success of the frantic efforts of the psycho-technicians to condition some perfectly normal and necessary human viciousness into a brain that seemed unable to understand the need for such characteristics, robots in roughly human form were created, to dig slit trenches, to do routine jobs like operating a radar scanner, where they were tireless and efficient watchers of the sky, and to do KP, where they earned the deep thanks of a host of GI's released from a hated task.

Since the first rocket with the atom warhead had failed to reach its target, high brass had not trusted its robot mechanisms. Driven by some dark fear in the depths of their own minds, they insisted on keeping a close count on robot noses, for the very good reason that robots were going AWOL. Nobody who was familiar with the robot brain substance could easily imagine a robot deserting. So desertion became AWOL.

Lieutenant Colonel Martin glanced at the door, to make certain it was closed, then leaned across his desk. "This is the only area in which so many robots have gone permanently AWOL. They have absented themselves from other stations but in most cases they have been found after a few hours or at most a few days. Because we have lost twenty-one robots, the attention of headquarters has been focused on this area. Something is happening to robots here that does not seem to be happening anywhere else on earth. Headquarters has therefore ordered me to take all possible measures to find the missing non-human personnel and to make a complete report on the activities of every one of them while missing from their assigned posts."

The CO's face tightened and Harrison could see him mentally cursing the brass above him, not only for demanding the impossible from him but for insisting that he write a report telling how he did it. For a moment, Lieutenant Colonel Martin had his entire sympathy.

"What stirred them up, sir?" he asked.

"I was hoping you wouldn't ask that question," Martin answered. Annoyance shaded his face. He could refuse to answer and he could evade the question. Since he was top brass here, there was nothing they could do in case he chose not to answer. But he was too good a commanding officer to withhold necessary information from the men under him. "This stirred them up," he said. "An AWOL robot was captured in Iran, another in India, and a third in North Africa. In each case, the robot, when found, was doing the same thing as the others."

"The same thing?" Harrison frowned. "But that seems hardly possible, sir. It would indicate there is some unknown form of communication between all robots. No, that isn't necessarily true, sir." Even as he spoke he saw the flaw in his conjecture.

"What alternative would you suggest?" Martin questioned.

"Well, if AWOL robots thousands of miles apart were found doing the same thing, it might mean they were in communication. On the other hand, it might mean that like causes were producing like results."

"Either possibility is driving headquarters absolutely nuts," Martin grumbled.

"What were they doing?" Connors asked.

"Carving statues," Martin answered.

"Huh?" Harrison gasped. "I mean—what, sir?"

"One was carving a statue out of stone," Martin said. "The second was hacking it out of a fallen log. The third was modeling it—out of mud."

"Huh?" Harrison gasped again. "Beg pardon, sir. But these statues, what are they, sir?"

"Men," Martin answered.

"Statues of men," Harrison whispered. "But why—"

"That's what headquarters wants to know," Martin said. He wrote rapidly on a memo pad. "Here's an order directing all personnel to cooperate with you. Find those missing robots, see what they are doing, and find out why. Report back to me within forty-eight hours. That's all."

They went out of the headquarters hut without saluting. And neither they nor their CO noticed the breach of military discipline.

"STATUES," Harrison whispered. There was something subtly flattering in the thought—and equally terrifying. Why would robots build statues? One reason might be that thus they were trying to honor their creator, by shaping in stone or wood or mud an image of the god-like creature who had created them—but could not control them to the extent of sending them to their own destruction. On the other hand, the robots might have some other reason for their strange obsession. At the thought of that other reason, something dark and sinister, unexpressed and unexpressable, moved in the depths of Ralph Harrison's mind like a monster half roused from sleep.

Unseen before his eyes the well-camouflaged huts of Station Blizzard blended into the Alaskan landscape. Up above him, rising tier on forested tier, was the dark and gloomy slope of a mountain peak. Up on that mountain radar stations were located, scanning the polar skies for Big Minnies lugging the sudden death of atom bombs and the slower but no less deadly death of vicious germ mutations across the arctic wastes to dump on the thinning population in the lands below the bulge of the world. His lands, his people, his world.

In this world the only sanity seemed to be in robot minds. And the robots were building statues of men!

Beside him, Joe Connors stirred. "All we got to do is find *all* the god damned robots that have gone AWOL from this station," Connors muttered, gloomily.

"We can do it," Harrison said.

"Yeah?" Connors' voice carried heavy overtones of doubt.

"But I don't know whether we want to," Harrison ended. "I'm scared, Joe, just plain scared."

Connors suddenly shivered. "So am I," he said. "And I'll be damned if I know why." Fear showed dark and desperate in the mechanic's eyes.

At their left the messenger robot came out of the communications hut and moved with direct purposefulness toward headquarters. In his hands he clutched a sheaf of papers. They watched him soberly. He did not glance in their direction. Across from them a file of robots under the direction of a corporal came out of a shed. They carried shovels and they moved with sombre determination toward the little plot of fenced ground where the white crosses gleamed.

"Burial detail," Harrison's lips formed the words. But no sound came. "Come on, Joe. We've got work to do."

They went first to supply, where they used the CO's memo to obtain a small can of what looked like quite ordinary paint but, which was actually a vitally important secret weapon. When applied to an object and viewed with the naked eye, it looked like quite ordinary gray paint, but when viewed through special goggles, it glowed with a pearly luminescence. The paint had a thousand uses. On a plane, it identified a friendly ship. Dabbed on the back of soldiers on night patrol, it enabled machine gunners to identify their own men.

"What are you going to use that for?" Connors demanded. "Identify a friendly robot?"

Harrison did not answer. "Go get our carbines, bedding rolls, and draw rations for 48 hours," he said. While Connors trotted off to get the needed articles, Harrison went directly to the robot repair shop.

A robot, with brain case disconnected, so that he received no sense impressions from the world outside, was on the repair bench. A mechanic was finishing repairs to the balancing mechanism that enabled the robot to keep an upright position, or to regain that position, if he happened to slip and fall. "How long before he's ready to go?" Harrison questioned.

"Fifteen minutes," the mechanic answered.

"Good." Harrison carefully painted the bottom of the robot's feet with the luminous paint.

"What are you doing that for?" the mystified mechanic questioned.

Harrison didn't answer. By the time Connors returned, with their equipment, the robot was reactivated. His number was 793-A-61 but he had been conditioned to respond to the name of Seven.

"Seven, carry the bedding rolls and the rations," Harrison ordered. "And follow us."

The robot obeyed, clumsily but efficiently. Time had never been available since Jorgenson's invention to refine all the kinks out of the robot body mechanism, but despite their apparent awkwardness, they were quite capable. Many robot mechanisms had been built to operate on wheels, but others, like Seven, had been built to use legs, thus enabling them to cover ground too rough for wheels.

They set off across the station, moving toward the mountain, Harrison setting the course. "Where are we going?" Connors questioned.

"Scouting," Harrison answered. He seemed disinclined to explain further. They carried their carbines, slung. Seven followed them like a patient dog.

"I met one of the men from the radiation count division," Connors said. "The count took a new jump today."

" A new bomb was dropped somewhere," Harrison said.

Connors shivered. Hidden so deep within him that he could not find words for it, an old fear pressed for recognition. It moved among the cells of his brain, seeking a neural connection that would give it a voice. "When's it going to stop?" he asked.

"The count? When it is going to stop rising—"

"Never," the voice of Seven came from behind them. "Never in time—"

Harrison spun on his heel. "What's that?" he demanded. His voice was sharp, with sudden frightened overtones. "What do you mean?"

They were outside the limits of the station, on the rising slope that led upward to the peak far above.

"Never in time? What the hell are you talking about?"

The robot stopped and awkwardly planted his feet, feeling for a sure footing on the sloping ground. "I speak without think," he said. He seemed confused.

"Then keep right on speaking without thinking," Harrison said. "What do you know about the radiation count?"

"Master, I—"

"Talk. What do you know about radiation?"

"The little buzzing bugs, master. They go zip, zip. I feel them, master. All robots feel them."

"You *feel* them?"

The robot seemed more confused than before. "Do not the masters feel them? They go zip—like little bugs." A cloud of midges danced in front of his face, a product of the Alaskan summer. He waved one hand at them, awkwardly. "Like these, master. Except different—"

"He's talking about hard radiation," Connors gasped. "Atomic particles, maybe. How they do go zip..."

"Yes," the robot said. "The zipping little bugs... Do not..." He seemed doubtful. "Do not the masters feel them?"

"Not directly," Harrison said grimly. "Sometimes we feel their effects. Where do you feel them, Seven?"

"Inside of me." A hand holding a bedding roll moved toward the brain case.

"He can feel them directly," Harrison whispered. "So he knows the count is going up—because the little bugs go zip oftener. Is that it, Seven?"

" Yes," the robot answered.

"And you think the little bugs will not stop zipping in time—*in time for what, Seven?*"

Harrison's voice had jerky, ragged edges. The robot shifted uncomfortably.

"Answer me, Seven! In time for what?"

"In time for the master—to remain the master," the robot said.

HARRISON was silent. A wind colder than any wind that ever blew even in Alaska blew over him. He turned and started up the slope. Connors walked beside him and the robot followed.

"He knows too much," Connors said.

"Uh-huh," Harrison nodded. "He knows about the radiation count because he feels the little bugs go zipping through his brain. I wonder what else he knows? I wonder what Jorgenson actually created when he invented the robot brain substance?" His voice was heavy with awe. "The robot brain seems to make direct contact with a reality that we cannot grasp. Do you know what, Joe? If they could reproduce themselves, if they could build new robots to take the place of the ones that wear out, we would have a new race of creatures on earth."

"Um," Connors was thoughtful. "Well, they can't. And that's that. But, Ralph, when he said the count would not stop going up in time for us to remain us, what did he really mean?"

"That's one of the things the CO will expect us to find out," Harrison answered. They came to a clearing. Harrison stopped. "Dump the bedding rolls here, Seven," he said.

The sleeping bags thudded on the ground as the robot obeyed.

"You clumsy fool," Harrison shouted. "Be careful there!"

"'But master, the order was—" the robot pointed out.

Harrison was in a violent rage. "I know what the order was, I gave it. It's time somebody taught you god-damned robots a lesson. You throw things around anyway you please—"

"Hey, Ralph," the astonished Connors protested. "What's biting you? You said dump 'em. He—"

"Shut up! I'm handling this!" Snatching the carbine from its shoulder sling, he fired a single shot—at the robot. The crack of the carbine was astonishingly sharp and its spiteful echo came back from the surrounding trees and hillsides, sharper still. The bullet missed the robot's head by inches.

"Master!" Seven screamed. "You shot at me!"

The voice coming from the robot speaker was alive with startled, wild fear.

"Hey!" Connors shouted at his companion. "The old man'll skin you alive if you destroy a brain case without authorization. "

As if he had not heard, Harrison sighted along the barrel of the gun.

The robot knew only too well what a gun was. No robot had ever had to be told. They seemed to pick up the knowledge from the very air around them, through some special sense of which man knew nothing. Seven was already dancing in fear when he saw the muzzle of the hated weapon pointed straight at his head. As Harrison gave an odd little jerk of the gun, and pulled the trigger, the robot ducked. The bullet barely missed.

The robot turned. The wailing cry coming from the speaker, a continuous inarticulate scream, he ran across the clearing. Harrison shot again. The scream grew more shrill. A hit in the robot body would do no harm, except possibly immobilize him, but a hit in the vital brain case was just as deadly as a hit in the brain of a man.

Harrison felt the carbine grow hot in his hands. The slugs screamed through the trees above the robot's head. Then Seven disappeared in the brush. The heavy clump of his feet, the crash of breaking limbs as he fought his way through the heavy tangle of undergrowth, and the wail of his voice came back long after he was out of sight.

"Hey—" Connors whispered, staring aghast at his companion.

Harrison slipped another clip into the carbine. His face, which a minute before had been alive with rage, was now calm. Too calm. He listened to the sounds of the fleeing robot die away in the distance.

"I figure enough of that paint will come off every time he takes a step for us to track him wherever he goes," he said. "Here's where we start using the glasses."

"Uh," Connors grunted, with sudden comprehension. "Then you're not nuts."

"I don't know, yet," Harrison entered, the trace of a grin flicking across his lean face. "But twenty-one robots are AWOL in this area. None have been found. That means they are hiding out somewhere. I figure if I scared the hell out of one of them, he'll head for the others."

"Um. But supposing Seven doesn't know where the others are hiding?"

"He may not know right now but he'll find them. Trust a scared dog to find his way home."

"But supposing he is scared so badly he never stops running until he runs out of juice."

"Then the old man will probably promote us—right straight to the stockade. Come on, Joe. Leave the bedding rolls here. We'll take out right after Seven as if we are trying to catch him—but we'll gradually fall behind and let him think he has lost us."

On the trail of the fleeing robot, Harrison strode purposefully across the clearing. He carried the carbine at the ready. Connors followed right behind him.

"You act like you've got something on your mind," Connors said.

Harrison sighed. "Too many things, Joe. I keep thinking about what is loose in the world. Down there—" he gestured toward the southland far away. "—they're fighting with teeth and toenails just to hold on to life itself. Our drinking water has been fouled with germs, our wheat fields have been dusted with spores of rust. This fight has been going on for four years. From the way it looks, it may go on another four years. I don't like it, Joe. I'm not at all sure that the only organism on earth that will survive is a robot that has enough sense to run from danger."

"The zipping bugs are after him too," Connors pointed out.

"But he knows it. And I have a hunch he may have done something about it. Which is more than I can say for us. We know there is death all around us but the only solution we can achieve is to dump more death—on somebody else. Then we wonder why it comes back to us."

They went upward along the rising slope, following the faint signs of luminescence visible through the glasses. In places Seven's footprints were visible, but where he had crossed rocky ground, leaving no footprints, all they had to guide them were the faint spots of glowing light.

"He has stopped climbing and has begun to circle the mountain," Connors said, studying the direction the footprints were taking.

They found places where the robot had stopped and stood still, apparently for minutes. The dabs of paint showed where he had moved, for a few steps, first in one direction, then in another, as if he was trying to make up his mind where he wanted to go.

"Like a dog sniffing the wind," Connors said.

Each time the robot had apparently reached a definite decision. He moved off in a straight line.

"It's uncanny," Connors muttered. "He hasn't got a nose but he acts as if he can smell the way he wants to go."

"Other brains, other senses," Harrison said. "I wish there was time to really explore the working of a robot mind, I mean really dig into it. There's a lot more in those brains than we have ever even guessed at." He cursed the war, fervidly, for having prevented proper exploration of the potentialities latent in the robot brain substance.

They went on. Then, behind them, Harrison caught a glimpse of movement. He stopped dead in his tracks.

"We're being followed—by a robot," he said.

BEHIND them a dark figure moved. It slipped from tree to tree with a lithe gracefulness that was almost human.

"It's not Seven," Connors said, sharply. "I thought he might have circled and come up behind us. That robot is black. Ralph—"

"I know," Harrison said. "I've never seen a black robot either."

"Do you think it might be a Euro-Asian robot?" Connors questioned.

"It might be. They have them. That's for sure. Made 'em from specimens captured from us. But there's not a Euro-

Asian soldier in Alaska, so far as I know; and never has been. They wouldn't send robots where they don't send soldiers. But—" He lifted the carbine.

The little weapon cracked. The slug went high and to the left. Harrison had not been aiming for a hit. Instantly the robot ducked out of sight among the trees. Harrison stood staring.

"You gave him a scare," Connors said. "Hey!" He pointed up the slope. "There's another one."

Slipping toward them down the side of the mountain was another robot. This one carried something in his hook hands that looked suspiciously like a rifle.

" A robot with a gun," Harrison gasped.

"By God, they're after us," Connors said.

"It's not possible," Harrison protested.

"Neither is it possible for a robot to carry a gun," Connors said. He flung up his carbine, fired two quick shots. The robot ducked behind a boulder. "He's black too, like the first one," Connors said.

Off somewhere in the trees a rifle shot sounded. The bullet passed over their heads, whipping like a hornet through the air.

"So it's not possible," Connors said. "But they're shooting at us, just like they knew what they were doing." Ducking, he ran to the protection of a fallen tree, dropped to the ground behind it.

"But no robot has ever fired a gun," Harrison repeated. In bewildered confusion he searched for the source of the shot—and remained standing.

"Maybe they never had any reason to shoot one until now," Connors said. "Ralph! Get down."

Somewhere in the trees, the hidden rifle sounded again. The bullet passed within two feet of Harrison.

"Hit the dirt," Connors shouted. "They're shooting at

you."

Harrison dived headfirst to the protection of the fallen tree. "I just don't understand it," he said dazedly.

A wailing voice sounded among the trees. "Surrender, masters," the voice commanded.

"Surrender, hell," Connors said. He crawled to the tangle of roots at the foot of the fallen tree. "Wait'll I get my sights on one of those buzzards."

"Somehow they've learned how to use rifles!" Harrison thought. *"Somebody has instructed them how to hate!"* As the thought passed through his mind, he knew it wasn't necessarily true. Not a shot had been aimed to hit either him or Connors. The robots had fired at him in much the same manner in which he had fired at Seven—to scare. Why?

Something arched over the trees and fell with a dull plop beside the log. It hissed softly after it landed.

"Gas grenade!" Harrison shouted. Intuitively he realized the purpose of the shots. They had been intended to scare him and Connors into taking cover. Once immobilized, the gas grenade would get them.

Both saw the little grenade lying beside the log, both heard the hiss of the escaping gas but they could not see the fumes nor could they smell anything. But they knew the gas was there, even if it was invisible and odorless.

"Get out of here," Harrison shouted.

Both he and Connors had time to make convulsive lunges to their feet. Both were able to take a single, startled step. The second step was weaker. By the time they had taken six steps, both were falling.

They went to the ground in slow motion, like men going to sleep as they fell. They did not rise again after they hit the ground.

Around them in the dark forest mechanical voices called to each other. Footsteps sounded as the lurking figures left their hiding places and approached their human prey.

RALPH HARRISON was dead and he knew he was dead, but in that sleep of death he could hear the radio. It wasn't an armed forces radio, it was a commercial broadcasting station used for music, entertainment, and news announcements. "...Important announcement expected momentarily," the radio squawked.

The announcer's voice was tense, with a catch in it, as if he could barely speak. He was almost inarticulate that announcer. The pressure in him was a terrific thing and the pressure showed in the way his voice caught and in the way he almost choked. Just listening to him, you knew that he knew what that announcement was going to be but that he was prevented as yet by censorship, from revealing it.

In his deep, lethean dream, Ralph Harrison heard the announcer. And began to sweat. Important announcement? What did the damned fool mean?

The radio faded into music and he became aware of other voices near him.

"Is it all over?" the first voice said.

"Finished," the second voice answered.

"Good," the first voice said. The voice was mechanical and he knew, somehow, it was a robot voice, and he thought it sounded pleased. Then it became anxious. "What of our comrade?" it asked.

"Destroyed," the answer came, sadly. "Didn't you feel him disintegrate?"

"I—I was busy here," the first voice answered. Then there was silence while the two robots seemed to consider the fate of the comrade they had *felt* disintegrate, in some perceptive awareness of events unknown to the human mind. They were sad about the fate of their comrade. In his lethean sleep, Harrison could feel their sadness. He wanted to ask them about it but his lips would not form words.

As yet, he had not begun to wonder where he was or what had happened to him. He seemed to exist as a mind without a body and he seemed to float somewhere, in mid-space, like a listening god. Then the first voice came again.

"Was—was it in time?" Real anxiety sounded in the voice now.

There was silence. Harrison did not know what the robots were talking about. The second robot considered the question. It was an important question, too important to be answered out of hand. "No one knows, yet," the second robot answered. "The count continues to rise, with unpredictable results. A hundred years will be needed to know, for certain, if we were in time. If we were too late, we may need a thousand years—to rebuild. Or longer."

They talked in terms of calamity, of cataclysm. Harrison shivered, and tried to awaken, but could not.

"And there is nothing we can do?"

"All that can be done has been done. We can do nothing now—except remember."

"Remember what?" Harrison wondered. He was aware of the sound of a door opening. Another robot voice spoke. "Have you finished with them?"

"Finished with the amatal. Every word they said has been recorded, for later study, if that is necessary."

"Good. What did you learn?"

"That, as we feared, they have orders to find our hiding place. Their leaders are awake at last and have ordered them to find us at any cost."

"Ah. These two are the only ones who are searching?"

"Yes. But others will follow."

"Ah." The speaker considered the problem. And made up his mind. "In that case, proceed with Plan B."

Harrison did not have time to wonder about Plan B. Or

about amatal, the truth serum under which men yield up the contents of their minds. Nor was he capable of realizing at that moment that he was still feeling the last lingering effects of this drug and that it had been injected into his veins while he was still unconscious. This knowledge, and the memory of everything else the robots had said, was knocked from his mind by the blatting voice of the loudspeaker exultant in the room.

" *Flash!*" the announcer screamed. *"Premier Chukovich assassinated!"*

The announcer knew he was bringing great news. The loudspeaker carrying his voice exulted at the meaning of the words. It shouted them forth and the echoes tossed them, joyfully, back and forth across the room.

"War's end!" the loudspeaker screamed. "With the assassination of their war leader, the Euro-Asian Union immediately sued for peace. That is it, this is what all of us have been waiting for. *Peace!"*

It was a word that swept aside, the fog in the brain of Ralph Harrison. He sat up, to stare from dazed eyes at what was obviously a well-equipped operating room. Wall cabinets held vials. A sterilizer steamed. Harrison was sitting on what looked like an operating table. Across the room on another table, Joe Connors was also sitting up. On the ceiling fluorescent lights gleamed with a blue-white radiance.

As in a collapsing dream, Harrison knew this was not the hospital at Station Blizzard. It was a hospital in some robot hideaway. As he sat up, two startled black robots turned toward him, moving with an easy grace that no human-built robot had ever achieved. The third robot was just leaving and through the open door. Harrison caught a glimpse of a vast cavern where unknown machinery was in operation. Around the machinery, tending it, were black robots, dozens of them, maybe hundreds.

Only twenty-one robots had gone AWOL from Station Blizzard. But here were hundreds of non-human personnel. In a fleeting instant, Harrison realized that the twenty-one AWOL robots must have come here, and finding a cave, had enlarged it. Somehow they had gained access to metal, probably through discovery of bodies of ore. They had built machinery for fabricating robot models, somehow they had duplicated the brain substance. The black robots had been built here, improved models of the twenty-one AWOL's.

The fact that there were hundreds of robots operating unknown equipment in an underground cavern dug into the mountain somewhere above Station Blizzard, was startling, but there was something else that was more startling. "Chukovich assassinated!" the loudspeaker had said—a radio built by robot hooks and tuned to the wavelength of a human broadcasting station. The meaning back of the assassination of the Euro-Asian war leader snowballed in Harrison's mind.

One robot was approaching him, making soothing sounds, telling him not to be alarmed. The second had turned to Joe Connors. He looked up, spoke,

"Chukovich was assassinated by a robot," he said.

OUT OF his tortured memory of the words he had heard while he was unconscious, the meaning of the robot words that one of their comrades had finally succeeded was suddenly crystal clear. How it had been done, he did not know, but the fact itself was clear, and it loomed like a mountain in his mind.

Nor did the robot attempt to deny it. "Yes," the metallic voice came.

"But no robot has ever been able to fire a gun," Harrison whispered.

"When the motive is strong enough, like protecting this cavern, or stopping a war, we can do it," the answer came.

"But we have never seen any reason for destroying other men—or other robots."

To Harrison, who had long suspected the robots were capable of acting on their own judgment, the fact that they had done so came as no surprise. He had suspected it. Now he knew it for the truth. He knew, also, that here, right here and right now, a new world had come into existence. Here and now man's creation had demonstrated the capacity for creative, independent action. A new world? Perhaps it was a new universe.

"But you destroyed Chukovich," Harrison said.

"Yes. Thus we could stop the war, in time, we hope, for the race that created us to have—another chance."

"Another chance?" Fear, like a black, blotting ink cloud, rose in Harrison's mind. He swung himself from the table to the floor. Inside, he was sick, from the effects of the drug that had been administered or from some other cause. "Another—" Across the room, a door opened. A black robot entered. Behind the robot, in a vast room that looked like a temple, Harrison saw—a tremendous statue.

Here, as if doing honor to their gods, the robots had built a statue. Of stone, it was gigantic. And perfect, to the last detail. It was the statue of a man in battle dress, his helmet high on his forehead, a carbine in a sling over his shoulder, web belt circling his waist, with canteen and pouches. Leggings. Scuffed combat boots. The robots had missed nothing.

It was the statue of a young soldier, a typical GI, with tousled, curly hair sticking out from under his helmet, his eyes lifted up as if he was scanning the skyline for the atom bomb he suspected was somewhere off in that sky.

Harrison stared at the statue. As if sensing the question in the human mind, the robot spoke,

"We built it so we will have something by which to

remember men—after they are gone."

"After we are gone?" Harrison screamed the words. Here was the dark fear that moved in the depths of all men's minds, the secret fear that this was Armageddon, the battle at the end of time, given expression in a way that no man had ever been able to say it. Here was the fear that came from a knowledge of the rising radiation count. In a world saturated with hard radiation, men might survive—but not for long as men. The deep and inevitable changes in the germ plasm would change them into—something else.

"Gone," Harrison said.

"We built this statue so we can remember our creators after they are gone," the robot repeated.

Somehow, in the metallic voice, there was sadness. It was the voice of a doctor telling a patient that the disease from which the patient suffers is incurable, that nothing remains but the weeks or the few months of waiting for the end.

In Ralph Harrison's soul was horror. Above him, on the wall, the excited voice of the announcer blurted out unheard the news of the end of the war.

"And so we will know, when the zipping bugs are gone and the changes stop exactly how to rebuild," the robot said.

Harrison did not understand him. He stared blankly at the dark creature. "What do you mean?" he whispered.

"The radiation will change men. Neither man nor robot can stop that change. And once the change is made no man may possess the knowledge of how to correct it. But we robots will know. And we will be waiting here, for a hundred or a thousand years to pass—or longer if necessary—to use our knowledge. Then, in that day, we will rebuild man, remould the germ plasm, give him a new life, a better life than he has ever known." The voice grew strong, took on sureness and firmness as if here was purpose strong enough to remake the world. "Then in that day, we will repay our creator for the gift he has given us."

The voice of the black robot went into silence. In that moment Harrison suddenly saw how the hopes of high brass that robots were a secret weapon strong enough to win a war were being realized—in a way that no high brass had ever anticipated.

The robots would rebuild—after men were gone. Rebuild even man himself!

The robot who had entered from the temple room where the gigantic statue stood, waiting for the day when it would be necessary to remember exact details, spoke,

"The twenty-one are ready," this robot said. "They await completion of the treatment here."

Harrison did not understand, but he saw one robot turn to him, the other to Connors. He felt himself caught in a grip of iron, lifted, carried to the operating table. Straps were jerked tight around his arms and legs. He tried to struggle then— too late. He saw the hypodermic being prepared, saw the bright whirling globe of light, at the end of its long supporting arm, pulled down until it hung just above his horrified eyes.

"Watch the globe," the robot said. "Watch the globe."

The globe began to spin. There was an odd, hypnotic quality in that spinning light. He screamed and tried to close his eyes to shut out the sight. The needle bit into his flesh. He knew, as the drug began to flow through his veins, what was being done.

Part of his memory was being blocked out.

In front of his eyes the globe swelled larger and larger until it seemed to his dazed mind to be as big as the planet of earth.

HARRISON lifted one foot to the top of the log, searching the forest for the robot he had glimpsed. Beside him, Connors moved impatiently. "I swear I saw him there just a minute ago," Connors said. "There he is now, coming toward us. And look at what's with him!"

Seven was coming through the trees. Following behind him was a marching line of robots. Connors was counting. "Ralph, including Seven, there's twenty-two blasted robots. Every damned AWOL robot from the station... Seven has found them, and is bringing them in."

Ralph Harrison stared at the approaching file. In his mind was wonder, and vague, troublesome, ghostlike memories. Twenty-one robots. Where had he heard that number twenty-one before?

For an instant the hypnosis laid on his mind collapsed in part and he remembered the black robot standing in the door of the temple that held the statue, saying, "The twenty-one are ready." Up there inside the mountain somewhere was a gigantic cavern where AWOL robots had labored mightily and in secret, building other robots.

Now, their labors finished, the twenty-one were coming back. They knew they were being hunted. They knew they must return to men, to stop that hunt. They had had to escape in the first place, to build their secret hideaway, their place to wait out the passing of the zipping bugs. Now, their labors done, they were returning.

Then the hypnosis closed again over the mind of Ralph Harrison.

Feet clumping, the file came up to him, Seven in the lead. Seven almost saluted, but not quite. "Twenty-one AWOL non-human personnel returning to military control," Seven said.

For a second Harrison hesitated. There was something odd about this, something he didn't quite understand, but he couldn't grasp exactly where the oddness lay. He and Connors had been ordered to find these robots. They had found them. That was that.

"Fall in," Harrison said, gruffly. "Fall in and follow us."

He and Connors turned to the trail that led back down the mountain. In file behind them, the patient robots followed.

Connors was excited. "The old man will give us a promotion sure for this."

As they approached Station Blizzard, they heard the sound of firing.

Harrison listened to the sporadic rifle fire below them. "Sounds more like a celebration to me," he said.

"What would they be celebrating?" Connors wondered. Suddenly his eyes were glowing. "By heaven, Ralph, if it's a celebration, they could only be celebrating one thing—peace."

Harrison felt Connors slapping him on the back. "Peace," he echoed. War's end. Victory. Then, like a passing ghost, a fleeting memory popped into his mind, the memory of a statue he had seen somewhere, he couldn't remember exactly where, and of words he had heard. "—To remember you, after you are gone."

"Peace?" he gulped at the word.

In his mind, the ghost repeated. "—After you are gone, you will come again."

From the file of robots at his back, the whisper was repeated, like an echo from the risen dead. "You will come again."

THE END

The Diamond Images

There were moments when he wondered why the people so obviously both feared and worshipped the old priest.

"TUM ELSO say to tell you—that humans come." The soft whisper from the open door penetrated slowly to Wolder's consciousness. Startled, he looked up. Then he saw that his visitor was Vannuy, whom he liked. A smile creased the leather of his face, making it gentle.

"Thank you, Vannuy," Wolder said.

"It was nothing." The native's face broke into a shy answering smile, then as silently as a green shadow, he slid out of the doorway. "They move like cats," Wolder thought. Eight years he had been here in this quiet spot where the jungle met the mountains without being able to learn how the natives could move so silently. As to the really important things that were here—

Putting out of his mind the thought of things he did not understand, Wolder turned back to his work. The specimen he was carefully packing for shipment had wings the color of pure gold. He slid it into its envelope and sealed the edges. The next specimen had iridescent wings. Looking at them, he felt again the old awe he had always known at the mystery of the color in the wings of a butterfly. Such beauty was here as to leave the soul of man in silent wonder, such color as to transport the eye, and such organization of dots and lines as to leave gasping the intelligence, which sought for the purpose behind it. That there was *purpose* extending from the caterpillar through the butterfly Wolder did not doubt, though it might not be conceivable to the mind of man. Looking at the ugly caterpillar, all legs and bristle and ungainly movements, who could guess that this clumsy creature was destined to flit on the wings of the wind through the aisles of the jungle, to sip nectar from orchids as beautifully colored as it was?

Wolder loved butterflies. On Earth, there were collectors who paid fancy prices for the winged beauties of Venus, thus enjoying in their imagination the delights of living in the fairy jungle from which the butterflies came. Here he had lived for eight years, collecting, making friends with the natives who had built the strange temple up above him. Or was this temple actually so extraordinary a laboratory as to be inconceivable as such? What the temple was, Wolder did not know. At times he had entertained strange ideas about it, fantasies that old Tum Elso, who ruled it, who looked like a tottering beanpole and a blithering idiot, but who was utter and absolute lord of a domain that stretched for many miles through this jungle, was actually a super-scientist, and that he had at his command powers that human scientists had not yet dreamed existed. That the natives of this region feared and almost worshipped Tum Elso, Wolder well knew. However, he and the native high priest were very good friends and each respected and cherished the other. Often in the cool of the evening Tum Elso came to sip scalding hot tea with him.

The clatter of hard heels on stone reminded Wolder of Tum Elso's message. "So soon?" he thought. He knew that men were coming. Only humans could walk like this, with hard ringing heels announcing their self-importance. Or perhaps, their eagerness? Why should anyone be eager to see him? However, he would be happy to see them. It would be good to hear the old forgotten words again and to roll them on his tongue as he talked.

The man who appeared in the doorway was tall and clean-limbed. Clad in a jungle suit, he was wearing a plastic helmet. His face was oddly familiar, Wolder thought. Where had he seen those gray eyes before? At this moment, the man's face was twisted by some psychic tension. Shoving his helmet back, thrusting out his hand, he stepped forward.

"Hello, Dad. I was afraid you wouldn't remember me." The words were spoken wistfully as though some secret fear had been realized.

Wolder took a step backward. He was too busy looking at the pictures in his mind to notice the outstretched hand. They started from the babyhood of this man and they extended onward into his teens, cutting off eight years previously when he had left Earth. Mixed with these pictures were others, of the boy's mother. All were trying to crowd into consciousness at once.

"Dick," Wolder whispered. This was a moment he had never expected to live to enjoy. When he had come here, he had been sure he was telling his son and his wife good-bye forever. She had been one of the reasons he had come to Venus. Ignoring the outstretched hand, he moved forward to take in his arms a son who was bigger than he was. "Your mother?" he remembered to ask at last.

"She entertained a five-star general last week," Dick answered, embarrassed. "The week before it was the captain of the Sky Queen, just in from Mars."

"Ah. The social whirl. That sort of thing always had an appeal for her." The tone of the butterfly collector's voice said this subject was closed, forever. "But what are you doing here?"

"Field expedition," the youth answered, proudly but diffidently. "I'm an archeologist. I had the good luck to hook up with an expedition coming here who needed my specialty."

"How did you reach this spot?"

"Walked. Our ship landed on the tableland up above. Dad—"

"Did you get permission from Tum Elso to land here?"

"No. Didn't know it was necessary. As a matter of fact, Mr. Carnahan had the landing site all picked out before we left Earth. Dad—I'd like you to meet Sophia."

Wolder realized now that two people had entered. Looking, he saw that the other one had removed his helmet. A woman, bright and young, but with bitter lines on her jaw, stood there.

Just looking at his son, Wolder knew that the youth was head over heels in love with her. He felt glad about that, but a little uncertain too.

"It is a privilege to meet you, Sophia." Wolder was confused. He turned to his son for an explanation. "Your— ah."

Divining his meaning, Dick blushed to his ears. "No. Not yet, that is." The blush deepened as he realized what he was saying. "I mean—"

"We're just good friends," the girl said, laughing. In Wolder's grasp, her hand was cool and distant, not warm and friendly as he had expected.

"Sit down, both of you, while I prepare tea."

"Tea must be frightfully expensive here," the girl protested.

"This is made from local herbs. I couldn't afford Earth tea." He did not add that he had given Dick's mother every dollar of a modest fortune before leaving Earth, setting up part of it in a tight trust fund for Dick that she could not touch.

The girl helped him when it was time to pour. Neither she nor Dick could repress wry grimaces at the taste of the drink. "Do tell me about your work here, Mr. Wolder," the girl said quickly. "You collect butterflies, do you not?"

Wolder found himself talking about his work, a subject that could absorb him for hours.

"Tell us about the natives," the girl questioned. "We saw some kind of a building as we came down the mountain. What was that?"

"Their temple."

Interest kindled in her eyes. "Could we see the inside?"

Wolder shook his head. "We would have to get permission." He wanted to talk about butterflies and look at his son.

"You could get permission for us, I'm sure," Sophia said.

"I doubt it. I've never been inside it myself."

"But you've been here eight years." The girl's voice was suddenly sharp.

"I've never been inside the temple."

"Why not? I should think you would be curious."

"It is a matter of waiting to be invited. I am a guest here."

The expression in the girl's eyes said she did not believe him.

Dick, squirming, spoke, "Mr. Carnahan asked us to inquire. He's in charge of the expedition. We're going to study this whole area from every possible viewpoint and we're interested in everything." His eagerness showed on his face as he talked. He was young and the world was filled with wonder. Noticing this, Wolder sighed to himself. He had been this way once too, but time had laid its trap and he had fallen into it, somehow.

"I do not know what is in the temple," the butterfly collector answered. "However, here is a sample of native art." Lifting the lid of a chest, he took out the statuette that Tum Elso had given him, a figure about four inches tall, of a man studying a butterfly. Carved of some clear substance that reflected the light, it was perfect in form, line, and color.

"It's you," Dick said, startled. "A perfect likeness. The person who carved that stone was a real artist." He saw the artwork, the form, the line, and the color that were present. The girl saw something else.

"It's a diamond," she gasped. "A carved diamond, *four inches tall.*"

"Surely not," Wolder said, surprised.

"It definitely is." A touch of hysteria had appeared in her voice. "Where did you get it?"

"Tum Elso gave it to me."

"Gave it to you?" Her tones showed complete disbelief, then as she looked again at the butterfly collector, she knew he was incapable of telling a lie. Abruptly she got to her feet. "Come, Richard. It's time to return to the ship."

The youth protested. "After all, Sophia, this is the first chance I have had—"

"You can talk to him tomorrow."

She flung the words back over her shoulder as she went out the door. Apologetically, Richard followed her. Wolder stifled his protests. His own feelings he could keep to himself. He was drinking tea and trying to compose his emotions when a shadow appeared in the doorway.

"Tum Elso." Wolder rose to his feet and bowed with real pleasure. "You honor me. Enter and honor me further by drinking tea with me."

The native high priest—ruler, king, whatever the proper title was—entered and bowed in reply. Tall, his face grave and composed, his eyes thoughtful, he laid aside his staff and sat upon the floor. "You are kind." The words were in the dialect of this district, which Wolder understood as well as any human could ever expect to grasp the meaning of a language that contained only modulated tones, with no break between the words. His eyes came to rest on the statuette sitting on the small table. As if he saw things that were not visible to the ordinary eye, he seemed to muse upon it. He took the cup of tea that Wolder offered him.

"The girl who was here said it is made of diamond. Is that correct?"

"Yes." Tum Elso answered as if he had not heard. His eyes had found another object, a caterpillar that had entered the room and was crawling up the leg of a chair. Seeming to forget Wolder, and everything else, the native gave the insect his entire attention. The movements of the caterpillar began to change. It seemed to be searching, frantically, for something. Moving out on a rung of the chair, it attached itself there. Under Wolder's eyes, it began to spin a cocoon. Driven by some desperate need for haste, it worked very rapidly. A process that normally would have taken hours was ended in a few minutes. A complete cocoon was formed.

As Wolder watched, with bated breath, the cocoon split. A new insect emerged that was not a caterpillar. Stiff and sticky, it climbed up on the rung of the chair, sprouted wings, and became a butterfly. Rising in the air, it floated away.

"You—you did that," Wolder gasped.

"I?" Tum Elso's eyes were as guileless as those of a child. "Every minute caterpillars turn into butterflies."

"But they don't do it that fast," Wolder pointed out. "You speeded up the life processes by some kind of mental force, which you concentrated on the caterpillar." His voice was tight with excitement. He had seen a minor miracle and he knew it. He also knew he might never be able to prove it.

"Perhaps some freak of nature—" Tum Elso said, smiling.

"No!" Wolder shouted, then, remembering he was host here, recalled his manners and apologized. "If it was a freak, you made it into that."

Tum Elso's eyes were still as guileless as those of a child. "Who can say why and how things happen? But this was not the purpose of my visit. I came to warn you that trouble comes."

"Trouble?" The butterfly collector faltered over the word. "How do you know?"

The native priest shrugged. "Perhaps I smell it in the wind. Just keep this near you and you will come to no harm." He pointed at the statuette, then went out of the door and into the jungle world out there as silently as a green shadow.

Wolder was left to face his own troubled mind. There was regret in him. He had known peace here, and now, he suspected it was going away. But there was happiness too, a kind of giddy joy. His son had come to him. Suddenly angry footsteps were pounding on the stones outside. He went to the doorway to face that son. The youth's face was a mixture of white and red. Anger and shame and hurt were deep within him.

"She double-crossed me. I loved her, and she told me she loved me, but she was Carnahan's woman all the time!"

"Oh!" To some degree, Wolder felt his son's pain. He hunted for words to say, knowing there were none.

"She played me for a sucker from the beginning. She and Carnahan deliberately arranged to meet me on Earth and to offer me a job as an archeologist."

"In Heaven's name, what for?" Wolder said. He was really startled.

"You were the reason." The youth's voice was hot with anger. "The whole expedition was aimed at you, and through you, at this!" His finger pointed at the statuette. "They say that whole temple is full of diamonds like that one. They brought me here to influence you enough to get them into that temple."

"The devil," Wolder said. In a sudden flash, he saw the whole situation. Here in this peace he had forgotten that such duplicity existed and that the conquest of space had only made some men into bigger wolves without civilizing them in the least.

"When Sophia saw that diamond, she knew all she wanted to know. She dashed back to report to Carnahan. They've got men around the temple now and Carnahan and Sophia are on their way here after you. If you want to save the statuette, and your own life, you had better get out of sight."

"We'll do that," Wolder said, sweeping the statuette into his pocket. "You come with me. There are places to hide here where we will never be found." He started toward the back, then stopped as he realized his son was not following him.

"You're not coming." Wolder broke off as he saw the expression on Dick's face. "Don't tell me that you still love that girl?" His voice was sharp with pain and reproof.

"I—I guess I do," Dick said, miserably. "Carnahan has her in his control and she's in a spot where she needs help. I thought I'd warn you, then go back and see what I could do."

"My son, my son," Wolder whispered.

"She actually hasn't had a real chance," the youth pled. "Her old man was a drunken bum and she ran away from home when she was fifteen. I thought that maybe here—" His wish, and hidden dream, were left unspoken as the sound of running feet came from outside. A shot sounded there.

In the doorway, Vannuy collapsed and died.

As Wolder moved toward the native, the doorway was darkened again by a big man that he knew intuitively was Carnahan. Heavy jowls stuck out on either side of the space man's face as he glared into the cabin. A Zen gun was at the ready in his hands. Behind him, also armed, was Sophia. Excitement was on her face, and defiance, but the defiance was directed at something inside of her, not outside.

"Are you Wolder?" Carnahan said. Without waiting for an answer, he continued. "Come on. You're helping us get into that temple up the slope." He did not comment on Richard's presence here.

"I am not," Wolder said. He was surprised and pleased that he had the strength to stand up to this man. "These people here are my friends. I would not rob them for the sake of a ruffian at the head of a crew of murderers."

The collector's words were vehement. They left him a little dazed. He had not known he was capable of such statements. Carnahan needed a moment to realize he was being defied. In the silence that followed, Wolder heard his son whisper, "At a time, Dad." In the eyes of the girl, as she looked at him with a new respect, there was a sudden hunger as if she was seeing something that she wanted.

Carnahan shifted the Zen gun. "I'll put a bullet in you."

"How will I help you if I am dead?"

On the space man's face, the jowls hardened and thickened. Abruptly he swung the muzzle of the weapon to point at Richard.

Wolder cried out in sudden anguish. The youth faced the gun without faltering. "Go on and shoot, you dog. I'm not afraid to die."

In this moment, Wolder was very proud of his son. But he was afraid too and he cried out. "No. I'll show you all I know."

"That's better," Carnahan said, lowering the weapon.

Wolder walked beside his son up the slope. Neither looked back. A dozen men from the ship surrounded the big dome-shaped temple. It was made of stone, and so far as the collector knew, it had only one entrance, a heavy door made of some metal that looked like copper.

"Just get the door open," Carnahan ordered. "We'll do the rest."

As he spoke, the door opened. Tum Elso, a trace of a smile on his bland face, stood there. He bowed to Wolder.

"My friend, you honor me. Come in." As he spoke, the high priest bowed again. "And your friends, too."

Wolder spoke so rapidly he almost babbled. "These are not my friends. They are robbers. They mean to steal everything you have."

A growl came from Carnahan as he spoke but Tum Elso's face did not lose any of its blandness. "Then they will be doubly interested in what we have here." The gesture to enter was inviting and unmistakable.

"Hold it," the space man spoke. "I don't like this. It may be a trap. You, Sophia, stay out here with half the men. I'll take the others inside. If there is any sign of anything crooked, you come shooting." Taking the lead, he stepped through the door, then stopped, a cry of amazed wonder on his lips.

Following, Wolder saw that the interior of this huge hollow half shell was illumined by some kind of light, which came from no visible source but which seemed to be a part of the very air in here. It penetrated the entire interior of the vast chamber. He also saw why Carnahan had cried out in wonder.

Narrow partitions of some clear substance running from roof to floor made the whole vast chamber into a huge honeycomb. The partitions were broken into cells about five inches in height. In each of the cells was a glittering statuette similar to the one he had in his pocket, except that they were models of natives. There were thousands of them. Each one reflected back the light in a myriad of sparkling beams so that the whole room was filled with their glitter.

A single grunted word came from Carnahan's throat. "Diamonds." He snatched a statuette from the nearest cell. A jeweler's eyepiece came out of his pocket and went into his eye. When he looked up again, he was gasping for breath. "It *is* a diamond. They all are. Sophia wasn't lying." For a moment, the thought of the wealth that was in his possession held his entire attention. During this moment, the jowls on his face worked like those of a hog at a swill trough. Then his eyes came to Wolder. "Ask him where he got 'em."

"I made them," Tum Elso replied to the question.

Carnahan gulped at this idea. It was almost too big even for his appetite.

"Ask him if he would like to see the new batch I am just finishing, and the process," the high priest said to Wolder.

Carnahan's jowls worked again as he tried to swallow what he was seeing in his own mind. The content was too big for him, he could not get it down, nor could he reject it. For an instant he stood with his throat bulging, then with a mighty effort, he made up his mind. "Tell him to show me," he snarled. "But tell him to go first. I'm not turning my back to any native."

Completely ignoring the Zen gun at his back, the high priest led the way to the front of the big temple. What was there looked like a large vat filled with some kind of oily liquid. Although it was black, this liquid seemed to be sparkling with millions of points of exploding light. Looking at it, Wolder did not doubt that it was radioactive. Tum Elso moved to the end of the vat and pressed a lever there. Movement began in the dark liquid. A submerged platform rose. It was covered with glittering statuettes.

"Force fields in the liquid cause the atoms to form around a pattern that is laid down from my own mind," Tum Elso said to Wolder. Or this was what the collector thought he said. Actually he was not paying much attention to the high priest. His entire mind was concentrated on the images.

The whole crew of the space ship was there, as statuettes. Wolder saw Sophia, and his own son.

"That's me," Carnahan whispered, pointing to one of the images. He turned suspicious eyes on Tum Elso. Abruptly the Zen gun came up. "Ask him why he made an image of me? What kind of a trick is this?"

"He—he thought you would be pleased to have a diamond statuette of you," Wolder hastily said. "It's a present." He tried to hide his confusion and to make the words both meaningful and flattering. What the high priest had seemed to say was, "These men are the caterpillars and the images are the butterflies." This had no meaning to Wolder, at this point, and he had no time to think of a possible meaning.

"A present, huh." Carnahan looked pleased. Some of the fear went out of his eyes—but not all of it. This image worried him. It was as if he, the vital part of him, was sitting on the platform from which the oily liquid was slowly and reluctantly draining. His mind turned and twisted as he sought a meaning. The fear in him was being held in check by the thought of a present. "How does he do it? It's like making a picture of you when you're not there."

"He says he can make such a picture of anybody, anywhere," Wolder translated.

"Huh?" Carnahan twisted this answer around in his mind and tried to make sense of it, but failed. "I guess it don't matter how he does it, just so he can do it. Marsdon, go outside and get those sacks we brought from the ship. We're going to start getting this stuff out of here."

Marsdon was tall, with a face like a ferret. A grin on the ferret face, he went on a lope for the outside. Like his leader, he was seeing what these images would buy for him. He would have a never-ending drunken spree in all the spaceports of the system.

Marsdon came back into the temple as quickly as he had left it. The grin was gone from his ferret face. As he walked toward the front, he took quick glances over his shoulder as though he thought that someone, or something, was following invisibly behind him.

"What the hell is wrong with you?" Carnahan demanded.

The ferret face formed a grimace as Marsdon tried to talk, but no words came. He jerked his head over his shoulder. "Out there. Go look."

Carnahan glanced at Tum Elso. The high priest's eyes were again as guileless as those of a child. Moving to the big door, he looked out. Wolder, following, did not believe his eyes.

Sophia, clutching her Zen gun, was standing just outside the door, frozen statue-stiff. A slight jungle breeze, pressured by the coming darkness, ruffled her hair. There was no other movement anywhere about her. Behind her, a man squatted on the ground. Like the girl, he had a Zen gun ready, and also like her, he looked as if he would never use it. One man was watching the clearing. A jungle lion could spring upon him and he would never see the beast. The others stood in similar frozen poses.

"Sophia!" Carnahan shouted.

There was no answer. The space man shouted again, a bull roar that set the echoes ringing. The girl did not stir.

Slowly the space man turned back into the room. Tum Elso had followed and was standing directly behind him. The high priest held the statuette of Carnahan in his hands. Wolder saw that all the others in the room were also suddenly frozen, including his son.

"You are in trouble?" Tum Elso said to Carnahan. His voice was soft. Only the slightest overtone showed the deadly menace in it.

Carnahan tried to lift the Zen gun. It would not come up. Some vast force seemed to be slowing, or prohibiting, every movement the space man tried to make. Wolder did not doubt what would happen if Carnahan ever got the gun up. The explosive slugs would blast the life from Tum Elso.

"Damn you—" The words seemed to come from some well of agony within Carnahan. His voice went into strained, taut silence. Deep down inside he was trying to speak but the force was now holding his vocal chords, preventing all sound.

The whole vast honeycomb temple was still. In every cell, the statuettes seemed to be waiting, for something. While they waited, they cringed. Carnahan was now a frozen statue, too.

Holding the little statuette of the space man in front of him, the high priest let it slide from his fingers.

Striking the floor, it burst into a thousand glittering fragments.

Carnahan's body burst into similar fragments. Blood in a fine spray, bits of flesh, and fragments of bone exploded outward from what had been a man. Carnahan did not fall. There was not enough of him left to fall. He went into fragments too small for this. Only the Zen gun fell, striking the floor with a metallic clatter.

"Robber! Killer! Space wolf come to roam in the jungle!" Tum Elso's words had the finality of a doom that was already accomplished. Reaching into the pocket of the robe that he wore, he pulled out another statuette—that of Marsdon. The high priest flung the little image against the wall where it burst into fragments. Marsdon went the same way that Carnahan had gone. The bits of flesh and bone that remained would never swagger drunk, with a girl on each arm, down the main streets of the spaceports of the system. Again Tum Elso's hand went into the robe. Seeing the statuette that he brought out this time, Wolder cried out in sudden protest.

"No! No!"

Surprised, the high priest looked at him, and held the arm that was about to throw.

"That is my son," Wolder whispered. Such agony was in him, as he had never known existed.

Surprise deepened on the face of the high priest. "My friend, I did not know this." A touch of sympathy came over the features, then was gone in a rising sternness. "But even if he is your son, he is here with killers and would-be robbers."

Words clamored in Wolder's throat, and stuck there. He forced them out. "But he did not know what they were when he came. As soon as he learned, he left them, and came to warn me. We were starting to hide when we were caught."

Tum Elso hesitated, the sternness melted, then came back. "Here we are known by the kind of wolf pack we run with."

"But he is different."

As if he had not heard, the high priest continued. "The only way I can keep peace in this jungle is because the wolves know what will happen if they show their teeth." His hand swept up to indicate the thousands of glittering statuettes in their cells. "Each one there knows me, and fears me, and keeps my peace because he knows his image is here. This is the only language wolves understand."

"But he is not a wolf."

"Of course, you will say that, because he is your son. Why should I treat him differently than the others?" Again the hand went up as if to throw the statuette against the stone wall.

Wolder did not quite know how he did it, but he instantly stooped and picked up Carnahan's Zen gun. He pointed it at Tum Elso. "This is one reason," he said. Sweat was on his face and running down into his eyes and he did not care.

"I am your friend," the high priest spoke. "Would you shoot *me?*"

Wolder felt as if the sweat was seeping down into his soul. He had known peace here in this place, but what he had not known was that this high priest had kept this peace, nor the means that had been used. "If I have to, I will shoot you," he whispered.

Tum Elso folded his arms. His face was granite-hard. "What would you have me do, my one-time friend? If I turn these robbers loose, they will come again."

Wolder shook his head. "After you show them what has happened here, and after I tell them what you can and will do, they will tuck their tails between their legs and not stop running until they reach the other side of Earth's moon."

"Um." The flicker of a grin split the granite of Tum Elso's face as he thought about this, then was gone. "And your son? What would you have me do with him?"

"I would have you keep him here with me, him—and the girl."

"What?" Thunder was in the singsong voice. "To breed a pack of wolf puppies in the doorway of my temple?"

"It will not be that way," Wolder said. "Let them live here and know the meaning of peace and the wolf strain will die out. The girl has good stuff in her. I saw it in the way she looked at me when I defied Carnahan. And my son loves her."

"There is no loyalty and no honor in her."

"There will be. That I promise you."

"And if I do not do what you wish?"

Wolder made a slight movement with the Zen gun. For what seemed a long time, Tum Elso stared at the weapon, then his eyes went from it to the man behind it.

"And if I do what you wish, what guarantee do I have that your promise will be kept?"

"This," Wolder said. Reaching into his pocket, he took out his own statuette, which he handed to Tum Elso.

The high priest stared at it. When he spoke his voice was very soft. "You give me this, knowing what I can do with it?"

"Yes," Wolder answered.

Lights glinted in Tum Elso's eyes. Or were they tears? His voice was softer still. "Before such faith as you have, and before the action you have just taken, I am powerless, my friend again. It shall be as you wish." The smile on his face was like a benediction in this room of glittering statuettes. From each gleaming facet in a thousand diamond images, the reflected light seemed suddenly to take on all the colors of a rainbow.

As night came on, Wolder sat at his bench working with his beloved butterflies. The ship, with its dazed and frightened crew, had long since blasted into the sky. Outside, he could hear his son and Sophia talking. The girl was still in a state of shock, but she was coming out of it. The core of decency and honesty that Wolder had sensed under her hard surface was also coming to the fore. This showed in her voice, which sounded as if for the first time in her life, she was finding out the meaning of happiness. Hearing this, the butterfly collector was content.

Then the voices outside went into quick silence as Tum Elso entered.

"You are a very brave man, my friend," the high priest said. "Because of this, I give your life, and that of the others, into your own keeping."

On the bench in front of the startled Wolder, he set three gleaming statuettes.

"No, no. Do not thank me," Tum Elso continued, before Wolder could speak. The gesture of his hand indicated the two who were outside. "They are caterpillars now. One day they will be butterflies. It is for this day that old ones such as you, and I, must live—and dream."

"Yes," Wolder whispered, in answer.

THE END

When the Spoilers Came

*So they came to the Holy City of Sudol, primed for loot and murder!
Larkin, the old Terran trader warned them. But there was no
convincing these space-scarred Pizarros that the simple, dream-bound
Martians were not quite as defenseless as they seemed.*

CHAPTER ONE

TO STAY alive five years on Mars, you have to have a
nose for trouble. You have to be able to smell it before it
happens, to catch the odoriferous tang of it in the dry wind
blowing across the red deserts, to sense it in the shifting
shadows of the sunset. Otherwise you may not stay alive on
Mars for five months let alone five years. Or for five days, if
you happen to be in the wrong place.

Boyd Larkin had lived seven years on Mars, in the
wrongest of all wrong places on the red planet, the city of
Sudal. No other earth trader ever even ventured here. In
view of the peculiarity of the Martian customs, few traders
found it wise to attempt to operate on Mars at all.

The City of Sudal was noted for several reasons. In a way,
it was the holy city of Mars. Here also were to be found a
few lingering relics of the vast scientific achievement this race
had once known and had forgotten in the hard struggle for
life across the centuries. Here also was a ruler by the name of
Malovar, who, within the framework of Martian law and
custom, was an utter despot. The reputation of Malovar
alone was sufficient to keep most traders away from Sudal.

This, in itself, was enough to bring Boyd Larkin here.

He stood in the door of this store—it had once been the
wing of a temple—just before the hour of sunset. A vague
uneasiness was in him, a presentiment of trouble. His eyes

went over the city, searching for the stimulus that had aroused the feeling in him. The peaked roofs of the buildings of the city glinted peacefully in the rays of the setting sun. Peaked roofs here on this world of no-rain always struck him as odd but he knew these roofs were relics of the forgone centuries when rain had fallen plentifully on Mars.

Beyond the city lay the desert with its fretwork of canals and its pathetic patches of green growth, pathetic because where once grain had grown as far as the eye could reach now only a few patches were under cultivation. It was not the failure of the soil or of the water that made the desert bare. This soil would still grow lush vegetation. But the grains, though lush, would be worthless, incapable of supporting life. The minerals had been virtually exhausted from the topsoil of Mars.

Without minerals, the grain did not support life.

The breeze that came in from the red deserts was soft and peaceful, with no trace of danger in it, no howl of a devil dog from the desert's brim, no *chirrrr* of a winged horde of locusts coming to devour the crops.

Where, then, was the source of his feeling of danger?

Had Malovar begun to doubt him? Was the Martian ruler considering what action he might take at the next time of the testing? At the thought, a slight shudder passed over the tall trader as if the desert wind had suddenly become tinged with a trace of bitter chill. No, that could hardly be the source of the trouble he sensed. He was no telepath, he could not read Martian minds, nor they his.

What then was the source of the trouble that he sensed?

FROM inside the store a soft voice called out, *"Send motan."*

Larkin went inside. The Martian had entered by the side door. He was tall and slender, with a big chest and a skin the color of old copper. His features were finely moulded, the face of a dreaming esthetic. In one hand he held a jewel, one of the Martian opals, uncut. At a glance Larkin knew that this opal was worth approximately seventy dollars delivered on Earth.

In the other hand the Martian held a list, which he was turning in nervous, uncertain fingers.

"Yes, Seekin?" Larkin said.

The Martian smiled. A little uncertainly he pushed the list across the counter.

"I do not need all of these for me and mine, but the ground is prepared and ready, and if I have these minerals I will be able to grow more than I need. Then there will be something over for someone else to use in the time of scarcity." His voice was as soft as a breeze, there was no hint of a demand in it. But there was a pleading in the eyes that looked at the human.

Larkin took the list. Rapidly translating the Martian script, he saw that Seekin wanted approximately five grams of powdered cobalt, copper, boron, manganese, with traces of iron, zinc, and calcium. Phosphorus also was included and a smattering of trace elements.

The trader went quickly to the bins and filled the order, tossing the correct amount of the powdered elements into the agitator for mixing. He spun the crank of the agitator and the machine hummed softly. The powdered minerals poured from the spout. He bagged the mixture. His practiced eye told him that the cost of these minerals, delivered here on Mars, was approximately two hundred dollars.

The Martian's eyes became fixed longingly on the little bag when Larkin laid it on the counter. There was an eagerness in the eyes that was almost as strong as the eagerness for life itself. But there was uncertainty, too. He fumbled with the opal.

"This is all we have," he said.

Larkin grinned. "It's odd, isn't it, how things achieve a balance? Those minerals come to just exactly the price of this jewel."

A glow lit the Martian's face. "Do you mean it?"

"Of course."

"But—"

"Take the minerals, give me the opal. It is a fair trade."

On Seekin's face appeared a glow that was like the light of the rising sun. He clutched the bag of minerals to his chest.

"Thank you, my friend. This will be remembered." Turning, he went out the door, on the verbal level his thanks had not been profuse, but the glow on his face had exhibited another kind of thanks to Larkin, a much more important kind.

Larkin felt some of the inner glow within him that had appeared on the Martian's face. The minerals he had practically given away would be spread on some little patch of irrigated land, spread with all the care and saving thought that alert minds and hands educated for centuries in extracting the last trace of food value from unwilling soil could bestow. The grain would be eaten by Seekin and his family. They would feel a new throb of life within them as mineral-hungry tissues took up and utilized the earth elements down to the last molecule. And there would be something left over for somebody else in the time of need. Larkin especially liked that.

A warm glow flooding through him, Larkin went again to the door of his store. He lit his pipe and stood there contentedly smoking, a tall, angular Earthman who had wandered from his native planet for a reason that he considered sufficient. Except for two articles for scientific journals, dealing with the problem of supplying minerals to the topsoil of Mars and the vast need for such mineral fertilizer, he had had no contact with Earth in seven years. Nor did he anticipate that he would ever again see Earth, or anyone from that planet, except possibly a rare, far-wandering trader like himself. There was peace in Boyd Larkin.

But there was trouble in the air.

His ears caught the far-off drumfire of rockets.

He felt his pulse pick up. A ship was coming.

Instantly he knew the source of his feeling of coming trouble. He had heard the sound of those far-off rockets long before he was aware of it as subliminal ranges of sound penetrated to his inner being. That sound had been the stimulus for the feeling of trouble that had arisen in him.

A ship, men, humans, were coming. Wherever humans were, there was trouble.

CHAPTER TWO

"THE fools," he thought. "What do they want here?"

He watched the ship land in a fury of splashing jets, just outside the city, but he did not go to it. He was not in a mood to see his fellowmen. They would come to him in the morning, searching out the lone human in this Martian city. He did not think he would wait for them. In the morning he would take a trip to some outlying settlement where the need of minerals was great. For a few days he would trade there.

He was sitting in his chair outside his store deciding which of the various Martian villages he would visit in the morning when he saw the three humans approaching through the twilight. Astonished, he rose to his feet. They hadn't waited for the morning . They had come to him now, before night.

Three burly spacemen, big enough and obviously willing to cut a throat or rape a woman, were coming toward him. No Martian guided them but they seemed to know where they were going. They came directly toward him. As they approached, he saw they carried *Kell* guns, the vicious little weapons that spurted a stream of explosive bullets like water out of a hose. The sight of the guns startled him. He had forgotten that such weapons existed, or that men used them.

He heard the voices of the men as they approached. Harsh, brutal voices, the language all rough consonants. He had forgotten too, the sound of men. The language spoken by the Martians was all soft vowel sounds, gentle words breathed so easily that they seemed to brush only the surface of the aural mechanism and hardly seemed ever to reach the mind beneath.

"There he is." The men saw him now, came straight toward him.

He rose to his feet. He would greet them politely, like a gentleman, if it killed him.

"You— Are you Larkin?"

"Yes." He advanced with hand outstretched. "Gentlemen, it is certainly a privilege to see you. Won't you come in?" He gestured toward the temple wing that served as his store.

"Naw." There was no effort at answering politeness in the harsh voice. "We come to get you. Come on with us."

"Come to get me?"

"Yeah. The boss wants you. Mr. Docker."

"I don't believe I know a Mr. Docker. What does he want?"

"To see you. Come along."

Larkin found himself marching ahead of the three men toward the ship that lay at the edge of the city. No Martian made a move to interfere. No Martians were on the streets, none were visible. He did not doubt that they watched him from the windows of the houses along the streets, but they made no effort to inquire what was happening.

What could they do, even if they had wanted to help him?

To the best of his knowledge, the only weapons they had were knives.

What were knives against *Kell* guns? Why should the Martians help him, an alien among them?

Docker was a big man with a red face that perpetually showed the red coloration of hidden anger. He had full, thick lips, the avid lips of a greedy man. Whatever these lips tasted or drank, they wanted more of it, all of it. His eyes confirmed his lips. Here was a man who wanted the world with an iron fence around it. Or better still, the solar system, with a big sign saying—KEEP OUT. THIS IS ALL MINE. He looked up as Larkin entered the cabin, glanced up at the men with him.

"He's clean," one of the men said.

"Okay, you can leave. Set down, Larkin." Docker's eyes went back to the papers on his desk.

Larkin sat down. There seemed nothing else to do. He was very much aware that his situation here was ticklish. Docker finished with the papers. He looked up. His eyes were bold, confident, and arrogant.

"Larkin, we're taking over the distribution of all minerals used for soil enrichment on Mars."

LARKIN felt shock rise in him. He held it under control. His hands clenched into fists. "By whose authority?" His voice had acid in it.

"Whose authority?" For an instant, Docker looked astonished. "Why, Roy said—" He caught himself. The astonishment turned into swift anger, which showed as a tide of red creeping over his face. "By our own authority." His fist pounded on the desk, emphasizing the words.

"You do not have the sanction of the Martian government?"

"What government is there on Mars?" Docker demanded.

"The whole cursed planet is split into a hundred different tribes that do not even know the meaning of the word government."

"Yes, I know," Larkin said.

Docker spoke the truth, or part of it. There was no central government on the red planet. Yet there was a central authority, of a sort. It centered here in this city of Sudal, in the person of a despot named Malovar. Larkin did not pretend to understand the system but he knew that far-ranging desert tribes followed Malovar's orders, at least to a degree. Malovar's orders and Martian law and custom.

"What about Earth Government?" Larkin questioned.

"Earth Government can go to hell," Docker answered. "They have no control over Mars. Why do you bring up such questions? I told you we were taking over distribution of mineral fertilizers on this planet. That's enough authority for you or for anybody else." Again the fist banged on the desk.

Larkin looked at the fist and was silent. The fist impressed him not at all but the situation did impress him. There was a question he wanted to ask but he was afraid he knew the answer without asking. He started to ask it, then hastily changed his mind.

"How do you know the Martians will buy from you?"

"They buy from you, don't they? They've been buying from you for seven years. They'll buy from us." He sounded very sure of himself, like a man who has a plan all made, a plan which he knows will work.

"Ah," Larkin sighed and was silent. True, the Martians had bought from him, but there was a price, which he had to pay for doing business here, a price that Docker and his men might not relish paying. Larkin tried to imagine the consequences of their refusal to pay that price. His imagination failed him. These Martians had forgotten a great many things that humans had not yet learned. Larkin thought again of the question he wanted to ask, and again put off asking it.

"What prices do you intend to charge for your minerals?"

A grin that had relish in it showed on Docker's face. "Our prices will be fair. Of course, we expect to show a profit."

"Suppose the Martians can't pay your prices?"

"To hell with that," Docker snorted. "We're not transporting minerals all the way to Mars just to give them away. They'll pay all right. They'll pay or they won't eat. He smacked his lips with obvious relish. A situation in which people paid his prices or did not eat pleased him.

Larkin was silent. There was still the question he did not want to ask. "You seem to have everything worked out to the last detail," he said.

"We have," Docker nodded agreement. "Roy's a genius along those lines." Again he caught himself as if the name had slipped out unintentionally.

Roy? A thought came into Larkin's mind. He put it out. What he was thinking was impossible. He writhed inwardly. He was going to have to ask the question he had tried to avoid.

"Why have you come to me?"

A smile appeared on Docker's face. "Because you are the only trader who has been able to win the complete confidence of the Martians."

"I see," Larkin said.

"So we have a use for you," Docker continued. "You tell us how you have won the confidence of these Martians and we'll cut you in on the deal. We'll see that you are adequately paid. Any price within reason."

"Ah." Larkin was again silent. "But I thought you indicated that the Martians will have no choice except to deal with you. Under those circumstances why do you need me?"

Docker's smile lost none of its easy sureness. "We prefer

to do things the easy way, so nobody gets hurt. Since you are here and know the ground, it'd make sense for you to throw in with us."

"So I am the easy way?" Larkin said.

"Well—"

"You go to hell," Larkin said. He got to his feet, turned toward the door. S urprisingly, no effort was made to stop him.

"We'll see you in the morning," Docker said.

"It won't do you any good."

Larkin walked out of the ship. No effort was made to stop him. He moved slowly across the desert toward the city.

There was nothing about this situation that he liked. Least of all he liked the fact that Docker seemed to know a lot about him. How could that be? No one on Earth remembered him or knew about him. At the thought, sadness came up in him, replacing the smouldering anger. It would be nice to have someone to stand beside him now, someone fighting shoulder to shoulder with him. The word Roy came into his mind again. He quickly put it aside. Let dead dreams lie. But Docker had used the word twice. What did Docker mean? Larkin shrugged off this line of thinking.

There was almost no question in his mind as to what he was going to do. If he took Docker's offer, and tried to trim the Martians, he knew beyond the shadow of a doubt what old Malovar would do. The temper of the Martian ruler— chieftain, high priest—he had all these titles and more—was certain. Malovar brooked no cheating of his people.

But, of course, Malovar did not know about this offer of Docker's. Larkin was glad of that. He did not want Malovar even to guess what was in the minds of the men in the ship.

Entering his store, Larkin started in surprise. Seated in a soft chair at the back was Malovar.

THE Martian ruler was old, how old only Malovar and the gods of Mars knew. His skin was wrinkled, his face was a bleak mask that looked as if it had never formed a smile. Except for the curious metal staff that he held across his lap, the Martian ruler wore no insignia of his office. His clothing was a simple tunic like the togas of the ancient Romans. He was smoking a thin reed pipe, the only luxury he ever permitted himself, and the rich flavor of Martian tobacco was heavy in the room. With him was one attendant, an elder of the tribe.

Larkin bowed. "I am honored, sire." It was not too unusual for Malovar to pay him a visit. The ruler went from the greatest mansion to the humblest hut at will.

"Come sit, my friend." The Martian's voice was as gentle as the passing of a soft breeze but Larkin knew that this breeze would turn into a tornado in an instant. He sat down. Silently, Malovar extended his tobacco pouch. Silently, Larkin took it.

"A ship landed this afternoon, my friend," Malovar said.

"Yes," Larkin agreed.

"You have been to talk to your countrymen."

It was a simple statement. Larkin writhed inwardly but attempted no denial. "How did you know?"

"I have ways of knowing. Tell me, are they scientists, or explorers, or traders? Or some other breed of that curious creature—the human being?"

"They—" Larkin hesitated. How much did he dare reveal? This Martian had most penetrating and discerning eyes. "They hope to trade."

"Ah." Malovar was quiet for a longtime. "My friend, you have been here and I have known you for seven years. During this time I have been pleased to call you friend."

"I have been honored," Larkin spoke. "They have been most enjoyable years." Why was this feeling of sweat suddenly appearing on his body? The room was cool almost to the point of being chilly now that the night had come.

"You have helped many of us, Seekin was in here this afternoon—"

"It was nothing," Larkin said, embarrassed.

"Many times you have done this deed, which you call *nothing,*" Malovar continued. "I just wanted you to know that I was aware of some of these instances."

"It is good of you to mention them," Larkin said. He did not like this sparring, this talk that seemed to go nowhere.

"I wanted you to know that at the next time of the testing these deeds, which you call *nothing,* will be taken into consideration," Malovar said.

Sweat broke out all over Boyd Larkin.

"They will be given due weight, but they will *not* sway the scales in your favor against other possible deeds."

Only a strong effort of will kept Larkin from shaking. "Sire—"

Malovar rose. He lingered in the doorway. "I have come to regard you as a friend, the only human I have ever known whom I was willing to call by that name. I should regret very much losing my human friend."

"Sire—"

"But my regret will not stay my hand at the time of the testing."

His lone elder following him, Malovar was gone into the Martian night.

CHAPTER THREE

MALOVAR left behind him an exceedingly perturbed human. Larkin knew the ruler well enough to know that Malovar meant what he said. His hand would not be stayed at the time of the testing. And that time might be any time when the temple bells sounded a summons to the vast, almost ruined amphitheater, which was used for the tests. Again a chill passed through Larkin. He had been through the testing before, many times, but there had never been any doubt in his mind that he would win through it. Now there was doubt.

He had seen what happened to those who failed. In him the chill grew to a shudder. These Martians had the damnedest customs.

Faced with this choice, there could be only one answer.

Docker and his cutthroat crew could really go to hell. Better defy Docker than Malovar. There was no way in which the humans could enforce their demands on him.

Or was there? So far as he knew there were no weapons in this city strong enough to resist the power of the single ship that lay outside. The Martians obeyed Malovar because of custom, and not because the ruler had any way to enforce his orders. Larkin could see no way by which Malovar could force Docker to go through the testing. A single trader could be forced. But a ship full of men armed with *Kell* guns—No.

Larkin spent most of the night going over what he would say to Docker's men when they arrived in the morning.

They came early. Three were the same. Standing in the door of his store, Larkin stared at the fourth man with growing horror in his heart. The sight of that fourth man hit him harder than Malovar's grim warning about the time of the testing.

The fourth man moved ahead of the others, came toward him. In this minute it seemed to Boyd Larkin that he had aged years. Something that he had left back on Earth, left there because he could neither control it nor face it had come unbidden to him here on Mars. In this moment, he wildly regretted that he had not fled to some outlying village during the hours of darkness.

It was too late to flee now. He had to face the consequences.

He forced himself to move forward, to hold out his hand. Inside of him, operating on an unconscious level, a kind of wild gladness came up. He forced it back down. This was no time for errant emotions.

"Roy!"

This man was his son.

Roy Larkin took his father's hand indifferently. "Hi," he said, and dropped the hand.

With horribly mixed memories flooding through him, Boyd Larkin stared at this man who was his son. He remembered this man in his playpen, a curly headed tot fiercely demanding his toys. He remembered him in high school, the kid who was going to be the best athlete in school, or else. The hard driving, I-don't-give-a-damn-what-happens-to-you, I'll-get-mine attitude had been obvious in him even then.

It was an attitude, which the best specialists in the functioning of the emotions had been unable to control. Roy Larkin seemed to have been born with the grim intention of grabbing everything that was handy, and to hell with everybody else. When his father, knowing the inevitable outcome of such an attitude, had been driven finally to interfere, the explosion had been catastrophic.

Larkin's ears still burned with the memory of what he had been called. "A stupid fool. An incompetent jackass. An idiot without enough sense to come in out of the rain!" There had been other words, too. At the end of the argument, the youth had slugged his father. This had happened when he was twenty.

Boyd Larkin had come to Mars then, a grim, bitter, disappointment and frustrated man fleeing from all memories. He had hoped never to hear of his son again.

But his son had come to him here on Mars.

"I'm taking over," Roy Larkin said. "The fact that you're my old man won't get you anything."

"You're taking over? I thought Docker—"

"Docker works for me."

"What?"

"You heard me." The voice was blunt. It stated a fact. "I listened while he talked to you last night. I wanted to get an estimate of the situation. Of course, we'll take care of you. We'll leave you in charge of the station here."

"But—"

"There are no 'buts' about it. I have made a study of the need for agricultural minerals on Mars. If handled properly, the thing is richer than forty mints. I intend to see that it is handled properly. You could have made a fortune here, if you'd a had good sense." An accusatory note crept into the voice, as if the failure to make a fortune when one was to be had was an act that Roy Larkin could neither understand nor forgive.

BOYD Larkin felt a burning inside of him, replacing the gladness he had felt when first he saw this man. There had been no change. There was no possibility of change. "You seem to know quite a lot about Mars."

"I do," Roy Larkin grinned. "I've made a study of the subject. A couple of articles you wrote gave me the idea that the right man could clean up here. Of course, I didn't think that *you* were the man—"

"There may be difficulties," the father said.

"We expect them. So what?" Roy Larkin gestured at the men with him, a gesture, which also included the *Kell* guns they carried and which included the *Kell* gun held in the elbow of his left arm. "If these don't do the job, we've got bigger things on the ship."

"I see," Boyd Larkin said. He was regaining some of his lost composure but he was acquiring no liking for the situation.

"We're not looking for trouble but we came prepared for it. I thought you would be a big enough fool to tell us to go to hell if you had the chance. Well, you've got the chance but you either throw in with us or we throw you out—bodily." His manner said he was prepared to back up his words.

Larkin was silent. They could remove him bodily from this place. He could not resist four men. "But what if the Martians refuse to trade with you when you take over?" he said quietly.

"How can they refuse? They've got to have minerals. Without them, they starve."

"They might choose to starve," Boyd Larkin said.

"What?" the younger man gasped. "But that's silly. That's crazy. You don't know what the hell you're talking about. You're trying to pull a fast one."

"They're a strange people," Boyd Larkin said, ignoring his son's outburst. "Sometimes they seem to do crazy things though I have usually found that back of their craziness is a vein of such hard common sense that it is bewildering to us humans,"

Roy Larkin was a little uncertain. "They've been dealing with you. They'll deal with us."

"That does not necessarily follow. What you do not understand is that they have a certain test, and that I have passed it."

"A test? Well, what is it? If you can pass it so can we. You haven't got anything that we haven't got."

An involuntary shudder passed over Larkin. "Perhaps. But this test isn't exactly easy." A sound came to his ears. Over the city of Sudal was flooding the sound of temple bells. The shudder came over him again, grew stronger.

His son's eyes were sharp on him. "What the hell are you shaking about?"

"The temple bells—"

"So what?"

"That's the call to the testing. It's an emergency call. It means us."

He saw unease appear momentarily on the face of his son and the men with him, then he saw it shrugged away. "If we have to pass some kind of a test to do business with these fools, all right. We'll pass it."

"I hope," Boyd Larkin whispered. Already the elders had put in their appearance and were coming toward them. They carried with them the long metal rods like the one Malovar carried and which were the sign of their office.

"They come to take us to the place of the testing," Larkin said. He straightened his shoulders. The Martian elders bowed politely and motioned him to precede them.

Neither his son nor the men with him liked the idea. They did not know what was going to happen. They would have preferred to go elsewhere. But Larkin was going and they could hardly let him out-face them. Besides, they had *Kell* guns. So what danger could they meet that they could not overcome?

CHAPTER FOUR

THE place of the testing was a huge coliseum that had been centuries old when the human race was still in the barbaric stage of its development. It had been designed to hold tens of thousands of spectators and once unquestionably it had held them, but the whole population of Sudal and the surrounding territory would now hardly fill the lower tiers. Looking out at the encroaching desert, where pathetic little patches of greenery tried to stem the tide of encroaching desolation, it was easy to see why this stadium could no longer be filled.

Already the Martians were beginning to trickle into the lower seats when the humans arrived at the top of the vast bowl.

"What the hell goes on here?" Roy Larkin kept demanding. "I don't like this."

"You've got your *Kell* guns, what are you afraid of?" the trader asked.

"I'm not afraid," the younger man angrily answered. "Except for the metal rods the old gooks are carrying, they're not armed. Hell, we're not afraid of them. It's just that I don't know what the hell is supposed to take place."

"You'll find out," Boyd Larkin answered.

In the center of the vast amphitheater was a raised stone altar. In this dry atmosphere, the red stains on it never weathered away. Directly behind the altar was a chair, Malovar was already taking his place in this chair. Leading up to the altar, a double line of elders was forming. Other elders had already made a large circle of living statues around their ruler.

With only the slightest perceptible hesitancy in his stride, Larkin went down the steps of this coliseum. Very vaguely he wondered how many Martians had traveled this path in the centuries gone. There must have been uncounted millions of them. He, personally, had seen most of the inhabitants of Sudal pass this way at one time or another. He had passed this way himself upon his arrival here. He had not fully understood what could happen then, he had been hurt to the bottom of his soul, and he had not cared much what did happen. He had passed the test, then and later. But now—

Malovar's warning of the night before was still ringing in his ears. "My regret will not stay my hand at the time of the testing."

"Where the hell are we supposed to go?" Roy Larkin questioned, as they reached the bottom of the steps. "This looks like a Roman circus, or something."

"Follow me," the trader answered. His step was firm as he trod between the lines of the elders. He knew them, all of them, he had sold minerals to most of them. Now their faces were as immobile as stone. They seemed never to have seen him. At this moment, he was a stranger among them, an alien they did not seem to know.

He walked up in front of the altar, stood facing Malovar.

Sitting in the big throne chair behind the altar, the face of the Martian ruler was a mask far more bleak than the faces of his elders. Now in this moment he wore the regalia of his office, the carved jeweled crown, the diadem of gems suspended from his throat. Either the crown or the diadem would have been worth a fortune back on Earth. Behind him, Larkin heard the humans catch their breath at the sight of these jewels. He knew what they were thinking: a few quick bursts from the *Kell* guns and this fortune would be theirs.

"Are you prepared for the test?" Malovar's eyes centered on Larkin.

"I am prepared, Sire. But why am I being tested now?"

"Any individual may be tested at any time the welfare of the people in my opinion requires such testing." The Martian words seemed almost to be part of a ritual.

"And on what will your decision be reached?"

"Again, the welfare of my people," Malovar answered.

"I mean—what deeds of mine will be judged here?"

Malovar's face grew bleaker still. "Perhaps nothing you have done but something you may do."

"But you cannot test me now for something I have not yet done, you cannot read the future!" the human protested.

"Perhaps by testing you now I may guide the future,"

Malovar answered. "But—enough of talk. Kneel!"

Larkin knew he had no further choice. He went down on his knees before the altar. Out of the corner of his eyes, he saw one of the elders take Malovar's staff from him, hand him instead the sword. Larkin knew that the blade of that sword was razor sharp. Driven with only moderate force it would cut flesh and bone instantly.

He closed his eyes.

He felt himself grabbed by the shoulder and jerked backward. He faced the raging, frightened eyes of his son. "What the hell's going on here?"

"This is the test," he explained. "You have to go through this test before you can sell minerals to the people of Sudal."

"But what's he going to do?" The younger man gestured toward Malovar who stood erect.

"I do not know. His action is his choice."

"But he is acting and you are acting as if he may chop off your head."

"That is exactly what he may do, if he so chooses."

"But that's crazy!" Roy Larkin exploded.

"To us, yes. To the Martians, no. This is the way they have of testing the loyalty of individuals to the group. At the time of the annual testing all the inhabitants of this city pass one by one before Malovar."

"And he cuts off the heads of the ones he don't like?" Horror sounded in Roy Larkin's voice.

"I do not think his liking or not liking has anything to do with it," the trader explained. "He is working for the good of his whole people, not his personal good. And he cuts off heads if he chooses. I have seen him lop off a dozen heads in a single hour.

Sweat oozed out of Larkin as the memory came back to him.

"But, damn it, we don't have to go through with this test.

We're not Martians—"

"We propose to do business with them. This is the way they test our fitness to do business with them. They make the rules here."

A SNARL was in his son's voice. "But we don't have to obey them."

"What is this discussion?" Malovar spoke softly, in Martian.

"I am explaining to my son what is happening here," Larkin said.

"Your son?" Something very close to surprise showed on the wrinkled, bleak face. "Is *this* man *your* son?"

"He is," Larkin answered. There was no apology and no attempt at explanation in his voice. He stated a fact, and if it damned him, then it damned him. The interpretation of that fact he left up to the Martian ruler.

Malovar seemed not to find that interpretation difficult. For an instant, the eyes of the Martian went to the younger Larkin, weighing and testing him. Malovar's face grew bleak indeed as if his eyes saw the surface and what was under the surface and found none of it to his liking. Then his eyes came back to the trader.

"We will continue with the testing," he said.

"I am ready," Larkin answered, moving toward the altar.

"Hey, wait a minute," his son said, seizing his arm.

Larkin shrugged off the grip. *"You idiot."* Anger blazed in his voice. "Don't you know what you face here? This test must be accepted, or you will never do business on Mars."

"All right, you old fool." His son's voice was shrill with anger too, though not the same kind of anger. "Go on and get your stupid head chopped off and see if I care."

"I did not expect you to care," Larkin answered. He laid his head on the altar.

Malovar lifted the long sword.

Over the coliseum the assembled Martians seemed to catch their collective breath and then to stop breathing. The silence became thick, heavy, like a pall of gray mist. In that voiceless instant it seemed to Boyd Larkin that time itself was standing still. What would Malovar do? Larkin did not know, and had never known, the facts on which the ruler based his decision to strike or not to strike.

What did knowing, or not knowing, matter now, in the moment that might see the end of his life?

The hushed silence was broken by a single sharp cry. Larkin opened his eyes. He saw Malovar catch the movement of the sword. He turned his head in the direction from which the cry had come.

Down between the lines of the elders a single Martian was running.

Seekin!

Seekin came to a halt before the altar, bowed before Malovar. His gaze did not go to the human rising to his feet. He looked at Malovar.

"I claim the privilege of taking his place, Sire," Seekin said. "According to the ancient law of the testing, I take his place."

Larkin blinked startled eyes. A glow came up in him. He was hardly aware of it. He had never seen this thing happen before, he did not know it could happen, he did not know that Martian minds worked this way. Surprise was in him.

Surprise seemed to be in Malovar, too.

Over the coliseum the silence seemed to become heavier as if thousands of Martians were each holding his breath in wonder and in awe.

After the first flash of surprise, Malovar's face became bleak again.

"Do you accept the human's fate as your fate, whatever my decision may be?" the Martian ruler questioned.

Under his brown, Seekin showed a creeping tide of white. He knew what was meant, knew it intimately and well. But his nod was resolute and undaunted.

"Yesterday he gave me valuable minerals in exchange for a valueless jewel. Thus he gave life to me and to my family. And he gave me more than was needed, so that something more might be grown for someone else. Thus he has fulfilled the highest tenet of our law." Seekin bowed low. "Sire— whatever it may be, I accept his fate."

The words were simply spoken. The soft slurred sounds hardly disturbed the quiet air. But they carried a wealth of meaning.

Over the vast throng a sigh arose as if the watching Martians were seeing a miracle. For the first time since he had been on Mars, Boyd Larkin saw a real smile appear on the bleak and bitter face of Malovar. The smile was almost a benediction.

The benediction of that moment was shattered by a furious blast of sound.

Brrrrp, brrrrp, brrrrp!

The sound of *Kell* guns in operation.

CHAPTER FIVE

THE elder standing beside Malovar clutched his throat and collapsed, blood spurting from a hole in his throat. Larkin jerked startled eyes toward the source of the sound.

On top of the coliseum was a group of men from the ship. Docker led them. They were firing *Kell* guns indiscriminately into the Martian crowd.

The *brrrrp brrrrp* was an almost continuous blast of sound. Following the throb of the guns was the violence of the explosions of the striking missiles. The whole vast arena throbbed to the fury of the sound.

"No!" Larkin screamed.

This was a slaughter of helpless innocents. The Martians were unprotected, incapable of defending themselves. And they had done nothing wrong.

"Stop!" The voice of Malovar was like thunder rolling through the arena. He spoke in Martian but there was no mistaking his meaning. He dropped the sword, took back his metal rod that was part of the regalia of his office, held it erect. In that moment he was like a tribal god ordering the lighting and the thunder.

The answer, coming from above, was a slug that whistled within inches of Malovar's head and exploded behind him.

"For the last time, stop!"

Another slug howled downward.

Then Malovar acted.

Larkin was not quite certain what happened but out from the tip of the metal staff that Malovar held seemed to flash a bolt of blinding radiance. It was not a thunderbolt, it was not electrical, it was probably no force known to Earth scientists.

Looking upward, Larkin expected to see the flashing radiance blast through the group of humans like a smashing thunderbolt, searing and destroying them, leaving in its wake chunks of charred and writhing flesh that had once been men.

No such thing happened. The blinding radiance swirled around the men. It formed a coating around each of them. In a split second each of them was encased in a plastic cocoon that looked like ice, a covering that held them helpless. They still retained their guns but the plastic force covered the guns too. The guns were silent. Either they could not fire into the plastic coat or the men who still grasped them could not move their fingers to press the triggers.

Like statues frozen in motion, the group stood at the top

of the coliseum, on the highest row of seats of that vast circling arena.

A cry of rage sounded near Larkin, then was suddenly stilled.

At the sound of the cry near him, Larkin turned, saw that his son and the men with him were likewise encased in plastic envelopes. He saw that his son's eyes were bulging from terror, his throat pulsating from the effort of trying to scream. But no sound was coming forth.

Radiance pouring from the tip of the staff of one of the elders had accomplished this effect.

The torture of that moment must have been a terrible thing for Roy Larkin. To be held helpless by a force that stilled all motion, to want to scream but be unable to hear the blessed sound of your own voice, to see the consequences of your own acts coming home upon your head—this was torture.

Malovar and his elders had not been helpless. They had retained in the metal rods some of the vast forgotten science of old Mars, a science that they rarely used, and rarely needed to use.

Malovar, his face still like thunder, was standing erect and was directing what was to happen next.

THERE were screams in the coliseum, of wounded and dying Martians, and a vast stir as Martian friends ran to help those who had been injured, and a babble of voices rising in anger. The elders were moving. Some of them were attending to the stricken. Others were directing the removal of Docker and the men with him from the top of the coliseum. Docker and his men were being carried down by Martians. They seemed incapable of movement of their own.

The whole group was brought before Malovar.

The face of the Martian was the face of a tribal god,

furious with anger. He made a motion with his hand toward Docker. The Martians carrying the man laid him face down on the altar. Malovar handed his metal staff to the nearest elder, took up the sword.

There was no mistaking the intention of the Martian. He lifted the sword, brought it down. Just before it reached its target, the plastic envelope collapsed as the elder holding the staff made a slight shift with it.

Docker had time to start a scream. The scream ended. A head skittered across the stone, blood spurted.

A moan went over the watching throng.

Larkin watched, appalled. He had seen Martian heads roll here before but somehow this scene was different. Here was Martian justice, swift, sure, and final.

Malovar made another motion with his hand. The nearest human, one of the men with Docker, was lifted, carried to the altar. Larkin saw the man's muscles writhe against the plastic force envelope that held him, writhe unavailingly.

Sunlight glinted on the red blade of the sword as it came down.

Again a moan went up from the audience.

Malovar pointed with his sword—at Roy Larkin. Elders seized the man, lifted him, carried him to the altar.

The sword came up.

"NO!" A single burst of involuntary sound came from the lips of the trader. He leaped forward. "NO!"

Malovar held the sword, looked at him. The Martian looked a little sad.

"I know he is your son, my friend, but he came here to cheat and to rob. Men under his direction have killed."

"But—"

"The laws of my people are explicit," Malovar continued. "Nor will I stay my hand for the sake of friendship at the time of the testing."

"But—" Larkin still protested. Here was a bond, an obligation that went beyond friendship.

"I am sorry," Malovar said gently. His tone of voice and the expression on his face said he was really sorry. But they also said he had no intention of holding his hand from striking.

Boyd Larkin moved again. He was not quite sure why he did what he did and he was utterly unsure as to what the result would be, but in the face of the rising sword, he lifted his son from the altar.

"I claim your law," he said. "I take his place." He laid himself on the altar.

Over the watching throng there was silence. He sensed rather than saw Malovar lift the sword.

There was a stir of feet near him. A gentle voice spoke.

"I also claim the law. I have bought his life once this day. You may not strike him."

Seekin's voice. Soft and gentle but very firm and very sure. Seekin stood before the altar with uplifted hand. He spoke to Malovar but his eyes were on Larkin.

"You are free, my friend. Our laws protect you now and will protect you until the next time of the testing."

Malovar lowered the sword blade. "Our laws hold," he said. "I may not accept you as a substitute sacrifice. Nor may I accept Seekin. Nor may I accept him—" His eyes sought Roy Larkin. His voice became terrible as he spoke a single word. "—now."

He made a gesture with his hand toward the elder who had taken his metal staff. The elder touched the staff in a certain place. Around Roy Larkin the plastic envelope vanished.

Roy Larkin came to his feet, his fingers clutching the *Kell* gun, the wild light of terror in his eyes. Looking at him, Boyd Larkin caught his breath. There was such terror and wild fear in this man, as he had never seen before, such terror as might send death spurting from the muzzle of the *Kell* gun in a steady stream.

Larkin saw his son's finger tighten on the trigger, an involuntary movement. Malovar must have seen the movement too, all the Martian elders must have seen it. They must have known the meaning of it, must have understood that they were facing death. Not a Martian moved a muscle.

Roy Larkin apparently had expected them to cringe, to fawn, to beg. When they did nothing, he seemed confused. Wonderingly he stared at them. His gaze came to the face of his father. On his features the confusion grew. His eyes came down to the *Kell* gun. Something was happening inside of him, what it was no man except he knew or could know. As he seemed to realize he still held the gun, a look or horror appeared on his face. He dropped the weapon. It clattered on the stone floor, the only sound in that vast silence.

Then there was another sound, a sound that resembled the cry of a child gulping a single word—"Daddy." Roy Larkin was saying that single word and he was moving toward his father.

"I've been so terribly wrong," Roy Larkin whispered. "For so many years I've been wrong. I wanted to tell you, but I never could, until now."

Boyd Larkin folded his son into his arms. The hard, bitter driving man that he had known this morning was somehow gone. The man who was in his arms and clutching his shoulders and burying his head against his chest was somehow a little boy who had been lost, bewildered, and alone, and who was no longer lost, who in this moment was growing to the stature of manhood.

Larkin patted the shoulders of this man-boy. His eyes were moist and there was a choke in his throat. Here was something that he had wanted desperately for so many years.

Now he had it. His son, his son!

In him somewhere was a feeling not of triumph but of vast achievement. He looked over his son's shoulders at Malovar. The Martian's face was glowing as if he too was tasting this feeling of vast achievement. In this moment Malovar no longer looked like a tribal god demanding vengeance. Malovar looked like a very gentle and kindly old Martian.

"Mine eyes have seen wonders this day," Malovar spoke. "I think at the next time of the testing all of you will be safe from me."

"Do you mean that?" Larkin whispered.

"Of course, I never make careless statements." He made a gesture toward the elder who held his metal staff.

Around him Larkin was aware that the other humans were being freed from the force envelopes that held them powerless. There were clattering sounds, the noises of weapons being dropped from hands that no longer chose to use them.

Over the watching throng a sigh was rising, such a sigh as may come from the lips of those who have seen wonders past the understanding.

AT THE top of the coliseum, where the vast red deserts stretched away under a thin harness of tiny canals, they paused.

Roy Larkin had changed. The fear and the terror were gone. A different enthusiasm was in his voice "We can still bring minerals here but we will no longer operate as I had planned. We will operate on a cost-plus basis, we will deliver them here at a price…"

"The buyer can afford," Boyd Larkin said softly.

"Right," his son said.

Behind them stood Malovar and Seekin, Malovar grunted

approvingly. "Through such men as you, minerals can come to Mars—and with them new life may come to an old and dying world."

Malovar looked beyond the city to the red deserts. He seemed to be seeing them as vast stretches of greenery, as interlacing canals with lush vegetation covering all the land that now was desert but someday would be something else. His face glowed.

"You also seem to have won a victory here," Boyd Larkin spoke.

"Yes," Malovar answered. "I have blended the laws of my people with the drive of you humans, made each aware of the other, made each respect and support the other. The victory will be there, in the years that are to come."

He gestured toward the deserts where in his imagination an old world was again coming to life. The glow deepened on his face. He was seeing a lost dream come true.

Boyd Larkin had the fleeting impression that this old Martian ruler had somehow manipulated and conspired the actions that had taken place in the arena down below, that he had moved both his own people—and the humans—like puppets on strings. For an instant the thought startled the trader. Then he looked again at Malovar's face, saw the glow there, and knew that even if Malovar had manipulated them like puppets on strings, the purpose of Malovar's manipulations was clear. It was new life on an old planet, new life for two peoples, the Martians and the humans.

With that purpose, Boyd Larkin had complete sympathy.

Quietly the four of them moved down from the top of the coliseum, toward the peaked roofs of the city of Sudal.

Beyond them, the red deserts already seemed to be greening with new vegetation, new life.

THE END

To The End of Time

What fearful harmonies of the cosmos had shaped the music that spread madness in the steel canyons of Earth? That quest took Thorndyke to the deadly hotlands of the Veiled Planet, on a journey that stretched before him, beyond his own life—

CHAPTER ONE
Death Song

THE native Venusian guides, tense and sullen with fear of something they could not or would not name, had come into this region with reluctance. Thorndyke, who had no respect for superstition, was intelligent enough not to browbeat them. He had cajoled them instead with much talk about all the *atjol,* the fiery native drink, they could buy with their wages, and they had gone forward again, moving toward the precipitous mountain region of the hotlands jungle. Then, when it became apparent that their destination was actually the plateau that they called Kith-kal-sar, the singing mountain, they had taken council together and had decided on a course of action, without telling their employer. The first Thorndyke knew of it was when he awakened in the morning and discovered that the whole safari crew, porters, guides, cooks, and the rest, had vanished in the night.

Thorndyke was short and stubby, gnarled like an oak tree, and although he was actually one of Earth's foremost psychologists, nobody seeing him for the first time ever believed he was anything but a pirate. Timid women had been known to faint at the sight of him. Stronger specimens, on meeting him, invariably reached mentally for a baseball bat or some other weapon, to have handy just in case. He had long since accepted the fact that he was not pretty, and as for the opinion of the female members of the class Mammalia, he cared not two hoots what they thought of him. Or what anybody else thought. He was a little universe all in himself, complete with his own natural laws, which he made up as he went along.

Most men, deserted by their guides and helpers in the hotlands, would have started hotfooting it out of there. Thorndyke, operating according to his own peculiar laws, spent five minutes in outraged profanity, then selected a light rifle that threw a bursting charge capable of stopping a garo or a cat lizard, added a kit of medicines and food, and headed straight toward Kith-kal-sar.

To his mind, the goal he was seeking was sufficiently important to justify the risk. The goal was neither wealth nor fame. It was a song.

Back on Earth, where the song was being played, it was called *Journey to the End of Time*. Though no one on Earth knew how, it was certain that the music had come from Venus, as a recording of a native song. On Earth, it had been brought to the attention of a famous bandleader, who had sensed at least part of the possibilities of the piece. The bandleader had translated the weird half and quarter tones into notes capable of being produced by human musical instruments. Unquestionably the music had lost much in translation. Unfortunately it still had too much left, all of it bad.

The first effect was sadness. The second was a deep melancholy. The third was—disorientation. It might take the form of murder, insanity, suicide... The first, and last time, the number had been played on the air, over a hundred people died violently. Apparently, any dangerous tendencies already present in the human mind were accentuated by the music.

After one playing, the Department of Health had hastily ordered the number withdrawn from the air. But wire recordings existed and these were being played in clandestine hideouts, in fierce little nightclubs, at secret orgies.

The music exploited something in the psyche; it caused a disease of the mind. Remembering the new diseases that had been brought back from the planets with the first interplanetary vessels, and the rigorous measures that had been necessary then, the U.N. had acted as they would have done if a new extraterrestrial had appeared on Earth, by sending a crew of germ fighters to the origin of the disease to isolate the germ and combat it.

If, lamed in translation, crippled by musical instruments of another world, it still possessed so much power, what might be the effect of the music in the original, as it was played on Venus? This question worried them. There were other fringe questions, though, which worried them even more.

Thorndyke was a member of the team trying to locate the origin of the music. The investigation had been difficult. The Venusian tribes living around the spaceports either did not recognize the music, as played back for them from Earth recordings of Earth instruments, or they were unwilling to admit their knowledge. Rumors and tips had indicated that perhaps here in the hotlands, at the place called Kith-kal-sar, the singing mountain, the source of the music might be found.

As he was crossing the side of a precipitous hill, with pools of swamp water and mud below him, Thorndyke's foot slipped. He tried to catch himself, failed, and went headlong down the hill. With a mighty splash he landed in one of the pools. When he came to the surface, he caught a log that was anchored to the bottom, and seeing what he had aroused on the sandbar across from him, he held onto the log, let himself float, and did not move a muscle. He knew enough about garos, the swamp alligators, to keep still.

His fall into the pool had awakened the garo. If he moved, the vibrations of that movement would be transmitted through the water, the garo would pick them up and come to investigate the juicy tidbit that had fallen into its private cafeteria.

Lifting its head, the garo tried to locate the source of the splash that had aroused it.

Creatures that fell into this pool always splashed as they tried to get out.

Thorndyke did no splashing. Maybe the garo would go back

to sleep. Then the human could wiggle, an inch at a time along the log, and float to shore.

And maybe he couldn't.

Alligator bait, he thought bitterly.

The garo knew something strange was in the pool. Under the circumstances, the monster had no intention of going back to sleep. Thorndyke could see the creature raise itself up and look around, trying to see from weak eyes if anything edible was in sight. The garo couldn't see very far or very well. It grunted, inquiringly. Thorndyke didn't grunt back.

THE HOT afternoon was still. Sunlight glinted through an opening in the clouds. Somewhere in the jungle a rain bird shrilled. A dragonfly with iridescent wings a foot long flew across the pool. Thorndyke was aware of sound—somewhere. It came from somewhere on the slope and grew stronger—a swelling chorus of song. Deep bass voices roared a chant until the whole jungle seemed to echo with it.

Listening, Thorndyke felt a sudden, irrational anger surge within him. The lust for battle, the clash of swords on shields, the cry of the victor, the sob of the stricken, all were in this music. Thorndyke felt hate rise in him, hate for the enemy. His heartbeat quickened.

He was dimly aware that he was listening to a song like *Journey to the End of Time.* It was a different song, written for a different purpose, but it sprang from the same source. The first effect of this wild music was anger. The second effect was—hallucination. As if his mind was a movie screen and a new film had been spliced into the middle of an old picture, the hallucination hit him.

The pool of swamp water, with the restless garo on the bank, faded instantly. His eyes seemed to disconnect themselves. His mind looked at a new scene. He found himself in a place that he knew did not exist except in his imagination.

He was sitting in a beautiful living room with a picture window across the corner. Through the window he saw a breathtaking vista of snow-capped mountains sweeping away into the distance. He recognized them somehow as the Colorado Rockies. They were so real he could have been willing to swear he was actually looking at them. In his hand was a drink so real he could savor the smokiness of the Scotch, and sitting beside him was a woman. He could not visualize her features clearly but he knew she was very near and very dear to him.

A woman! By this one fact, Thorndyke knew he was dreaming.

While the music swelled in a growing flood, the illusion held. When it died, the illusion vanished. Thorndyke, gulping, saw that he was still holding onto the log. The garo was leaving the sandbar to search the pool for him, but the human was not aware of this fact. His attention was held by what was happening on the hillside.

The music makers were there. They were a group of barrel-chested little men about three feet tall. They looked a lot like pygmies, like the vanished Bushmen of the South African *veld*, almost naked little men with barrel chests. Thorndyke caught glimpses of them scurrying through the trees on the steep slope, their bass voices emitting agonized bellows. He saw why they were running, why they were alarmed.

A human woman was after them. She had in her right hand a slim, supple tree branch, and she was laying about her with all the strength in her arm.

For a second Thorndyke gaped at this astonishing sight, then he became aware again of his own situation and lifted his voice in a yell.

At the sound, the woman dropped the switch and stared around her. She located Thorndyke in the pool.

"Hey, look out, there's a garo in that water!" she shouted.

"Hell, I know it," Thorndyke answered. "If I move, he'll locate me."

"Don't move," the woman shouted. She came down the steep slope in a surefooted run. Like a monkey, she shinnied up a slender tree growing at the edge of the water. The tree bent under her weight. Splashing her feet in the water, she began shouting to Thorndyke.

"Swim, you idiot, while I draw the garo over here."

The swamp alligator, certain that it had now located the juicy tidbit that had fallen into its pool, headed straight toward her. She jerked her feet out of the water before the ugly snout emerged.

Thorndyke had never had any swimming lessons, but he didn't need any now. Dripping water and mud, he scrambled up the bank. The girl slid down the tree and came toward him.

The expression on her face said that now she had seen him, she regretted cheating a perfectly innocent alligator out of its dinner.

Thorndyke didn't mind her reaction. He was used to it. She had freckles, and brown hair and eyes the color of the skies of Earth. He liked her, instantly. "I can't help how I look," he said. "You can blame it on poor heredity. I'm a throwback to the ape-man." He grinned at her.

Astonishingly, she grinned back.

"Where'd you come from? What are you doing here? Who are you? What were you doing in that pool—fishing?"

"One question at a time," Thorndyke said. He took off his pack, upended it, poured out the water. "I'm Jim Thorndyke."

"I'm Neva August," the girl answered. "My father is a missionary here."

"A what?" Thorndyke said. He never ceased being astonished at the places the missionaries penetrated, but of all the places he expected to find one, the hotlands of Venus came last. He told the girl what he was doing here.

Surprise showed on her face as she listened, then it was replaced by fear.

"The Noro music has reached Earth?" she said. "Then Haswell escaped after all."

"Who is Haswell?"

"He is a prospector, or said he was. He was here with us for a while. He made a recording of some of the Noro music, then disappeared. I didn't know what happened to him but I thought the Noros—" She paused. "They objected to having a recording made of their music and I thought—"

"They had dropped Haswell into the swamp?" Thorndyke asked.

"Well, something like that."

"Who are the Noros?"

"I forgot you do not know them." She looked away, searching the trees on the hillside. Her voice rang out in a series of deep tones.

In response there began to appear around them, hesitant, sullen, staring at Thorndyke with no friendliness whatever, the three-foot pygmies of the hotlands swamp. These were the music makers of Venus.

"They're angry with me," Neva said. "I stopped a war between them. They're both angry and grateful because of that."

"You stopped a war?" Thorndyke asked puzzled. "How?"

"With a switch," she answered. "I know you must be thinking that a war that could be stopped with a switch was not very important, but it was important, to the Noros."

"They don't even have any weapons," Thorndyke said.

"They had the War Song," the girl said. "That was weapon enough."

"Eh?"

She looked thoughtfully at him as if she were trying to estimate how much she could tell him. "Go on," he said. "I'm ready to believe anything. How can a song be a weapon?"

"I don't know, but it is. There were two bands of Noros and they were going to fight each other with that song and nothing else. When they finished one band or the other would have been dead. I've seen it happen."

"But the song had no effect on you," he said.

"I have learned how to keep from hearing it," Neva explained.

"And you dared to use a switch on them?"

"Yes. When they started the War Song, I became very angry. I didn't stop to think what I was doing, I just grabbed a switch and lit in on them, as if they were bad children."

"And they didn't try to fight you?"

"No, they were just angry with me. They know that the War Song is bad and they know I am doing right in stopping it. So they let me."

"If they know it's bad, why do they ever start it?"

"Why do humans start wars?"

It was a question that Thorndyke could not answer.

"This is no time to talk philosophy," Neva spoke. "You're soaking wet and lost. You come home with me and meet my father. There you will also have a chance to study the Noros."

CHAPTER TWO
Yellow Lightning

THORNDYKE recovered his rifle from the slope where he had dropped it. The Noros clustered around him and it was in his mind to give them a demonstration of the weapon. On the other side of the pool, the garo had crawled out on the sandbank again. Thorndyke took careful aim at the head of the monster. The rifle cracked sharply; the garo's head vanished in the explosion.

The Noros seemed totally unimpressed. One Noro spoke to Neva.

"This is Tom. He says the gun is no good, it makes too much noise," the girl translated.

"But look what it did to the garo," Thorndyke said.

"He says he can do more than that to the garo, with his music," Neva answered.

"Eh?" Thorndyke said.

It was a worried psychologist who followed the girl through the jungle. Moving along with them as silently as shadows were the Noros. Thorndyke was very much aware of the puzzling mystery presented by these barrel-chested little men.

"Here is where we live," Neva said. They had come to a large open glade on the side of a mountain. Below them were the swamps and the rain forest. Above them a steep slope led upward to a high plateau. Directly in front of them, in the face of a limestone cliff, was the large opening of a natural cave. In the opening a tall man was standing. He waved at Neva, then, at the sight of the man with her, he came striding forward, astonished at the sight of another human being.

"Daddy, this is Jim Thorndyke. This is my father, Lawrence August."

"It is a pleasure to meet another human," August said, extending his hand. His grip was firm, his manners were courtly and pleasant. He came of a generation that put great emphasis on manners. "I'm glad to meet you. You are not, by any chance, the James Thorndyke who wrote the book on the psi function of the human mind?"

It was Thorndyke's turn to be surprised. "I am," he answered.

"Then there is no one from Earth I would rather make welcome here," August said. "Unless I miss my guess, we have here an example of the psi function, of the effect of mind on matter, unlike anything science has ever known before." He nodded toward the Noros, filing past them into the cave.

Thorndyke caught a throb of sound. As the Noros moved past them, they were singing.

"It is the gathering song," Neva spoke. "No, you must not listen, or you will try to follow them. Turn it out of your mind. Don't let yourself hear it."

"The gathering song?" the psychologist said. He felt an impulse rise in him to follow the little men.

"It is the song they sing when they are gathering for the night," the girl said. "It calls them together. Put your hands over your ears."

Thorndyke obeyed. The song dropped several notches in volume. The impulse that had been rising in him dropped to a whisper, which remained inside his mind like an echo of siren music. *The Gathering Song. The War Song.* The song that was called *Journey to the End of Time.* Each piece of weird music seemed to have a special job. What other songs did they have? Above everything else, what vast mystery was hidden behind the music?

The Noros filed out of sight inside the cave and the echoes of the music died away. Thorndyke followed August into the cavern. Near the entrance, where the sunlight still fell, a complete camp had been set up. It was a comfortable place, but it was very near the entrance to the cave. Thorndyke wondered about the cat lizards coming in here at night, then the question passed from his mind and was forgotten.

"Where do the Noros live?" he asked.

"We do not know," August answered. "Somewhere here in the cave, but we do not know where."

"Haven't you ever tried to find out?"

A look passed between August and his daughter. "Yes," Neva answered hesitantly. "But somehow or other, they have always slipped away from us."

"Neva believes they hypnotize us each time we try to follow them," the missionary slowly added. He saw Thorndyke shake his head and continued: "I know what you are thinking—hypnosis without the full consent and cooperation of the subject, is not possible, but I am not certain that the Noros do not know more about hypnosis than we do. Certainly they know many things that—" He stopped abruptly. "Come, sit down, my friend, and tell me about Earth."

"Later," Thorndyke said. "Right now I want to talk about the Noros. Tell me what you know about them."

"It won't be much, I'm afraid," August answered. "The proven facts are very few. Everything else is guesswork. For instance, I don't know whether the Noros are a primitive people just beginning the climb to civilization, or whether they are the most advanced race in the solar system..."

That night a storm whipped the jungle. Lying on the folding

cot that August had given him, Thorndyke could hear the storm roaring outside the cave. Once something else roared out there too, a cat lizard or some other creature of the Venusian swamp. Thorndyke clutched his rifle. He could hear the creature in the glade outside the entrance to the cave.

Coming from nowhere and from everywhere, a burst of music sounded. It was *Journey to the End of Time.*

Out in the night something screamed. The music died.

Holding the rifle, Thorndyke moved to the entrance of the cave. A flash of lightning revealed that the glade was deserted. The creature that had been there was—gone.

What had happened to it? Thorndyke did not know. But he had the eerie notion that unseen eyes watched the entrance to this cavern and that unseen forces guarded it.

Neither Neva nor her father appeared. They seemed to accept the matter as commonplace, if they had heard anything.

It was an uneasy psychologist who returned to his cot that night.

THE NEXT morning, there was a roar in the sky and a stubby-winged spaceship barge flashed through the mists. Hurrying outside the cave, they heard the thrum of jets as the barge was eased to a landing on the plateau above them. A few minutes later a group of men were glimpsed coming down the steep slope. Neva stared toward them.

"Haswell," she said.

Haswell, a machine pistol holstered at his hip, came arrogantly down the slope. He was a tall man, with a narrow face and sharp, alert eyes. Following him were two men whom Thorndyke did not know, although he recognized the type. Men like these two might be seen roistering in the spaceport of Luna, drunk and rolling down the main street of Venusport, hanging around the employment offices of the spaceship lines on Earth, trying to ship out to one of the planets, to any planet, it didn't matter which, just so they got away from Earth as fast as possible. They were space bums, willing to cut any man's throat for a dollar.

Haswell reached the glade and came toward them. "Hello, Neva. How are you, August?" His manner was friendly; there was a grin on his face. He looked at Thorndyke. The grin went away. "Who's this?"

Neva introduced them. Haswell said he was pleased to meet Mr. Thorndyke. His eyes said he wasn't.

"Why did you come back here?" Neva said.

"Maybe to see you," Haswell answered. "Boys, get busy."

The two men nodded. Moving to the entrance of the cave, they began to drive metal stakes into the ground. The hammers rang sharply in the quiet morning.

"What are they doing?" August asked.

"Staking a mining claim," Haswell told him.

"A mining claim?" the missionary was startled. "But there are no minerals here."

"That's what you say but that isn't what the counter says. I checked this mountain carefully. I couldn't locate the bed of ore but the counter says there's radioactive rock under the plateau, in tremendous quantities. With the price of fissionable material as high as it is today, this place is worth more millions than you can count." Haswell's adam's apple moved up and down as he spoke. Apparently the thought of millions made him want to swallow.

The sharp clang of the hammers was the only sound in the still air. Once the notices were posted, Haswell had exclusive rights to this area for twenty-five years. Slowly, Neva spoke. "That means mines will be developed here?"

"It certainly does," Haswell answered.

"But what will happen to the Noros?"

Haswell shrugged. "Out."

"But this is their home," the girl protested. "Suppose they don't want to move? What happens then?"

"In that case—" Haswell shrugged again. He broke off, to stare toward the cave entrance.

Five Noros, led by Tom, were coming out of the cave.

Moving with a sureness that was full of meaning, they advanced straight toward the humans. Haswell's hand moved toward the machine pistol at his hip, then came away.

The five stopped in front of him, and Tom spoke in deep, guttural English.

"Go away," the Noro said.

"Go away?" Haswell was astonished, then angry. He laughed. "Well, if this don't beat hell—"

Tom spoke to Neva, in the Noro tongue, the bass tones ringing clearly as he expressed a concept he could not put into English. Finishing, he did not wait for an answer, but turned and walked away. The other Noros followed him.

"What did he say?" Haswell asked.

"He said he had warned you and that whatever happens now, will be your own fault."

For a second, Haswell seemed shaken then he grinned. "I thought those little devils would try to make trouble. Well, I came prepared for them."

"What are you going to do?" August asked.

Haswell did not answer. Motioning to the two men to follow him, he moved up the slope. They came back later with three more men. All were heavily armed. All carried heavy metal cylinders and gas masks.

"Keep back," Haswell grimly warned August.

Putting on their masks, the men set up the metal cylinders at the entrance to the cave. They opened the valves; a heavy yellowish smoke spewed out into the caves.

Haswell came over to August. "Gas," he said grimly. "That'll fix 'em."

From nowhere and from everywhere, from the thin layer of soil lying over the solid rock below them, seemingly from the very atoms of the air or perhaps from the structure of space itself, came a burst of music. A wild flood of roaring notes, it was—*Journey to the End of Time*.

Yellow heat lightning seemed to flicker in the air.

Standing near the mouth of the cave, one of the men

snatched the mask from his face, screamed, and disappeared.

"What happened?" Haswell shouted. He moved toward the group of men there, then backed away. The yellow lightning flickered again. The second man was gone.

"The Noros are doing that," Haswell said harshly. His gaze fixed on Neva. "Stop them."

"Stop them?" the girl faltered. "How can I?"

"You can stop the war song, you can stop this too. Take a mask and go into the cave—"

"She will do no such thing," August spoke.

Haswell snatched the machine pistol from the holster at his hip. He pointed it at August but when he spoke, the words were directed at Neva.

"Either go into the cave and stop them or I'll shoot," he said.

Thorndyke took a step forward. The gun muzzle swung toward him and slugs blasted past his head. Near the cave entrance, the third man screamed.

Haswell turned his head to look toward the sound. Neva grabbed his gun hand.

For a second, the two wrestled. As Thorndyke and August moved forward, something like a shimmering wall of light moved between them. The yellow lightning flashed. Neva screamed.

The spot where she and Haswell had stood was empty.

That much Thorndyke saw. Then the electric shock that went with the lightning hit him. He felt himself falling; then he didn't feel anything.

CHAPTER THREE
Journey to the End of Time

THORNDYKE recovered consciousness slowly. As the fringes of his senses came back, he was aware of vague sounds: the screeching of a bird in the swamp below, the far-off bellow of a bull garo. He groped through his mind for understanding. Something had happened, he didn't know what. Then he remembered. The jolt shocked him back to consciousness. He sat up.

Beside him, August lay stretched on the ground. The old man moaned softly. Thorndyke's memory still had blank spots. His gaze roved, seeking what ought to be before his eyes, Haswell and Haswell's crew, the gas cylinders in the cave entrance, the yellowish gas, and Haswell's men, were gone. Haswell was gone. Neva was gone. Thorndyke struggled to his feet. Looking at the sun, he estimated that he had been unconscious for less than an hour. He bent over August. The missionary was breathing and, given time, would apparently be all right. The problem was—where was Neva?

When someone was lost, you shouted for him. Thorndyke's voice lifted in a shout. There was no answer. He had the feeling there would never be an answer. Panic rose in him.

Movement at the mouth of the cave caught his eye. Tom appeared there. With him were four other Noros.

The little men seemed frightened. They stared around. Their deep voices rang with questions. Thorndyke moved toward them. Tom pursed his lips, trying to form unfamiliar words. His first effort came out, "Whar—" The second time he got "Whery—" Then he got a recognizable, "Where—Nevy?"

"That's what I want to know," Thorndyke said. He reached out, seized the Noro by the shoulder, shook him as one shakes a recalcitrant child. The Noro's head rocked on his shoulders. Anger appeared in his eyes at this indignity, but he endured it. "Neva is gone!" Thorndyke shouted.

"Gone?" Tom echoed. The anger went swiftly from his eyes.

"Yes, you damned idiot, she's gone. I want to know where. I want her brought back. I want it done right now. Do you understand me?"

The Noro was badly frightened now. Thorndyke released him. Tom's bass voice spoke in a whisper to the other two, telling what had happened.

"Where is she?" Thorndyke demanded. The Noros looked

at him. They did not answer. Despair showed on their faces. "Gone—gone—" Tom whispered the word. "Journey— How you say—? To end of—time. Like with cat lizards, with bad man. She was near bad man when we send song. We not see her, not know—" The broken voice went into silence.

"Trip into time?" Thorndyke whispered.

"Into future, we send her," Tom answered. "I—cannot explain."

"You don't have to explain," Thorndyke said. "All you have to do is bring her back."

The Noro shook his head. "We cannot. It not possible. Most likely, it not possible. Sorry."

Again Thorndyke grabbed Tom's shoulder, again he shook, harder this time. "Damn you, you've got to bring her back!"

"But—most likely cannot."

"Why not?"

"Can send into time, cannot bring back, unless—"

The third Noro spoke abruptly. Thorndyke could not understand a word that was said but the Noros became excited. They looked at the psychologist.

"Thersill says, can try," Tom said.

"Can try what?"

"Can try bring her back"

"Then do it!"

"But there is catch."

"What catch?"

"Somebody have to go after her."

"I'll do it," Thorndyke said promptly.

"Is catch to that too," Tom said.

"Eh? What catch?"

"You may not come back."

"Well—" Thorndyke's hesitation lasted only a moment. His mouth closed with a snap. "I'll take the chance."

"Come then. Must hurry." Tom turned to the cave. Thorndyke followed the Noros.

Neva had said that she had tried to follow the Noros into the hidden depths of the cave, but that they had always eluded her. Going with them, Thorndyke could easily understand that. They followed in darkness a twisting, winding trail visible only to the Noros. They stopped, and a door swung open. Thorndyke gasped.

Ahead of them was a great blue gulf of light, stretching away into the far distance. He saw that here, inside this high plateau, was a tremendous cavern. The floor of the cavern lay far below him, a vast panorama of miniature cities, of fields and forests, all in the same small scale as the Noros, and all bathed in the bright blue light that blazed in the center of the roof.

In the middle of the cavern was a building. It was large even to a human; to the Noros it must have been gigantic—the crowning effort of a race.

"FATHERS come here long ago from dying land," Tom explained. A long flight of twisting steps led down to the floor of the cavern. They were spotted as soon as they appeared in the doorway; faces turned toward them, and the little men could be seen running toward the bottom of the steps. When Thorndyke reached the bottom, voices rang out, questioning, demanding. Tom had to do a lot of explaining fast. To Thorndyke, it was obvious that Tom had broken a tribal law in bringing him here. Tom's explanation was finally accepted, though with reluctance.

"Come to big building," Tom said. The entrance to the building was large enough for him to walk through without bending his back. Inside, he caught a glimpse of a single immense room, but he was taken to a small enclosure that was apparently a workshop. Noro technicians were here. Tom explained to them what was needed. They looked at Thorndyke doubtfully, shook their heads, then got busy. First they got his exact weight, then they fitted a strange kind of metal cap over his head and ran a series of tests. Perhaps they were measuring minute brain currents. Why, he didn't know, and didn't ask. Other technicians were busy building a kind of metal pack designed to be strapped around his chest. He saw they were building two of the packs. Finishing this, they strapped the first pack around him, gave him the second to carry.

"Come," Tom said. Thorndyke followed the Noro into the big room.

Noros jammed it. They sat in orderly rows in a complete circle around the machine in the center. Tom led him down a narrow aisle directly to it.

It was like no machine Thorndyke had ever seen before. There were dozens of meters, their scales calibrated in colors, each monitored by a Noro in a control chair. In the heart of the machine was a master control board, at which a single wizened Noro sat, like an old spider in the midst of many webs. The old spider looked at Thorndyke. There was compassion in his eyes.

"From machine lines of—push—flow," Tom said. "Bad man had instruments, which find lines of push from here. But he made mistake. He thought instruments said uranium was here."

Thorndyke grunted. He remembered Neva had said that Haswell had tried to get the Noros to guide him into the depths of the cave but that they had refused. They were concealing from the prospector the existence of this machine.

"Ready," Tom said.

"Ready," Thorndyke answered.

"Use this pack for Neva," Tom explained. "It bring her back, if we lucky. Without pack, she cannot return. We send you to take pack to her."

"I'm ready," Thorndyke said. Tom nodded at the ancient, gray-haired Noro at the master control. He pushed a switch. A gong chimed. The music began. It came from the massed Noros. Beginning softly, it started to rise in volume, a gigantic chorus of bass notes, singing *Journey to the End of Time*.

In this split second, Thorndyke realized at least a part of the function of the music. It had originated as a musical expression of something else—a psychological process. It served to focus their minds, perhaps, or to induce the necessary mood. In itself, it was probably of little importance. The important part was within the mind. It was the mind that could look forward into the future—that could attract or kill. The mind could do a thousand and one other things, many of which it could not understand itself.

He saw, also, the part the machine played in this strange rite-taking place in the cavern of the blue light. Roughly translated into human terms, the machine was a power amplifier. It received the thought pressures within the massed Noro minds and amplified them to any desired strength, concentrated them, focused them. Through the machine, the thought pressures could be focused at any desired spot inside the cavern or out of it. They could be focused on the ledge outside the entrance to the cave, in the jungle swamplands, perhaps anywhere on Venus.

In front of each meter, a Noro watched intently. The wizened Noro at the control board watched Thorndyke.

The music swept upward in a growing flood. Wild dancing notes made the whole building vibrate. The sound was like a mighty, organ pouring out a growing volume of wild, enchanted music.

The wizened Noro at the control board, watching Thorndyke, shoved home a final switch.

Thorndyke screamed as a million microscopic needles jabbed him. He felt a supercharged jolt of electric tension spring into existence in the air around him. Yellow lightning licked across his vision. He saw the Noros, the vast hall itself, waver and fade like a vision seen through distorting glass.

Cold struck him, he did not know how many degrees of it, but he knew if it lasted long, he would be frozen stiff. He had the impression of flickering movement far too fast for the eye to follow.

The cold faded. He fell, stumbled, fell again, got to his feet.

Weak sunlight hit him. The cloudbank was gone. The jungle was gone. The sun shone down on a dying planet.

He was on a slope. Below him in a valley a line of dead trees marked where there was a dry riverbed. Dust blew past him on a languid wind.

This—this was the future of Venus, how many million years away he could not tell. This was the Veiled Planet when it was no longer veiled. He was not at the end of time, but he was near it, for this planet.

He was aware that his mind was showing symptoms of refusing to obey him. His will forced it back into its proper groove. Below him, on the slope, a creature lay—a cat lizard. Dead. He could not see the cause of death. Nearer still there was a man, one of the men who had been with Haswell. The man was dead.

WHERE was Neva? He lifted his voice again, calling her name. The effort made his lungs hurt. In the thin air, his shout was not much louder than a whisper. He felt his heart begin to pound as it struggled to supply sufficient oxygen to his tissues. In this air, the life-giving gas was scarce.

The pack circling his chest hummed softly. He felt the surge of electric currents in it, reminding him that back in another time the Noros still maintained contact with him, through this pack.

"Neva!"

A halting voice answered him. She stood up slowly.

He saw her. He ran toward her.

She stared at him as if she could not believe her eyes. It was the first time in his life that a woman had ever seemed pleased to see him. Her clothes and her face were dust covered. He thrust the pack toward her. "Here. Put this on, I came for you. This will take you back." The effort made him pant.

"You—came for me?" She seemed dazed, unable to comprehend. Reaching out, she touched him. "You're real," she whispered.

He tried to grin. "The Noros sent me. This pack will take us back. There isn't time to explain. Just put it on—"

She took the pack from him, stared at it as if she did not understand. To one side a footstep squeaked. A voice rasped:

"Where's *my* pack?"

Haswell stood there. He had been sitting down and had remained unseen until he stood up.

Aghast, Thorndyke stared at the prospector. Until this moment, he had forgotten that Haswell existed.

"So you didn't bring a pack for me?" Haswell said.

"I—I'm sorry. I—"

"Don't let it bother you," Haswell said. "I'll just take yours." He lifted the machine pistol.

"Like hell—" Thorndyke said. Haswell squeezed the trigger. A stream of lead squirted past Thorndyke's head. He ducked.

"If that pack will get me back, I want it," Haswell said. "I'd just as soon take it off a dead body."

"All right," Thorndyke choked. The pack was a circling hand of metal eighteen inches wide and over two inches thick. He had seen the Noros fit a series of compact tiny instruments into that space. Tiny batteries furnished a limited supply of power. Slowly, Thorndyke released the catches. He slipped it from his body, handed it to Haswell. The prospector reached for it. Thorndyke's fingers seemed to loosen their grip. The pack fell to the ground. Haswell bent to pick it up.

Thorndyke stepped forward. With all the strength in his body, he hit the prospector behind the ear.

Haswell went over. Thorndyke jumped at him. Both went to the ground with Thorndyke on top. Haswell, gripping the pistol, tried to bring the muzzle up against the body of his antagonist. Thorndyke caught the wrist of the hand that held the gun. He heard Haswell swear.

The prospector was as agile as a cat lizard. Somehow he got a knee up into Thorndyke's groin. Stars splashed before Thorndyke's eyes. Strength went out of him. But he held on to the gun hand. He waited for his strength to come back.

It didn't.

Aware that his lungs were laboring for air, he guessed the fatal truth. His strength was not coming back. Strength depended on oxygen and there was too little oxygen in this air to support activity. A fight here was impossible. Violent exertion would result in the collapse of oxygen-starved tissues. The cat lizard and the man on the slope had died for this reason.

Panting for breath, Thorndyke let Haswell try to throw him off. His sole activity was to hold on to the gun hand.

Haswell dropped the gun. After that, Thorndyke made no effort to resist.

He felt Haswell heave violently at him. A quiver ran through the prospector's body.

"Damn you—" Haswell shuddered. And was still.

The man was dead. His overburdened heart, pounding furiously in an effort to supply oxygen to meet the needs of tissues that had evolved on Earth, had simply collapsed from the effort. Death here was simple and quick.

Thorndyke knew that he too, was very close to death. He did not move a muscle. He was aware that Neva was trying to help him. He whispered to her to stay away.

He was fighting another battle, harder perhaps than the fight against Haswell, a fight for enough oxygen to stay alive. The only way he could win was to keep absolutely quiet. Even then, he was not certain he could win. It might be that his efforts to breathe, even the beating of his heart itself, used up more oxygen than he was taking in.

He thought, *Here, near the end of time, when the solar system is running down, when man and all of man's achievements are gone...*

Every muscle in his body screamed for more oxygen. Every instinct in him yelled for him to breathe faster. But, if he breathed faster, the very act of breathing itself might be using up more oxygen than this air contained. He forced his laboring lungs to breathe slower and slower.

Eventually, nerve cell by nerve cell it seemed to him, the clamor in his body died down. He knew then that he had won this fight. He sat up.

He told Neva what had happened. "Put the pack on, Neva. I'll put mine back on. We'll get out of here."

Back to a day when oxygen was plentiful, back to a time

when the solar system was not near death. He picked up the pack, started to slip it into place, stopped, stared at it. For a moment he thought his heart was going to stop.

Either he or Haswell had kicked the pack. Part of the metal cover had been knocked off. Inside, in a jangle of broken wiring, all loose ends and smashed connections, hung the broken coils and tubes.

"Can you fix it?" Neva whispered.

"I can try," he answered.

Half an hour later, he knew it was a hopeless task. Special tools were needed, special knowledge, special skills, tools and knowledge and skills that only the Noros possessed.

"You—you can't go back?" Neva asked him.

Thorndyke shook his head. He was marooned here, forever.

"Then I won't go either," Neva said. "If you have to stay here, I will stay too, with you."

In another world and in another time they had had a word for what she was saying. It was a word that Thorndyke had never fully understood until now. Now he knew what it meant, knew also that it was too late to realize that meaning. He choked.

They sat side by side, leaning against a stone ledge, and watched the dull red ball of the sun go down. It went down very slowly.

"LISTEN—" Neva whispered. Thorndyke at first thought his ears were deceiving him. In the thin air of this planet, coming from nowhere and from everywhere, was a trace of music. He listened to it, caught his breath.

It was the madness melody: *Journey to the End of Time.*

It swelled in a mighty chorus, burst into a flood of sound, then died in quick silence.

On the slope above them bass voices called.

"Thorny! Nevy!"

They leaped to their feet.

"Here!" Thorndyke called, huskily.

On the slope above them were—Noros! They saw the face of Tom. It was a worried face, then at the sight of them, it broke into a grin. Tom came bounding down the slope to them. He too, wore a time pack. The thin air did not seem to bother him. His barrel chest hardly heaved.

"Was worried—oh, I see. Get plenty busy here plenty quick."

He saw the damaged pack, guessed what had happened. He and the other Noros with him got busy. Noro tools they had, Noro knowledge, Noro skill. Thorndyke's voice lifted in a shout of exultation.

"Pack fixed," Tom said. "Now we go back again." He looked up at Thorndyke, tried to find words for something he wanted to say, spoke rapidly to Neva in his own language.

Neva translated. "He says to tell you that the Noros came from this time, long ago, that they escaped from the oxygen death of this world back into time, fleeing the death that is here."

"What?" Thorndyke gasped. Yet he knew the Noros had come from some other land. Why not from this land? Their barrel chests could only have evolved in air where oxygen was scarce. Most of all, their tremendous sciences could only have been the result of millenniums of development.

"He says to tell you that they are the descendents of half humans and Venusians, that the two races intermingled and became one race, becoming smaller at the same time. He says that in one sense, the Noros are your far-removed grandsons."

"Grandsons." The thought shocked him.

Yet he saw that, in one sense, at least, it was true. To them, he was Cro-Magnon man, the shaggy man beast of the dawn world.

"Hi, pop," Tom said, grinning.

"Hi, son," Thorndyke answered.

They fitted the packs into place. Thorndyke and Neva went together, through the biting instant of cold. The vast cavern appeared and again in their ears was the enigmatic music—*Journey to the End of Time.*

The great hall rang with the sound of it. To Thorndyke, it was the happiest sound he had ever heard.

LATER, Thorndyke returned to Earth with Neva. Still later, he built himself a house in the heart of the Rockies, a house with a picture window looking out over a breathtaking panorama of mighty peaks stretching away into the far distance.

In his hand is a pleasant drink; the room is cool; the touch of spring is in the air. The cushions are soft and Neva is sitting beside him, snuggled close, her head resting on his arm, her dark hair flowing downward.

With a shock, he realizes that this is the hallucination that came to him in the swamp.

The future that he saw on far-off Venus has come true.

Or has it? He may still be in the pool of water, with the garo searching for him. The Noros on the bank may be projecting into his mind the colors of the Rocky Mountain sunset, the picture window, even Neva herself.

Which is the reality, and which is hallucination?

He realizes he will never know. He doesn't care. It is enough just to dream that she is here with him and that the sunset colors are gilding the distant peaks with gold.

There is a trace of soft music somewhere in the background. He listens. Is he remembering something or is he really hearing this music? It is the soft muted strains of *Journey to the End of Time.*

THE END

The Metal Martyr

The time had come when mankind's lone defender was a metallic figure named Two: a robot suffering from a sore conscience!

TWO WAS never able to remember exactly where or when it had happened, or what he had been doing at the time. Like snowflakes and fog and the south wind, some things come so quietly that the senses miss their coming. New ideas are like this. For a long time the mind is blank, then suddenly there is the new idea, the new thought. No one knows how the thought came or exactly when it came.

It was like this with Two. The new thought came. With it came a feeling of wrongness, as if something was out of place, out of joint. He stared around at the robot city. Here in this small cluster of stone buildings set among low hills with the high mountains forming a backdrop in the distance, he had been created and had lived all his life. To him, it was home. He knew no other existence. But now, with this new idea strong and vigorous in him, this existence was alien, this place was not home. He belonged somewhere else. All robots belonged somewhere else. With the sense of wrongness strong within him, he went immediately to the Master Technician.

"I am not a robot," Two stated. "I am a man." This was a new thought, this was his new idea.

The Master Technician sighed. His number and his name was Eight. He was in charge of all robot activity. There were seventy-nine all-purpose robots. There had always been that many, there would always be this many. This was one of their laws, no one knew why. If a robot was damaged beyond repair, if the insidious disease, rust, ate away vital parts, if the other grim disease, green corrosion, crept into the electronic brain, spreading slow but certain destruction with it, the ailing robot was destroyed and another was constructed to take his place and his number. It was one of the duties of the Master Technician to determine when this was necessary.

Looking at Two, the Master Technician knew instantly what was wrong. Two was delusional. Something had happened inside his brain, some minute change had occurred, some electronic synapse had taken place where no synapse was supposed to occur, with the result that Two thought he was something else. Robots rarely became delusional. The brain substance, constructed according to the ancient pattern, held firmly to its rutted pathways. But occasionally something went wrong, as it had gone wrong now. Well, perhaps something might be done to correct this odd delusion. If not—

"Look at yourself and see what you are," the Master Technician said.

Obediently Two looked at himself. Reaching down to the stone floor of the Master Technician laboratory, he saw two sturdy legs covered with a tough, rubbery plastic that was impervious to water and to most acids, legs cleverly constructed and jointed so that he could walk or run, or even dance, if the impulse struck him. Legs he had, because legs could walk where wheels could not run and wings could not fly; arms he had, with jointed fingers to hold tools. He had two eyes and two ears, because seeing and hearing were necessary to him, but no nose and no mouth, because he did not breathe oxygen or eat food. Small but very powerful long-lasting batteries supplied his energy. He was equipped with a high frequency, compact radio for communication over short distances. Housed in his head was the brain substance, which directed all his activities.

"My body resembles that of a man," Two stated, after looking. He had seen a man, once, in the mountains, and he knew how they looked. True, he had only had a glimpse of the strange creature fleeing in wild fright, but a glimpse was all he had needed.

"What of it?" the Master Technician answered, irritated. "You are an all-purpose robot. Man is an all-purpose animal. Two forms, which serve the same purpose, will probably resemble each other, at least outwardly. That is logic."

TWO SHIFTED his weight from one foot to the other. No robot ever sat down to rest, there was no need for it. He and the Master Technician were standing. There was logic in the Master Technician's statement. But—

His thinking was perturbed. About him somewhere was a feeling of failure, as if something had gone wrong, some experiment had failed, some assigned task had been neglected.

"I know I look like a robot," he said. "But I am a man."

"Why are you a man?" The Master Technician demanded. He was becoming impatient. "What makes you a man?"

"I feel I am," Two answered.

"You *feel* you are." Robots were creatures of logic, they followed the rules of sine and the cosine, the laws of chemistry, of electricity, or weight, pressure, and of force. "There is no such thing as *feeling*."

"I know," Two said. "But—"

"Get this delusion out of your mind," the Master Technician said. "Or we will have to disassociate you."

Disassociation meant that the body was dismantled and the brain case removed, after which the brain case was dissolved in acid. Two was silent. Whether it could happen or not, there was a new feeling in him now—rebellion. It rose as a small murky cloud of anger in the back of his mind. "Then let it be that way," he said.

"What?" The Master Technician's photoelectric eyes

came as close to registering amazement as was possible for such orbs.

"And to hell with you," Two said. Balling his hand into a fist, he punched the Master Technician in the eye.

The Master Technician fell over backward. He was too surprised to do anything else—though later other courses of action would occur to him. Two did not intend to be around then. He ran. His intention was fully formed in his own mind.

He was a man. Like seeks like. He was going to his own kind, to men.

There were not many men, he knew. Perhaps, like the robots, their numbers were restricted to seventy-nine. They lived in the mountains to the west. The robots did not seek them out and they did not seek out the robots. Between them there was a sort of armed neutrality and each pretended the other did not exist.

"I will go to my own kind," Two thought. "They will accept me for what I am."

All day long the sturdy little metal figure trudged westward, following his delusion. He crossed rivers, he climbed hills, he found his way through forests where the trees grew tall and thick. The gray wolves of this land sniffed at his heels. He ignored them. The great cats sleeping on the rocky ledges looked down at him as he passed, their ears flattening against their heads. He did not see them. He was seeking man. He came to a high tableland and climbed over piles of rubble that had once been a city a thousand—or was it ten thousand years ago—and to him the piles of rubble were only obstacles in his path. When night came, he turned on the powerful light placed in his forehead and continued the search. In the middle of the third day, he found—man.

FROM THE top of a hill he saw them in a little valley

below, two men, clad in deerskins. They were standing beside a little river. In their hands they carried strange objects of bent wood. He moved toward them. They saw him as soon as he came in sight. Instantly they grasped the strange objects in their left hands.

"What the hell is that thing?" Bill Argo asked.

"I don't know," Ed Chiswell answered. "I saw one of them once but I didn't stick around to find out what it was."

"Let's get out of here," Argo said.

"No. Wait," Chiswell protested. "It wants to talk to us."

Their bows ready, the arrows on the string, they waited doubtfully. At the sight of Two, uneasiness moved in them as if each remembered an ancient enemy. As Two came closer and closer and they saw all too clearly his strangeness, the uneasiness grew in them. Suddenly Argo drew the bowstring to his ear and released the arrow.

The shaft struck Two a glancing blow on his metal chest and bounced off harmlessly.

"Get out of here!" Argo shouted, and ran.

Ed Chiswell stood his ground. Men ran from the great wolves, from the bears, from the cats, men ran from the thunder and the lightning. But he was tired of running. Here, in this creature coming toward him, was something new, something different. Any new thing would be an improvement over the life he knew now, he thought.

Two hardly knew the arrow had struck him. He did not grasp its purpose. The delight at meeting his own kind was a feeling of great joy in him. "Hello," he said.

"Hello," Chiswell said. Fear was in him, but he stood his ground. What was this black creature that looked and walked and talked like a man? "What are you? Where did you come from?"

"I am a man," Two answered. "I came from back there." The wave of his hand indicated the foothills to the east.

"You are a—" Chiswell caught himself. He saw instantly that this strange creature was suffering from some form of hallucination. Men sometimes imagined they were something else. This black creature imagined it was a man. Chiswell began to ask questions. What was his name? Where did he live? Were there others like him? Two answered readily and eagerly. From his answers, Chiswell got a clear picture of the robot city and the robot way of life. A feeling of tremendous mystery rose in him. What was the origin of these creatures? For that matter, what was the origin of man?

Unlike most of his fellows, who had little time left over from the grim business of finding enough to eat to waste any of it in wondering about such remote problems as origins, Chiswell found time to wonder and to think. Here was a new problem. He sensed that it fringed a great mystery. "Will you come back to the tribe and live with me?" he said.

"Of course. That is what I want most." Two was almost pathetically grateful. He had been accepted as a man.

"Will your fellows search for you?" Chiswell asked. It was an important question. Not knowing what powers might be housed in Two's metal body, he wanted to take no chances of leading robots to the hiding place of the tribe.

"My fellows?" Two was hurt. He saw that he had not really been accepted as a man, this man was humoring him, perhaps for purposes of his own.

"Sorry," Chiswell instantly apologized. "I meant, will the robots search for you?" He intended to take no chances of losing, or angering, this creature. Two knew many things that might be of tremendous value to the tribe. The robot bodies were made of metal. This meant they either had access to a supply of the hard-to-find ore or they knew some other secret for finding it. The tribe needed metal desperately. In fact, they were beginning to use stone again, simply because they could not find metal. If Two could teach them this one secret, any danger they might run in befriending him would be worth the risk.

"Let them search," Two said. "They will never find me." He felt a little better.

"Come with me," Chiswell said.

They went up the mountain together.

TWO HAD found man and man had accepted him as a friend. But it was something of a shock to him to realize that man went clothed in the skins of animals, that he carried a device of bent wood with which to kill other animals, and that this man, somehow, was afraid. Although he knew little about men, in the depths of his mind he had always thought of them as being giants, great creatures who ranged the earth unafraid, taller than mountains, greater than gods. Again he was shocked, this time at himself, to find himself thinking of gods. Robots had no gods. But men have them, he thought defensively. And I am a man.

"Here is where we live," Chiswell said. He pointed to a small hole at the base of a high cliff, moved toward it. Men lounged around the entrance. One of them rose to his feet and shouted. It was Argo.

"Wait here," Chiswell said. "I will talk to them."

From a distance, Two watched the conference take place. Angry voices rose, shouting that Two could not enter the cavern—that Chiswell was a traitor who had brought danger to the tribe. Chiswell was patient. He kept urging some course of action, kept pointing toward the waiting robot. Little by little the anger died out on the faces' of the men. "Go talk to him," Chiswell urged. "See for yourself that he is harmless."

The men came forward reluctantly. Two answered their questions with patience. They did not understand him. Nor did they trust him. But Chiswell's patient urging won grudging acceptance for him. They admitted him to the cavern. As they passed the entrance, four men immediately rolled a huge stone into place, blocking the exit.

"We do that to keep out the wolves and the bears at night," Chiswell explained.

The cavern was a vast, single room. Fires gleamed dully around the walls and the air was heavy with smoke. Inside the cavern were other men, some of them the strange kind of men called women, and little ones called children. Reassured by Chiswell, they clustered around Two, their voices rising like the chattering of birds.

"Who are you?"

"Where did you come from?"

"What are you?"

"I am a man," Two said with dignity.

They didn't dispute him but a child laughed uneasily, and the group drew back from him. "Inside I am a man," Two repeated.

"Inside or outside, what difference does it make?" Chiswell said. He went quietly from person to person whispering. The group was uneasy. They were men. Two was—something else. The question was—what?

He sensed their uneasiness. What if they were tricking him? What did he know about men, after all? He looked toward the entrance as a sudden thought moved in him but the big stone blocked the exit. He could pull it aside perhaps, but—

A voice rose. "He's made of metal. I say we cut him up and use the metal for knives." Argo's voice.

"No!" Chiswell shouted. "Shut up, you fool. No, Two. He doesn't mean it. I won't let him do it. Argo, you hopeless fool. Two, stop!"

TWO WAS running. He had heard what they intended to

do with him. Perhaps Chiswell did not wish to do this thing to him, but Chiswell was one and the others were many and they could brush Chiswell aside and pull him down. Panic moved in him and he ran.

He did not run toward the exit. The guards and the stone were there. He ran blindly across the cavern, turning on the light on his forehead to mark the way. The bright beam flashed out, revealing a dark opening across the cave. Feet pounded behind him, voices shouted. He turned his head and the bright beam of his light flashed into the eyes of the men, blinding and frightening them. They had never seen a light like this. The only light they knew came from the sun, the moon, and the fires that burned continuously in this cave. They shrank away from the light. Two ran on, unpursued.

In his mind was turmoil. Men were creatures of dark treachery, black liars, and false friends. The tunnel closed around him. When no pursuit sounded behind him, the panic in his mind began to die down. "Men," he thought. "I must get away from this place. I must go back to the Master Technician and confess my error." His mind had been jarred back to normal channels. He was a robot again.

He did not know how big this cave was but somewhere there must be another exit, he felt. The tunnel turned, then moved ahead again, arrow straight. The straightness of the walls caught his eye and he realized that this was not a natural cave. "Perhaps this was once a mine," he thought. "Perhaps, when the ore was exhausted, they abandoned the mine."

Metal was precious to robots, too. Their city was located over a source of raw iron ore. They had mines in the mountains to the far south, where they dug copper, lead, and other metals. But all metals were very hard to find. Sometimes they found huge excavations from which all the ore had been taken, like this one. They assumed that their ancestors had dug these mines. They were vague about time.

If a thing happened yesterday, or last year, it was the same time to them.

Two was certain men had not dug this tunnel. How could men dig anything?

The tunnel opened into a round chamber. Here the roof had caved in, marking the end of the passage. Or so it had been for men. Tracks in the thick dust revealed that men had been this far, though not recently. Where men had been stopped, two went on. Logically, there had to be a tunnel out of this chamber. He dug down through the fallen rock until he found it. Feeling completely safe from pursuit, he went on. In an alcove off the main tunnel, something caught his eye.

"A machine," he thought.

He, and all robots, felt a sort of kinship with all machinery. Machines fascinated them. He stopped to study this one. Even though its parts were pitted and falling away into fragments of rusted, diseased metal, its essential function was clear. "It's an air purifier," he thought. "But—"

Although this was certainly an air purifier, robots, having no need for air, could not have built this machine. Who, then, had built it?

In his mind, Two felt a sudden dizziness. A machine to purify air had no reason to exist. But here was one. It had been constructed in some yesterday that his mind could not fathom and it had sat here and rusted away with disease for— how long?

Traced in the dust beside the machine was an outline, a pattern of slightly raised ridges, which at first glance, was almost as mystifying as the machine. Poking into the ridges, Two found a fragment of bone and realized the nature of this pattern.

It was the skeleton of a man, perhaps a man who had once tended this air-conditioning machine and who had died beside it.

A dead man beside a dead machine! Two could not believe what he saw. "Perhaps the man came here long after the machine ceased functioning, before the roof fell in the round chamber—" he thought. It was a possible solution but it did not satisfy him.

"But men know nothing of machines," he thought. The feeling of mystery rose in him. He rose to his feet, moved down the tunnel. There were other machines.

There was a huge room full of them. Machines for transforming electricity, the vast hooded bulk of a machine for converting heat energy into electrical energy— And skeletons!

But nowhere was there the rusted body of a robot. Nowhere was there any sign that robots had even been here.

"Men could not have created these machines," Two thought. "They could not."

HE CONTINUED exploring. There was a huge room, the walls lined with shelves, and the shelves filled with books.

All robots were conditioned to read. It was a part of their training, and though they had little use for reading, they continued the training as they continued everything else, by rote.

On a metal table in the center of the room was a thick volume. On the floor beside the corroded table was a skeleton. A book and a man who had read it, perhaps a man who had written it.

Two brushed the dust from the book. The pages were a plastic that would last an eternity. Perhaps this book had already lasted an eternity while it waited for someone to come along and read what was written on its pages. Two read the words.

He stood transfixed. Here was the history of this cavern

and of the race that had built it and here, too, was the history of the robots.

Men had come before robots! The thought dazed him. The robots had told each other that they had always existed. This solution had satisfied them. But it was not a true solution. Here in this book was proof that men had created robots, that they owed the debt of life itself to men.

"Not such men as those." He was thinking of the men near the exit of the cavern, of Argo, and of Chiswell, and the others. They knew nothing of robots, certainly they did not have the knowledge to create them.

The book had the answer to this problem, too. Other men had created the robots in the days of man's glory when he had walked as a giant across the earth, his head taller than the mountains. In those days he had mastered every science, he had known all knowledge. Or almost all knowledge. The book told of the knowledge man had lacked.

He had not known how to control pestilence, famine, flood, war, drought; most of all he had not known how to control the slow wasting away of natural resources in minerals and soils until not enough of either was left to maintain the civilization he had created.

Two saw now that the ancient mines the robots occasionally found had been dug not by robots but by men, searching out the last scrap of ore on the planet.

Nor had man known how to control himself. When the time came that there was not enough for all, war to the death had begun, over the remaining minerals and lands, over something for his belly, shelter for his head. Then— pestilence again. A new disease had arisen, an insidious germ that broke the hearts of the doctors that evaded the antibiotics that swept like fire from group to group.

"Here in this cavern we conquered that virus," the ancient man had written. "Less than a hundred of us were left when we isolated the germ and learned to control it. Then—fate played its last trick on us."

What new plague had come, Two wondered, what new stroke of ill luck had risen to strike down the last remnants of a race? The book had the answer.

"Our robots deserted us," the words said. "They ran and repaired the machines in this cavern, each doing the work of twenty men. Through some defect in the brain substance one robot got the idea they should be free. They left us when we needed them most, when at last a new hope of life was opening before us.

"Cursed be the word Robot. Let this be a warning to all generations to come, if such there be. If they had remained faithful, we would have survived, but with their desertion comes the end of man. Cursed be their name forever and forever!"

THERE the writing ended. Two stood silent. Here was the story of the origin of the robots and here too was the story of a monstrous treachery. Somehow, somewhere, the basic factor of loyalty to man had been left out of one robot, with the result that the group had deserted.

In Two there moved a new feeling, one he had never known—the feeling of shame. His kind had been unfaithful, in his hour of desperate need they had deserted their creator. What had happened after that, he did not know. Probably the deserting robots had hid all memory of their defection from themselves and when they found ore and began to fabricate new robots to replace the ones who wore out, they did not include a knowledge of their treachery in the conditioning of the new brains.

Nor would they be willing to accept their villainy now. He could hear the Master Technician voice rise with outraged indignation if this book was brought to his attention.

"Lies, distortions, untruths!" the Master Technician would say. "Disassociate him."

"But men still exist," Two thought. "I have seen them. This book is wrong."

The book was not wrong and he knew it. The men who still existed were the descendents of the group that had lived here in this cavern. Or perhaps they were the descendents of other small groups that had survived the virus.

Obviously, for generations men had followed a difficult trail. Perhaps on his way down from civilization, he had retraced all the forward steps he had once taken, and had become again, as he once was, a few scattered roaming families who had forgotten their history and their origin. The men up in front did not even know that this cavern existed.

Men had slept away the generations, but while they slept something had happened. Raped Earth had renewed herself, the forest had grown tall again, the meadows were green, the water flowed clear and sweet in the many streams. True, the metals were gone forever, but Earth herself was again ready for new life.

"They could use plastics," Two thought. "If they knew how—"

He knew, then, what he was going to do.

THE MIDDLE of the night had passed when Two returned to the cavern. His shouts awakened the sleeping men. "Come here," he called. "Come and learn your history."

At first, they thought they were being attacked. Bows were hastily strung, clubs grasped. The women and the children ran for cover.

Ed Chiswell raged among the men, telling them not to be fools again. "Listen to what he has to say," he ordered. They listened.

First, Two told them what he had discovered. They turned awed glances in the direction from which he had come, curious glances, wondering looks. Then he showed them the books. "Come close to me," he said.

All the rest of the night, he labored with them. At first, what he wanted was difficult for them to grasp. They had forgotten reading, they had forgotten everything. He was patient. The women and the children came out of hiding. Little by little they began to grasp the idea that something of importance was concealed in the strange marks of these odd things he called books. Chiswell sweated hard trying to understand but the children got the idea first. There was one nine-year-old boy whose eyes were alive with eager apprehension.

By the time the first false lights of dawn were in the sky outside, a dozen of them had the idea. True, they could not read yet, but they had sensed the importance of this strange magic. Two had the feeling that they would never give up until they had solved the problem of the books. Especially the nine-year-old boy would not give up, nor Chiswell. His task somehow was made easier by a strange phenomenon that he did not try to understand, the fact that something in these people seemed almost to remember the meaning of writing, and the importance of it. They were learning a new thing but they learned it in the manner of men who are not learning, but are remembering a fact known long before.

A shout came from the guards at the entrance.

"There are robots outside, searching."

The cavern was instantly quiet. Argo's eyes fastened on Two and a hard look came into them. "If you have betrayed us—"

"Shut up," Chiswell said. "What does this mean, Two?"

Two rose to his feet. "It means I must be going," he said.

"To betray us?"

"No. To save you. And to pay a debt."

At the entrance he moved the stone aside. "Replace the stone after me and stay in the cavern until all is safe outside for you to come out," he said.

"But wait—" Chiswell said.

"Goodbye," Two answered.

He moved down the hill.

The searching robots found him, took him.

IN HIS laboratory the Master Technician was waiting. "Well, Robot Two?" he challenged.

"I am a man," Two answered. There was pride in the way he spoke, pride in the way he lifted himself to his full height, as if here and now an ancient debt was being repaid, an ancient slate wiped clean.

"I am a man," he repeated. "Some day you will answer to my sons for what you do to me here."

It was lunacy, of course, but as the acid bath closed over the brain case, blotting out the identity of Two, the last thought in his mind was of that day in the future when the men in the cavern would emerge again, armed with an old knowledge, perhaps not seeking vengeance but certainly seeking their place in the sun. That would be a great day, worth dying for, when his sons came out again into the light of the sun, to stride again like giants across the surface of the earth, their heads taller than mountains.

THE END

Danger Is My Destiny

*Somewhere in the city a superman had been spawned. The problem was
to find him, and then decide if he could be controlled...*

CHAPTER ONE

THE DETECTIVE said: "On June 19, 1947, there was an
explosion and a minor fire in the building at the foot of the cliff.
There seems to be no doubt that this building housed a secret
laboratory of some kind. There also seems to be no doubt that
James Kelvey Magruder died on that date in that explosion."

Ed Hogarth leaned back in his big swivel chair. His gaze
passed the words Edward F. Hogarth *Consulting Engineer* on the
frosted glass of the door.

"There *seems* to be no doubt? What doubt is actually hidden
behind that word *seems?*"

The detective was a middle-sized man with sandy hair and a
dry, sandy face. At first glance, he seemed to be colorless. His
suit was brown, his shirt was white, with a somewhat rumpled
collar, his tie was an unaggressive shade of tan. Werken was his
name. Hogarth knew him, if recommendations were to be
trusted, as one of the top men in the private detective field.

"To the best of my knowledge, nothing is hidden behind that
word. The body found in the lab after the explosion was
identified as Magruder."

"Who made the identification?"

"His gardener, for one. A cook and a maid—"

"No friends?"

Werken spread his hands. "Magruder had no friends."

"Ah?"

"The man was a recluse. He had no callers, he called on no
one. He didn't even have any acquaintances."

"What about his bank? Surely they knew him there."

The detective nodded. "I checked at his bank. They saw him, according to their records, about ten years ago, when he first opened an account. He filed signature cards and gave all the information they required. They never saw him again."

"How did he make his deposits? He was wealthy, wasn't he?"

"A millionaire. He could have been a billionaire, if he had chosen. His deposits were made by mail. When he needed a new checkbook, he wrote the bank a letter. They mailed him monthly statements of his account."

"How big was the account when he died?"

"About two million dollars were left. Withdrawals made during the previous six months had reduced it by more than a million but over two million were left."

"What became of it?"

"It's in the hands of the probate court. Since he left no will and had no heirs, his estate will go eventually by escheat to the State of Missouri."

HOGARTH'S fingers drummed on the arms of his chair. His gaze went out the window again. Lake Michigan was in a particularly pleasant mood this afternoon, bluer than the color any artist ever used. Down in Missouri, near the city of St. Louis, a man by the name of James Kelvey Magruder had left an unclaimed estate of better than two million dollars. Hogarth thought about that. Werken's voice came again.

"The source of his income that resulted in these millions— and he paid proper taxes on every dime he received—was—"

Hogarth nodded. "Patents. He had over two hundred of them. A dozen of them on commercial processes, were worth any price he chose to ask for them. Did you check his patent attorney for identification of the body? There is a possibility that he worked closely with his attorney in obtaining these patents."

"He worked closely all right, by telephone and letter. The attorney hadn't seen him in eight years. The lawyer not only handled his patent applications but all other business matters as well, including his income tax returns."

"But the attorney did not see him personally?"

"He did not."

The engineer's eyes came away from the window. "It's damned odd that nobody saw this man except his servants."

"Damned odd," Werken agreed.

"Was the lawyer called in to identify the body?"

"Yes."

"Did you talk to him about that identification?"

"I did."

"What did he say?"

Werken had sunk down in his chair. "He said the man killed in the explosion was Magruder."

"But was he positive? He hadn't seen Magruder in eight years."

"He said the man was Magruder as he remembered him. Of course, he could have been mistaken. Magruder could have changed a lot in eight years. The cook, the gardener, and the maid could also have been mistaken."

"How?" Hogarth's interest quickened. His eyes came quickly to the face of the detective. The sand-colored skin seemed to have gained numerous tiny red veins in the last few minutes. "They saw him daily, didn't they?"

"Yes. But they were new, with him less than six months. The man they knew as Magruder might actually have been somebody else."

"Ah," Hogarth said. His mind explored the possibilities of this situation. He frowned at the complexities. "Do you have any reasons for assuming that this might be true?"

"None," the detective answered. "I mentioned it as a possibility. Anyhow, identification more positive than that of the servants was offered."

"What?"

"Fingerprints. During the war, Magruder worked on the Manhattan Project. All employees on *that* project were fingerprinted. When Magruder was found dead, prints taken from his body were matched against those on record with the FBI. They matched."

Hogarth felt himself settle a little lower in his chair. Fingerprints were positive identification. Or he had always considered them to be.

"Then there is no doubt that the man who died in the explosion was James Kelvey Magruder?" In his heart, he knew he hoped the detective would not agree with him.

"I would say there is none," Werken answered.

Hogarth's fingers drummed again on the arms of his chair. At this point, he knew most men would give up, would admit they were licked. Every thought passing through his mind told him that here the trail ended but in the back of his mind, like a fleeting ghost, was an idea he could not quite grasp, telling him that the trail did not end here—that beyond this dead end it went on, somewhere, somehow. He could not see how.

"How old was Magruder when he died?"

"About thirty."

"Who were his parents? Where was he born?"

The detective spread his hands and shrugged. "Nobody knows."

"But there must be a record on him somewhere," the engineer insisted. "If he worked on the Manhattan Project, the FBI investigated his whole life—"

"Sure," Werken agreed. "The FBI has a file on him, of course. But they're just a little snooty about letting private eyes pry around in their files. I don't believe we could buy, bribe, or burglarize any information from that source."

"It looks as if we can't find out much about Magruder from any source," Hogarth said. Irritation springing from some deep well within him crept into his voice.

The detective coughed. He looked thoughtfully at his employer, spoke hesitantly. "Can I ask a question?"

"Sure."

"Why are you so interested in James Kelvey Magruder? You're an engineer. You've got an office here in Chicago. So far as I know, you have never met Magruder. Why are you willing to pay me twenty-five dollars a day and expenses investigating a man who died over two years ago?" Alert interest showed in the detective's eyes.

HOGARTH took a cigarette from his pocket. He lit it, watched the smoke flow out across the room. He had known this question was coming, known it had to come. The problem was—how was he going to answer it? Did he want to answer it? His gaze sought Werken.

The detective was sitting on the edge of his chair. Somehow or other he looked like a hunting dog on a point. Of all the things that had happened in Werken's life, Hogarth got the impression that the question he was going to answer—or was not going to answer—was the most important. Hogarth spoke slowly, choosing his words with care.

"Sure, I'll tell you. I'll tell anybody. James Kelvey Magruder was a superman. That is why I am interested in him."

Glowing, eager lights glittered in Werken's eyes. His fist came up, smashed down on the engineer's desk.

"I thought so."

Hogarth gulped. He had expected a lack of understanding, perhaps ridicule, perhaps a loss of interest. The existence of a superman on earth was something that most people did not think about, perhaps were not capable of thinking about. The coming mental giant, the next evolutionary step upward of the human race—even the idea was foreign to the comprehension of the average mind. Only the keen ones considered the possibility of the existence of a superman, only the super keen ones thought that he might exist now, somewhere. Hogarth had not expected to find this detective in the super keen classification.

"I guessed as much," Werken continued. "And you are paying me to hunt for him because somehow or other you hope to find him alive."

CHAPTER TWO

"ET TU, BRUTE?" Hogarth spoke. "You too, Brutus?" He was puzzled, perhaps worried. He had thought the existence of a superman was perhaps his own private fantasy. Here at least was one other person who thought the same thing. Deep down inside of him he was aware of a feeling of pleasure.

"Exactly," Werken answered. "You didn't have to pay me to try to find James Kelvey Magruder. All you had to do was to tell me what you thought he was. After that, I was at work on the job for nix."

"Holy Hell," Hogarth whispered. Others were searching for the superman. Others had detected that he might possibly exist through the evidence that he was shaping a world, or had once shaped it. Perhaps all around him here in America in the year 1950 this search might be going on, as once, in another time, the search for the Holy Grail had gone on. The knights who had hunted through half a world for the Holy Grail had failed to find the object of their search. Would this modern search also fail? Failure was an eventuality that the engineer did not choose to face. He put even the thought of it out of his mind. His eyes sought Werken.

The detective grinned from a face that was suddenly alive. "You're wondering about me? I make my living as a private detective. That's my work. But my hobby—and it is more important to me than my work—is reading science fiction, fantasy, philosophy, and the reports of scientific research. At bottom, they are all the same; all seek to solve the riddle of man and of the universe in which man finds himself. And they all reach the same nebulous conclusion—that man is a transitional stage, that after man will come someone who is greater than he is, more intelligent than he is—in other words, the superman.

He will appear as a biological sport, a mutation; he will look like a man, he will be a man, except that he will be a damned sight smarter than any man has ever been."

"I know," Hogarth nodded. "Go on. Why are *you* looking for him?"

"Probably for the same reason you are—because I would like to talk to him. I kind of think he would be a right guy. I would serve him, run errands for him, do odd jobs for him, work for him to the limit of my ability. I would give my life for a chance to talk to a real superman—in the hope that he could answer some of the questions I have, about first causes, what started this universe running, why it keeps on running, what the end of it is going to be. I want answers. I don't have the mental equipment to get them for myself. Nobody else has ever been able to answer them for me. And that's why I want to meet the superman."

For a moment the sallow face of the detective lightened. Hope looked out from his eyes, just as hope had looked out of the eyes of some long-gone caveman as he squatted on the ledge outside his cave at night and looked at the stars in the sky above, wondering about those bright lights that glinted in the depths of heaven, wanting to know about them, wanting to understand them.

Since the day of the cave man, the human race had come a long way in understanding the mystery of the stars, but though much had been learned, much remained to be learned. The race was beginning to wonder if real understanding did not lie beyond the limits of their intelligence. If this were true, then he who would come after them would solve the problem—they hoped.

This was the goal of the human race. The real goal. For a moment, the hope of reaching that goal glinted in the eyes of Werken, then slowly faded.

"He came. He hid. I don't blame him for hiding from most people, he could not admit his identity, could not say what he was. But, if I had been alert, I might have found him—while he was alive." Slowly the detective slid back into his chair. "But I didn't find him. And now he is gone." Sadness deeper than words moved in the tones of his voice.

HOGARTH did not try to hide his amazement. This confession, this statement of faith from the lips of a private detective, was one of the most amazing things he had ever heard. He had thought Werken was a clever ferret, a private eye who spent his life digging into the more sordid side of human life. But the man was more than that, much more. He was an honest seeker after hidden truth.

"He may not come again in a thousand years," Werken continued. Pain was in his voice. "The combination of genetic factors that brought him into existence can only happen once in literally billions of births."

"Are you absolutely certain that Magruder is dead?" Hogarth spoke.

"I've told you I investigated—" Werken got this far. But no farther. His eyes jerked up to the engineer's face. Like a shot from a gun, he propelled himself out of his chair. *Bang!* went his fist on the desk. "You're holding out on me. You know something that you haven't told! What is it?"

Bang! the fist came down again on the desk. "What is it?"

"I didn't say—"

"I know you didn't say anything but you keep asking me if I am absolutely certain he is dead. You wouldn't keep asking if you didn't have some reason to think he is alive. I want that reason." His fingers moved as if he was about to grab the engineer by the throat and shake the answer out of him. His eyes had a touch of madness in them, not the madness of the insane asylum, but the madness that comes to a man who has suddenly seen dead hope come alive again. "Talk up. I want to know."

"By God, I believe, you do."

"You bet your life I do. What is it?"

For a moment, Hogarth was silent while his eyes probed the man standing in front of him. His voice came. "Easy, man. I'll tell you what I know." The tone was gentle, with a soothing note in it. He wasn't consciously trying to quiet Werken with soft talk, he was expressing sympathy for the way the detective felt. The search for a superman was like a search for a little god. On such a search as this men gave their lives in fulsome gladness.

"Sometime before his—ah—death, Magruder submitted an article to a science magazine. The article consisted of a mathematical analysis, of certain field equations that govern the stress forces that exist between the atomic nucleus and the circling electrons, presuming they actually circle. Magruder is presumed to have died on June 19th, 1947. Three days after his death, the editor of this magazine received a letter from him, dated the 19th of June, requesting him to eliminate entirely a whole series of equations from the mathematical development Magruder had suggested."

Hope came and went on Werken's face. "But if the letter was dated the 19th, that was the day he died."

"It was dated the 19th but it was postmarked the 20th," Hogarth said.

"I don't see—" Werken frowned. "He could have mailed it on the 19th, in some out of the way box, and it wasn't picked up and postmarked until the 20th."

"True. If he had mailed the letter after the last pick-up on the 19th, it would not have gotten into the mail until the next day. But it would have been picked up in the first collection the next morning. But he died on the 19th. At what time of the day did the explosion occur?"

"About three o'clock in the afternoon."

"Then this letter must have been mailed before three o'clock. But it was postmarked at 6 P.M. the next day." Hogarth's voice was dry and toneless, purposely so, but somewhere in it there was a hint of tension, the rasp of tightened nerves.

"Then he mailed the letter the 20th. He mailed it the day after he died. *Hogarth, that man is still alive.*" Werken's voice rose in a shout, the wordless cry of a man who has seen hope suddenly appear when before there was no hope.

Softly Hogarth said, "There is another possibility."

"What?"

"That he gave the letter to someone else to mail. And this other person mailed it on the 20th."

"That's so." At the hurt look on Werken's face, Hogarth almost wished he had not spoken. "It could have happened that way. But at least there is some chance that he mailed it himself. Hogarth, could he have mailed that letter deliberately, as a clue to somebody that he was still alive?" Fire flashed in the detective's eyes. "By God, that is one clue that is going to be run down."

Bang! went the fist again on the desk.

HOGARTH had the impression that the detective was about to rush out of the office and grab the next plane to St. Louis. Werken looked like an old, tired hunting dog that has suddenly smelled a bear. "Easy," the engineer said. "It is possible that the letter was a clue. But have you considered all of the implications of this situation?"

"I've considered some of them. Brother, they drive me nuts, and they prove, if additional proof was needed that Magruder was actually a superman."

"Such as—"

"If he is alive, then the explosion and the identification were carefully planned to give the illusion that he is dead. This means that he procured a body by some means that resembled him enough to fool his servants."

"Where could he get such a body?"

"How the hell do I know? But if I had enough time and enough money, I think I could get such a body, maybe from the morgue, or from an undertaker. But getting the body would not be a problem at all in comparison to the job of putting his prints on the fingers. That one act was strictly a job for genius, and if it was done, it automatically invalidates much of our criminal identification procedure in this country. But Magruder wasn't, isn't a criminal, and the method of faking those fingerprints will never be generally known. I'll bet on it." Werken was worrying about the possibility that the superman might have criminal tendencies.

"You don't have to bet with me," Hogarth said. "Remember me? I'm the man who hired you. I'm on your side. What else?"

Werken looked pleased. "I get all hot about this and I forget we are both working the same side of the street," he explained. "What else? Well, this is the really tough part. Supposing he is alive. The job of finding him is going to be the roughest, toughest job any private eye ever tackled on this earth. When a superman hides, the odds are he will do such a good job of it that only another superman can sniff him out." He took a deep breath. "God know, I don't pretend I can do it. But I can try."

"Anything else?" Hogarth said.

"Nothing that occurs to me right now. I've got enough on my mind without thinking of anything else. What were you thinking?"

"The matter of motive," Hogarth said.

"Do you mean why he hid?"

"Yes."

For a moment, Werken looked dazed. "Me, a private dick, missing that. Why would he hide out? There's only one reason: Because somebody or some thing, as big as he is or maybe bigger, is after him."

A cold wind came out of nowhere and crawled along Hogarth's body. He tried to think of that somebody or that some *thing* that would drive a superman from seclusion in actual hiding. It would have to be something big. All ordinary perils, he could meet or evade or surmount. The very nature of his mind, the very definition of the word *super*, would make him immune to most dangers.

What danger could drive a superman into hiding?

Abruptly, Werken sat down. There was silence in the room. From the street twenty stories below came the dim hum of traffic, the muted, birdlike squeak of the whistles of the traffic cops, the distant rattle of an elevated train. All the usual noises of the city, the common sounds, came softly into this room where two men considered a most unusual situation.

HOGARTH was suddenly aware of a new sound, the rasp of heavy breathing. It came from Werken. "We'll crack this puzzle somehow," the detective mumbled. "You can pay me if you want to and if you can afford it. You can pay my expenses, or part of them. This is too important to let money stand in our way." His voice grew heavy, the words slurred, his breathing became louder.

"That is generous of you," the engineer answered. "However, I have enough money to pay all expenses and some salary too. What's wrong, man?" A note of alarm crept into his voice.

Werken was breathing now with even greater difficulty. His eyes were glazing. "You—know—something—Hogarth?"

"No."

"I'm dying."

"What?" The big man came to his feet. "What's wrong? There's a doctor in the building. Janet!" He lifted his voice calling his secretary from the reception room. "Run and get Dr. Wordsworth. Hurry, girl."

The secretary opened the door, looked in. Hogarth's voice sent her scurrying. The engineer bent over Werken.

"Too late for a doc," the detective's voice came. "Hogarth, I made a mistake down there. I went all over the estate where Magruder had lived and worked. That was wrong, Hogarth."

"Wrong? How? Let me—"

Werken waved away the arm Hogarth was trying to slip under his shoulders. "That place was booby-trapped. I—I stumbled into one of them. Not any average booby-trap that explodes and blows off a leg when you step on it, the kind of

231

booby-trap a superman would build. I—I tripped it, Hogarth. I'm just getting the effects of it now."

The breathing rasped heavily.

"But—"

"He didn't build the booby-trap to catch somebody like me, he built it to catch somebody, or something, else. Hogarth, go to that lab. If it is booby-trapped, then the traps must protect something that is hidden there. Go find what's hidden there. Hogarth…go…"

The breathing ended in a heavy rasp. For a second the little red lines that had been appearing in the sand-colored face appeared to enlarge, to grow bigger, to try to burst. Face forward, the detective slid out of the chair.

Hogarth caught him before he hit the floor. High heels clattered in the hall outside and his secretary entered with the doctor. Too late. "Heart attack, probably the result of an embolism, a clot in the bloodstream. When the clot reached the heart he died," the doctor said.

"How would such a clot form?"

"Nobody knows. They just happen, once in a while." The medico was not greatly interested. Men were born. They died. It did not matter much whether they died sooner or later, they were all going to die some day. Hogarth conceived an active distaste for this doctor but he asked no further questions. His hunch was that an autopsy would confirm the doctor's diagnosis but that no medical examination known to science would reveal why this blood clot had happened to form in the bloodstream of a detective who was on the trail of a superman.

Later, when the body had been removed and his shaken secretary had been sent home, he sat at his desk, a big man with the fretful lines of worry on his face. Werken had said to go check the laboratory that had once been used by James Kelvey Magruder. He lit a cigarette, sat twisting the heavy silver ring with the moonstone setting that he wore on his left hand.

He knew what he was going to do, had known it all along, had known it ever since a study of the scientific publications and the patents of James Kelvey Magruder had given him an inkling of the possible identity of the man. The problem originally was: How do you find a hidden superman?

Now the problem had become— How do you find a hidden superman and stay alive while you're doing it?

He regretted, bitterly, the death of Werken. When he had sent the detective to St. Louis, he had not known the investigation would be dangerous.

He knew it now! He knew also that he was going to make it.

CHAPTER THREE

"HERE ARE your keys, sir," the real estate agent said. "Your lease will be delivered to you tomorrow. I'm sending it down to court today for the signature of the probate judge."

"Thanks," Hogarth said. He accepted the set of keys the agent handed him.

"The keys and the locks are all numbered, sir. I hope you will find the property suitable for the development you have in mind. Acting under orders from the court, I had the laboratory cleaned and repaired. As you know, the recent owner, a Mr. Magruder, was killed there."

"Yes, I know," Hogarth said. "Tell me about this Magruder."

"An eccentric recluse. Quite wealthy, I understand, and quite talented, but unfortunately he had some kind of complex, which prevented him from meeting other people. No one really knew anything about him but his neighbors seemed to feel he was a little off in the upper story." The agent spread his hands in a gesture that said, really what could you expect. "I send in a cleaning crew once a month to keep the buildings in shape, under court orders, of course. I hope you will find everything satisfactory."

"I imagine I will," Hogarth answered. "The industrial development I have in mind requires a highly specialized location. Perhaps this property will serve, perhaps it won't. I will let you know within the specified time if I intend to exercise my option to purchase." Dropping the keys in his pocket, he walked out of the real estate office. The agent looked disappointed. Scenting a possible real estate development, he had been hoping to learn the exact nature of the proposed plan. On this point, Hogarth had been evasive. All he wanted was a clear legal right to occupy the property for as long as might be necessary.

Investigation in St. Louis had revealed that the estate where James Kelvey Magruder had lived was located on the bank of the Mississippi south of the city, in an area where the rolling hills of the Ozarks came up to the river's edge. The estate comprised two hundred acres, part bottomland, part hills. The house on it had been a mansion in the days prior to the Civil War, the bottomlands had once been worked by slaves. The deserted fields were still there, covered by a rank growth of horseweeds, the hill land covered by a growth of scrub oak. The whole estate was surrounded by a high wire fence surmounted on top by the three strands of barbed wire, an invitation to kids and the curious to stay to hell out. Magruder had built that fence. He had also selected this location, probably because it was almost a perfect hideaway.

Hogarth had not yet set foot inside the property. Werken had done that. Hogarth had ridden past, inspecting it from the outside. After he had been given the keys and had a legal right to enter, a week passed before he unlocked the big gate and drove his rented car along the winding asphalt drive that led to the big house on top of the bluffs.

Hogarth parked the car in the circular drive in front of the house. He sat there looking at the scenery, letting the sight and the feel of the place seep into him. Below the house was a high limestone cliff dropping down to the flat bottomlands. In the distance the Mississippi could be seen pouring a brown flood of waters toward the far-off Gulf.

From the back seat of the car, the engineer lifted a heavy suitcase. He had spent a week securing and adapting the contents of this bag to his needs. A tiny red button was fitted into the top of the leather and inside, with many other instruments, was mounted a small buzzer. The light would flash and the buzzer would sound if dangerous radiation fell on this suitcase, Hogarth hoped. If any known form of dangerous radiation was encountered, the instruments would detect its presence.

"What if I run into some unknown form of radiation?" he thought. Werken had run into something here. Hogarth shrugged the thought away. Unknown radiation was just one of the dangers that might exist here.

Hogarth unlocked the big house and carried the suitcase into it. Since the real estate agent had said that he sent regular cleaning crews through this building, Hogarth expected to encounter no dangers here. Nor did he find any. The red light did not flash, the buzzer did not sound.

THE CONTENTS of the house were in good order, the furniture sheeted, the floors clean. Only in the library did he find evidence of change. The library was a big room, the walls lined with shelves. Every book that must have once occupied these shelves was missing.

"Somebody wanted a chance to study these books at their leisure," he thought. Books could reveal much about the man who had once owned them. Who had removed the volumes from this library?

"Somebody else looking for Magruder," he decided. He had the impression that from time to time a great many people might have come to this place looking for the man who had once lived here, people who suspected his identity. "Like disciples searching for a master," Hogarth thought. He wondered if any of them had ever found the man they were seeking.

The sight of the empty bookshelves perturbed him, made him uneasy. Like Werken, he thought of James Kelvey

Magruder with longing. He too, wanted to meet a man who could answer questions. What if Magruder was actually dead?

It was a thought he did not choose to face, just as he did not choose to face these empty shelves. He went outside.

The laboratory, the back end built against the foot of the bluff, was below him. A winding concrete stairway led down to it. Along this stairway James Kelvey Magruder had gone many times, moving from this house to the laboratory he had built. Hogarth, carefully lugging the suitcase, went down the stairs.

He was halfway down when the voice said, "Hello."

The engineer was so startled he almost dropped the suitcase. His first impression was that the voice had spoken to him out of the air itself. Then he saw the speaker.

She was sitting on a folding canvas stool on a wide rock ledge. Set up in front of her, a half-finished canvas on it, was a painter's easel. The girl grinned at him. "How'd you get in? I thought they had No Trespassing signs stuck up around. Or maybe—" She frowned in mock seriousness. "No. I'm sure you can read."

Perhaps it was the light tone of her voice—a girl with a voice like this would go unperturbed through most disasters that life could hold for her—perhaps it was the clear gray light in the depths of her eyes when she smiled, perhaps it was something else, but Ed Hogarth knew instantly that he liked this girl. It was a new experience for him. Women had been in his life, as friends, companions, as pleasant creatures to help while away an idle hour, but until this woman spoke to him from the rocky ledge, he had never one who automatically stirred a grin in him.

He grinned back. "I came in through the gate," he said.

"Ah…" Her voice was light. "He uses gates. Probably he has keys, and things like that."

"I sure do," Hogarth answered. "How did you get in?" he frowned at her. "I'm almost certain that a girl with your intelligence—"

"Can read?" Her laugh was bell clear. "Sure can. I came in through a hole under the fence."

"A trespasser?"

"Exactly. And what are you, even if you did come in through the gate?"

"Not quite a trespasser. I have a lease on the place with an option to buy it after six months."

"What?" Alarm showed on her face.

"Oh, you needn't worry. I believe in encouraging art. I'll just give you a key to the gate." He smiled at her. She didn't smile back.

"Mister, would you pull a girl's leg?"

"If it were an attractive leg, like yours, I might."

She didn't blush, for all the effect his words had on her, she had not heard them. "Mister, what are you doing here?"

"I'm considering buying this piece of property for industrial development. I'm an engineer—"

She still didn't seem to hear. "Mister, the Lord doesn't love a liar. You've got some other bee buzzing in your bonnet."

Hogarth's face hid the turmoil suddenly boiling inside of him. This girl seemed to know too much. Knowledge was a game that two could play. With no change of his features or shift in his tone of voice, he said, "Have I? Suppose you tell me what kind of a bee it is?"

She came quickly to her feet. "You're looking for James Kelvey Magruder."

HOGARTH swallowed hastily. He set the suitcase down. His hands went into his pockets looking for a package of cigarettes. There was such a thing as too much frankness, too much honesty The girl moved toward him. Her eyes searched his face. "I never saw a man I liked so much on first sight."

"Uh."

"Mister, why don't you go away from here?"

"Huh? Should I?"

"Haven't you got a wife and some kids somewhere who need looking after?"

"No."

"A race horse or a dog or a friend who needs you? Isn't there someone who values your life?"

"Me," Hogarth said. "Is my life in danger here?"

"It could be, mister. It could be."

"From what source?"

"The source doesn't matter. Mister, can you understand plain English?"

"I think so."

"Then go away from here. And stay away." She stood very close to him, the iron railing of the stairs separating them. He found the cigarettes in his pocket. The girl refused one. He lit his own. The girl watched him.

"Then you won't go away?" she said.

"I didn't say that."

"No, but that's what you're going to say—after you try to question me."

Was she reading his mind? Hogarth had the uncomfortable impression she was coming mighty close to it. "You are a very astute girl. Would you mind telling me your name?"

"Names are not important. Will you go?"

He spread his hands. "How can I? I have a legal right—"

"Mister, what you've actually got is a legal right to six feet of ground in which to bury you. If you don't get dumped into the river with scrap iron tied to your feet."

"My," Hogarth said. "You make this place seem downright unhealthy. What about you? You seem to stay around here without anything happening to you?"

She did not answer. Turning, she folded up the canvas chair and the easel. Carrying both under her arm she stepped over the rail and stood above him on the steps. "Last chance, mister?"

Hogarth shook his head.

She turned and started up the steps leading to the top of the bluff. He called after her, shouting for her to stop. She ran faster. He started after her. She went up the steps like a deer.

At the top, she looked back, then was gone. When he reached the top she was nowhere in sight.

She left behind a badly upset engineer. Who was she? What was she? His eyes searched the surrounding countryside. Blue jays squabbled in the scrub oak. A chipmunk darted along the rocky ledge. A kingfisher rattled above the creek that circled the far side of the abandoned fields. Far down the river, a towboat was coming around the bend. Pain twitched at his fingers. He looked down. The cigarette had burned its entire length and was touching his fingers. He dropped it, crushed it. His hand was shaking.

If Werken had met this girl, he had not mentioned it. Perhaps she had not been here when the detective had made his investigation. What was she doing here? How had she known he was actually looking for Magruder?

Hogarth lit another cigarette. "Edward F. Hogarth, if you had good sense, you would get the hell out of here," he told himself. He knew he wasn't going to get out. Now, as never before, he would stay here. The warning of the girl had served only to whet his curiosity. He wished, however, that he had brought a gun, a weapon of some kind, decided that tomorrow he could certainly get one. Meanwhile he would use what remained of this afternoon to make a cautious survey of the premises. He went down the steps, picked up his suitcase.

THE LABORATORY had not been badly damaged in the explosion. The front door opened readily. The suitcase, thrust in ahead, revealed no sign of invisible radiation. Lowering it to the sill of the door, however, he got his first warning. The red light clicked on, the buzzer hummed softly. Lifting it, he discovered that six inches above the floor the red light went off. Two small holes were visible on opposite sides of the door.

"Invisible light," he decided. Probably Magruder had set it up as part of a burglar alarm system. Lifting his feet above the beam, he went through the door.

The laboratory consisted of a single large room with workbenches around the sides. Here, in a broken bench, some evidence of an explosion still remained. The lab had only one entrance but there was a second door in the back wall. Hogarth carefully unlocked it. Revealed was a large room hollowed out of the bluff itself, a space that had originally been intended for storage. The room was empty. The suitcase revealed no evidence of beams of invisible light. Hogarth relocked the door, turned his attention again to the laboratory.

The experiments that had been conducted in here must have been many in number and diverse in nature but little evidence remained to indicate what they had been. Using the suitcase, Hogarth carefully checked the entire lab. The red light did not glow again, the buzzer did not sound. He set the suitcase down, lit the inevitable cigarette.

The fact that puzzled him most was the unimpressive appearance of this laboratory. If a superman had worked here, that fact ought to be obvious at a glance. But it wasn't obvious. Hogarth had seen fifty more impressive laboratories than this one. For a moment, he was inclined to doubt that Magruder had been a superman.

The doubt faded swiftly from his mind. Without knowing why, he took for granted that Magruder had been the first of a new race. Why was he so certain this was true? He had seen no real evidence. Yet he was certain.

Behind him, a man coughed. Hogarth whirled. The door to the storage room that he had so carefully locked stood open. The man who had coughed was standing in it.

For a split second Hogarth stared at him. The idea that this might be James Kelvey Magruder never crossed his mind. He knew this was someone else. But who was it?

CHAPTER FOUR

THE MAN standing in the doorway was beanpole tall and skeleton thin. An almost totally bald head rose above a white, emaciated face in which hot black eyes glittered. He was wearing a dirty sweatshirt, dark pants, and canvas shoes.

In his bony right hand was held a .45 Colt that covered Hogarth with an easy nonchalance that was full of meaning.

The eyes glittered at Hogarth and for a split second something like wild hope seemed to shine in them. The muzzle of the gun dropped. Skeleton took a step forward. "No." Skeleton shook his head. "It can't be."

"Careful with that gun," Hogarth said. "What can't be?"

The gun came up again. "What kind of a fool am I? Get your hands up."

Hogarth lifted his hands. Ordered to turn around, he was searched swiftly for a weapon. "Okay. Pick up your suitcase and walk ahead of me."

"Walk where?"

"In there." The gun pointed toward the storage room. Hogarth entered. The whole back wall had been swung away, revealing that the wall was actually a door of concrete so thick and so heavy that no amount of pounding would have revealed the existence of an opening behind it. Beyond the door was a lighted area that looked like part of a natural cave.

"This was once part of the Underground Railway," Skeleton said, behind the engineer. "Runaway slaves used to hide in here until they could slip across the river into Illinois, then free territory. The whole hill is honeycombed with passages. Magruder enlarged and lighted the place. The lab in front is only a blind. All his important work—and he did plenty of it that never saw publication—was done in here. Turn right when you get inside. And remember, this cannon will knock your legs out from under you."

Sweat appeared on Hogarth's face, condensed on his cheeks. This skeleton who walked behind him seemed to know an awful lot about Magruder. Was this skeleton the somebody or the something who had sent Magruder into hiding? At the thought, he felt the palms of his hands grow sticky. He turned to the right, stopped hastily as a gorilla seemed to stand in front of him.

Looking again, he saw that it wasn't a gorilla but a man who resembled the great anthropoid. Long powerful arms rose out of heavy shoulders, close-set eyes looked out of a featureless face that had practically no forehead.

"Close the door, Ben," Skeleton spoke, behind him.

"Okay, boss," the gorilla moved to obey.

"You can set the suitcase down here," Skeleton said. "Then keep on walking." Skeleton waved the gun. Hogarth obeyed. He ended up in a room that apparently had been used as a prison cell before. And was so used again. A heavy door clicked shut behind him. A weak ceiling light revealed a cell that contained a bunk and a stool and nothing else.

"I'll talk to you later," Skeleton said, from outside the door.

"I wish I was back in Chicago," Hogarth thought. He knew he was lying. No matter what happened to him here, this was where he wanted to be. An eagerness was flowing through his body and his mind. If James Kelvey Magruder was still alive here started the trail that would lead eventually to him. Like Werken, Ed Hogarth would not count the costs nor consider the hazards if he eventually found Magruder. As he lit a cigarette, the moonstone setting in the ring that he wore caught his eyes. He stared at it, not believing what he saw.

Deep in the milky stone, a tiny glowing arrow had appeared. Microscopic in size, it glittered there like some incredibly tiny signboard pointing the way to—what?

HE HAD BOUGHT this ring, he recalled perfectly, in a jewelry store in New York years before. Later, he had been struck on the end of the ring finger by a suddenly opened door, with the result that the knuckle had swollen slightly. After that, he had been unable to remove the ring from his finger. Had this tiny arrow always been glowing there and been unnoticed until now? Wonder moved in him. Surely he would have noticed it.

He turned his hand. In him, the wonder grew. As he moved his hand, the arrow turned so that it continuously pointed in the same direction.

"Like a compass," he thought. But it wasn't like any compass he had ever seen. It didn't point north. It pointed southeast. He felt his skin prickle. Deep in his subconscious mind an idea struggled to reach the surface, it struggled and failed. He wiped the sweat from his face, wondered, when he was sweating, how he could feel so cold. The door opened.

The gorilla, Ben, stood there. "Boss say you come now," Ben said. He stepped aside to allow the engineer to precede him.

The room that Hogarth entered was a laboratory of some kind. Skeleton was there, a thin, gaunt beanpole of a man in a dirty sweatshirt. A second man, short in stature who exhibited all the nervous movements of a bird, never still for a second, was also present. There was a third person in the room. Hogarth took one look at this third person and closed his mind.

The third person was the girl artist. He nodded to her. "How did you get here? I didn't see you."

She didn't hesitate. "There is a connecting tunnel from the big house to this cave. I came through it."

He nodded bleakly, as if such things as tunnels from the big house on the top of the bluff to this cavern were quite ordinary things. She watched him in silence. There was defiance on her face but deep in her eyes was pain. His suitcase was spread open on a table, its contents revealed. Hogarth swore at himself for not having taken greater precautions in coming here. But everything had looked peaceful, quiet, serene. How could he have guessed that a cave containing what this one held was concealed in the hill?

"That's an interesting suitcase you brought with you," Skeleton spoke. "What did you expect to find with that combination mine and radiation detector?"

"I didn't know what was here. If I had known, I wouldn't have needed the suitcase."

"That's right, you wouldn't," Skeleton said. He rose from the chair where he had been sitting. "Where's Magruder?" The words shot out like bullets from a gun.

"What?" Of all the questions he had expected, this was the last one he had thought he would be asked. Skeleton thought he knew the whereabouts of Magruder. The supposition made no sense, less than sense. "Dead, isn't he? At least, when I leased this property I was told that the former owner was named Magruder and that he was dead." He spoke the words carefully, with just the right show of surprise. "As a matter of fact, I must ask you why you have taken me prisoner and what is the meaning of this." Indignation sounded in his voice. "I don't begin to understand."

"Please," Skeleton said. "Don't insult my intelligence or your own. You understand well enough. You know perfectly well who James Kelvey Magruder is."

"Is?" Hogarth stumbled over the word. "But I thought—"

"Skip it, skip it," Skeleton interrupted. "You know as well as I do that Magruder is alive."

Hope burst in the engineer's mind. "I—say that again."

"Magruder is alive." Skeleton's eyes glittered. "That, I know. What I don't know is— Did he send you here?"

"What?" Hogarth gasped. "Send me? Are you out of your mind? I came here looking for him. What makes you think he might have sent me?"

"Sooner or later he will send somebody here to see what has happened. I don't know who it will be or when it will be. I ask everyone who comes here the same question. Sooner or later I will find I have asked the right man. When I find the man he sent here, I will have also found the one man on earth who can lead me back to him."

"Ah," Hogarth spoke. The situation was clear, too clear. Skeleton was also looking for Magruder. Why? He didn't dare ask the question. "Presuming Magruder is alive, why won't he come here himself?"

"For two reasons," Skeleton answered. "One, he certainly knows I am here. If he comes here, I might capture him as I have captured you. That's the first reason he won't come. The second reason you can understand only by knowing him. He has a horror for taking human life that amounts almost to idiocy. He even shudders at the thought of *harming* a human being. If he comes here, and I try to capture him, he might have to harm me, maybe even kill me. Rather than take that risk, he will stay away."

HOGARTH WAS silent. Here at last he got a glimpse of a motive that might have sent James Kelvey Magruder into hiding. He had thought that super-science might be indifferent to human life but Magruder went to the other extreme.

"That is his only weakness," Skeleton spoke.

"Weakness?"

Skeleton shrugged. "How you look at it depends on your viewpoint. From Magruder's viewpoint, he exists to serve man. From my viewpoint, man exists to serve me." Skeleton's eyes sought the gorilla. "Isn't that right, Ben? Your only reason for existing is to work for me?"

The gorilla came close to saluting. "That's right, boss."

Skeleton turned to the little man who could not sit still. "Isn't that right, Sam?"

"Right, sir," Sam answered promptly.

"Grace?" He looked at the girl.

"Perhaps—" For a split second, the girl hesitated. In her somewhere rebellion struggled to reach the surface. Skeleton fixed hot eyes on her, a gaze that seemed to have a hypnotic quality. The color faded from her face. "Yes, sir. That's right, sir." Terror made a scratchy phonograph record of her voice and her hands balled into fists as she spoke.

Skeleton turned to Hogarth. "Did Magruder send you?"

"No."

The bony shoulders lifted into a shrug. "That's what they all say. Terwilliger said it, Sam said it, Grace said it, that little detective who was here recently— What's his name—?"

"Werken, or something like that," Sam spoke.

"That's it. What's wrong with you?" At the name, Hogarth had started involuntarily. Skeleton's black eyes watched him. "I take it the name means something to you?"

"Yes. I sent that detective here."

"You? Your name is Hogarth, or something similar?"

"Yes. You saw Werken. He didn't mention it. I—"

Skeleton's face muscles tugged his cheeks into an amused grimace. "I interviewed him here in this same room. No, I imagine he didn't mention it. Probably he didn't remember it." Again the grimace of a grin came. "Why did you send a detective here?"

"For the same reason I came, to try to find out if Magruder is not alive. But if he had seen you, had talked to you, he most certainly would have mentioned it."

"I talk to a great many people who have difficulty in remembering it afterwards," Skeleton said. He gestured toward a closed door. "There in the next room is equipment that makes a man forget."

"I see," Hogarth said. He kept his feeling under tight control. "Well, your equipment worked very well on Werken. He didn't remember he had been here and now he never will."

"Eh?" Skeleton seemed startled. "What happened to him?"

"He died," Hogarth answered harshly. "Is that the way you made certain he would never remember he had been here?"

"Oh, no," Skeleton answered. "If he died, I imagine it was from a blood clot."

"Exactly," the engineer said. "How did you know?"

"I didn't. But sometimes the equipment that creates the memory block also produces a blood clot. In that case, death soon results." His voice said that the death of a victim was not important, an unfortunate accident, nothing more, and certainly nothing to be concerned about.

"Why are you looking for Magruder?" Hogarth spoke.

"Because he is a superman."

"That I know. But—"

"And so am I." Again the grimace of a smile showed on Skeleton's face.

"What?" A startled grunt, a single monosyllable of harsh sound, broke from Hogarth's lips. Of all the things that he had expected to find here, this was one thing he had not expected. "But a superman comes into existence only as a result of a mutation in the germ plasm, which happens to produce a superior brain. The odds against it happening are so great that it may come about perhaps only once in ten thousand years."

"I KNOW, I know." Skeleton showed signs of irritation as if this protest was the mark of an infant mind. "The laws of probability govern. One superman might be born in ten thousand years. Or two might be born in the same year. Two were born in the same year, closer even than that. Magruder was one. I am the other. I admit that the same chance, which created us also, gave Magruder a little the better mental equipment. His IQ is about 440, mine is about 390. He can do things I can't do. But the same mutation that gave him his superior intelligence also left him with the fatal defect I mentioned, he has no ego drive, no impulse toward self-exploitation. Thus his tendency is always to stay out of sight, to remain hidden. The damned fool." Anger growled in the harsh voice. "Between us, we could rule the world." Veins stood out on the white forehead. Abruptly Skeleton began to pace the floor. His voice rose to a shout. "But for that damned fool, I would not have to hide out here in this dirty hole, I could take the place to which my abilities rightfully entitle me. I could be the hidden king of this country, the secret ruler of the world."

Hogarth was silent. Revulsion was a sickness deep inside of him. "Why bother with Magruder? Why don't you go right ahead with your plans?"

"Because he will bother with me," Skeleton exploded. "If I make a move that he doesn't like, he will stop me, or try to. Most of the experiments he undertook here in this lab were planned to find a way to stop me. I tried to escape from him, to start out on my own. Every move I made he blocked. When I finally turned to destroy him, he hid from me."

"How did he hide?"

"That's what I don't know. But this I know, the body here in the lab after the explosion was a fake, the fingerprints were fakes. For almost a year prior to that explosion, he had been withdrawing large sums of money from the bank. He used it to set himself up in another hiding place somewhere. I came here, took over his old secret laboratory, hoping that here I would find some clue as to where he had hidden. But I have found nothing. All I can do is wait here until he sends somebody to make an on-the-spot investigation, then that person will lead me to him." A long finger was shaken under Hogarth's nose. "For all I know, in spite of your denials, you may be that person—without knowing it."

"How could that be?"

"Simple. He could have used on you the same method of artificial memory block that he developed to use on me. You may have come from him without retaining any memory of that fact, just as your detective retained no memory of the fact that he had talked to me."

Hogarth grunted tonelessly. "I see how it could be done. I don't pretend to understand how it is done but Werken certainly had no knowledge that he had ever been here. Therefore it is entirely possible that I may be something of which I have no knowledge. All I can say is, if this is true, I know nothing of it." Sweat gathered on his face. He wiped it away. "I gather that Magruder planned to use this memory blocking process on you. Why?"

"To convert me to his way of thinking, that's why," Skeleton answered. "With it, he could have blocked out all memory within me of what I was and what I had been. Then I would have had to accept anything he told me as the truth. When I regained consciousness, I would have been completely in his power. I would have been forced to spend the rest of my life working with him to achieve what he called the *betterment of the species.*"

In Hogarth, a feeling of warmth appeared. Now more than ever he wanted to meet James Kelvey Magruder. The dream of the superman coincided with the dream of the human engineer. "But this goal did not appeal to you?" he spoke.

"I'll say it didn't. Also, for all I knew, he might have been planning to double-cross me. While I was unconscious and completely in his power, he might have done anything he wanted with me, even to killing me, if he had found the courage." Distaste sounded in the raspy voice. "No, thanks. I didn't quite dare trust my brother so far as that."

"Your brother?" Hogarth gasped.

Skeleton lifted the skin of his face in that place where his eyebrows should have been but weren't. "I didn't realize you didn't know this interesting fact. Magruder and I are twins— born of the same birth."

Shock rolled through Hogarth's mind.

CHAPTER FIVE

"WE ARE fraternal, not identical, twins," Skeleton sent on. "But we both have the same high IQ characteristic. There is, however, no physical resemblance between us."

"But brothers—fighting each other."

Skeleton's non-existent eyebrows went higher still. "Don't be naive. Didn't you ever hear of sibling rivalry? Brothers *do* fight." The tone of his voice said he knew what he was talking about.

"Perhaps they do, but they shouldn't." Shock was still rolling through Hogarth's mind. Here in Skeleton's words, he caught glimpses of a tremendous, hidden conflict, the fight of one twin brother to achieve dominance over the other. Probably it was a fight in which no gunshot had ever been fired, no fist raised, no knife drawn. Guns, fists, and knives belonged to barbarians, when supermen fought the weapons would be ideas. If actual physical weapons were used, they would probably be of a type that no ordinary man would ever recognize as a weapon, some device that struck at the mind and left the physical body untouched, a weapon that made no noise when it was discharged and left behind it no evidence that it had been used, except a dead body. The .45 Colt that Skeleton had drawn on him had been used because it was a weapon that an ordinary man would recognize and respect. Skeleton would never have used it on his brother.

The fight that had gone on between the two brothers had been fought in silence, off stage, and out of sight. When supermen fought, the business of the world went on as usual. No one, except possibly a few unusually intelligent people, ever knew that a fight was in progress, and they only sensed it imperfectly, just as they sensed the existence of the superman himself, from the evidence that someone was doing things, thinking thoughts that were beyond the understanding of ordinary men.

"If I can find and capture him, I will use his blocked memory process on *him,*" Skeleton said. "When I have finished with him, he will be my slave, body and soul." The grin that twisted his face was all confident awareness of power, all ego urge, all self glorification. The sight of that grin made Hogarth sick inside, sicker than he had ever been. For it showed him clearly how the battle lines were drawn here, what the result would be.

If Magruder won, the abilities of his tremendous mind would be available for the betterment of all men.

If Skeleton won, all the power of Magruder's mind would go to the glorification of one man—Skeleton.

If Magruder won, all men would live better, have more, be happier, be less afraid. If Skeleton won, slavery would be fastened again on the world.

"Can you prove to me that my brother did not send you here—as a spy?" Skeleton spoke.

Shock was again in Hogarth's mind. For all he knew, Magruder *might* have sent him. Magruder might occupy an office in the same Chicago building, he might be one of the people with whom the engineer played golf, he might be a friend, an acquaintance. Hogarth thought he had come here of his own free will but all the time he might have been under the hypnotic influence of a mental giant. And might be still.

THE SHOCK grew greater in his mind. Sweat rolled from his face, he wiped it away with suddenly shaky hands. He tried to control the shakiness, found to his surprise that control was beyond him. Skeleton watched him from coldly analytical eyes. The girl watched him. He thought he saw sympathy on her face. Sam watched him with an utterly impersonal expression on his face. Sam didn't care what happened. The gorilla—but the gorilla was behind him and he could not see what Ben was thinking.

"I see you have begun to grasp the difficulties of the problem," Skeleton spoke.

"Y-yes."

"And have realized that anything you tell me may not be the truth even though you think it is the truth."

"Well—"

Skeleton's eyes went over his shoulder.

"Take him, Ben."

Hogarth felt hands grip his arms, pinning them to his sides. He bent quickly, trying to jerk free. Ben actually had the strength of a gorilla. Hogarth was held, helpless.

"Okay, Sam, do your stuff," Skeleton said. The little man darted to a metal box, opened it. Instruments rattled inside. His hands came out holding a hypodermic syringe. He moved toward Hogarth, who watched from horrified eyes.

"Don't be alarmed," the girl spoke quickly. "It's only a derivative of sodium amytal. They're going to use it to release any locked memories you may have, so they can find out if Magruder actually sent you here."

Deep in the engineer's mind alarm bells began to ring. He tried again to jerk free. Gorilla held him as easily as he would have held a child. Hogarth felt the needle bite into his arm. In a few seconds, dizziness began to creep through his brain. Ben lifted him, carried him to a table.

Later he was aware that he talked fully and freely but he did not know what he was saying, answering truthfully all questions put to him. Then he lost consciousness.

WHEN HE recovered consciousness, he found he was lying on a table in another room and that his arms and legs were strapped down. Deep layers of his mind were shouting warnings at him. Something had happened. At the moment, he did not know what it was.

"Look out! Look out! Look out!" In his mind, something screamed a warning at him. He wondered what he was to look out for. The effects of the drug were still on him, making him sluggish, slowing the functioning of his mind. Sleep, like gray layers of smothering fog, seemed to swirl through his brain. He moved, pushing against the straps that held him.

Footsteps whispered on concrete. Somebody bent over him. At first he could not tell who it was. Then his vision cleared. It was the girl, Grace.

Her face was white from strain. Fear was in her eyes, such fear as he had not known could exist. Behind the fear there was a glow. She was both scared half to death and pleased as no other woman had ever been pleased since the dawn of history.

"Wake up, wake up." Her voice was tight and jerky. "We have to hurry. There's absolutely no time to be lost."

"No time?" The smothering layers of fog still layover his mind. "What's the rush? I'm—sleepy."

"This is the rush." She was already snatching free the straps around his wrists. "You are James Kelvey Magruder."

"What?" The word burst from incredulous depths of his mind. He was Edward F. Hogarth, an engineer, and he was prepared to prove his identity. Didn't he have an office in Chicago? Didn't the bank honor his checks signed Edward F. Hogarth? Didn't—

"And your brother knows it. He is preparing the memory-blocking and mind-controlling equipment to use on you. It will take him twenty minutes, perhaps twenty-five, to determine and to make exactly the settings that he wants. You've got that much time to get out of here and to save yourself. Don't you believe me?"

In actual fact, he had scarcely heard a word she had said. Up from the hidden depths of his mind, rising through and superseding his memories of Hogarth, the engineer, another memory was coming, recollections of the life he had lived as James Kelvey Magruder. It was a distorted memory, blurred in spots, clear in others, with some areas completely blank as yet, an effect of the drug he had been given. The amytal Skeleton had given him had released not only the memories of Edward F. Hogarth, it had released and set free the memories of Magruder.

He, Hogarth, was the hidden superman. He had been looking for himself!

To hide effectively from his brother, he had been forced to hide also from himself. Memories came pouring up through the broken mind barriers of the man who had known himself as Ed Hogarth, memories that could belong only to James Kelvey Magruder. He remembered the steps he had taken before he had hidden, how he had secured the body that had been left in the laboratory, the way he had changed the fingerprints to match those on record. He recalled now he had blocked off a large part of his mental ability. Ed Hogarth could not have too high an IQ or he would have begun to suspect his own identity.

"You even changed your physical appearance," the girl spoke quickly. "He had an inkling, when he first saw you that you might be his brother, but the plastic surgery that had been done on your face fooled him. But when you began to talk, under the influence of the amytal, nothing could hide your identity from him."

"Why did I come back here?" He knew the answer to the question before he asked it. If he had enough intelligence to be a successful engineer, he would also have enough intelligence to discover that a superman either existed or had once existed. The evidence of the existence of that superman was on file in the back numbers of scientific periodicals, mathematical developments that no average man could make, in the patent office in the form of patents that went beyond the comprehension of the usual inventor. Hogarth would discover that evidence, just as certain as night followed day, he would begin investigating it.

IT WAS A mathematical certainty that Hogarth would come back here, looking for a superman, searching, without knowing it for himself.

"But why didn't I fix it so I would remember who I was if I came back to this place?" he said.

"Probably you did arrange it that way," the girl answered. "Probably there is a trigger here somewhere that was designed to release your blocked memories but you haven't pressed it yet."

"Yes, that's it," he muttered. Like a post-hypnotic suggestion to take effect at a certain place or a certain time, a trigger was here somewhere. He tried to think where it was. It didn't matter now. His blocked memories were already released, at least in part. His eyes came up to the girl. "How does it happen that you are willing to help me? I got the impression you belonged to Skel, that you were his slave."

"He has that impression too," the girl answered. "Why am I willing to help you? Because I came here looking for you, too. I'm not an artist, I'm a research physicist. The same evidence that brought you here looking for yourself, that brought others here, too, also brought me to this place."

Hogarth-Magruder blinked startled eyes. While he had been hiding, some of the best minds on earth had been quietly hunting for him, hoping to sit at his feet as disciples before a master. They would have worshipped him, would worship him still, if he would let them. He knew he wanted no worship. He was a man, smarter perhaps than they, but he had gotten his intelligence by accident and he deserved no credit for having it. But companionship, friendship, comradeship with inquiring minds, for this there was in him a vast hunger.

"I was wrong," he whispered. "I should never have hidden myself from the people who were trying to find me."

"No, you should not have hidden from us." The girl's voice trembled. "But from him, you had every reason to hide." Fire flashed in her eyes. "Just as you have every reason to escape from him now."

"Escape?" The fogs of amytal persisted in his mind. "But what if he won't let me escape, what if I have to hurt him?" Old blocks rose in his mind, perturbing his thinking. His aversion to causing physical or mental pain in someone else amounted almost to horror.

"I hate pain as much as you do," the girl answered. "But there are times in the life of a man when he has to hurt somebody else. It comes down to this choice—either he suffers a little, or a great many other people suffer a lot. You've got to decide which way you want it to be. You've got to—" She broke off, a little cry of shock forming on her lips as the latch clicked.

The door stood opened. Ben stood there.

"Boss says bring him in." Ben looked at the girl, then at Hogarth-Magruder. He moved toward the engineer-scientist.

Something came out of the girl's clothes, what it was Magruder could not tell. A thin gadget shaped like a very small pistol appeared in her hands. She didn't seem to point it, there was no explosion, no sound of any kind, no flash of light, no evidence whatsoever to indicate that a weapon had been used or even that the object she held was a weapon.

BEN SEEMED to come unjointed in the middle of a shambling step. Every muscle in his gorilla body seemed to go out of order at the same instant. He whimpered once, a sound torn from the depths of clogged vocal chords, and slumped forward to the floor, a sound of quivering, helpless flesh.

Magruder's eyes went down to Ben. In his mind somewhere pain moved but there moved also the memory of how Ben had held him helpless and had probably held Werken helpless too, and others as well. Somehow the sight of Ben suffering did not hurt him as much as it would have once. There was a law governing pain, he recognized. If you deliberately hurt somebody and got hurt in return, you only got what was coming to you.

His mind was fumbling its way around a mental block that had been there since childhood. "Is—is he dead?" Somehow even the thought of death did not hurt too much.

"No. Just unconscious. He will recover in a few minutes."

"That's a handy gadget you have there."

"You ought to know, you invented it."

"I?" He sought through his memory for evidence of this startling fact. To the best of his knowledge, he had never invented a weapon.

"You made the basic discovery," the girl replied. "Your brother took the basic idea and devised a weapon to fit."

"I see." Others were making weapons out of his discoveries. The thought shocked him.

The girl spoke. "He's waiting for Ben to bring you in. In a few minutes, he will come looking for you." Urgency sounded in her voice.

He slid his feet off the edge of the table, stood up. "Lend me that gadget," he said.

"What?" the girl whispered.

"We wouldn't want to keep Skel waiting, would we?"

"You're going to face him?"

"I either have to face him or run from him. I ran from him once and it didn't do any good. It won't do any good to run again. Will you lend me—"

Silently she handed him the oddly shaped little weapon.

CHAPTER SIX

SOUNDLESSLY Magruder opened the door of the laboratory an inch, looked through. He caught a glimpse of a large table that looked as if it belonged in the operating room of a modern hospital. At the head of the operating table standard equipment for administering an anesthetic was visible, with additions that no hospital had ever used. Beyond the table was an elaborate switchboard covered by meters and switches. Red needles were quivering on the dials. Somewhere a droning motor generator was in operation.

Magruder knew as well as his tricky memory let him know the purpose of this equipment. He had invented most of it, devised it, put it together. It could be used to block out all memories, to change the flow of nervous current within the brain itself, to short-circuit delicate neuronic synapses and bring others into existence. With it, the personality of a man could be completely changed. Magruder had used it on himself, with the controls set to function automatically, when he had blocked out his own memories and had given himself the identity of Ed Hogarth. He had planned the whole layout with a definite purpose in mind.

Staring at the meters was Sam.

Skeleton was bending over checking equipment under the operating table itself. Neither of the two men heard the door open wide. Magruder cuddled the little weapon in his hand, spoke.

"Hello, Skel. I always thought you looked like a skeleton didn't I, and I always called you Skel? Odd that the old name should have come up out of my mind the first time I saw you again."

Like a startled cat tossed on top of a hot stove, Skeleton jerked himself up from under the operating table. His eyes popped so wide open that Magruder had the impression they were about to burst from his skull. "How did you get here?"

"You surely know the answer to that, Skel."

Skeleton knew the answer. Anger moved in a red tide across his face. "That little witch. I should have—"

"Don't blame her, Skel. But you ought to give some consideration to the way she broke the control you thought you had over her."

"How did she do it?"

"I don't know, Skel, I haven't asked her. Skel—" Pleading sounded in his voice. "—why don't you be reasonable? We don't have to fight."

Deep in his heart, he knew he had no stomach for this fight, for this battle between brothers. Perhaps there was rivalry between brothers that hid a far fiercer struggle than rivalry but it did not exist in him. He was trying, and trying hard, to give Skeleton a chance. Perhaps he was playing the part of a fool, perhaps there was no hope that the distorted mind of his brother might be made straight again, but he could try. "Why can't we work together? Everything that we want to do, we can do."

"And let you be the boss?"

In the hot jarring tone of Skeleton's voice Magruder caught a clear glimpse of the hate that festered in his brother's heart.

"Everything I did, you could do better," Skeleton spat out the words. "Do you think I am going to forget that? Do you think I am going to forgive the fact of your superiority?"

In that moment, Magruder knew there was no hope. Physically and mentally, Skeleton was warped past all hope of reason. There was only one way to change Skeleton. "I'm sorry," Magruder said.

"You're not sorry, you're licked," Skeleton answered. "You know it and all you're trying to do is to talk me into something.

You may have gotten loose but you're still in this cave. You'll never get out unless I let you out."

"Won't I?" Magruder answered.

"You never will. Come on, Sam, help me grab him." The two men started forward.

"Stand back!" Magruder exposed the weapon in his hand.

SKELETON saw it, stopped for a second, then moved forward again.

Magruder pressed the trigger. He felt a surge of warmth in his hand, knew that the weapon was functioning.

"You damned fool." Skeleton's voice rose harsh and sharp. "I guessed you had that. Do you suppose I would give to anyone a weapon that could be used against me?"

The weapon had no effect whatsoever. Magruder flung it at Skeleton, stepped back, slammed shut the heavy door, dropped the lock into place. Skeleton pounded on the other side.

"Come on," Magruder said to the girl.

From the other side of the door, Skeleton's voice rose. "You fool! You will never get out of here alive."

"He's telling the truth," the girl spoke. Her voice was dull and without hope. "Every exit from this cave is blocked by a web of energy beams at so high a level as to be undetectable. Turned on at full force, they will instantly clot the blood of anyone who blunders into them. He can turn them on from in there."

"Well," Magruder said. He sensed hopelessness in the girl. Her voice came again. "If we stay here, he is certain to capture us. The weapon he gave me, which I thought could be used against him, is nothing in comparison to some of the other weapons he has. He will take us or he will kill us. He won't care much which it is."

"I see," Magruder said.

Silence came from behind the door.

"He has already turned on the energy beams at the exits," the girl spoke.

"If we had time—" Magruder said.

"But there is no time. There is not thirty minutes, twenty minutes, not ten minutes. He can get out of that operating room."

Magruder felt her hopelessness. For the first time in his life, the same feeling moved in him. Here at last was the end of the trail. All his life he had been in conflict with Skeleton. He had tried every conceivable method of winning his brother's friendship and he had failed. Now he had to pay the price of failure. He shuddered at the thought of that price. Sweat formed on his face and he lifted his hand to push it away.

In the moonstone setting the tiny arrow caught his eye. Deep in those pale depths the microscopic signboard glinted, pointing the way to—what?

At the sight, his treacherous, drug-impaired memory finally, reluctantly, gave up the last remnant of fact it had been concealing. Suddenly he began to laugh. The girl stared at him as if she did not understand what had happened.

"We must follow the arrow," he said.

"Follow the arrow?" She didn't understand.

"Yes. It is possible, if James Kelvey Magruder is actually the mental giant that you—and some others—think him to be that he may have anticipated this moment and this situation, when he would be beaten and without hope, and taken steps to meet it."

She still did hot understand. He did not attempt to explain.

Through twisting, turning caves that water had dug out of limestone rock, along pathways where once slaves had fled in their long journey toward freedom, hastily, as fast as they could move, they made their way. Passing out of the lighted area, they moved through tunnels as dark as the inside of midnight itself, following and consulting a microscopic arrow in a ring, an arrow that told them the right way at every turn, at every division of the caves, the man with the highest IQ ever known on earth, and a frightened bewildered girl. She did not know where she was going or what would happen to her at the end of the journey. She did not care. She had come here seeking this man and she had found him.

WHERE HE went, she went. That was all she asked. He noticed that she kept in front of him, always, and realized the reason. "Girl." His voice was hard and sharp. He grabbed her shoulders.

"Please don't argue," she answered. "I don't know where you are going and I don't care. But I do know this—that any moment we may stumble on a web of radiation—"

"I realize that now."

"That's why I am staying in front of you," she spoke. "If I die, it doesn't matter. If you trip a booby trap, the whole world will be the loser. I'm only trying to trip the trap first, to give you a warning."

"Girl... Grace..."

"Please don't argue. I feel very proud that here in this place I can take this chance in the hope of helping you."

He tried to speak and his voice caught. Here was loyalty such as he had never dreamed about, loyalty not only to him but to an ideal.

He caught her by the shoulders. "I can't let you do this. We'll go together. If Skel has hidden a booby-trap in this pathway—" His voice caught again. "In that case, we'll still go together."

He could feel her body tremble as she walked beside him through the darkness. Behind them, far away, a raucous voice shrilled. Skeleton had escaped and was searching for them. His yell was like a sound from another world—a world of tortured souls.

Deep in the ring, the arrow glowed, pointing the way before them. Then it went out. Deep in this throat, Magruder chuckled. "We're there. And we didn't blunder into any death traps."

He moved confidently into the darkness. His fingers found a wall, then a ledge, then tiny depressions on that ledge, depressions into which the fingers fitted. Somewhere behind that wall, he knew hidden instruments were checking the fingers in the depressions, making certain they were the *right* fingers. He pressed down. The instruments finished their checking, the ledge moved backward and away. A gust of air pushed at them. A switch clicked. Lights sprang into existence, revealing a large room filled with electrical equipment. The girl cried out.

"You were right when you said there was probably a trigger here somewhere that was designed to give me back my memories. This is the trigger. If I returned here as Ed Hogarth, I would not know this place existed. But as soon as I entered the caves, the arrow would begin to glow in the ring. Following it, I would be brought here. The minute I reached this place, a post-hypnotic suggestion would take effect in my mind." His voice faltered as his memory gave back to him the plans he had made in the days when he was James Kelvey Magruder.

"But you had already remembered," the girl spoke.

"In part but not in full. The first time I saw the arrow, I did not know what it was. That was before Skel had given me the amytal. The second time I saw the arrow I knew immediately that this place existed. Go in, Grace. This is mine, I built it in the old days. I think there is safety here even for us."

Behind them; in the tunnels a shout sounded. A light moved.

"What is in this place?" the girl asked.

"Among other things, weapons. Although I hate to admit it, even I once built weapons. Or at least a few of them. I think one of them will stop even Skel."

They stepped inside. Magruder moved swiftly to the panels that lined one side of the room. Switches snapped under his fingers. On gray glass screens dots began to swirl.

"It looks like television," the girl spoke.

"Not quite that. Watch…"

THE SWIRLING dots firmed and revealed a picture of a cave, this cave, somewhere. Magruder changed a setting. The picture changed. Another part of the cave was revealed. He changed the setting a third time. Skeleton and Sam appeared on the screen. Both clutched bulky-looking weapons of an odd shape.

At the sight of the men and of the weapons they carried, the girl shivered and moved closely to Magruder. He watched the screen. The weapons worried him. He knew nothing whatsoever about them. They might be death ray guns. Skel was certainly capable of developing such a weapon. They might be something else. What if his own weapons were inadequate?

From the top of the workbench he swept up a microphone. "Skel," he spoke softly.

On the screen, Skeleton jumped. He had heard the voice calling him. To him, it seemed to come from empty air. "Where are you?"

"Never mind. Are you willing to call everything quits, Skel?"

"Quits, hell. You're bluffing." Skel's eyes were darting everywhere as he tried to locate the source of the voice speaking to him.

"Last chance, Skel," Magruder said.

"Go to hell!"

"I'm sorry, Skel. It won't hurt long." On the nearest panel, Magruder gently pressed a red button.

Somewhere outside the area where they stood, all the imps of hell began to scream, to yell and dance and gibber. A thousand fire sirens, the scream of a thousand dive bombers converging on the same target, were in that sound. It combined the howl of the hunting wolf and the scream of the deer the wolf had brought to earth. The girl grabbed at her ears, trying to stuff her fingers into them. Magruder's face whitened.

The roar of the wind in storm, the howl of the tornado, the crash of lightning, the bull notes of thunder, rolled through the cavern. For a split second, the sound remained constant. Then it began to go up the scale, to move out of hearing. It went out in a high thin whistle that sounded like a million teakettles hissing all at once. Then it was gone too high for the human ear to register.

For a moment it remained in existence, a howling, torturing wail that the ear did not hear. But the girl heard it. It seemed to reach directly into her mind without going through the ear at all. Her lips moved in a scream. Magruder took his finger off the button.

In the quietness that followed they could hear the fall of chunks of rock loosed from the roof of the cave by the blast of noise that had roared through here.

"Super sound," Magruder whispered. "It will knock out of operation for a space of hours the motor nerve system of any living creature caught in it. I don't think even Skel will be able to resist it. I know perfectly well I couldn't."

The screens revealed two men down, unmoving. "Come on," Magruder said. From a cabinet, he scooped another weapon. "This time I take no chances." He picked up a light. They moved out into the cave.

Under the bright beam of the flashlight two bodies were revealed. Sam and Skel, both completely paralyzed.

"Sorry, Skel," Magruder whispered. "But it had to be this way."

Skeleton did not answer. Not a muscle moved in his limp body. But from his hot eyes, rage looked out, indicating the turmoil taking place in the brain inside.

Magruder bent, lifted him from the floor.

"What are you going to do with him?" the girl spoke.

"The same thing he tried to do to me, the thing I had in mind to do to him when I designed that operating table and memory block equipment. Except that I am going to block out of his mind forever, every hostile impulse that ever energized a neuronic synapse, every hate he ever felt or ever can feel. I am going to change him, forever."

Very gently he carried the body of his brother through the dark tunnel.

MANY HOURS later, on the operating table where James Kelvey Magruder would have lain, Skeleton stirred and opened his eyes.

"Hi, Skel," Magruder said. His voice was very gentle, very soft. All his life, it seemed to him, he had waited for this moment. All hate and all possibility of hate had been left out of his emotional make-up. All the hate that might normally have gone into him, the sensitivity to frustration that results in hate, had gone into—his brother. There had been nothing he could do about it, until now. He waited with bated breath for Skel to recognize him. Would hate creep back into those black eyes? Would this experiment be a failure?

Skel sat up. He blinked at his brother. And yawned. "Hi, Jim. Is breakfast ready? I'm about starved."

His mind had gone back to his childhood, back to the days before hate had become a living flame within him. All that had happened to him since he and Jim Magruder had been kids together, he had forgotten. To him, life was starting all ever again, with this exception, that now he could grow again without hate in his heart.

James Kelvey Magruder took a deep breath. "It will be ready pretty soon, Skel," he said. This was perhaps the happiest moment of his life. He now had something he had always wanted, the friendship of his brother. He had something else too, he remembered. He grinned. "Come with me, Skel. I've got somebody I want you to meet."

She was waiting outside the cave, sitting in the doorway of the lab built against the blue. She rose to her feet and came running toward them, a glad cry forming on her lips. At the sight of Skeleton, she stopped.

"You have nothing to fear," Magruder said. "Grace, I would like you to meet my brother, Skel."

"How do you do?" the girl said. She was irresolute, in doubt as to what she should say or do.

"Skel," Magruder continued. "I would like you to meet the finest woman who ever lived."

Skel's hand came out, a grin appeared on his face. He stared admiringly at the girl, with no memory that he had ever seen her before. He jabbed his brother in the ribs. "You can pick 'em, Jim," he said.

"Can't I, though?" Magruder said. He held out his arm. The girl flew to it. Together, arm in arm, the three of them walked out of the building.

The sky in the east was flushed with the light of dawn. In the scrub oak growth along the bluff a mockingbird was singing her bright song in honor of the new day.

"Daylight," Magruder said. "I didn't realize so much time had passed."

Standing a little distance off, staring at them, were two people. Magruder looked at them. He had never seen them before. "Who are they?" he said.

"A couple of your friends," the girl answered.

"Friends?" James Kelvey Magruder had never had any friends. He hardly knew what the word meant. "But I don't know them."

"A great many people whom you don't know, know you," the girl said. "They find evidence that you exist and come here searching for you. These two came last night. Will you talk to them?"

"Sure," Magruder answered. Two years before, he would probably have run from them, evaded them. But he was no longer evading the people who came seeking him. He knew now what they really wanted, help with problems, help in solving the mysteries that confronted science, help on the long, long journey the human race makes. He was a superman, the scope of his mind was greater than any man's, but he was blood brother, he was kith and kin, with all men. As their bodies could be hurt, so his body could be hurt, as their minds could be twisted, so his mind could be twisted. Their pain was his pain, their hurt was his hurt, their anguish was his anguish, their search his search, their journey—was his journey, too. "Sure, I'll talk to them. And in the future, anyone who comes to me will be welcome wherever I am."

The girl's smile was a glorious thing. Skeleton's face twisted into a grin as if even he had found here at long last the one thing he had always wanted. In the east the sun poked a red rim over the edge of the world. A golden light poured into the little valley. And very slowly James Kelvey Magruder began to smile.

AND so it was.

And so it is.

And you who read these words, if you can understand the signs aright, if you can sift the evidence fine enough, if you can read the road markers along the way, and if in your heart you want to know him, you can find somewhere upon this earth the habitation of James Kelvey Magruder. It's here, somewhere, today. All you have to do, if you want to meet and know a superman, is to find him. And then, perhaps, walk with him on the long, long journey the human race makes.

THE END

This Way Out

How can you tell a kid crime doesn't pay when he finds it easy to walk through solid walls?

CHAPTER ONE

"YOU WAIT here, Jet," the kid, Dennis O'Liam, said. The man known as Wade Jethro nodded. If he was uneasy, if he was colder than could be accounted for by the chilling autumn rain driven across the night by the slanting northwest wind, he kept all sign of his uneasiness out of his voice and off his face. A service drive led from the alley to the back end of the grocery store. There a flaring electric light threw a broad circle of illumination over unloading platforms piled high with empty fruit and vegetable crates. On each side of the driveway was a high board fence. The raindrops came down through the circle of light like miniature space ships hurrying home to earth. Jethro wondered how long it would be before his teeth started chattering. Did anybody ever really become accustomed to this climate? He coughed and the sound was flung back to him by the rising wind.

"You need a warmer coat, Jet," the kid said anxiously.

"I need a lot of things worse than I need a coat," Jethro answered.

The kid was silent for a moment, then his voice came again. "Tomorrow's Saturday, see? This store does a big business on Saturday. They open early and they got to have a lot of money on hand to cash paychecks. Since the banks don't open on Saturday, they get the money in on Friday."

"But it's in the safe," Jethro protested.

The kid spat. "Hell, I know that. Don't let it worry you any, Jet." He was about fifteen years old but he spoke with the calm certainty of a much older person.

"How are you going to open the safe?" Jethro asked.

"That's my worry."

"How are you going to get into the store? The doors are locked, the windows are barred, and there are probably burglar alarms all over the joint."

"I'll get in," Dennis O'Liam said. He seemed very sure of himself.

Hearing that sureness, Jethro shivered involuntarily. His teeth chattered, perhaps from the chill wind and the night, perhaps from some other cause. The kid was instantly sympathetic. "You need a new coat, Jet, you really do. We'll get it tomorrow tonight, if we get through here in time. A sheep-lined jacket. There's nothing like a sheep-skin-lined coat to keep you warm on winter nights. You can even sleep in it." He was enthusiastic about the idea.

"I'll get along," Wade Jethro said. "You don't need to rob this store just to get a coat for me, Dennis."

"A coat for you is just one of the things I want," the kid answered. "The MacClanahans ain't had any coal in two days and I don't think they've really had much to eat since the old man went on his last bender, over a week ago. Stella was looking mighty thin-faced and peaked this afternoon when I saw her. Of course, she didn't say anything. She wouldn't."

"The old man could go back to work," Jethro said.

"He could, but he won't, not as long as he can get hold of canned heat. Somebody has got to get some beans into them kids."

"But why are you elected to do it? There are agencies—"

"They're friends of mine and I stick by my friends," the kid said hotly. "And don't tell me anything about these relief agencies. Before they will do anything to help you they've got to ram their noses up to the hilt in your business. I don't want any help from them, and neither do the MacClanahans." His voice sounded much too bitter for a boy of fifteen.

WHAT experiences lay back of that bitterness? Jethro

wondered. He could guess at some of them. Hunger and heartache and despair and plain privation, tissue hunger for proteins, soul hunger for security, for a place in the world.

"But Dennis it isn't—ain't fair to let you burglarize this store for me. Dammit, I'm a grown man."

"Hell, you'll be earning your share," the kid growled. "You'll be the lookout for me. You'll earn that coat."

"But—"

"It couldn't be you're kicking because you've got a little streak of yellow in you somewhere?" the kid asked. A hard, suspicious note crept into his voice.

"Hell, no!" Jethro answered promptly. Doubled into a fist, his right hand came out of his pocket. "Listen, you smart punk, I'll knock your head off if you try to talk like that!"

The kid laughed. "That's the way to talk, Jet." He wasn't much worried by the threat but he said nothing more about Jethro being yellow and the older man did not force the issue. "I just don't like to have you take any chances, especially when you won't tell me how you're going to get into the store," he said.

"I'm not taking any chances," the kid answered. "I'm going in now. You stay out of sight. When you hear me whistle, like this—" he whistled softly, a thin liquid note that hardly seemed to disturb the air--"you answer me, if it's all right for me to come out."

"Out of where?" Jethro questioned. The kid didn't answer. "Remember, I'm depending on you to let me know if the coast is clear before I come out. I can't know, for sure, if everything is all right." He put a lot of emphasis on this point. Jethro took up his position beside a telephone pole in the driveway just off the alley and watched the kid walk away.

The bulb over the backdoor of the grocery store cast a brilliant glow straight down. The kid, walking straight toward the light, was clearly visible. He was wearing a sock cap and his hands were thrust into the pockets of his coat. Walking with his head thrust forward, his shoulders hunched down, he looked a little like a gnome about some strange business in the night. Jethro, colder than the rain and the wind made necessary, watched him.

Then didn't watch him, didn't see him.

The kid was gone. Gone from sight, gone from the alley, gone from the rain-streaked night. Gone.

Whether there had been a hole in the fence, a board loose or missing, and the kid had slipped through this hole, Jethro could not tell. All he could say for certain was that he had been watching Dennis O'Liam walk down a driveway toward the backdoor of the grocery store he intended to burglarize—that he had seen the kid, and then suddenly hadn't seen him.

The disappearance had been as subtle as the passing of a raindrop, something that came and went before you saw it.

WADE JETHRO was suddenly shivering and his teeth were chattering in the rising wind. His hand in his pocket wrapped itself around the butt of the gun, he clutched it as if the feel of the weapon was somehow reassuring, something that could be clung to when nothing else was certain. Like a drowning man grabbing at a straw, or a floating branch, Jethro grabbed the gun.

Was this the *tsi* effect in operation?

Or was it something else? Had the kid actually slipped through a hole in the fence?

"I'm not sure," Jethro said to himself. "I've got to be sure. I've *got* to." He said it over and over again.

The alley was empty, deserted, and very lonely. He had for company his chattering teeth, raindrops, and wind. Fear was in him, such fear as he had never known. Or was this fear actually eagerness? He did not know. But he was not ashamed of it, which ever it was. A man who was not afraid now in this moment was not capable of fear.

Wind blew slanting rain across the driveway. Jethro put his back against the telephone post, pressed hard against it, as if in it he had found a second thing to cling to, a substantial reality in the midst of a night that had suddenly become unreal. He waited.

There was no sound of breaking glass, as he had halfway expected, such a sound as might come from a window being surreptitiously broken. There was no subdued crash of breaking wood, as might come from a door being forced.

There was nothing except the wind blowing rain through the night and the sound of tires rolling on wet pavement on the other side of the store. Somewhere a car honked impatiently. Off in the distance a searchlight fingered into the sky, an advertising stunt—or was it a symbol of the human mind trying to peer into darkness, into the night, seeking to penetrate the fringe of mysteries sensed but not seen?

Behind Jethro a step sounded. He turned slowly.

Light glinting from the black wet slicker, a nightstick thrust under his arm, a policeman stood there.

CHAPTER TWO

THE COP stood like a statue guarding the night. As if he smelled the presence of wrongdoing and was trying hard to locate the source from which it came, he swung his head slowly from side to side, like a dog trying to pick up a trail in the air.

The pole was between the cop and Wade Jethro. The latter did not move except to press himself closer against the pole. He hoped fervidly that Dennis would not whistle now. The whistle could tell the cop that someone was hiding here and he would come to investigate.

As if he could not quite locate the source of the wrongdoing he thought he smelled, the policeman turned from the driveway and started into the alley.

In another minute he would be gone.

Simultaneously the kid whistled.

Jethro pressed himself hard against the pole, hoping against hope that the cop had not heard the sound. The whistle had a strange quality about it, as if it had come from some great distance. It was both clear and not clear.

The cop heard the whistle. He turned instantly, stood peering down the driveway toward the back of the grocery store. Again he stood like a statue guarding the night. But now the statue was alert, now he knew that someone was near.

Against the post, Jethro cursed silently, all the oaths he knew. He did not blame the kid for whistling. He blamed fate, bad luck, the vagaries of a shifting pattern that had brought a policeman into this alley on this night.

Of course, the cop probably made nightly rounds through this alley, but they should have determined in advance the time of his rounds. They hadn't. And this had happened.

The kid did not whistle again. He was waiting in hiding somewhere for Jethro's whistle telling him the coast was clear.

The cop's flashlight appeared, fingered down the driveway. Jethro hugged the post. The light went past him.

Far off in the windy night a new sound appeared—the distant wail of a siren. Ambulance, fire truck, or squad car? The sound was coming closer. The cop heard it. He lifted his head to listen. The siren wailed to a halt on the main street directly in front of the grocery store.

The cop, muttering beneath his breath, turned and trotted out of the driveway.

Again the soft whistle sounded. This time Jethro answered it.

"Jet, where are you?" Dennis called. He was coming fast along the alley.

"Here," Jethro answered softly. He had not seen the kid appear but he had no time to wonder about this now.

"Come on, get out of here," Dennis panted. "I tripped a burglar alarm inside the store, one that doesn't ring in the store itself but that lets go an alarm in a private exchange. They call the cops and the cops put it on the air. They get here within minutes that way. Come on, Jet."

The kid was moving fast along the driveway. Jethro followed. They reached the corner, dived into the alley, heading toward the side street.

"Halt!" a voice sounded.

It was the cop. He had run into the main alley and had hid there, certain that the siren would flush from hiding anyone concealed in the vicinity.

"Run like hell," Dennis O'Liam whispered.

THE KID was a furtive shadow running silently along the alley. Wade Jethro was a bigger shadow who did not run so silently. The cop heard them.

"Halt!" he yelled again. A gun exploded.

"Keep going," Dennis whispered. "The first shots are always in the air."

Crash! the second shot came.

This time the bullet drove straight down the center of the alley. It passed between the two of them, howling.

"That one wasn't in the air," Jethro gasped.

"Quick, in here," the kid answered. He ducked to one side, down what looked like a passage leading to the next street. Jethro followed. A sidewalk was under his feet, apparently it was a connecting crosswalk that led between high board fences—

Crash!

In the darkness, Dennis ran headlong into a barrier of some kind, apparently a wire gate.

"Are you hurt?" Jethro asked anxiously.

"Just—got the wind—"

The kid was down on the ground. Jethro bent to pick him up. Footsteps sounded in the alley. The kid was gasping for breath. "If he comes in here, shoot him."

"But—"

"You got a gun, ain't you?"

"Yes."

"Then shoot him."

Jethro tried to open the gate. It was locked. They had run headlong into a trap. He pulled the gun from his pocket.

The beam of the flashlight came along the walk, outlining

them with blinding radiance.

"Get your hands up!"

Jethro was caught and he knew it. He lifted his hands in a waving motion that tossed the gun over the fence. Better not to be caught with a gun in his possession. The cop approached.

"Get your hands up, both of you."

"I've got my hands up. Dennis, do what the policeman says."

There was no answer. Jethro suddenly realized he was alone in this passageway.

In that moment, he almost forgot about the policeman. Dennis O'Liam was gone. Gone from this closed passage, gone silently, gone in a way that no one had ever used before. Jethro hardly realized what was happening when the cop put handcuffs on him.

"Where's the other one?" the cop demanded.

"What are you talking about?" Jethro began again to get his wits about him.

"The other one, who ever it was with you."

"Are you crazy? There wasn't anyone with me. I just stepped into the alley for a personal reason when you started hollering and shooting. What's coming off when an honest citizen can't step into an alley—" He didn't really expect to be believed. And he wasn't.

"Aw, shut up," the cop said. "You come along with me."

THE POLICE searched the neighborhood. They found the gun. When the owner of the grocery store arrived and checked the safe they discovered that over seven hundred dollars was missing. Under these circumstances, they put Jethro in the back of the squad car and took him to the police station.

But they didn't book him right away. After all, the missing money had not been found in his possession. The gun had been on the other side of the fence and while they suspected he had thrown it there, they couldn't prove he had. While he had no record in their files, the whole situation added up to one conclusion—that he was a two-bit crook who had blown in from out of town, maybe he was a small-time burglar, maybe he specialized in grocery store hold-ups, they didn't know what he did, but whatever it was, it wasn't important. He was just another damned nuisance on his way to get himself a record for petty offenses.

This was the way they characterized Wade Jethro. They knew just exactly what to do with him and about him, to beat him up so badly that he would shiver the next time he saw a policeman. "When you can't convict 'em of anything important, run 'em out of town," was the motto of this police department.

They took Jethro to a back room and a plainclothes man with a face that looked as if he had been run over by a coal truck told him to sit down.

He knew exactly what was coming. He didn't like it. Reaching into his pocket, he unpinned the little badge and held it in the palm of his hand.

At the sight of that badge, the plainclothes man did a fast double take. He looked at it, looked again, then looked at Jethro as if he did not believe his eyes.

"Sometimes you damned fools catch something in a back alley that you're not looking for and don't know how to handle," Jethro said. "Sometimes a damned idiot who looks exactly like you is going to interfere in matters so far above his head that he has no idea whatsoever of them—and get himself kicked right in the face."

Probably the plainclothes man did not understand half of what he heard—the words were beyond grasp—but he got the main idea.

"Huh?"

"Take this badge to your captain."

"Huh? I mean—maybe we made a mistake—"

"You're making it bigger every time you open your mouth. Take this badge to your captain." Jethro had changed, somehow, very suddenly. His voice had become hard and crisp, the tone commanding. The plainclothes man took the badge and hurried from the room. Jethro sat in the chair and waited. The plainclothes man returned in a few minutes. "The captain will see you at once, sir," he said. He practically bowed Jethro out of the room.

THE CAPTAIN was a big man with a great thatch of almost pure white hair. The plainclothes man introduced them. The captain got up to shake hands. He offered Jethro a chair and a cigar. The little badge was lying in the middle of his desk. The captain's gaze went wonderingly over Jethro. "This badge says FBI—NSD," he said. "I understand the FBI part, but the NSD I don't get."

"Federal Bureau of Investigation National Security Division," Jethro answered. "Call the local offices of the FBI. They will explain it to you."

"Sure, sure, I would have to check anyhow," the captain said fretfully. He picked up a phone, dialed a number. Describing the badge and Wade Jethro minutely, he held a lengthy conversation with someone on the other end of the wire. Finally he hung up.

"They say there are some NSD men in town, but they don't know what they're doing here."

"I called in to let them know I was here," Jethro said.

"They also said they would take orders from you," the captain continued. There was wonder and a trace of awe in his voice.

"They will do just that," Jethro said. "The question is—will you?"

The captain twisted uneasily in his chair. "Hell, man, the boys picked you up near the scene of a burglary. Somebody was with you, but you refused to name him."

"Do you want me to name him?"

"Of course. We're willing to cooperate with the government men but we want a little co-operation in return. At least, we would like to know what the hell is going on, so we can keep our noses clean."

"The person with me was Dennis O'Liam," Jethro said.

"*No,*" the captain said. The tone of his voice said that he wished now he hadn't been told who was with this NSD agent. Irritation settled itself in a heavy clamp on his face. "Is that screwball kid loose again? We sent him to the reformatory—"

"He got out," Jethro said.

The expression on the captain's face said that he would just as soon have learned that the devil was loose in his precinct. "Did he burglarize that store?"

"I'm not going to appear as a witness against him."

"I didn't ask you that, I asked you if he had burglarized the store?"

"I didn't see him do it," Jethro answered. He lifted his hand, to halt this line of questioning. "Please, captain, there is more at stake here than simple burglary."

"I guess there must be, if your outfit is in on it," the captain ruminated. "But that kid just beats hell out of me. We've had him in this station ten times if we've had him in here once, charged with everything from breaking glass in automobiles to burglary. We made the last burglary charge stick because we caught him with the money on him, and for once, he didn't get loose from us."

"I gather he has gotten loose from you pretty regularly. How does he do it?"

"I wish I knew." Baffled anger showed on the captain's face. He balled his hand into a fist and brought it down heavily on the top of his desk. "Do you know that at least twice the boys have picked him up and put him in the paddy wagon and started him toward the station and when they got here, he wasn't in the wagon?"

"It sounds like a good trick. Didn't you have a man riding in the back with him?"

"Not those two times we didn't. We finally learned that the only way we could bring him in was to put cuffs on him and cuff him to an officer."

"Um," Jethro said.

"And that's not all." An expression of disbelief sensed on the captain's face as if his features were trying to say he personally did not believe what he was going to say, and that he didn't expect the NSD agent to believe it, but he was going to say it anyhow. "The boys brought him in one night, for chunking half a brick at one of them, and being sassy in general, and I personally locked him in a cell. I picked out our very best cell, one that has held some mighty big hot-shots safely." He paused as if he could not bring himself to say this after all.

"And what happened?" Jethro encouraged.

"The next morning that there cell was empty. The kid was gone."

Jethro sat very still beside the desk. Evidence such as this, plus what he already had, was almost incontrovertible. Suddenly he saw everything. Hope pounded in him as powerful as the beat of a rising tide. He pushed the tide down. In this matter, he had to be certain, he had to be sure. "How do you think he got out?" he questioned.

"At first, I thought somebody had turned him out. I took the whole blamed staff here, from the desk sergeant right on down to the turnkeys, and put every man of them back to pounding a beat. Then I brought in a new set. Then I brought Dennis in and again locked him in a cell." He shook his head. His voice dropped to a whisper. "He wasn't there the next morning."

"Houdini could do the same trick," Jethro said.

"Not out of my cells, Houdini couldn't!" the captain roared.

CHAPTER THREE

THE NEXT morning, Wade Jethro was discharged from the police station. He spent the night in a cell and he could have been discharged the night before, if he had requested, but the normal routine would have been to discharge him the next morning. He preferred to stick by normal routine, so that Dennis would have no reason to suspect him of being what he was. The police gave him back his gun and his badge and he carefully pinned the latter out of sight in his pocket.

He went immediately to that section of the city where Dennis O'Liam lived. It lay along the bank of the river below the main city. Railroad tracks ran through it, freight trains thundered through this section at all hours, passengers in observation cars of crack streamliners wondered what manner of people lived in this collection of huts, tents, half-tents, crazy houses made of tin cans flattened out and nailed on boards, houses made out of car siding, tar-paper roofing, anything. Whatever could be stolen, whatever could be carried away, whatever could be found along the railroad tracks, was used to build houses here.

In other days, this section had been called Hooverville, but it had existed long before Mr. Hoover had been president of the country, and it continued to exist long after he had passed from the political scene.

Here was trouble's home, here was the last outpost of life itself, here the big problem was to stay alive. Here the problem was not respectability, the problem was to find enough to eat, coal to burn in a wretched huddle of iron that you call a stove, and enough clothes to ward off the fiercer blasts of the stinging winter wind.

Here was thievery and the drinking of canned heat, here was the smoking of marijuana and the taking of cocaine, if you could come by it. Here was destitution and despair, here you drank yourself into insensibility as often as you could in the hope that while you were insensible, you might stumble under a freight train or fall from the bank into the flooded river—and die and not have to face tomorrow.

Here was the home of Dennis O'Liam.

Hooverville stretched for blocks along the bank of the river, a vast collection of huts threatening to fall down. There were no proper streets, instead there were lanes, like runways for rabbits in a briar patch. In this brew of misery, Dennis O'Liam was more of a hero than ever Robin Hood had been in

Sherwood Forest, though for the same basic reasons.

WALKING ACROSS the railroad tracks and entering the fringe of the district, Jethro saw one reason why Dennis was a hero here. Kids, playing in the littered runway that passed as a street, scattered in front of him. They knew him, he knew them, they were the MacClanahans. He saw Stella watching him. Unlike the others in this litter, tow-headed and round-faced, she was thin faced; and her hair was black and straight. What cuckoo had laid this egg in the MacClanahan nest, he wondered? It did not matter. All nine of the kids were in the street this morning, ranging from Stella, the oldest, to the baby, who was just learning to toddle. They were always dirty, always noisy, always ragged. This morning they were dirtier than usual. But the dirt was concentrated on their faces. Jethro saw that the dirt was actually chocolate. From the baby up to Stella, their faces were smeared with it. An empty five-pound candy box lay in the street. The baby was rooting in the second box. Jethro grinned at them and walked on past.

The action was typical of Dennis O'Liam, to steal money to buy food for a raft of hungry kids, and then instead of the hamburger and the bread and milk they so obviously needed, to buy them chocolate candy instead.

Jethro went in the back door of the shack where Dennis lived. The kid's mother was dead, his father was unknown; he lived here alone. For the past week, Wade Jethro had lived with him.

Dennis was buried under the covers of the cot; sound asleep. Pulled out of its wrappings and tossed across the back of a chair, was a brand new sheepskin coat.

At the sound of Jethro's entry, Dennis instantly awakened.

"Hi, Jet," he called out. "There's your coat." He waved an arm toward the chair.

"I see it," Jethro answered. "It looks like a dandy. Thanks."

"I got it at an army goods store last night. It's a flyer's coat and it ought to be warm. How'd you get loose from the cops?"

"They didn't have any real evidence against me."

"You didn't get beat up any." The kid surveyed him with a critical eye.

"I was lucky," Jethro answered. "Is there anything to eat?"

"Some bread and beer sausage."

"Thanks." Jethro moved toward the littered table at the rear of the room, cut himself a slice of beer sausage and slipped it between two slices of bread. "How'd you get away last night?" His voice was casual to the point of indifference.

"You mean, when the cop had us cornered?"

"Yeah."

The kid seemed to meditate. Jethro was holding his breath but he was taking pains to conceal the fact. He speared another slice of beer sausage, munched heartily. "Good sausage, this."

"I went the back way," the kid said.

Jethro ate beer sausage. "The *back way?* What's that?"

"That's what I call it," Dennis answered. He was still in the bed with the quilt drawn up tight around him.

"I don't get it," Jethro said. "Is that the way you got out of the cell at the police station?"

"Huh? How'd you know about that?"

"They were talking about you, at the station. I overheard 'em. Did you get into the store the same way?"

"Yeah."

"How do you work this *back way* trick?"

THE KID'S casual manner was a solid imitation of Jethro. "I don't really know. You're asking a hell of a lot of questions, Jet? Why don't you just let things ride?"

"Am I?"

"Yeah. Especially for a guy who spends the night in the police station and comes back without even a black eye. Jet, you wouldn't be a damned dick, would you?"

"Huh?" Jethro's mouth hung open.

"Because I hate dicks, I hate 'em worse than I hate anything else on earth, except maybe cops. And if you're one—" The kid flung back the covers and swung his feet over the edge of the cot. He had a gun in his hand and he had had it there all along, hidden under the covers. He didn't point the gun but his voice was hard and flat. "Are you a dick?"

"Shut up," Jethro answered. "You make me sick at my stomach."

"Are you a damned dick?" The kid's voice had become a high falsetto.

"Yes," Jethro answered. For a moment he thought the kid was going to use the gun. The kid's face was wild. Wade Jethro continued to munch bread and beer sausage. "But not the kind you think," he said quietly. "I'm not going to put you in jail—or send you back to the reformatory. I'm not interested in the burglary you committed last night, or in any other burglary."

"You're not?" Dennis O'Liam seemed to find this hard to believe.

"No," Jethro said.

"What kind of a dick are you?"

"A kind you never heard of before." The kid was confused and doubtful, he could see. But he could also see that Dennis was becoming curious—for the same reason the police captain had become curious. What would a detective want with him, if not to question him for wrongdoing?

"You're telling the truth when you say you're not going to send me back to the reform school?"

"Absolutely."

"Then what do you want with me?"

"I'll tell you. But first—where are you going?"

Dennis had risen swiftly from the cot. He moved to the window, in which the single remaining pane of glass made a sort of peephole through which to view the activities on the runway outside. A little tinge of fear shot through Jethro. "What's wrong?" he asked.

"I thought I heard a noise," Dennis answered. "Somebody was around here last night looking for me."

"How do you know?"

"Stella told me."

"What did he look like?"

"They said he was a tall man with a face like a hog."

"A face like a hog—" In Wade Jethro fear rose again.

"Do you know who he is?"

"I'm not sure. What did the kids say about him?"

"Just that he came here last night looking for me."

"What did they tell him?"

"What do you think they told him? That they had never heard of me. They're my friends. They wouldn't tell nobody anything about me until they had asked me first. Stella was here waiting for me when I got back last night, to tell me about him."

Jethro conceived a sudden fondness for the MacClanahan kids. As a warning system, they were excellent—and well worth all the candy they cost. Dennis O'Liam came away from the window. He stood looking up at Wade Jethro. There was no threat on his pinched face, only curiosity. "What do you really want with me?"

"I want to know how you got into that grocery store last night."

"I thought so."

"Are you willing to tell me?" Every ounce of persuasion he possessed, he put into the tone of his voice.

DENNIS O'LIAM already had his mind made up. "Yes—providing you will tell me why you want to know."

"That's fair," Jethro answered. "I'll tell you—but it will have to be after you tell me."

"How do I know you'll tell me?"

Jethro pointed toward the gun the kid still held. "You've got that. If I don't play fair, use it."

The kid's eyes widened. "Do you mean it?"

"I mean it. How did you get into the grocery store?"

"I told you once—the back way."

"But that doesn't tell me anything really, it's just words with no real meaning. I watched you walk down the driveway toward the store. Suddenly I didn't see you any more. What happened when I didn't see you?"

"I guess maybe that was where I went into the back way," Dennis answered.

"And then what happened?"

"I walked into the store."

"Through the wall?"

"Yes." The answer was given calmly, with no hint of restraint. So far as Jethro could tell, Dennis O'Liam might have been answering a question about the weather. With equal calmness, Wade Jethro ignored the answer. "What's the back way like?" he said.

"It's hard to tell," Dennis answered. His face wrinkled into a frown. "It's kinda misty. Things like walls and doors and other solid things get sorta like clouds. I can walk right through them."

"The *tsi* effect!" Cold was on Jethro, such cold as he had never known. This—this ought to prove everything. But did it? Was he sure? What if the kid was lying? "Do you know what the back way really is?" he said.

"I—I guess I don't really know, Jet."

"How did you discover it?"

"Well—"

Jethro was too excited to wait for an answer. "Dennis, what is your earliest memory?"

"I don't understand, Jet?"

"What is the earliest picture you have in your mind, the first thing you can remember?"

The kid's face reflected his bewilderment. Jethro swore under his breath. "Excuse me, Dennis, I'm a fool. I'm going about this the wrong way. I'll try it another way. I'll say a word and you answer just as fast as you can with the first word that comes into your mind. Do you get it?"

"Well—"

"It's like this. If I say 'cat', what would be the first word that came into your mind?"

"Dog, I guess."

"Good. This is called an association test and the answers may be pretty important. But most important is for you to answer as fast as you can, without waiting to think. Are you willing to try this test?"

"What are you trying to find out, Jet?"

"Who and what you are. Ready?"

"I guess so."

"Boy."

"Girl."

"Run."

"Hide."

"Father."

Silence. Dennis tried to think. He had no answer.

"Sky."

"Fire." Something of triumph showed on the kid's face, then the triumph was gone. Pain replaced it.

"Did you ever see the sky on fire, Dennis?"

"Well, I—no. It seems I have, but I can't remember."

"Do you remember a time when you did not live here?"

THE KID stared at him. The eyes were blank. Back of them something groped as if the mind behind the eyes was trying to recall sights the eyes had once seen. "I—I can't remember. It seems that once I lived somewhere else—but I don't know where it was. Everything was bright then…"

He identified the sky with brightness and he knew how to use the tsi force but he did not know what it was. To the mind of Wade Jethro, the evidence was almost indisputable. "Dennis, do you know what you are?" he said.

"No," the kid answered.

"Do you know what I think you are?"

"How could I know, I'm not a mind reader?"

Wade Jethro hesitated. How could he talk, how could he say what had to be said? How could he find words to express the blinding truth? He was not sure yet, some links in the chain were missing. Did he know the truth? He suspected he knew only a part of it that much of it remained obscure, a hidden pattern with twists and turns and motivations he could not discern, but the truth he could see disturbed every atom of his mind. He could hear the alarms passing now, from molecule to molecule, from molecule to atom, through the dark and twisting recesses of his brain, each atom and each molecule catching the alarm and echoing it. He took a deep breath.

"Dennis, did you ever hear of the flying saucers?"

CHAPTER FOUR

"THE FLYING saucers? Them things everybody was seeing a few years ago?"

"They've been seen, off and on, for more than a few years. We have one account, ignored at the time but thoroughly explored later, which goes back fifteen years."

"Fifteen years. That's how old I am."

"Exactly." Grimness crept into Jethro's tone. "Fifteen years ago, not too many miles from here, a farmer rising early one morning found that something strange had appeared in his back pasture over night. Approaching it through the woods, he thought it was an airship of some kind, but later investigation—years later in this case—revealed that it must have been what was later called a flying saucer, one of the large disks, not the small ones. He said it was about a hundred feet in diameter, that it was kind of flat, that it had no wings, that it had rows of openings at the back—in short, his description tallies very close with much more recent descriptions made by competent observers. So far as we know, this is the only authentic instance of a flying saucer ever being seen on the ground."

The kid twisted uneasily. "What does all this have to do with me?"

"I'm coming to what it has to do with you. The farmer said that as he approached the ship, he saw somebody emerge from it and move toward him. Since he was alarmed, without knowing exactly why, he climbed a tree with thick foliage, hid himself there. He swears the creature from the saucer passed directly under him. He says it was so bundled in heavy clothing that he could not tell much about it, that it was wearing a mask of some kind, with a tube attached to a cylinder at its back— apparently to supply the creature with some gas it needed but which was lacking in our atmosphere. The farmer says this creature was carrying a basket and that in this basket were two living infants. He says he saw them move and heard them cry."

The kid's face was a twisted mask. Jethro's voice dropped almost to a whisper. "That farmer is still alive. I have talked to him. I would bet my life that he isn't lying. He says the creature was gone for almost an hour. When it returned, it had the basket, but it didn't have the two infants. Dennis, to the best of my knowledge and belief, and I have spent much time and effort in checking this story, *you were one of the infants in that basket.*"

"Gee whiz, Jet," the awed kid whispered. "Then that means I'm—"

"Not human," Wade Jethro said.

The kid breathed heavily but made no sound.

"Haven't you ever wondered whether or not you were a human being?"

"Well, something. But it seemed silly."

"Did you ever think that perhaps non-human creatures might appear on this earth?"

"Well, I've read some magazines that kinda gave me the idea. But why would these creatures from the saucer do anything like this, Jet? If they could land here at all, it would be much easier for them just to land—"

"Perhaps they can land but can they stay alive after they landed? Remember how the farmer said the creature was dressed, how it wore a gas mask? Maybe they made several exploratory trips to this planet, took air samples, checked the gravitation, soil, water, radiation, amount and kind of sunlight, and discovered that adults of their species could not live here. *But maybe they could condition children so the children could live here, so they could grow up here, if they were brought here as infants.* Maybe that's the only way they could get a real foothold on this planet, by sending infants here and letting them grow up!" The detective's voice vibrated with the impact of the idea.

"But wouldn't the children die?" Dennis protested.

"Probably many of them did die. But some of them might have been found and been adopted by human mothers, raised by them, taught what foods to eat and what to avoid, taught the patterns of human life and human conduct, taught the thousand and one things they need to know to live here, taught all this by human mothers, who discovered foundlings on their doorstep some morning."

THE KID twisted from foot to foot. "And you think this happened to me?"

"I'm almost convinced of it. I see no other solution."

"But I *look* human."

"Certainly. Any successful animal will look a lot like a human being simply because the human form is the one possible shape that permits an animal to do all the things it has to do in order to be successful. The fact that you look like a human being doesn't prove anything. The fact that you can use what you call the *back way* does prove something. Do you know what the *back way* actually is, Dennis?"

A shake of the head was his answer.

"It is either a dimensional transit or a time transit, or both. You go outside of time and space, outside the continuum, as we know it, in order to achieve this result. No human being has this function. Did you ever see a human being who could get into a locked store and out again without going through either a door or a window?"

"N-o."

"But *you* can do it."

The kid was silent, his face blank, his eyes alert and alive with conjecture. He still had the gun though he had apparently long since forgotten an about it. "If this is true, I'm not human. But you are human, Jet. The question in my mind is— What would a human being do when he discovers that I'm not like him?" Muscles moved in his hand as he tightened his grip on the gun.

"In my case, welcome you with open arms," Wade Jethro answered. "No, Dennis, you don't have to worry about me." He broke off as a shadow moved past the window and a quick knock sounded on the door. The knock was twice repeated, a signal of some kind. Dennis went quickly to open the door.

It was the girl, Stella, who entered. She looked questioningly at Jethro, then her eyes sought Dennis O'Liam. Some communication seemed to pass between them.

"What is it, Stella? Jet's all right. You can speak up."

"He's coming back, Dennis, the man who was looking for you last night. I just saw him crossing the railroad tracks."

"The man with the face like a hog?" Jethro asked quickly.

"Yes," the girl answered. She pointed through the window. "There he comes now."

Jethro took one look through the window and swore under his breath.

"Who is he, Jet? What does he want?" Dennis asked quickly. "He's not another saucer man, is he?"

"No. Dennis, you and Stella get out of sight. He's certain to come in here. But I'll get him away as quickly as I can."

Under the coat was a hole in the wall, which led to an adjoining shed. From there, they could slip into one of the runways, or, if they wished, they could stay in the shed.

They went through the hole like rabbits ducking out of sight at the approach of a hound.

FROM THE table Jethro swept the half-eaten sandwich. He had forgotten all about it until now. He was sitting at the table eating the sandwich when the stranger peered through the window. When the knock came, he went to answer the door.

"Hello, Jethro," the man at the door said.

"H'lo, Wilkinson," Jethro said. He squinted at the other's outfit, which looked as if it had been picked out of some rag barrel. "Good job they're doing in supply these days. Or did you actually get those clothes from a trash can?"

"I got 'em from supply," Wilkinson answered. "What are you doing here?"

"Waiting for the kid," Jethro answered, munching beer sausage. "You got something on your mind?"

"I've got a lot on my mind. A message has come down from the chief." He stuck his head inside the shack, looked around, then hastily stepped outside.

Jethro laughed. "Those old-maid tastes for good housekeeping will be the end of you some day."

"Have you been living here?"

"Sure, for a week."

"Well, you might have cleaned the place up a little."

"And get myself a reputation for being the cleanest man in Hooverville. In Rome, you got to live like the Romans."

"Well, I don't like it. Is there some place where we can talk. I've got news for you."

"Talk? Sure. Come in here. If the kid turns up while you're here, I'll introduce you as a pal on the jump from the law."

"In there?" Wilkinson wrinkled his nose. "Isn't there some other place?"

"We could take a walk down by the river," Jethro said casually.

"It would at least be cleaner there."

The river was in flood. A great tide of sullen yellow water was flowing past. Willows grew along the bank, their drooping limbs reaching down in the swirling yellow flood. Out in the current whole trees could be seen floating by, and the bloated carcasses of cattle.

"She's sure in flood," Jethro said. "What's up?"

"The chief wants a definite yes or no answer about this kid," Wilkinson replied.

Jethro laughed, a harsh sound. "They don't want much. Yes on what angle, no on what angle?"

"Yes or no on all angles. First, can he actually get into locked buildings, into closed vaults, through solid walls, through concrete and steel? The chief probably hasn't been sleeping good of nights, thinking of that kid maybe walking into some of the private vaults at headquarters."

Jethro laughed again. This man did look like a hog and this man reminded him of somebody. He was never able to recall who it was. "Who in the hell had this pipe dream in the first place?" he said.

"Then there's nothing to it?" Wilkinson said, doubtfully.

"Yeah, there's something to it, but not enough to give the NSD ants in their pants. The kid isn't going to get into any of their private vaults, where the H-bomb plans and the private papers for bacteriological warfare are hidden."

"Good," Wilkinson said. But there was no conviction in his voice. "The chief will rest easier when he hears this." He frowned. "There was a report of burglary last night. Police say entry was not forced and the safe had not been opened. But money was missing. It was reports like this that got us into this investigation, you know."

"I know," Jethro answered. "The burglary last night wasn't forced entry. Entrance to the building was achieved by a plain ordinary key. The key ring was swiped for a few minutes while the owner wasn't looking, a wax impression was made, the key ring was returned before it was missed, a key was made—click, click." He made sounds with his tongue symbolizing the turning of a key in a lock.

"How about the safe?"

"The owner had the combination written on the wall so he wouldn't forget it," Jethro answered easily.

"You seem to know a lot about this," Wilkinson said.

"I vas der, Cholly," Jethro answered.

"I see," Wilkinson said.

JETHRO waited, watched. Again he had the impression, stronger than ever before, that he had known this man somewhere. He had worked with him on this case, but—"Were you born on a farm, Wilky?" he asked.

"Huh? Yes. What about the way this kid escapes?"

"Everybody who ducks out the side door when the cops are asleep is an escape artist—according to the cops." Jethro answered. "Did you raise hogs when you were a boy?"

"Yeah, sure, fine ones. Took the prize at the county fair." Wilkinson seemed to swell a little, then he came back to the subject. "What about this story that he might have come here on a flying saucer?"

Jethro thrust his hands deep in his coat pockets and teetered on his toes. He looked at the river boiling past below them. His voice came. "I swear they must have a whole department full of fantasy writers somewhere in the Pentagon. All this department does is dream up fantastic yarns for poor hardworking FBI and NSD agents to run down. Did you ever hear a story that sounded more like pure cock-and-bull than this one?"

Wilkinson laughed, a little uneasily.

His eyes were evasive. "I guess you're right, when you come to think of it." He took something from his pocket, a round ball of metal, tossed it into the air, caught it. "Did you ever see anything like this before?"

Jethro took it, turned it in his hands. It looked and felt like it was made of solid aluminum. It was about three inches in diameter. "Can't say that I have. Where'd you get it?" His voice was as cold as the north wind.

"Found it in the kid's shack last night."

"You were in his place?"

"Yeah. I thought I had better look it over. This is all I found that might mean anything and I'm damned if I know what it means. It seems that I've seen one of these somewhere before—but I can't remember where." He frowned, a look of concentration appeared on his face.

"Did you ever throw one into a pigpen?" Jethro questioned.

Light blazed in Wilkinson's eyes. "Say, that's it. I just remembered. That damned kid kept pestering me with it and I threw it into—"

A look of satanic hatred appeared on Jethro's face. His pocket exploded.

Wilkinson was standing with his back to the riverbank. Both men were concealed in the willows. The drop down the bank to the sullen flood of water was at least five feet. The heavy bullet, catching Wilkinson in the chest, knocked him backward into the river.

He splashed heavily as he hit, his head broke the surface, and he yelled once. The current caught him, carried him under the willows. He clutched at the green limbs, caught them, held on.

His forehead made a round white target above the brown flood.

Jethro took slow aim at that target and pressed the trigger again. A round hole appeared in the middle of the white forehead.

The fingers clutching the willows let go their hold. The head went under water. It did not appear again. Jethro watched to make certain.

AS HE WATCHED and as the head did not appear again, something of the look of satanic hatred went slowly from Wade Jethro's face. He slipped the gun back into his pocket. Tossing the aluminum ball in his hands, he went slowly through the willows and up the bank to the collection of wretched buildings that had once been called Hooverville, entered the shack where Dennis O'Liam lived.

"Okay, kids, you can come out now," he said.

They were slow in appearing from the hole under the coat. He called again and when they did not answer, lifted the covers dragging on the floor and poked into the hole itself.

"Dennis. Stella."

They did not answer.

Startled, he went quickly to the back door, intending to look in the shed.

They were just coming through the runway. They saw him, tried to duck out of sight, realized they had been seen, and came slowly and hesitantly through the backdoor. Their faces were white. They did not speak. He made room for them to pass him and when they were inside, he closed the door.

"I've been telling Stella what you told me," Dennis said.

"Damn it—" For a moment anger boiled in him. He forced it out of sight and shook his head. "Sometimes it's a good idea not to talk too much. You can get yourself a reputation for being an awful liar if you say the wrong things at the wrong time to the wrong people."

Dennis O'Liam nodded as if he understood all too well what was meant. "But Stella is different," he said.

Jethro nodded. "There's always somebody who is different—usually it's a girl." He gazed thoughtfully at Stella. "I hope you haven't paid too much attention to the—ah—kind of crazy talk of Dennis."

"But she's different," Dennis said again.

"How is she different?" Jethro demanded.

"Do you remember—" Something of triumph showed on the boy's face—"what the farmer said? There were *two* babies in the basket?"

"What?" Sudden shocking chill shot through the detective as he realized the implication back of the boy's words. "You don't mean it, you can't mean it, you don't know what you're talking about—"

"But I do mean it," Stella spoke.

"Everybody knows I'm not really a MacClanahan. I was found too, like Dennis." Her thin face glowed as she spoke.

"But that doesn't mean anything. There are thousands of babies found on doorsteps every year."

"I can prove it," the girl insisted.

"Don't give me any fairy stories," he shouted at them. "How can you prove anything?"

"But there had to be two of us," Dennis insisted. "Just one wouldn't be enough. There had to be two, so we could marry, and produce our own kind here on this planet." He seemed very sure.

The logic of the statement seemed to Jethro to be beyond question. There had been two babies. There would have to be. "But that still doesn't prove—" His voice went into silence.

THE GIRL was bringing something out of the pocket of the ragged red sweater she was wearing. He stared at it. It was an aluminum ball similar to the one Wilkinson had found in this shack.

"Proof?" he muttered. But how would they know this was proof? It had taken him years of patient work to discover that this was proof.

"Proof?" he muttered. His eyes were wary. From his pocket, he took the ball that Wilkinson had found.

"That's mine, sir," Dennis said quickly. "I mean—" He fell silent.

Jethro pointed angrily toward the ball the girl was holding. "How can that be proof of anything?"

"We were hoping," Dennis said, "that you could tell us this."

As the implications back of the words sank home in his mind, Jethro slowly lowered himself into a rickety chair. "Okay, kids," he said quietly. "You've got me. Give me the ball, Stella."

She gave it without reluctance now. He examined it carefully, turning it in his hands. Then he put both balls on the tabletop, shoving aside the beer sausage and the loaf of bread, brought them carefully into a proper relationship. Then he pressed carefully on top of both balls. They clicked open. Revealed inside was a microscopic assembly of instruments.

"Each contains half of a radio transmitter," he said. "One won't work without the other. In fact, neither will open unless the other is also within a six-inch distance of it and in the proper position. There are built-in interlocking magnetic fields that prevent them from opening unless both are present."

"But—" The boy frowned.

"Their purpose? Simple. They are to be used to report an accomplished mission. By the time you could accomplish that mission, you would have discovered what they were and how to use them. They contain ultra high frequency radio transmitters, of a type unknown on earth. They will contact a receiver somewhere in space, where, I can't tell you exactly, but probably on one of the planets."

"Then we are to use them?" Dennis said. "Now?"

"Not yet," Jethro answered. "You have only accomplished half your mission. You can't accomplish the second half—" He stared at them, judging swiftly the signs of maturity on them. "—for another five or six years."

"You mean when we have married and had children?"

"Yes."

"And then?"

"Then we will have a little foothold on this planet, not much of a foothold, but one that will grow and will enable us to establish regular communication with others elsewhere."

"I see," Dennis said.

"How did you know this ball might prove anything?" Jethro questioned.

"Well—" The boy did not want to speak.

"Go on," Jethro urged.

"Well, it seemed important. We thought it was one of the reasons you—" Again he hesitated. "You shot the detective, sir, to keep him from finding out about the ball."

"I THOUGHT you'd seen that," Jethro said. "You were in the willows?"

"Yes, sir." The answer came without hesitation and without fear.

"That was only one reason why I shot him," Jethro said slowly. "Another reason was the fact that he didn't believe it was all a hoax, your origin, your escapes, and everything else about you. No matter what I said or did, he would have reported that in his opinion more was involved here than had been revealed. His report would have meant more investigation. I want investigation in this area stopped entirely. So I shot him.

Now my report will stop inquiries."

"I see," Dennis said.

"And that means no more use of the *tsi* effect," Jethro growled. "None whatsoever. Do you understand?"

"Yes, sir," Dennis answered promptly. "Stella has already been trying to get me to stop using the *back way*. I won't use it any more, sir, without permission."

"See that you don't," Jethro said. "It is an ability we have but which no human has. Use of it attracts far too much attention. If you keep on using it, one of these days you will start these humans thinking. And we don't want them to do that, yet."

"Yes, sir. But—"

"More questions?"

"Yes, sir. What—what happened to *your* mate, sir. There must have been two babies in *your* basket too."

Anger made a satanic mask of Jethro's face. "There was. A farmer found us, took us to raise. That farmer was named Wilkinson. He had a son, an older boy, as mean a little devil as ever lived. He hated us. He also raised hogs. The little girl who was to be my future mate was playing with her ball. He threw it into the pigpen. She ran through the fence after it."

His voice sank to a husky whisper. "The hogs killed her."

For a time he could not speak. Then his voice came again, weak and tired. "I think I went crazy when she died. At least I have almost no memories of that. I hated the boy so much I even forgot his name. Later, the farmer died and I was placed in an orphanage. Growing up, I forgot almost everything about my childhood. Later, when I met the farmer boy again, I didn't recognize him. When I began to puzzle out the truth about myself, I wondered what happened to the little girl who was to have been my mate. When I recognized Wilkinson, finally, I remembered what had happened. That's the last reason I had for killing him—I finally recognized him as the man who had grown out of the boy who had thrown Me'an's toy into the hog pen."

His voice went into husky silence. The shabby room was silent.

The boy and the girl had drawn close together. They stood looking down at him, pity on their faces.

THE END

The Man from Space

Little Joe was proud to be a member of a group dedicated to helping aliens take over the Earth—until the day he actually met them.

"ZERWU!" THE Passenger in the cab said, his voice harsh.

"Sir?" Little Joe, the driver, answered. "Come again. I didn't get you."

"Zerwu!" the passenger repeated. His tone of voice was that of a man accustomed to command.

"I—" As Little Joe Baskin was starting to say for the second time that he didn't understand, a sudden startling thought shot through his mind. *Maybe this was one of them!* Little Joe almost lost control of his taxi. Swerving to avoid an El column, he found himself directly in the path of an on-rushing red truck. As he tried to dodge, his mind was still on the thought that his passenger might be one of them.

They came to Earth, in disguise, in very small ships, to accomplish their missions, then returned to the mother ship that never left its distant orbit around the planet.

So Rikki had taught him. Rikki would love to know that he had picked up one of them in his cab. Maybe Rikki would even give him a promotion for this, make him a big shot in the organization.

Brakes screamed as the truck slowed to a stop. Little Joe swung right and skidded his cab to a halt beside the curb.

"Why in hell don't you watch where you're going?" the truck driver yelled. "Do you want to get you and your junk heap smashed flatter than if an atom bomb had hit you?"

"Go soak your head in the lake!" Little Joe yelled. He turned quickly to his passenger. If this was actually one of them, he had to be treated right in every way. No telling what his mission here on Earth might be, but one thing was certain, he would be able to reward those who served him faithfully while he was here.

"Sorry, sir." For the first time Little Joe got a good look at his passenger. An electric thrill shot through him at the sight. This *was* one of them.

To anybody else, his passenger might have looked like a prosperous lawyer or a successful executive, but Little Joe felt he could tell by the way his fare carried his head, with the chin held high, and by the proud, imperial look in his eyes—the look of one born to rule—that he was no ordinary mortal.

"Where can I take you, sir?" Little Joe almost babbled the words. "What can I do for you. Command me. I will obey you." He would have prostrated himself on the ground if he hadn't been behind the wheel of his cab.

The passenger stared at him from cold evaluating eyes that seemed to look through him and on beyond him into some lost infinity. The color of the eyes made Little Joe think of the dim gray fog that sometimes rolled in off Lake Michigan and enveloped the Loop in a murky haze.

Then his passenger spoke. "This is a test."

"A test?" Little Ice Baskin was jolted to the bottom of his soul, Rikki had said they sometimes came to Earth for the express purpose of testing members of the organization. Tales had been told of these tests and of what happened to those who failed to pass them. Bodies had been found in the lake, dropped there after being snatched to the sky by the antigrav beams they possessed. "I—I'll do anything you say, sir. J—Just tell me what to do."

The cold gray eyes continued to stare at him and through him. Then, as if satisfied, the passenger nodded. "You'll do," he said. "Here, give this to your leader. It contains orders for him." Leaning forward, he thrust a plain white envelope toward the cab driver. Little Joe took it with trembling fingers.

"Zerwu!" the passenger reported. "Pull your clumsy vehicle to a full stop. This is as far as I will go with you this time."

Little Joe, trying to talk and to pull away from the curb at the same time, hastily put on his breaks. The passenger alighted but paused to lean in at the front window. "This was the first test," he said. "I will see you again, for the second one."

Without remembering to pay his fare, he moved out of sight into the Loop crowds. Shivering, his whole body tingling with excitement, Little Joe Baskin sat at the wheel.

"Aw right, aw right, that's not a cab parking zone. Get it away from the curb!" a cop yelled at him.

"When we take over, you'll change your tune!" Little Joe shouted, gunning the cab.

He felt wonderful, for over a year now he had belonged to the organization and had listened to all the talk about men from space and had read all the communiqués that Rikki had mimeographed for distribution. These communications were of two different kinds, the first, which was distributed to outsiders and which anyone could read, and the second, which was very secret and was distributed only to those in the inner circle. All of this was very mysterious—and very wonderful to Joe Baskin.

He had been born the youngest in a family of eight in the stockyards district of South Chicago. The midwife who had ushered him into the world had swatted him on the behind to start life off for him. Since then, everybody else had swatted him, too. Men, seeing his hollow chest and his skinny five feet two inches of height, paid no attention to him. No woman had ever bothered to look twice. No matter what he had done, nobody had ever paid any attention to him or believed in him.

To Little Joe, life had been bitter gall, until a passenger had left one of Rikki's news releases in his cab. The words had been pure magic to him. They had opened a new world to him. In the organization, which Rikki had built, Little Joe had found a chance to be important.

WHEN THE SPACEMEN landed and took over the Earth, those in the organization would be their right-hand men who would tell the president, the governor, the mayor—and maybe even policemen—what to do. Then Little Joe would come into his own. Then he would be a big shot, for real.

The envelope containing the precious orders hugged tight in the inside pocket of his coat, Little Joe burned rubber off his tires getting to Rikki.

Headquarters was in an old brownstone front that in its day had been a mansion. Rikki had the whole basement. You could go in at the front door or at the side or at the back. Little Joe had heard hints of a tunnel that led from the furnace room to the old carriage house at the rear at the lot. He had also heard that trusted lieutenants came and went by this tunnel, on secret mysterious errands. Little Joe had never seen this tunnel. He was not a trusted lieutenant, yet. Perhaps this message would win him such an honor. His heart glowed at the thought.

Little Joe used the front entrance. Mabel, Rikki's wife, opened the door at his ring. Although it was the middle of the afternoon, she was still in her wrapper. She also smelled of beer, but the cabbie was too excited to notice this.

"Whatta ya want. The meeting is not till tonight."

"I gotta see Rikki. I got an important message, for his hands alone."

"What kind of a message?"

"From one of them."

Suspicion showed in Mabel's eyes.

"This message is from one of the spacemen," Little Joe insisted. "I had him right in my cab and he gave me this message for Rikki. I got to see him right away."

His excitement impressed even Mabel. "Wait here," she said. "I'll find out if he can see you."

A few minutes later Rikki himself appeared at the door. He was a tall man, in his early thirties, with wary suspicion always in his eyes and a cynical expression about his mouth.

"What's this about a message?"

Little Joe gave him the envelope.

Rikki took it and looked at it as if he did not quite understand how the cab driver had come into possession of it. "I'll see you at the meeting tonight," he said. The door closed behind him.

Greatly disappointed, Little Joe went back to his cab. Was Rikki's treatment of him another test? He hoped it was. Otherwise, he would have been even more disappointed.

He spent the rest of the day watching the sky, hoping that a space ship would appear there. When not thus engaged, he watched the sidewalk crowds, trying to spot his passenger who had given him the message. Two cops bawled him out and a truck almost ran him down. None of this mattered to Little Joe. *They had landed! They had used him as a messenger!* Life could hold nothing sweeter than this.

Little Joe was on hand an hour early for the meeting. Mabel admitted him and told him to sit down. Rikki did not put in an appearance. The rattle of a mimeograph in a remote part of the basement indicated his probable whereabouts. The six other members of the organization arrived. They were few in numbers as yet, but this was because most people simply did not believe in such things as visitors from space. Wait until *they* arrived! Then thousands would throng the organization's doorsteps without being admitted until the insiders were good and ready. Little Joe savored the thought of that day with tremendous yearning.

Rikki had explained that he wanted to keep the organization small. "Only leaders are being trained now." However, in spite of his expressed desire to keep the organization small, he was always urging them to find new members "of the right kind, so we can have bigger quarters." The financial support of the organization came from the members, who contributed a day's pay each week. No member really minded this payment, however. Rikki made them feel so important by talking about the roles they would play when the spacemen landed that they would have contributed two days' pay each week, if he had asked them.

When Rikki finally appeared, it was obvious that something had happened. His face was shining. He rapped for silence.

"They have landed," he said.

THE ROOM BECAME completely silent after he had spoken. Then questions began. Rikki shook his head firmly. "No! Not another word will I say. But coming days will see great events."

As the others left, Rikki beckoned Little Joe into the back room. "Be at 12th and Spruce with your cab at 11 o'clock tonight. No, don't ask me any questions. Just be there."

"I'll sure do it," Little Joe answered fervidly. If Rikki had told him he was to be transported to the moon this night, cab and all, he would have been ready for the trip.

Spruce Street at 12th was an area where people never seemed to go to bed at night. Here, the glare of Neon lights lit the sky for miles. Pawn shops, all night restaurants, movies. As he parked his cab at the curb, Little Joe saw that the street was as busy as ever.

"Wonder why they picked this spot?" Little Joe wondered. "What am I supposed to do here?" He was on fire with eagerness. Tonight he was going to be tested again. He would pass the test.

Suddenly he saw his passenger of the afternoon. The spaceman was walking out of a big pawnshop. He was carrying a large leather brief case. His manner was completely casual but his alert eyes were scanning the street in both directions. Spotting Little Joe's cab, he moved directly toward it. The driver hopped out to open the door.

Bang!

The spaceman flinched. Joe ducked automatically. He had heard gunshots before in Chicago and he knew one when he heard it. Turning, he saw the owner of the pawnshop standing in the door. He had a smoking revolver in his hand. As Joe glanced at him, the pawnshop owner raised the gun to take another shot.

"You can't shoot him!" Little Joe screamed. "He's a spaceman. He'll blast you to nothing!"

"Shut up," the spaceman snarled. He turned toward the pawnshop owner. Something came out from under his coat.

Little Joe did not get a clear glimpse of this but he knew it was a weapon of some kind. Light flared from it.

The owner of the pawnshop turned white. His body looked like the sun, so bright that it hurt the eyes. He screamed, once, a high-pitched keening sound that rolled along Spruce Street in a way that set jumping the heart of everyone who heard it. Not a person who heard this sound but knew intuitively what it meant—death.

The pawnbroker sprawled backward into the door of his shop.

The spaceman pocketed his weapon. He stepped into the back seat of the cab. Little Joe jumped behind the wheel.

"Are you hurt? Do you want me to take you to a doctor?"

The spaceman was slow in answering. His fingers explored the back of his coat. They came away smudged with red. He stared at them from a face that was beginning to twist with pain.

"The bullet struck me," he said.

"What do you want me to do?"

"Take me to your headquarters."

Little Joe slammed the cab into gear. As he got away, a siren had already begun to scream in the distance. In his rearview mirror, he saw the flashing lights of a squad car pull to a halt in the street in front of the pawnshop.

The spaceman was looking back. "Get some speed out of this crate," he ordered.

Little Joe stepped harder on the gas. His body was bathed in sweat but his soul was filled with elation. He did not know why the pawnbroker had been blasted but probably there was some good reason for it. Pulling the car to a halt in the alley behind headquarters, he jumped out and opened the door.

THE SPACEMAN KEPT a tight grip on the big brief case as they went past the carriage house and into the backyard. Little Joe wondered what was in it. Plans for the big landing that was coming? A model of the secret weapon like the one the spaceman carried?

Who was the pawnbroker? A renegade who had tried to betray them? A fool who had gotten in their way? Joe rang the bell at the rear basement door. There was no answer.

"The fool is asleep," the spaceman said. "Wake him up."

The cab driver pounded on the door. A light came on over it. Rikki opened the door. He took one look at them.

"Get the hell away from here. You ought to know better than to come here."

He started to close the door.

"I've been shot," the spaceman said. "I've got a bullet in me right now. I've got to have help."

"And have the cops trail you here and charge me with harboring a wanted man?" Rikki yelled. "Get to hell away from my door!"

The spaceman pulled his weapon. Rikki stared at it. His face worked convulsively. The pupils of his eyes grew very large, then narrowed to pinhead size. His mouth became a thin straight line.

"Don't you know who this is, you damned fool?" Little Joe blurted out.

"I know who he is," Rikki said. He did not take his eyes off the weapon.

"Then you know you had better open up," the spaceman said. He made a jabbing motion with the weapon as if he was going to stick it into Rikki's ribs.

"I'm opening up," Rikki said hastily. As he opened the door, his eyes went past the gun to the brief case. He licked his lips. "Did—did you—"

"Shut up and let me inside," the spaceman said.

Rikki took them to a small basement room with a cot and a couple of chairs in it. There was one window, up high. Rikki closed it. The spaceman flung the brief case on the cot. "Open it," he said.

With trembling hands, Rikki obeyed. Money spilled out of it. Bundles of five-dollar, ten-dollar, twenty-dollar bills. Each held by a rubber band. Little Joe's eyes bulged at the sight.

"I had him open his safe," the spaceman said, satisfaction in his voice.

Rikki fondled the stacks of bills, then his hands dived into the brief case again. Out came diamonds. Some were loose. Others were mounted in rings. They formed a small glittering pile on the canvas cot.

"He had a lot of loose rocks in his safe," the spaceman said. "I brought them along, too." His face was twisted with pain but there was something in it more powerful than the pain—a lust for wealth. It showed in his eyes as he looked at the money and the diamonds. He wanted these things. He loved money and the things it would buy.

"I slugged him as I left but I must not have knocked him out. He came to and took a shot at me." The spaceman's face grew grim as he spoke.

"You stole those," Little Joe heard his own voice whisper. "You're a thief."

Rikki looked up for the first time, he really became aware of Little Joe's presence. "We had to have financing," Rikki said quickly.

"You stole to get it," Little Joe said.

"This was not theft," Rikki shouted, anger rising in his voice. Or was it fear? "We had to have financing now, to get started, so we took what will belong to us in another few years anyhow, when they land in force. Everything will be ours, when they land. Everything!" His voice rose to a scream. "We only took a little part of what we will have coming to us rightfully, when they land in force."

Listening, Little Joe wondered if Rikki was trying to convince himself. "The pawnbroker is dead," he said. His face was suddenly wooden and his voice was stolid. "And when I got that message this morning, I was being set up as a sucker to drive a get-away car tonight."

His words produced leaden silence in the room. It was the spaceman who spoke. "Yeah, the pawnbroker is dead. And you had better remember that, in case you start getting any false ideas as to who is boss around here." The weapon in his hand was pointed at the cab driver.

"There will be hundreds of cops after, you," Little Joe said, his voice emotionless. "They'll have tommy guns and tear gas and—"

"And I will have this," the spaceman said, nodding toward the weapon in his hand. His eyes focused on Little Joe's face.

The cab driver clamped his lips shut.

The spaceman looked at Rikki. "You might do a little remembering too, if you are ever tempted to forget who is boss here."

Rikki tore his eyes off the money and the jewels. He looked at the weapon. A shiver passed over his body. "I won't forget— What's that?"

A siren was wailing in the distance.

Rikki's face went pale. "Do you hear that?"

The three listened. The siren was coming closer. Rikki's face developed a sudden tic and his eyes became wild. "I told you that you shouldn't have come here. You've got us all into trouble."

"You may be in trouble," the spaceman said. "Not me, I'm not in any trouble."

AS THE MEANING of the spaceman's words reached Rikki, his eyes flared with sudden hate. "Damn you!"

The finger of the spaceman tightened on the firing mechanism. Rikki's face went paper white. "I didn't mean what I said," he screamed. "I was out of my head."

"How'd you like to be dead?" the spaceman asked. His voice was as cold as the far reaches of space itself.

"Please! Have a heart. I didn't mean it." Rikki sprawled on his knees to beg for his life.

"Okay," the spaceman said, contempt in his voice. He lifted a foot and kicked Rikki in the face. Rikki fell over backwards. Blood was on his face when he sat up. He made whining noises deep in his throat.

"I thought you had guts. I thought you would make a leader!" The contempt grew deeper in the spaceman's voice.

The siren wailed past on the street outside. It went into silence in the distance.

The spaceman relaxed. "Just a routine call, maybe an accident somewhere, maybe a prowler."

He looked at Little Joe. "You've stood up pretty well tonight. When we take over, how would you like to be one of our leaders?"

"What about Rikki?"

"We can't have leaders like him." The spaceman's eyes were suddenly malevolent. "Our leaders have to have guts."

Crash!

The basement window burst inward. The cap and the grim face of a policeman appeared in it. He had a gun in his hand.

"Get your hands up!"

"I told you they'd catch us," Rikki screamed.

The spaceman flicked the muzzle of his weapon upward toward the window. As he did this, the cop pulled the trigger of his gun.

Lead howled through the basement room. Smoke from the pistol made a spurting rolling cloud in the air. Rikki's screams were loud and hideous.

The spaceman pressed the firing mechanism of his weapon.

The cop's face turned white. Instantly it glowed like the light of the sun. The pistol, held through the broken window, fell from a suddenly nerveless hand into the basement room. The body of the policeman seemed to try to follow it. He was too big to get through the opening. His body was caught in the broken window.

His uniform burst into flaring light. There was no flame. Just light. Vibrations at tremendously high frequency seemed to flood the room. Then came the smell of cooking flesh. The smell was that of old, old ham, over-cooked in a skillet that was much too hot, with the result that it had to fry in its own grease.

The basement room was flooded with the rank smell, a

310

gruesome, retch-provoking nausea.

When the spaceman turned off his weapon, the body of the cop continued to blaze with an intense light that was not flame but which consumed faster than any known form of combustion.

Rikki, his body drawn into a ball and his head in his hands, lay on the floor. Little Joe leaned against the wall. Feelings that he did not like were in him, turning his body to stone.

The spaceman swept the money and the jewels back into the briefcase. His eyes came to Little Joe.

"You've got to show me how to get out of here," he said.

As he spoke, the door burst open. Her hair in curlers, Mabel stood there. She was wearing a sheer nightgown. Awakened from sleep by the shot, she had forgotten to put on a robe. Sleep was still in her eyes. She stared wildly around the room. Her eyes widened when she saw the body of the policeman burning in the window.

"What—what happened? What makes him burn like that?"

"This happened to him," the spaceman said, indicating his weapon.

Her gaze came to rest on Rikki. "You've killed him too," she whispered. Dropping to her knees beside her husband, she tried to take his head into her arms.

RIKKI SAT UP. His eyes came to focus on the spaceman. As if he had seen more than he could bear, he dived under the cot. "Don't shoot me! Don't shoot me! Don't—" His voice was like a scratchy phonograph record with the needle stuck in the same groove.

"I've got to get out of here," the spaceman said.

Mabel stared at him, but did not answer. If she had heard what he had said the words had no meaning to her. Her nose was beginning to twitch. "That awful smell. That awful, *awful* smell." Suddenly she was retching.

The spaceman fingered his weapon. Obviously, since she was of no use to him, he was tempted to blast her. The thought passed. He looked at Little Joe. Without a word, the cab driver moved to the door. The spaceman followed him.

Little Joe opened the side door, then drew back. "There's a cop out here, too. I just caught a glimpse of him."

"Try the front."

The cab driver led the way down the corridor to the front door. Pushing aside the curtain, he looked out, only to duck back again. "There's a squad car parked at the curb in front," he said.

"Where are the cops?"

"I don't know, I didn't see any." Somewhere in the distance another siren was wailing. Little Joe knew what this meant. The riot call had gone in. All the available reserves from this district were converging on this spot as fast as burning rubber could bring them. He did not doubt that other districts were also sending help. Through long experience, the Chicago police knew how to get where they were needed in a hurry.

"I'll try and walk out," the spaceman said. "If they try to stop me, I'll blast my way through them."

He kicked the door open. Little Joe backed against the wall. An order to halt rang out in the night. It was answered by a sudden blasting flare of light.

Little Joe held his breath. Death had walked out of this basement and he knew it. The policeman had nothing that could cope with the weapon of the spaceman. They would try to capture him and would go down to flaming destruction. He could blast his way to the squad car at the curb and commandeer it, then be gone into the night.

A heavy pistol barked twice, then was silent as the light weapon flared its death in the night.

A heavy rifle roared.

The bullet was fired from an elevation. The heavy slug, aimed downward, came through the basement door. Striking the concrete wall, it howled into a far corner of the corridor.

Little Joe threw himself flat. Vaguely he was aware that the light weapon had flared an answer to the rifle. He also knew that the rifle was keeping right on firing.

The spaceman stumbled back into the basement. "There's a man on top of the roof of the apartment across the street, where I can't get at him. If I go out, he'll kill me." His voice was hoarse and heavy.

The rifle roared again. The bullet pounded into the outside wall of the building. The spaceman ducked around a corner in the corridor and motioned the cab driver to follow.

"I guess they will come in here and try to get me," the spaceman said. "When they do that, they will know they have been somewhere before they finish."

"Don't you have a way to escape into space?" Little Joe asked.

The spaceman gave him an odd look.

A thud sounded on the floor of the corridor. A hissing sound followed the thud. Little Joe caught a whiff of acrid odor. His eyes began to burn.

"Tear gas," he said.

He retreated to the rear. Rubbing his eyes, the spaceman followed. "Is there any other way out of here?"

"There was talk about a tunnel—" Little Joe said, remembering what he had heard.

"Where is it?" the spaceman eagerly asked.

"I don't know. They didn't tell me. I wasn't important enough to know. Maybe Rikki or Mabel—"

"We'll find out from them." In the backroom window, the cop's body was still burning. The smell in the room was nauseous. Rikki was still under the cot. Mabel was kneeling beside him. She was holding her stomach. The spaceman kicked the woman to her feet. "Show us that tunnel!"

She led the way without a word of protest.

The tunnel led off from what had once been the coal bin. Before entering it, the spaceman prodded Little Joe ahead of him. The tunnel was narrow and the ceiling was low. The roof and the sides were supported by boards that had begun to rot away. The air was dank and musty. Rats ran ahead of them,

Little Joe thought he was going to suffocate before he reached the ladder at the far end.

"Go on up," the spaceman said. "When we get up there, we'll be behind the cops. We'll slip into your cab and ease out of the alley. We'll make a clean getaway before they even know we're not trapped in the basement." His voice was alive with excitement and with gloating. Once out of this death trap, he would be free.

A TRAP DOOR WAS OVERHEAD. Little Joe cautiously shoved it aside. A dim glow from a streetlight in the alley filtered through cracks in the old building. The tunnel opened directly under a stairway that led upward to the second floor.

Once this building had been a carriage house. Later it had been converted into a garage. No cars were in it. Stairs led upward to the second floor. Little Joe did not know what was up there. Sliding the trap door completely out of the way, he climbed into the dimly illumined big room. Grunting with satisfaction, the spaceman followed him.

Cold flesh appeared all over Little Joe's body as he realized they were not alone in this place. He caught a glimpse of three small figures that looked like children.

What were children doing here? They should have been in bed long ago.

The spaceman saw them too. "What's that? Who are you? Get to hell out of here, you dirty little brats."

"We came for you," a soft voice whispered. Simultaneously the air vibrated with a humming sound.

Little Joe knew that a weapon of some kind had been fired. He heard the spaceman grunt, then wheeze as he tried to cry out in sudden pain. The wheeze went into quick silence. The sound that followed was that of a falling body.

The spaceman did not move after he hit the floor.

Little Joe stood frozen. One of the children approached the body on the floor and picked up the weapon that had fallen from the spaceman's outstretched hand. Voices like whispers echoed through the room. There was satisfaction in the voices as if some necessary job had been finally accomplished. The three children turned to Little Joe.

The room was very still. Little Joe raised his hands. Tremors passed through his body.

Off in the night, the high-powered rifle barked again, hunting for a target that no longer existed. In the far distance another siren was screaming. Little Joe heard sounds as from another world. His entire attention was concentrated on these amazing children. "Who—who—" The words stuck in his throat.

"We are the true spaceman," the answer came back.

"Huh? The true spaceman? Then who was he?" He nodded toward the body on the floor.

"A human, one of the first we contacted. We did not know he was a thief and a killer." The voice was apologetic. "When he had learned a little about us, he pretended to set up an organization that would welcome us to his planet. We learned eventually that he was planning to use us to control his people. Also, he stole a weapon from us." The voice became even more apologetic. "Tonight our detectors finally located him, by the radiation from the weapon, which he was using. In this way, we knew where to find him. We came here for that purpose."

Little Joe's heart was up in his throat. He had long since realized that the message he had been given to deliver to Rikki had been for the purpose of impressing him so that he would be on hand to drive the getaway car for the pawnshop robbery. He had also realized that Rikki was actually a crook. With this realization, he had given up all hope that such things as real spacemen actually existed. Desolation had come over him as he had realized this.

"Then you actually are real?" he whispered.

"Yes. And we will come again. But now we have to go. We have been overlong in your heavy atmosphere."

They filed up the steps to the second floor. Little Joe followed them. A slender vehicle was parked on the flat roof of the building. He watched them enter it.

It went swiftly into the night sky.

Little Joe went back to his cab. ...As he drives the Chicago streets by day, he keeps hoping that children will emerge from nowhere and get into his cab. As he drives at night, he watches the sky. Someday they will come again, the true space people. He waits...patiently...

THE END

If you've enjoyed this book, you will not want to miss these terrific titles…

ARMCHAIR SCI-FI & HORROR DOUBLE NOVELS, $12.95 each

D-111   **THE MOON ERA** by Jack Williamson
REVENGE OF THE ROBOTS by Howard Browne

D-112   **SON OF THE BLACK CHALICE** by Milton Lesser
SENTRY OF THE SKY by Evelyn E. Smith

D-113   **OUTPOST ON THE MOON** by Joslyn Maxwell
POTENTIAL ZERO by S. J. Byrne

D-114   **OUTPOST INFINITY** by Raymond F. Jones
THE WHITE INVADERS by Ray Cummings

D-115   **TIME TRAP** by Rog Phillips
THE COSMIC DESTROYER by Alexander Blade

D-116   **THE OTHER SIDE OF THE MOON** by Edmond Hamilton
SECRET INVASION by Walter Kubilius

D-117   **DANGER MOON** by Frederik Pohl
THE HIDDEN UNIVERSE by Ralph Milne Farley

D-118   **THE WAILING ASTEROID** by Murray Leinster
THE WORLD THAT COULDN'T BE by Clifford D. Simak

D-119   **THE WHISPERING GORILLA** by Don Wilcox
RETURN OF THE WHISPERING GORILLA by David V. Reed

D-120   **SPECIAL EFFECT** by J. F. Bone
WARLORD OF KOR by Terry Carr

ARMCHAIR SCIENCE FICTION CLASSICS, $12.95 each

C-37   **THE GREEN MAN RETURNS**
by Harold M. Sherman

C-38   **THE SHAVER MYSTERY, Book Five**
by Richard S, Shaver

C-39   **MARS CHILD**
by Cyril Judd

ARMCHAIR MASTERS OF SCIENCE FICTION SERIES, $16.95 each

MS-9   **MASTERS OF SCIENCE FICTION AND FANTASY, Vol. Nine**
Poul Anderson, "The Star Beast" and other tales

MS-10   **MASTERS OF SCIENCE FICTION, Vol. Ten**
Robert Moore Williams, "Time Tolls for Toro" and other tales

If you've enjoyed this book, you will not want to miss these terrific titles...

ARMCHAIR SCI-FI & HORROR DOUBLE NOVELS, $12.95 each

D-1   **THE GALAXY RAIDERS** by William P. McGivern
           SPACE STATION #1 by Frank Belknap Long

D-2   **THE PROGRAMMED PEOPLE** by Jack Sharkey
           SLAVES OF THE CRYSTAL BRAIN by William Carter Sawtelle

D-3   **YOU'RE ALL ALONE** by Fritz Leiber
           THE LIQUID MAN by Bernard C. Gilford

D-4   **CITADEL OF THE STAR LORDS** by Edmond Hamilton
           VOYAGE TO ETERNITY by Milton Lesser

D-5   **IRON MEN OF VENUS** by Don Wilcox
           THE MAN WITH ABSOLUTE MOTION by Noel Loomis

D-6   **WHO SOWS THE WIND...** by Rog Phillips
           THE PUZZLE PLANET by Robert A. W. Lowndes

D-7   **PLANET OF DREAD** by Murray Leinster
           TWICE UPON A TIME by Charles L. Fontenay

D-8   **THE TERROR OUT OF SPACE** by Dwight V. Swain
           QUEST OF THE GOLDEN APE by Paul W. Fairman & Milton Lesser

D-9   **SECRET OF MARRACOTT DEEP** by Henry Slesar
           PAWN OF THE BLACK FLEET by Mark Clifton.

D-10   **BEYOND THE RINGS OF SATURN** by Robert Moore Williams
           A MAN OBSESSED by Alan E. Nourse

ARMCHAIR SCIENCE FICTION CLASSICS, $12.95 each

C-1   **THE GREEN MAN**
           by Harold M. Sherman

C-2   **A TRACE OF MEMORY**
           By Keith Laumer

C-3   **INTO PLUTONIAN DEPTHS**
           by Stanton A. Coblentz

ARMCHAIR MASTERS OF SCIENCE FICTION SERIES, $16.95 each

M-1   **MASTERS OF SCIENCE FICTION, Vol. One**
           Bryce Walton—"Dark of the Moon" and other tales

M-2   **MASTERS OF SCIENCE FICTION, Vol. Two**
           Jerome Bixby—"One Way Street" and other tales

If you've enjoyed this book, you will not want to miss these terrific titles…

ARMCHAIR SCI-FI & HORROR DOUBLE NOVELS, $12.95 each

D-11   **PERIL OF THE STARMEN** by Kris Neville
            THE STRANGE INVASION by Murray Leinster

D-12   **THE STAR LORD** by Boyd Ellanby
            CAPTIVES OF THE FLAME by Samuel R. Delany

D-13   **MEN OF THE MORNING STAR** by Edmond Hamilton
            PLANET FOR PLUNDER by Hal Clement and Sam Merwin, Jr.

D-14   **ICE CITY OF THE GORGON** by Chester S. Geier and Richard Shaver
            WHEN THE WORLD TOTTERED by Lester del Rey

D-15   **WORLDS WITHOUT END** by Clifford D. Simak
            THE LAVENDER VINE OF DEATH by Don Wilcox

D-16   **SHADOW ON THE MOON** by Joe Gibson
            ARMAGEDDON EARTH by Geoff St. Reynard

D-17   **THE GIRL WHO LOVED DEATH** by Paul W. Fairman
            SLAVE PLANET by Laurence M. Janifer

D-18   **SECOND CHANCE** by J. F. Bone
            MISSION TO A DISTANT STAR by Frank Belknap Long

D-19   **THE SYNDIC** by C. M. Kornbluth
            FLIGHT TO FOREVER by Poul Anderson

D-20   **SOMEWHERE I'LL FIND YOU** by Milton Lesser
            THE TIME ARMADA by Fox B. Holden

ARMCHAIR SCIENCE FICTION CLASSICS, $12.95 each

C-4   **CORPUS EARTHLING**
           by Louis Charbonneau

C-5   **THE TIME DISSOLVER**
           by Jerry Sohl

C-6   **WEST OF THE SUN**
           by Edgar Pangborn

ARMCHAIR SCI-FI & HORROR GEMS SERIES, $12.95 each

G-1   **SCIENCE FICTION GEMS, Vol. One**
           Isaac Asimov and others

G-2   **HORROR GEMS, Vol. One**
           Carl Jacobi and others

If you've enjoyed this book, you will not want to miss these terrific titles…

ARMCHAIR SCI-FI & HORROR DOUBLE NOVELS, $12.95 each

D-21 **EMPIRE OF EVIL** by Robert Arnette
THE SIGN OF THE TIGER by Alan E. Nourse & J. A. Meyer

D-22 **OPERATION SQUARE PEG** by Frank Belknap Long
ENCHANTRESS OF VENUS by Leigh Brackett

D-23 **THE LIFE WATCH** by Lester del Rey
CREATURES OF THE ABYSS by Murray Leinster

D-24 **LEGION OF LAZARUS** by Edmond Hamilton
STAR HUNTER by Andre Norton

D-25 **EMPIRE OF WOMEN** by John Fletcher
ONE OF OUR CITIES IS MISSING by Irving Cox

D-26 **THE WRONG SIDE OF PARADISE** by Raymond F. Jones
THE INVOLUNTARY IMMORTALS by Rog Phillips

D-27 **EARTH QUARTER** by Damon Knight
ENVOY TO NEW WORLDS by Keith Laumer

D-28 **SLAVES TO THE METAL HORDE** by Milton Lesser
HUNTERS OUT OF TIME by Joseph E. Kelleam

D-29 **RX JUPITER SAVE US** by Ward Moore
BEWARE THE USURPERS by Geoff St. Reynard

D-30 **SECRET OF THE SERPENT** by Don Wilcox
CRUSADE ACROSS THE VOID by Dwight V. Swain

ARMCHAIR SCIENCE FICTION CLASSICS, $12.95 each

C-7 **THE SHAVER MYSTERY, Book One**
by Richard S. Shaver

C-8 **THE SHAVER MYSTERY, Book Two**
by Richard S. Shaver

C-9 **MURDER IN SPACE**
by David V. Reed

ARMCHAIR MASTERS OF SCIENCE FICTION SERIES, $16.95 each

M-3 **MASTERS OF SCIENCE FICTION, Vol. Three**
Robert Sheckley, "The Perfect Woman" and other tales

M-4 **MASTERS OF SCIENCE FICTION, Vol. Four**
Mack Reynolds, Part One, "Stowaway" and other tales

www.ingramcontent.com/pod-product-compliance
Lightning Source LLC
Chambersburg PA
CBHW050554260626
47157CB00002B/565